IRON LAKE

"I can't remember reading a better first novel than this one."

—*The Drood Review of Mystery*

"*Iron Lake* is where it all began, when Cork O'Connor walked off the page, tough, vulnerable, hardened and shattered, and into our lives. His creation is a brilliant achievement, and one every crime reader and writer needs to celebrate. With this novel, Kent Krueger elevated the crime fiction genre into something very special."

—Louise Penny, #1 *New York Times* bestselling author of *Kingdom of the Blind*

"There's a feel that you get from a master craftsman, a saddle that sits right, a fly rod that casts with its own agility, or a series of books written with a grace and precision so stunning that you'd swear the stories were your own—Kent Krueger's Cork O'Connor novels fit that bill."

—Craig Johnson, author of the Walt Longmire series

"Among thoughtful readers, William Kent Krueger holds a very special place in the pantheon. Upon introducing Cork O'Connor in *Iron Lake* twenty years ago, Kent showed the mystery-reading world that a protagonist need not be a chain-smoking loner with lots of emotional baggage but he could be an honest and admirable family man doing his best for all the right reasons."

—C. J. Box, #1 *New York Times* bestselling author of *The Disappeared*

"For readers new to William Kent Krueger, this twentieth anniversary edition of *Iron Lake* will be an eye-opening discovery. For those of us who have been reading his wonderful Cork O'Connor novels since their beginning, this volume will be a welcome pilgrimage to the birthplace of one of our favorite characters, a journey down Krueger's icy, mysterious, and singular memory lane."

—T. Jefferson Parker, Edgar Award–winning author of *Swift Vengeance*

"In August 1998, the same month my own first book came out, I heard about this other debut novel called *Iron Lake*. I can still remember the night I stayed up late finishing it. When I closed the book, I thought two things: This is the best mystery I've read all year. And how in *hell* am I ever gonna keep up with this guy? Twenty years later, I'm still trying."

—Steve Hamilton, Edgar Award–winning author of the Alex McKnight series

"*Iron Lake* is an explosive brew: one part James Ellroy, one part Stephen King, one part Jack London, and all parts terrific. . . . A truly remarkable first novel."

—David Housewright, Edgar Award–winning author of *Penance*

"If you don't know Cork O'Connor, get to know him now."

—*Booklist*

"Minnesotan Krueger has a sense of place he's plainly honed firsthand in below-zero prairie. His characters, too, sport charm and dimension. . . . This first-timer's stamina and self-assurance suggest that O'Connor's got staying power."

—*Kirkus Reviews*

PRAISE FOR WILLIAM KENT KRUEGER'S CORK O'CONNOR MYSTERIES

DESOLATION MOUNTAIN

"Elegiac and frightful detail . . . dynamic action scenes."

—*The New York Times*

"Krueger skillfully combines the otherworldly setting of the Minnesota wilds with Native American lore to create a winning mystery with more than a few surprises."

—*Publishers Weekly*

"Kent Krueger keeps upping his game with each thriller featuring O'Connor . . . fans will not be disappointed."

—*Pioneer Press* (Minnesota)

SULFUR SPRINGS

"Remarkable . . . masterful . . . book from an author who never disappoints."

—*Book Reporter*

"Realistic and believable . . . Cork O'Connor is a worthy protagonist."

—*New York Journal of Books*

"Totally un-let-go-able, a can't-miss for fans and a new obsession for new readers."

—*Globe Gazette*

MANITOU CANYON

"A remarkable tale. . . . The characters, story and plot will haunt you long after you've read the last page."

—*Book Reporter*

"A mystery made up of several shiver-inducing levers . . . [with] a plot that keeps tightening around O'Connor and the granddaughter—and the reader's nerves. A first-rate addition to this series."

—*Booklist*

"A gripping thriller."

—*Milwaukee-Wisconsin Journal Sentinel*

PRAISE FOR *NEW YORK TIMES* BESTSELLER
ORDINARY GRACE
WINNER OF THE EDGAR AWARD
FOR BEST NOVEL

"Krueger's elegy for innocence is a deeply memorable tale."

—*The Washington Post*

"A pitch-perfect, wonderfully evocative examination of violent loss. In Frank Drum's journey away from the shores of childhood—a journey from which he can never return—we recognize the heartbreaking price of adulthood and its 'wisdoms.' I loved this book."

—Dennis Lehane

"Once in a blue moon a book drops down on your desk that demands to be read. You pick it up and read the first page, and then the second, and you are hooked. Such a book is *Ordinary Grace.*"

—*The Huffington Post*

Also by William Kent Krueger

This Tender Land
Desolation Mountain
Sulfur Springs
Manitou Canyon
Windigo Island
Tamarack County
Ordinary Grace
Trickster's Point
Northwest Angle
Vermilion Drift
Heaven's Keep
Red Knife
Thunder Bay
Copper River
Mercy Falls
Blood Hollow
The Devil's Bed
Purgatory Ridge
Boundary Waters

WILLIAM KENT KRUEGER

IRON LAKE

POCKET BOOKS

New York   London   Toronto   Sydney   New Delhi

Pocket Books
An Imprint of Simon & Schuster, Inc.
1230 Avenue of the Americas
New York, NY 10020

This book is a work of fiction. Any references to historical events, real people, or real places are used fictitiously. Other names, characters, places, and events are products of the author's imagination, and any resemblance to actual events or places or persons, living or dead, is entirely coincidental.

This Pocket Books paperback edition February 2021

POCKET and colophon are registered trademarks of Simon & Schuster, Inc.

For information about special discounts for bulk purchases, please contact Simon & Schuster Special Sales at 1-866-506-1949 or business@simonandschuster.com.

The Simon & Schuster Speakers Bureau can bring authors to your live event. For more information or to book an event, contact the Simon & Schuster Speakers Bureau at 1-866-248-3049 or visit our website at www.simonspeakers.com.

Manufactured in the United States of America

10   9   8   7   6   5   4   3   2   1

ISBN 978-1-9821-6408-9
ISBN 978-0-6710-3690-4 (ebook)

This one was always for Diana.
Because she always believed.

PROLOGUE

Cork O'Connor first heard the story of the Windigo in the fall of 1965 when he hunted the big bear with Sam Winter Moon. He was fourteen and his father was dead a year.

Sam Winter Moon had set a bear trap that autumn along a deer trail that ran from the stream called Widow's Creek to an old logged-over area full of blueberries. He'd found scat at the creek and along the trail and in the blueberry meadow when the berries were ripe. The trap was made as it had been in old times. Against a tree, Sam built a narrow enclosure of branches with a single opening. Over the entrance he suspended a heavy log secured to a spring pole. The trap was baited with a mash of cooked fish, fish oils, and a little maple syrup. It was the first time Sam had ever built a bear trap—a nearly lost Ojibwe tradition—and he'd invited Cork to help him with the process. Cork had no interest in it. Since his father's death, nothing interested him. He figured Sam's invitation had nothing to do with both of them learning the old ways together. It was just another good-intentioned effort to make him forget his grief, something Corcoran O'Connor didn't want to do. In a way, he was afraid that to let go of the grieving would be to let go of his father forever. Still, out of politeness, he accepted Sam Winter Moon's offer.

Late in the afternoon, they found the trap sprung, but the bear was not in it. They could see where the animal had fallen, slammed down by the weight of the great log, which, when they'd hauled and set it, Sam had calculated at over three hundred pounds. The log should have broken the bear's back. Any normal black bear should have been there for them, pinned under the log, dead or almost dead. The trap was sprung. The log had fallen. But the bear had shrugged it off.

Sam Winter Moon turned to the boy gravely. "I expect it's hurt," he said. "I got to go after it."

He looked away from Cork and didn't say anything about the boy going.

"A bear like that," Cork said, "a bear that can bounce a tree off his back, he'd be worth seeing."

Sam Winter Moon knelt and ran his hand over the deep indentation the animal's great paws had made in the soft ground. "Risky," he said. He looked up at the boy. "If you come, you got to do exactly as I say."

"I will," Cork promised, feeling excited about something for the first time in a year. "Exactly."

They fasted the rest of the day and breathed in the smoke of a cedar fire. At first light next morning, they blackened their faces with the cedar ash, a sign to the spirits of the deep woods that they had purified themselves. Sam tied back his long black-and-gray hair with a leather cord ornamented with a single eagle feather. They smoked tobacco and red willow leaves mixed with powdered aster root as a hunting charm, then covered themselves with tallow made of various animal fats to disguise their scent from the bear. In a small deer-hide sack that Sam hung on his back, he packed more tallow, matches, a whetstone, and a box of 180-grain cartridges for his rifle. He looked a little doubtfully at the cartridges. His was a .30-06 bolt-action Winchester. Fine for deer and small bears, he told Cork. But a bear like the one they were after, a bear that could shrug off a tree, that was something else. He gave Cork a canvas pack with bedrolls, cooking utensils, cooked wild rice, coffee, salt, and deer jerky. Finally he put in several long leather cords so that if they were given the bear, they could lash its body to a travois and cart it to a road where he could retrieve it with his truck. He hung his Green River hunting knife on his belt and slung his rifle over his shoulder.

At the sprung trap, they made a circle, looking for vegetation flattened in the bear's passage. Sam found a sign, a clear line where the fallen birch leaves were pressed into the soft earth underneath, and they followed north, where the bear had gone.

Every fall Sam Winter Moon killed one bear. The smoked bear meat he shared with the other people on the Iron Lake Reservation, especially the elders who could not hunt or trap anymore but who still enjoyed the taste of the fat, richly flavored meat. He also shared the meat with Cork's family. Cork's mother was half Anishinaabe, and his father, although he was white, had been Sam's friend for many years. The skins Sam sometimes sold for bounty, but more often he kept them for himself. He was grateful to the black bears for the meat they gave to him and the people of his band, but he told Cork, as they followed the trail that fall, that he would be grateful even for just a glimpse of this great animal who'd shrugged off the log trap as if it were no more than a small bothersome thing.

Bears, Sam cautioned him, were the most difficult animals of the woods to track and to kill. They had decent eyes, good ears, and the best nose of any animal alive. They were smart, too. And if they were hurt, there was no thing a man would ever go against that was more dangerous. He loved hunting the bears. He appreciated the ritual of the hunt that joined hunter and hunted together with the land that was the mother of both man and bear. He enjoyed the challenge of tracking, using his own knowledge of the animal and the woods instead of hunting with dogs the way white men did.

Sam stopped occasionally to look carefully at the soft earth or vegetation. Near noon, they found a stump where the bear had dug for grubs, and later a branch from an oak broken off to get the acorns.

The sky was clear blue, the air cool and still, the great woods full of the russet and gold of late fall. They moved quickly and Cork was filled with excitement. His stomach growled loudly from the fasting and he rustled the dry leaves as he walked. Sam said not to worry too much about the noise he made. A bear, especially a big one, would not be much concerned with sounds. The smell of a man, that was the thing to keep from a bear. Sam hoped they would be able to come at the animal from downwind. If not, he hoped the tallow would mask them.

They were led into the late afternoon. Cork realized he had no idea where they were in the great forest. He asked Sam if he knew these woods, and Sam said no. They'd passed out of reservation land and were now in what the white men called the Quetico-Superior Wilderness. This part of the forest Sam had never been through. But he didn't seem worried. At sunset they stopped and built a fire at the edge of a stream. Sam heated the wild rice, which they ate with the deer jerky. When the sky turned black and full of stars and the chill of the fall night crept over them, he made coffee and poured it into tin cups for them to drink.

"Will the bear get away while we sleep?" Cork asked.

Sam settled the old coffeepot in the embers at the fire's edge. He stirred the fire with a stick. "The bear's got to sleep, too. We've been guided well today. I think that's a good sign." He paused while the flames sprang up around the end of the stick. "But, you know, I been thinking. This bear's moving pretty good. Doesn't seem like that log hurt it much after all. A bear like that, well—" He glanced at the boy. "I been thinking it'd be a shame to kill it. If we even could."

"I'd like to see it," Cork said.

"Me, too." Sam smiled. "And I believe we will."

Suddenly the old pot hopped and slid across the coals, startling Cork so that he jerked and spilled his coffee.

Sam Winter Moon looked around them, then up at the sky. His voice dropped to a whisper. "A Windigo's passing close by."

Cork wiped at his leg where the coffee had burned him through his jeans. "What's a Windigo?"

In the firelight, Sam Winter Moon's dark eyes were deadly serious and a little afraid.

"You don't know about the Windigo?" he asked the boy. "You've lived in this country all your life and you don't know about the Windigo?" He shook his head as if that were a dreadful thing.

Corcoran O'Connor sat on the far side of the campfire and stared at the blackened coffeepot that only moments before had jumped and rattled and moved across the coals without a human hand near it.

"I suppose," Sam Winter Moon said, looking cautiously at the tin pot himself, "I should tell you, then. For your own good." He carefully eyed the sky again and the stars, and he kept his voice low. "A Windigo's a giant, an ogre with a heart of ice. A cannibal, a cold and hungry thing. It comes out of the woods to eat the flesh of men and women. Children, too. It doesn't care."

"Is it coming for us?" Cork scanned the shadows that jumped at the edges of the firelight.

"The way I understand it, a man pretty much knows when the Windigo's coming for him."

"Can you fight it?"

"Oh, sure. Can even kill it."

"How?"

"Well, the Windigo's a powerful creature, and there's only one way so far as I know." The ritual ash of the morning had worn off the smooth parts of Sam's face, but it still blackened every deep line and crevice, so that in the firelight he looked like a fractured man. "You got to become a Windigo, too. There's a magic for that. Henry Meloux'd most likely know the magic. But you got to be careful, because even if you kill the Windigo, you're still in danger."

"What danger?"

"Of staying a Windigo forever. Of being the ogre you killed. So you got to be prepared. You got to have help for what follows the killing of a Windigo. Someone's got to be there with hot tallow ready for you to drink to melt the ice inside you, to melt you back down to the size of other men."

"I hope I never meet the Windigo," Cork said, eyeing the old tin pot.

"I hope so, too," Sam agreed.

Cork was quiet a moment while the fire snapped

and popped and sent smoke and glowing embers upward into the dark. "That's just a story, right?"

Sam rolled a cigarette and considered while he sealed the paper with his tongue. "Maybe. But in these woods it's best to believe in all possibilities. There's more in these woods than a man can ever see with his eyes, a lot more than he can ever hope to understand."

Although he was tired, Cork stayed awake by the fire a long time while Sam smoked and told stories about Cork's father. Some of the stories made them both laugh. That night, as Cork lay in his bedroll, he thought about the bear they were after. He was glad Sam had changed his mind about killing the great animal, but he hoped they would at least see it. He thought about the Windigo, which was something he hoped he would not see. And he thought about his father, whom he would never see again. These were all elements of his life, and although they were separate things, they were now intertwined somehow like the roots of a tree. All his life he would remember the bear hunt with Sam Winter Moon. In some manner he didn't quite understand, the hunt had opened a way in him for the grief to begin passing through. All his life he would be grateful to his father's friend.

Almost thirty years would pass, however, before he would have cause to remember the Windigo. Thirty years before he heard it call his name.

CHAPTER 1

For a week the feeling had been with him, and all week long young Paul LeBeau had been afraid. Of what exactly, he couldn't say. Whenever he tried to put the finger of his thinking on it, it slipped away like a drop of mercury. But he knew that whatever was coming would be bad, because the feeling was exactly like the terrible waiting had been before his father disappeared. Each day he reached out into the air with all his senses, trying to touch what was coming. So that finally, on that morning in mid-December when the clouds rolled in thick and gray as smoke and the wind screamed over the pines and tamaracks and the snow began falling hard, Paul Le-Beau looked out the window of his algebra class and thought hopefully, Maybe it's only this.

Shortly after lunch, word of the school closing came down. Students quickly put on their coats and shouldered their book bags, and a few minutes later the yellow buses began to pull away, heading onto roads that threatened to disappear before them.

Paul left the Aurora Middle School and walked home, pushing into the force of the storm the whole way. He changed his clothes, put on his Sorel boots, took five dollars from the small cashbox on his dresser, and left his mother a note affixed with a butterfly magnet to the refrigerator door. Grabbing his canvas newspaper bag from its hook in the garage, he headed toward his drop box. By two-thirty he was loaded up and ready to go.

Paul had two paper routes covering nearly two and a half miles. He began with the small business district of Aurora and ended just at the town limits out on North Point Road. At fourteen, he was larger than most boys his age and very strong. If he hustled, he could finish in just under an hour and a half. But he knew this day would be different. The snow had been accumulating at a rate of more than an inch per hour and the bitter wind that swept down out of Canada drifted it fast and deep.

He took the routes in the time when his father was drinking heavily and his mother needed money. Delivering the papers, especially on days like this that seemed impossible, was a responsibility he took seriously. In truth, he loved the storms. The energy in the wind and the ceaseless force of the drifting snow thrilled him. Where another boy might see only the plodding task ahead of him, Paul saw challenge. He took pride in his ability to battle against these elements, trudging through the drifts, leaning hard into the wind in order to complete the job expected of him.

He was an Eagle Scout. Order of the Arrow. Member of Troop 135 out of St. Agnes Catholic Church. He had made himself capable in a hundred ways. He could start a fire with flint and steel; hit a bull's-eye with a target arrow at thirty yards; tie a bowline, a sheepshank, a slip knot; lash together a bridge strong enough to bear the weight of several men. He knew how to treat someone for shock, drowning, cardiac arrest, and sunstroke. He believed seriously in the motto "Be Prepared," and often as he walked his paper routes, he imagined scenarios of disaster in Aurora that would allow all his secret skills to shine.

By the time he neared the end of his deliveries, lights had been turned on in the houses along the way. He was tired. His shoulders ached from the weight of the papers and his legs felt leaden from wading through knee-deep drifts. The last house on his route stood at the very end of North Point Road, a pine-covered finger of land that jutted into Iron Lake and was lined with expensive homes. The last and most isolated of the houses belonged to Judge Robert Parrant.

The judge was an old man with a hard white face, bony hands, and sharp, watchful eyes. Out of fear Paul treated him with great deference. The judge's paper was always placed securely between the storm door and the heavy wooden front door, safe from the elements. Whenever Paul came monthly to collect for his service, the judge rewarded him with a generous tip and more stories about politics than Paul cared to hear.

The judge's house was almost dark, with only the flicker of a fireplace flame illuminating the living room curtains. With the last paper in hand, Paul threaded his way up the long walk between cedars laden with snow. He pulled the storm door open, plowing a little arc in the drift on the porch, and saw that the front door was slightly ajar. Cold air whistled into the house. As he reached out to draw the door closed, he heard the explosion from a heavy firearm discharged inside.

He edged the door back open. "Judge Parrant?" he called. "Are you all right?" He hesitated a moment, then stepped in.

Paul had been inside many times before at the judge's request. He always hated it. The house was a vast two-story affair built of Minnesota sandstone. The interior walls were dark oak, the windows leaded glass. A huge stone fireplace dominated the living room, and the walls there were hung with hunting trophies—the heads of deer and antelope and bear whose sightless eyes seemed to follow Paul whenever the judge asked him in.

The house smelled of applewood smoke. The sudden pop of sap from a log burning in the fireplace made him jump.

"Judge Parrant?" he tried again.

He knew he should probably just leave and close the door behind him. But there had been the shot, and now he felt something in the stillness of the house from which he couldn't turn, a kind of responsibility. As he stood with the door wide open at his back and the wind blowing through, he glanced down and watched tendrils of snow creep across the bare, polished floor and vine around his boots like something alive. He knew that a terrible thing had happened. He knew it absolutely.

He might still have turned away and run if he hadn't seen the blood. It was a dark glistening on the polished hardwood floor at the bottom of the staircase. He walked slowly ahead, knelt, touched the small dark puddle with his fingertips, confirmed the color of it by the firelight. There was a bloody trail leading down the hallway to his left.

Pictures from the manual for his First Aid merit badge that showed arterial bleeding and how to apply direct pressure or a tourniquet came to his mind. He'd practiced these procedures a hundred times, but never really believing that he'd ever use them. He found himself hoping desperately the judge wasn't badly hurt, and he panicked just a little at the thought that he might actually have to save a life.

The blood led him to a closed door where a dim light crept underneath.

"Judge Parrant?" he said cautiously, leaning close to the door.

He was reluctant to barge in, but when he finally turned the knob and stood in the threshold, he found a study lined with shelves of books. Along the far wall was a desk of dark wood with a lamp on it. The lamp was switched on but didn't give much light and the room was heavy with shadows. On the wall directly back of the desk hung a map of Minnesota. Red lines like red rivers ran down the map from red splashes like red lakes. Behind the desk lay an overturned chair, and near the chair lay the judge.

Although fear reached way down inside him and made his legs go weak, he forced himself to move ahead. As he neared the desk and saw the judge more clearly, he forgot all about the procedures for a tourniquet. There was nowhere to put a tourniquet on a man who was missing most of his head.

For a moment he couldn't move. He felt paralyzed, unable to think as he stared down at the raw pieces of the judge's brain, pink as chunks of fresh watermelon. Paul didn't even move when he heard the sound at his back, the soft shutting of the door. Finally he managed to turn away from the dead man just in time to see the second thing that night his Scout training could never have prepared him for.

CHAPTER 2

"Cork?" Molly said from the bed.

He heard and he didn't. Standing at the window with his hands poised at his zipper, Corcoran O'Connor watched drifts rise in the yard. His old red Bronco parked in the drive was already hub deep in powdery white. Farther down through the pines, the abandoned resort cabins by the lake were nearly invisible behind a gauzy curtain of blowing snow.

"You're not really thinking of going, are you, Cork?" Molly asked. "Not into that."

"What would folks say if I ended up snowbound here?"

"The truth. That you were screwing Molly Nurmi, that shameless slut."

He turned to her, frowning. "Nobody calls you that."

"Not to my face, anyway." She laughed when she saw his anger. "Oh, come on, Cork. I've lived with that most of my life. It doesn't bother me."

"Well, it bothers me."

"I'm glad it does." She pushed the hair from her eyes, dark red hair damp with sweat. "Stay, Cork. I'll fire up the sauna. We can get hot and wet, roll in the snow, come back to bed, and make love again. How does that sound?"

He finished zipping his pants, buckled his belt, and came away from the window. He went to the bed and took his red corduroy shirt from the corner post where it had been hastily draped. Slipping it on over his long johns, he slowly worked the buttons through. He bent and tugged on his socks. The cold floor had nearly frozen his feet. "Hand me a cigarette, will you?"

Molly took one from Cork's pack of Lucky Strikes by the bed, lit it, and handed it to him. "They'll kill you."

"What won't anymore?" He glanced around the room, looking for his boots.

"You seem distracted today."

"Do I? Sorry."

"Feeling a little guilty?"

"Always."

"There's no need to," she said.

"Easy for you to say. You're not Catholic."

"Come on. Relax here beside me a minute while you finish your cigarette." She patted the bed at her side.

He looked out the window. "I should get going. It'll be hard enough getting back into town as it is."

Molly drew the blanket and sheet around her and pushed herself up against the headboard. She pulled her knees up to her breasts and hugged them as if she were cold. "Why are you always so concerned with what people say about you, Cork? It's not as if you're still the golden boy."

"I don't care what people say." He knelt and fished around under the bed for his boots. "It's not me I'm worried about." He found them and sat on the bed.

"Your wife?" she asked innocently.

Cork exhaled and shot her a cold look through the cloud of smoke.

"You know what I mean," she said.

Molly took the Lucky Strike from his fingers and tapped the ash into a little tray shaped like a pair of red lips on the nightstand. She left the cigarette there while Cork concentrated on lacing his boots. She reached out and let her hand drift down the knobby ridge of his backbone. "What is it that you think we do here, you and me? I'll tell you what I think it is. This is grace, Cork. This is one of those things that God, when He created it, said, 'That's good.'"

Cork kept lacing his boots as if he didn't hear, or if he heard, as if it didn't matter.

"Can I tell you something, Sheriff?"

"I'm not the sheriff anymore," he reminded her.

"Can I tell you something," she went on, "without you getting cold and stomping out?"

"Do I get cold and stomp out?"

"You get quiet and make excuses to leave."

"I won't get quiet," he promised.

"Cork, I think you miss your family."

"I see my family all the time."

"This is different. This is Christmas. I really think you miss them more than you want to admit."

"Bullshit," he said, standing up.

"See, I've made you mad. You're leaving."

"I'm not mad. I just finished tying my boots. And you know I have to leave."

"Why? What difference would it make if you stayed and people found out about us? It's not as if you're being unfaithful to a loving wife."

"It's a small town and I'm not divorced. People would kick us around in their talk like a couple of soccer balls. I don't want my kids having to listen to that."

"Fine." She slid down and pulled the covers tight around her. "Have it your way."

He picked up his cigarette, took a last drag, and ground out the ember on the red lips of the ashtray. He slipped the pack of Lucky Strikes into his shirt pocket. "Going to see me out?" he asked.

"You know the way."

"Now who's cold?"

"Go screw yourself," she said.

"The world would be a dreary place, Molly, if that's the way things worked." He leaned down and gently kissed the top of her head.

"Go on," she said, pushing him away softly. But she smiled in spite of herself. "I'll be right down."

He walked along the hallway of the old log house, over Molly's braided rugs, creaked his way down the stairs and into the kitchen. Molly had fed him. Some sort of light brown sprout bread and lentil soup. Yogurt and strawberries for dessert. She drank Evian springwater, but she'd given Cork a Grain Belt. A few swallows were left in the bottle and he drank that down. The beer was still cool but had gone flat. He lifted his parka from the peg beside the back door and put it on, then settled his black watch cap over his ears. As he worked his gloves onto his hands, he glanced at a small plaque that hung on the wall. It was homemade, wood-burned by Molly's father long ago. It contained an old Finnish saying her father had roughly translated into English:

> *Cold, thou son of Wind,*
> *Do not freeze my fingernails,*
> *Do not freeze my hands.*
> *Freeze though the water willows.*
> *Go chill the birch chunks.*

Like most magic charms of the people of Molly's heritage, it suggested to the evil of the world—from hiccups to death—that it visit instead other things, such as the loom or the needle or the thicket or, in a pinch, one of the neighbors. When Cork turned around, he found Molly watching him from the doorway. She'd thrown on a red chenille bathrobe and pulled bright red wool socks on over her feet.

"Will I see you at the Pinewood Broiler?" she asked.

"You won't be plowed out in time to get into town tomorrow."

"I'll probably ski in."

"Waitressing means that much?"

"This time of year the company does."

Cork went back and kissed her. "If I don't see you, I'll call."

"I won't hold my breath."

He pushed out the back door onto the utility porch, then out completely into the hard cold and the snow. He waded to the Bronco, cleared the tailpipe and the driver's door, scraped the ice from the windshield, and got in. He cranked the engine. Wiping where his breath had fogged the windshield, he saw Molly standing at the kitchen window, her arms locked across her breasts. The light was on at her back and filtered through her hair making it like wisps of red smoke. She was a beautiful woman, large-boned and strong, ten years younger than Cork, though she'd taken such good care of herself—didn't smoke, didn't drink, didn't eat red meat—that she looked even younger. Cork was a dozen pounds overweight, smoked far too much, and was beginning to go a little bald on the crown of his head. What she saw in him, he had no idea.

Women, he thought with a warm flare of gratitude. Go figure.

He slipped the Bronco into four-wheel drive and began slowly to move through the first of the drifts toward the county road that would take him to the highway into town. As he headed off, he glanced back at the cabin window, prepared to wave, but Molly was no longer there.

The state highway was no better than the county road through the woods from Molly's. Except for the Bronco, not a thing moved in the white hillocks the wind had bulldozed across the asphalt. From the weather reports he'd heard, Cork was pretty sure it was like that from the Canadian border all the way across the Arrowhead of Minnesota into Wisconsin. He drove slowly, steadily, a little blindly. After twenty minutes, he came on a figure hunched in a red-plaid mackinaw and wading toward town. He slowed to a full stop, stepped out onto the running board and hollered, "Get in!"

The figure, so bundled Cork couldn't even see a face, slowly turned and came toward the Bronco. When they were both safely inside, Cork started once again for Aurora.

"Hell of a day for a constitutional." Cork peered into the slit between the wool muffler that came above the nose and the knitted cap that was pulled down to the eyebrows.

The mittens were drawn off and Cork saw old veined hands stained with liver spots. The hands went to the muffler, whose ends were tucked securely inside the collar of the coat. As the muffler came loose, Cork recognized Henry Meloux, whom white people around Aurora sometimes called Mad Mel. Cork knew he was in fact one of the Midewiwin, an Anishinaabe medicine man, who lived by himself on a remote point around the northwest end of the lake. He must have been walking most of the day in the blizzard to have come so near town.

"Shoot, Henry, what could be so important it would bring you out on a day like this?"

Meloux stared beyond the wipers that shoved the snow into little heaps off to the sides of the windshield. "Snow, not snow, the day is the same to me."

"Noble philosophy, Henry, but one that could get you frozen to death."

"I seen more storms than you could imagine. And worse. I seen storms and other things."

Cork reached inside his parka for his pack of Lucky Strikes. "Cigarette, Henry?"

The old man took one; so did Cork. But before Cork could light up the old man sniffed at the air inside the Bronco. He gave Cork a grin full of teeth remarkably good in a man so ancient. "You smell like the good, deep part of a woman."

"I think that wind's frozen your nose, Henry," Cork told him.

"No." The old man kept on grinning at him. "It's a good day for a man to be inside." Meloux laughed softly. "Understand?"

The old man lit his cigarette with the lighter Cork offered and grew quiet again. They had come to the edge of Aurora. They passed the big new corrugated fence of Johannsen's salvage yard, put up when the Chippewa Grand Casino was being built so that the gutted frames and rusting wreckage of the junkyard wouldn't sully the image of the town. A little farther on was the Iron Lake Best Western, brand-new, with 150 rooms and an indoor swimming pool with a Jacuzzi and sauna. The big marquee out front welcomed gamblers and informed them that Lyle Porter was playing piano in the Kitchi-Gami Room eight to midnight. The parking lot was nearly full. Next to the Best Western stood a new Perkins restaurant and across the road a glittery twelve-pump Food-N-Fuel gas station.

On the streets of Aurora not much moved except a few pickups with wide traction tires. The shops had closed early and most of the windows of the small downtown were dark. For the most part, it looked as if the town's 3,752 citizens had simply crawled inside to wait out the storm.

The old man had been quiet a long time, smoking the Lucky Strike reflectively. Finally Cork asked, "What brings you into town on a day like this, Henry?"

The old man said, "I seen it."

"What?" Cork asked. "What did you see?"

The old man looked straight ahead. "It jumped over my cabin two nights ago, headed northwest, going toward the storm before the storm come in. I seen the black where it ran through the sky and covered the stars."

"Seen what?" Cork asked again.

"I heard it, too. Heard it calling names."

From the way Meloux's voice dropped to nearly nothing, Cork figured that was bad. "Heard what calling names?"

But the old man clammed up on the subject. "I can walk now," he said.

"You're not thinking of going back to your place before the roads are cleared."

"I walked here a long time before there were roads."

"That was a couple of centuries ago, Henry."

The old man took one last drag on his cigarette and crushed it out in the ashtray. "Thank you, Sheriff O'Connor."

"Christ, I'm not the sheriff anymore."

Meloux put on his mittens, opened his door, and stepped out. "The smell of you alone has been worth the time." He grinned once again, then shut the door.

Cork watched him tuck the ends of his muffler into his mackinaw and turn toward the lake, toward the glittery dome invisible behind the storm where everyone who came to Aurora these days was headed, where the bright neon of the huge new casino blazed night and day, and where, even in the worst of weather, the doors were always ready to swing wide in a warm, smoky welcome promising easy fortune.

When Meloux was gone, vanished in the white, Cork smiled to himself and said the name of the thing the old man had dared not utter.

"Windigo."

CHAPTER 3

Stu Grantham stood before a large framed photograph of Split Rock Lighthouse that hung on the wall of the law office of Nancy Jo O'Connor. He clasped his hands behind his back as he stared at the famous landmark on the North Shore of Lake Superior. He'd been that way for nearly a minute—thoughtful, silent, unmoving—and Jo simply let him be. She had him cornered. She knew it, and if he thought about it awhile, he'd know it, too, and they could get on with things.

A tapping at the door and Fran, Jo's secretary, peeked in. "Jo, I'm sorry. I know you didn't want to be disturbed, but the state patrol's just closed Highway 1. I heard it on the radio."

Jo glanced out her window. The parking lot of the Aurora Professional Building was nearly empty. Her blue Toyota Cressida was covered with snow and hung with icicles and looked like some kind of Arctic beast hunkered down to wait out the storm. Beyond that the world was white and nothing moved in the sea of snow.

"Thanks, Fran," Jo said. "Why don't you go on home before you get stuck here."

"What about you?" Fran asked. She glanced at

Grantham, who seemed oblivious to the news she'd brought.

"I'll finish here with Stuart and be right behind you."

Fran stepped toward her and handed her several pages from a phone memo pad. "I held your calls as you asked. Here are the messages."

"Thanks. Drive carefully."

"You, too."

Jo scanned the phone messages. One from Frank Monroe at the department of natural resources. Call him about the Rust Creek variance for the casino. Two from Judge Robert Parrant. Simply call him. One from Dorothea Hayes about the easement for the new pulp mill. One from Sandy Parrant. No message.

Stu Grantham walked silently to the small table where Jo kept a stainless steel coffee server and several mugs, poured himself some coffee, and sat down. Grantham was a realtor by profession and head of the county board of commissioners by choice of the electorate. In his late fifties, he was white-haired and still handsome. Talc softened his cheeks. He smelled of musk aftershave. Jo wondered if he'd shaved just before coming. Men sometimes did that for her, believing it might make a difference.

Jo was a rigorously slender woman. She had hair so blonde it was almost white and eyes blue-white like glacial ice. She'd been separated from her husband, Cork, for several months. Some men, Grantham apparently among them, saw that as an opportunity.

"What is it with you, Jo?" Grantham finally asked. "Whenever I try to use your services, you're always going on how you're so busy you can't hardly see straight. But here you are still taking on the cases of these—" He stopped himself abruptly.

"These what, Stu?"

"You know. These pro bono Indian cases. They've got the casino now. Let 'em hire their own damn attorneys."

"The casino is owned by the Iron Lake band of Ojibwe. Louise Willette is Lakota. She gets nothing from the casino profits. She has to work hard for what the county pays her. What she doesn't need is the constant harassment of her coworkers."

"For Christ sake, Jo, she's the only woman on a road crew of men. What does she expect? These guys can't watch every word that comes out of their mouths."

"When it applies to my client, or to women in general, they'd better." Jo put down the phone messages and folded her hands patiently on her desktop. "Look, Stu, I could easily have started an action against the county. The evidence is overwhelming. But I brought it to you first because I'd like to save you and the rest of the board a lot of embarrassment. My client is willing to settle this quietly. Come election time next November, I'm sure you'll be glad Louise and I didn't splash this across the headlines of the *Sentinel*."

"Doing me a favor." Grantham grinned, showing an incisor outlined in silver. He set his coffee mug on the desk and began to twirl a heavy, gold Aurora High class ring on his finger. Class of '52 or '53, Jo guessed. Aurora good ol' boy. "Know what I'm thinking?" Grantham said. "I'm thinking Wanda Manydeeds put her up to this."

"Nobody put her up to anything. But, yes, it was Wanda who told Louise to see me. And why shouldn't she? I'm the best attorney in Aurora."

"Ever since you and that Manydeeds got together,

Tamarack County hasn't been the same," Grantham lamented.

"And amen to that."

Jo kept her reply amiable. She'd handled Stu Grantham and others like him since she'd first hung her shingle in Aurora nearly a decade before. But it hadn't been easy.

They'd moved back to Cork's hometown to raise their children in a place that was not like Chicago. Cork warned her things would be difficult; she was an outsider and a woman. She hadn't realized just how hard it would be until she'd gone nearly three months without a single client.

Then one spring day Wanda Manydeeds stepped into her office.

She was a large woman—not heavy, but tall and solid—dressed in faded jeans and a blue flannel shirt rolled up to her elbows. Her long black hair was done in a single braid and ornamented with a feather. She wore brightly beaded earrings and a beaded bracelet and possessed one of the most confrontive gazes Jo had ever encountered in another female. A young woman, probably twenty, though she was hardly larger than a girl, stood behind her, slightly hidden.

"What kind of lawyer are you?" the large woman with the earrings and bracelet asked.

"A good one," Jo replied.

"Are you a lawyer for money or for justice?"

"Given the choice between those two, I lean toward justice."

"Good. We don't have any money."

"Maybe we should talk about justice, then. Won't you both have a seat?"

The women accepted the chairs Jo offered. The large woman sat proudly, with her back held very straight. The younger one sat a little slumped and wouldn't look at Jo directly.

"You know me," Jo said. "My name's on the door. You are—?"

"I am Wanda Manydeeds," the large woman replied. "This is Lizzie Favre." The young woman glanced up and then lowered her eyes quickly.

"What is it you wanted to see me about?" Jo asked.

"We want to fight some powerful people," Wanda Manydeeds replied.

"Who exactly?"

"We want to fight the Great North Development Company."

"Great North." Jo sat back, a little tug deep in her stomach. "Robert and Sandy Parrant. What's your complaint against them?"

"They won't hire Lizzie."

Jo looked at the young woman. "Because you're female?"

Lizzie hesitated, then replied quietly, "And because I am Ojibwe."

"The man who hires for Great North, a man named Chester, I've heard he calls us squaws," Wanda Manydeeds said.

"But not to your face," Jo said.

The large woman shook her head. "He is a coward."

"That kind of man always is." Jo picked up a pencil and idly tapped the sharpened lead on a legal pad as she considered the situation. "Judge Robert Parrant. Sandy Parrant." She liked the taste in her mouth, the slight dryness in anticipation of a good fight. "Going at the old man would be like taking a swing at barbed wire. But the son—" She leaned toward the other women confidently. "Word is, he's poised for a run at the state legislature. I think we might have him there."

"You'll do it?" Wanda Manydeeds asked. Her face, which was hard and tawny as sandstone, showed no emotion. But there was a flash in her eyes that Jo interpreted as satisfaction.

"We'll do it," Jo replied.

And they had.

"How's Sandy's transition to Washington going?" Stu Grantham asked.

"What?" Jo brought herself back to the moment, to Stu Grantham stalling on the far side of her desk.

"Our new senator. Is he ready for Washington?"

"He will be."

"You read the article in the *Pioneer Press*? Another Jack Kennedy, they're saying. Harvard-educated, liberal, good-looking. A lady's man." Grantham paused a moment, twirling his heavy class ring. "You going with him?"

"I beg your pardon?"

"I heard he wanted you to be part of his staff in D.C."

"My practice and my family are here in Aurora," Jo replied coolly. "I have no intention of leaving."

"I just thought, with things the way they are between you and Cork—"

"What about my client?" Jo swung back to the real issue. "Are we going to be here all night or do you agree to the terms I've proposed?"

"All night with you?" Grantham leaned across the desk, grinning. "Now, that's a thought."

"You know, Stu," Jo replied calmly, "that's exactly the kind of statement that landed your road crew in deep shit."

"Ah, look, Jo—"

"No, you look." She drove a finger at him, and although she didn't touch him at all, he sat back abruptly. "I want an answer and I want it now. Will you advise the board to accept our terms? Or do we drag this through the courts and air all the dirty, sexist linen in public? If you want to know the truth, Stu, I'd just as soon do this in court. I'd just as soon make an example of this crew and maybe the whole leadership of this county while we're at it."

Jo would have gone on, but the phone rang. She turned from Grantham and answered it with an irate, "Yes!"

It was her sister Rose.

"Have you heard from Anne?" Rose asked, speaking of Jo's eleven-year-old daughter.

"No. Isn't she home with you?"

"She checked in right after school let out and said she had an errand to run. I didn't think anything of it. But that was three hours ago, and I haven't heard from her since."

Jo looked out her window at the furious energy of the storm. She worked at keeping her own voice calm. "Does Jenny know anything?"

"No."

"Friends?"

"I called everyone I could think of."

"Have you tried Cork?"

"I left messages on his machine."

"Maybe he took her ice fishing," Jo suggested, although she was certain Cork wouldn't have done that without calling first.

"Jo, I'm worried."

"Are Stevie and Jenny there with you?"

"Yes."

"Keep them there. I'll be right home."

Jo hung up the phone. She glared at Grantham. "Well?"

The telephone call had broken Jo's momentum. Grantham was straightening his tie. "Trouble at home?"

"Nothing I can't handle."

"I don't think I want to rush a decision here, Jo," Grantham said. He wandered back toward his chair and seemed prepared to settle in again.

Jo went to the door and held it open, signaling Grantham their meeting was at a definite end. "I'll be in touch."

"I'm sure you will." The man smiled as he left.

Jo threw a few things into her briefcase. She pulled on her coat, locked up the office, and headed out to the empty parking lot. Under the snow, the windshield of her Toyota was coated with a thick layer of ice that broke her plastic scraper. She turned the defroster up full blast, and while the engine warmed and the air grew hot enough to begin melting a clear patch, she labored to brush snow off the rest of the car.

Suddenly, out of the cold of the storm, she felt the touch of a deeper cold on her back, as if an icy hand had reached through her coat and touched her skin. She swung around, a shiver running down her spine, and peered into the swirling white behind her. She strained to look at the line of cedars that walled the corner of the lot a couple of dozen yards away.

"Is anyone there?" She knew it was ridiculous to think a human hand could have reached so far. But what had touched her had not felt human at all.

No voice answered except the bitter howl of the wind. She left off brushing the snow, got into her car, and locked the doors. The defroster had cleared only a small area low on the windshield, but it was enough for Nancy Jo O'Connor. She left the empty lot as quickly as she could.

CHAPTER 4

Cork pulled up alongside a snow-covered Quonset hut that stood next to the lake. The front of the hut had been reconstructed as a burger stand, with two sliding windows and a long, narrow counter for serving customers. Pictures of ice cream cones decorated the side of the building up front. The serving windows had been boarded over with plywood, and above that a sign painted in red letters on a white board read, "Sam's Place."

Cork parked near the back door and went in. The back half of the hut had been converted into a space for living—one large room that held a stove and refrigerator, a sink, a table with two chairs, a sofa, a bunk, a small desk, and a bookshelf. One corner had been partitioned for a bathroom with a toilet, a sink, and a shower stall. During World War II, the hut had been part of a complex used by the National Guard. After the war, the complex was abandoned and all but the single Quonset hut had been bulldozed. Cork wasn't sure why the hut had been spared, but it had been purchased by Sam Winter Moon, who'd made it over into a business serving cones and shakes and burgers to the summer tourists. Sam had lived in the back during the season. Late fall after he closed up, he lived in his cabin on reservation land. In his will, Sam had left the Quonset hut to Cork.

Inside, the place was cool, much cooler than it should have been. Cork stepped down into the cellar and found that the burner on the oil furnace wasn't running, a chronic problem. He hit the red reset button. Nothing happened. He kicked the tiny motor. The burner came on with a small roar. Mentally Cork crossed his fingers, hoping the burner would last the winter. By next fall, if Sam's Place had a good season, he could afford to replace it.

Back upstairs, he stepped through a door into that part of the hut that was the burger stand. Boxes of nonperishable supplies sat stacked, waiting for spring. The big ice-milk freezer stood sparkling clean and idle next to the small grill. Propped against the wall near the door was a sack of dry corn with a plastic bucket and scoop inside it. Cork scooped out a quarter bucket of corn, headed back through the hut and outside again.

The lake was lost behind the snow. Cork trudged through the drifts toward a tall Cyclone fence that edged Sam's property. My property, Cork still had to remind himself. On the other side of the fence was the Bearpaw Brewery, the buildings big and dark and indistinct through the blowing snow. He followed the fence to the edge of the lake. Although the rest of the lake had been frozen awhile, a large expanse of water near the fence stayed open year round because of the runoff from the brewery. Warning signs had been placed on the ice, and safety stations with sleds and life rings stood along the shore. Cork was surprised to see a figure in a familiar red coat hunched at the water's edge.

"Annie?" he called. "Is that you?"

His daughter turned. She was big for her age, and

freckled year round. She'd inherited the wild red hair of her Irish ancestors, but from her Anishinaabe genes came dark thoughtful eyes that regarded her father with concern.

"I was worried about Romeo and Juliet," she said. She looked out at the lake.

The open water was choppy in the wind, and looked cold and gray. Two Canadian geese huddled together twenty yards from shore, their bodies pointed into the wind, riding out the storm. The bird Anne called Romeo had injured a wing late in the summer. When the other geese had gone south, he'd stayed, and his mate, whom Anne had named Juliet, also stayed. They never left the lake. The open water kept them there. Cork had taken to feeding them when he'd realized their plight. Anne had adopted them as well, taken them into her heart of concern.

Cork gave her the bucket. "Why don't you feed them," he suggested.

The geese had turned at Cork's approach, anticipating the corn he carried in the bucket. They paddled nearer, but held off coming ashore. Cork kicked at the snow with his boots, clearing a circle all the way to the frozen ground.

"Just pour it in there, Annie," he said.

She spread the corn around the circle, then they walked away a dozen steps. Romeo and Juliet waddled through the snow to the corn and began noisily to feed. They watched Cork and Anne carefully.

"Do you think they'd ever eat from our hands?" Anne asked hopefully.

"Most animals can be tamed, I suppose," Cork replied. "The question is, do you really want to? Make them tame and they become easy prey for people not as kindly disposed toward them as you are."

"People would hurt them?" she asked, appalled at the idea.

"Some would. Just for the pleasure of it. Come on. They'll be fine now." He started back to the hut.

Inside, Cork took a moment to listen to his answering machine. He frowned at Annie after he heard the worried voice of his sister-in-law.

"You didn't tell your aunt Rose you were coming?"

"I did," Anne insisted. "She was reading a recipe, so maybe she didn't hear."

It was possible. Rose would be oblivious to a nuclear attack if she were deeply involved in the intricacies of a new recipe. But it was also possible that Anne had used her inattention to sneak away. It wasn't that Rose would have minded her coming, but, given Rose's ability to see disaster at every turn, she probably wouldn't have allowed her niece to come so far from home in the storm.

Cork called and explained to his sister-in-law, who sounded so relieved she forgot to be angry. Cork said he'd bring Anne right home.

As they stepped outside to the Bronco, Annie looked through the blowing snow toward the open water of the lake.

"Will they be all right?" she asked.

"I expect so. As long as the water doesn't freeze and we give them plenty of grain."

"I worry about them. I pray for them. Do you think it's all right to pray for geese?"

"It's all right to pray for just about anything, I suppose."

She looked at him, her face red from the wind and the cold. "You don't."

"I let you do the praying for both of us these days, sweetheart. You do a better job of it than I ever could."

They got into the Bronco. Cork pulled out across the tracks toward Center Street.

"Know what I pray for most?" Anne said, staring through her window at the snow as it swirled around them.

"What?"

"That you and Mom get back together."

Cork was quiet. Then he said, "It never hurts to pray."

The house on Gooseberry Lane was big, two stories, white with dark gray shutters and a wraparound porch. Out front stood a huge American elm, and in the backyard, a red maple nearly as large. Lilac bushes formed a tall hedge on the north side, and south was a grape arbor. The house had been the home of his mother's parents, then had belonged to his own parents. When Cork's father was killed, his mother had turned it into a boardinghouse. It was never a luxurious life, and Cork always worked to help bring in income, but they managed to keep the house and to hold together and, as Cork remembered it, to be happy.

All the houses on the block were similar—old, shaded in summer, quiet. There wasn't a single fence to be seen, and Cork had always taken issue with the assertion that fences made good neighbors. Until Jo had asked him to leave, Cork had been quite happy to call Gooseberry Lane his home, and the people who lived there his neighbors.

He used his garage door opener and parked next to Jo's blue Toyota Cressida. Her car had two bumper stickers. One said, "Sandy Parrant for U.S. Senate" and the other, in true political jingoism, said, "Just look at the candidates. The difference is aParrant." The election was long over. Parrant had won. Cork thought it was high time Jo got rid of the bumper stickers.

He made his way to the back door with Annie. Stepping into the kitchen, he was greeted by the aroma of baking ham.

"Smells delicious, Rose," Cork said. He hung his parka and cap on wall hooks beside the door.

He could tell his sister-in-law was trying to be upset with him. She nodded in response to his complimentary greeting, then went to the oven, opened the door, and bent to check inside. She was wearing floral stretch pants that didn't at all flatter her wide hips and thighs. She had on a baggy red sweater and old blue canvas slip-ons. Her hair was dull brown like road dust, and her fleshy arms were covered with freckles. She was nothing like her sister, Jo, in appearance or temperament, and if Cork hadn't known better he'd have guessed that one of them had been adopted.

"Sure miss your cooking." Cork grinned.

Rose smiled despite herself. But she set stern eyes on Annie, who was trying to slip through the kitchen unnoticed. "I was worried sick, Anne."

"I told you where I was going, Aunt Rose," Anne argued politely. "But I guess you didn't hear. You were reading that recipe for Christmas pudding."

"I was?" Rose glanced at a cookbook open on the kitchen table. "Still, you should have called when it got to be so late."

"My fault, Rose," Cork said. "She was helping me with some chores."

"Well." Rose considered Anne a moment more. "Go clean up. Dinner will be ready shortly. And you—" She turned to Cork with a scowl, then smiled. "Would you like to stay? There's plenty of food."

"Where's Jo?"

"Down the hall in her office. She'd like to talk with you."

"I might not be welcome for dinner after."

"You know that's not true," Rose said. "Just let me know and I'll have Jenny set another place." She turned back to the stove, picked up a wooden spoon, and began stirring something in the saucepan.

In the living room, Cork found his five-year-old son, Stevie, on his belly playing with Legos. The television was on, tuned to cartoons. Stevie rolled over at his father's approach and shouted, "Daddy!"

Cork knelt down. "What's up, buddy?"

Stevie held out a Lego creation, something like a house. "Jail," he said.

"Good one, too," Cork told him. "Who's it for?"

Stevie's eyes turned devilish. "You."

"*Hmmmm.* Am I the sheriff of this jail?"

Stevie shook his head.

"I'm the crook? Well then, let me show you what they put me in for."

He wrestled with his son awhile. "You're getting too tough for an old man like me," he finally said.

"Feel." Stevie flexed his skinny arm. Cork felt mostly bone but made a face full of admiration. Stevie turned his attention back to cartoons.

Jenny, Cork's fourteen-year-old daughter, came into the room from the hallway. She gave her father only a glance before she curled up on the sofa with a book in her lap. He could tell by the way she looked at him that she was reflecting some of her mother's mood. The whole house seemed suffused with the quiet cold of Jo's anger.

"Hi, kiddo. Where's your mother?"

"In her office, working. She's waiting to talk with you."

He looked at the book in her lap. "What's that?"

"Mrs. Cavanaugh asked me to do a reading for the Christmas program next week."

"What reading?"

"Whatever I want. A poem, I think. I'm going to read something by Sylvia Plath."

"Didn't she kill herself?"

"She was a very intelligent woman."

"What poem?"

"I haven't decided yet."

Cork sat down beside his daughter. She edged away. "Have you discussed this with Mrs. Cavanaugh?"

"She said the choice was mine."

"Sylvia Plath. That doesn't sound very Christmasy. Maybe we should talk about it," Cork suggested.

"The choice is mine," his daughter said emphatically.

Jenny was becoming more like Jo all the time. Even at fourteen her face already had the same too-serious shadowing. She was small, precocious, and full of radical energy. Her eyes were like her mother's, too. A cold blue-white. But there were many things Jenny had done to make sure she was not like her mother. Jo had marvelous taste in her dress, yet Jenny chose to wear clothing bought at secondhand stores—old dresses and combat boots and ratty sweaters. With the help of a friend, she'd pierced each of her ears in two places, and she kept discussing the possibility of putting at least one hole in her nose. She streaked her hair with purple and sometimes wore it in short spikes that looked as if she'd grabbed hold of a live power line. She had given up smiling in favor of an attitude of disgust or sometimes simply ennui that was exaggerated by the sleepy look from her full-lidded eyes, part of the genetic Ojibwe legacy of her father.

"Guess I'd better see what your mother wants, huh?"

"Guess you'd better," Jenny agreed.

"Wish me luck," he said.

"Luck," she offered him dourly.

He found Jo at her desk in her office bent over papers. The room was walled with law books and smelled of leather bindings. Jo looked up as he came in. Her eyes seemed big and startled, but as soon as she took off her thick glasses, they resumed their usual deceptively languid calm.

"We were worried about Anne."

"My fault," Cork said. "She was helping me with some things."

"What things?"

"Am I under oath, counselor?"

"I'm just wondering if this was a mutual plan or one of Annie's spur-of-the-moment inspirations."

"Why don't you ask Annie? She'll tell you the truth."

"I'm asking you. Because if it was something you knew about, I wish you'd have checked with me first."

"There's no court order dictating I have to do that."

"Maybe there should be."

She pushed away from the desk, stood, and turned her back to Cork. She stared out the window at the backyard, where the snow flew around the trunk of the maple tree and piled up against the lilac hedge. Her hands were clasped tightly behind her.

"I think it's time we began discussing a divorce."

"Annie was just telling me how she prays for us to get back together."

"Cork, we have to help them see things as they are."

"If I always knew how things are, I suppose I'd do that."

She turned back. "You know, it's funny. Last year I could have sworn a divorce was exactly what you wanted."

"I never said that."

"No," she agreed. "But you also didn't object when I asked you to leave the house." She faced the window again, studying the storm outside.

"It was what you wanted, wasn't it?" When she didn't reply, he walked slowly to her desk, then carefully came around and stood beside her. "Maybe it's time you and I stopped thinking so much about what we want and thought a little more about the kids."

She swung around angrily and threw her glasses on the desk. "You think I don't worry about them? I work long hours to make sure the bills are paid and Annie gets her braces and Jenny might not have to work her way through college. I don't get any help from you on that."

"I wasn't talking about finances," he countered coldly. He walked away and stood staring at the rows of legal books, tomes that attempted to spell out justice, something he no longer believed in. He fought against the hopeless, cornered feeling they gave him.

"Look, we can't go on the way we've been going," Jo said. "It's not good for anybody, especially the children."

"And a divorce would be better?"

"Cleaner."

"Like antiseptic."

"It's what's best for everybody. I think deep down you know that, Cork."

They were both quiet. The wind rattled the window, and from beyond the door came the sound of the television in the living room.

Cork put his hands deep in his pockets and balled them uselessly into fists. "Fine."

"When?" Jo pressed him.

"Whenever you want."

She put her glasses back on and looked down at the papers on her desk. "After Christmas will be fine. You'll want to get yourself an attorney. I can give you some recommendations if you'd like."

"Don't do me any favors," he replied.

There was a knock at the door. Rose peaked in. "Dinner's ready," she said, looking them both over tentatively.

"I've been invited," Cork told Jo.

"All right," Jo agreed, not happily.

Near the end of dinner, the telephone rang. Rose answered it. She held the phone against her ample bosom and said, "It's for you, Cork. It's Darla LeBeau."

"Darla?" Cork got up from the table and took the phone. "Hi, Darla. What's up?" He listened and his face grew serious. "I'm sure it's nothing. He's a responsible boy." He listened again. "Look, how about if I come over? No, it's no trouble."

"What's no trouble?" Rose asked as soon as he hung up.

"Paul LeBeau went off this afternoon to deliver his newspapers and hasn't come back. He's been gone almost five hours."

"You don't think he's still out there in the snow somewhere?" Rose asked.

"I don't think so," Cork said. "Even if he was struggling, he could easily knock on a door. Anybody in Aurora would let him in. Darla's afraid Joe John's come back and taken him."

Rose shook her head. "I don't think Joe John would do something like that. Do you, Cork?"

"It's a possibility."

"He'd kidnap his own son?" Rose looked astonished.

"Jesus, Aunt Rose, it happens all the time," Jenny said.

"Don't swear," Anne told her sister.

"Jesus Christ." Jenny smiled cruelly.

"Jenny!" Rose said.

"Jenny's right," Cork broke in. "Most common form of kidnapping. The truth is, if a kid's going to be taken, I'd rather he was grabbed by someone who's doing it out of love."

"That's not love, Cork," Jo said.

"It might be to Joe John." Cork started for the kitchen.

"You don't mind going?" Rose asked.

"No," he said over his shoulder. And it was absolutely true. It had been a long time since anyone needed him this way, and if felt pretty damn good.

CHAPTER 5

Darla opened the door even before Cork had a chance to knock. Her eyes were puffy and red from crying, and tears had left a trail through her face powder down both cheeks.

"It's Joe John, Cork." she said. "I know it's Joe John."

Darla worked at the casino in public relations and was still dressed for the office in a dark blue blazer and skirt, a cream-colored blouse. There was gold around her neck and on her wrists.

Cork stepped in out of the cold and wiped melting snowflakes from his face. "What makes you think so, Darla?"

"Because it's just like him to drop off the face of the earth for two months, then pull this kind of stunt. It's just the kind of thing he'd do on a drunk." She took his coat and brushed the snow onto a mat in the hallway, then hung the coat in the closet there. Cork slipped off his boots and left them on the mat.

He'd known Darla LeBeau since high school, when she was a cheerleader with long blonde hair, nice legs, and a lot for a boy to notice under her sweater. In her sophomore year, she began going steady with Joe John LeBeau. Joe John was a full-blooded Anishinaabe bussed in from the Iron Lake Reservation ten miles outside Aurora. Dating someone from the reservation would have caused Darla a lot of trouble, but Joe John was different. Joe John was a celebrity, a basketball player of amazing ability. The *St. Paul Pioneer Press* had dubbed him the next Jim Thorpe, and he'd been heavily recruited by colleges all over the Midwest. He accepted a basketball scholarship to Indiana, but just before he was to begin his second year, as he was crossing a street in Bloomington, an old woman who failed to stop her big Cadillac at a red light ran him down. His right leg was shattered from his ankle bone to his hip, and although it was reconstructed, he always walked with a limp after that. With no hope of playing basketball again, he came home to Aurora. Shortly after that, he and Darla were married.

"You probably should have called the sheriff, Darla."

"I didn't want to get Joe John in trouble. I just want Paul home safely."

"Have you tried calling Paul's friends?"

"I've called everywhere I can think. His friends, my folks, the neighbors. I even called Pizza Hut because sometimes he'll play video games there after he's finished his routes."

"Nobody saw him?"

"Nobody. I've got coffee. Want some?"

"Thanks."

He followed Darla to the kitchen.

"You're sure he went to deliver his papers?" Cork asked.

"He left a note on the refrigerator telling me where he was going. He's so good that way."

Cork sat on a stool in her spotless kitchen. He'd sat here with Joe John many times after he brought him home from a drunk. Joe John wasn't a mean drunk.

Mostly he was nostalgic. Very often Cork would find him on the basketball court in Knudsen Park shooting hoops. Even drunk, he had a nice touch. Or sometimes Joe John would disappear for a while, usually no more than a week or two, and he would come back sobered up and contrite and full of assurances that he was through with the bottle forever.

A lot of the whites in Aurora were quite happy to see Joe John fail. *Indians*, they said with great satisfaction. *Drunks*. It didn't matter that Joe John had given Aurora some shining moments, that the signs posted at the town limits proclaiming "Home of the Warriors, State Basketball Champions" was entirely due to Joe John's talent, and that Joe John had suffered a significant disappointment through no fault of his own. That he was Indian explained it all.

Joe John had tried many times to beat the booze. It was his sister, Wanda Manydeeds, who finally helped him. Like Henry Meloux, she was one of the Midewiwin, a member of the Grand Medicine Society. She convinced Joe John to let Henry Meloux treat him in the old way. She could have treated Joe John herself, but the Midewiwin never ministered to their own relations. The treatment was something neither Meloux nor she nor Joe John would talk about, but it seemed to work. For over a year, Joe John had been sober. He had begun a business of his own, a janitorial service, contracting to clean offices in Aurora. It was a good business. Things seemed to be going well.

Then, two months ago, Joe John up and vanished, leaving his truck smashed into a tree on County Road C and the cab reeking of whiskey. He'd simply walked away from the accident and never come back.

"Have you heard from Joe John lately?" Cork asked.

"Not a word." Her hand trembled as she poured out his coffee. "I was always afraid something like this would happen. Joe John hated it here, Cork. When he was drunk, he used to talk about how he'd take Paul away someday, somewhere where nobody knew who he was and wouldn't make fun of Paul for being the son of a drunk Indian." She looked at her trembling hand and put the pot down.

"You told me on the phone he's been gone about five hours. How do you know?"

"In his note he said it was two o'clock when he left. I don't know why he thought he had to deliver on a day like today. Nobody would care if the paper wasn't delivered today. People would understand." Her shoulders sagged wearily. "I make good money at the casino. He doesn't have to deliver papers at all. I think he just wants to show people he's not like his father."

"How have things been between you and Paul lately?"

"What do you mean?"

"Any tension, arguments?"

"You mean, did Paul run away?" she said. "He wouldn't do that."

"I don't think he would either," Cork reassured her. "It's just one of the possibilities we have to consider." He sipped his coffee. "Has he talked about his father lately? Maybe said something about wanting to find him? I'm only asking because I know how it feels to lose your father at that age. I know I would have done anything to bring him back."

"No, nothing. He's been quieter lately, but I just figure it's his age."

"Have you called Wanda? If Joe John's back, she'd know."

"I tried. The lines must be down."

Cork thought for a moment. The refrigerator clicked on and the bottles rattled inside it. The wind howled past the kitchen window in the breakfast nook.

"Okay, we know he left the house. Do we know if he actually started his route? Or finished?"

"No."

"Do you know what route he follows, who his customers are?"

"No," Darla said, shaking her head with exasperation. "No."

Cork reached out and touched her hand across the counter. "That's all right, Darla. There's no reason you should. Does Paul keep any kind of record of his customers?"

A sudden, hopeful look lit her face. "He has a receipt book he uses when he collects for the papers every month."

"Good. Let's have a look."

"I'll get it," she said.

Cork didn't see any reason yet to be worried about Paul's safety. Aurora was a small place and children didn't just disappear. Probably Joe John was responsible, too ashamed to face Darla but anxious to see his son, particularly as it was the Christmas season. Cork also knew from experience that more often than not when teenagers vanished, they left of their own accord.

Darla LeBeau returned with a dark blue receipt book and handed it to Cork. Paul kept good records, and from the order of the addresses, which began on Center Street and followed one another geographically out to the last address on North Point Road, Cork figured Paul probably collected from his customers in the same order he delivered their papers.

"What are you going to do?" Darla asked.

"I'll start by calling a few of his customers, find out if the papers were delivered, and maybe when. That will give us a little more to go on than we have now. And you never know. Someone might have seen something."

He began with the last address in the receipt book. Judge Robert Parrant. The line was fuzzy and Cork didn't even get a ring at the other end. He moved back through the receipt book, making half a dozen more calls. North of the tracks, nothing connected. South, everyone who answered had received a paper, although no one had actually seen anything of Paul.

"Seems to be a problem with the lines to the north," Cork told Darla. "I wish I'd been able to get through to the judge. That would tell me if Paul had actually finished his route."

Darla brightened a moment. "Sometimes Paul stops there a while. The judge seems to like him. Tells him stories and things. Paul hates it, but I've told him to be polite."

"I suppose it's possible Paul's stranded there and because of the problem with the telephone lines, he has no way of letting you know. Maybe I ought to head over to the judge's house. At least I'd be able to tell if Paul finished delivering his papers."

"I want to go with you," Darla said.

Cork shook his head. "You need to stay here by the phone just in case Paul calls. I'm sure he's fine, Darla. He's a good, responsible kid who knows how to take care of himself, okay?"

"What if he's not there?"

"Then he's somewhere else and he's okay and we'll find him," Cork assured her. At the front door, Cork said, "Call someone. It isn't good for you to be here alone. Call someone you can talk to. Okay?"

"Okay," she said. She put her hand on Cork's arm. "Find him, Cork. Please."

The judge's estate wasn't easy to reach. The plows hadn't touched any of the outlying roads yet, and Cork went slowly, with the front bumper of the Bronco nosing through drifts. The estate occupied the whole tip of the finger of land called North Point. The house itself was a huge stone affair, more than a century old, surrounded by gardens in summer and a sea of snow in winter. In its way it was like the man who owned it. Isolated.

The judge had once been a powerful figure in the politics of Minnesota. The scion of a family grown rich from clear-cutting the great white pines of the North Woods, he viewed himself as a rugged individualist and stubbornly clung to the view, as had those Parrants before him, that a man became what he made of himself. Only the hand of God—not an interfering government—should direct men's destinies. In the Iron Range, an area noted for its independent, unpredictable, and generally cantankerous population, his message was well received.

His personal influence had reached its zenith more than two decades earlier when he made a nearly successful bid for the governor's mansion. Five days before the election, with the judge carrying a slight edge in the polls, the *St. Paul Pioneer Press* published photographs of him leaving a motel room in the company of the wife of the chair of the party's central committee. Minnesota may have been liberal in its politics, but it was pretty Lutheran in its morality. The judge lost by a landslide.

He retired from the state political arena after that,

but he still maintained his influence in the Iron Range. Except for the election of Cork as sheriff, which the judge had opposed, no one in Tamarack County was elected without the judge's benediction.

As sheriff, Cork had occasionally found it necessary to call on the judge at his estate on North Point Road. But it was never a duty with any pleasure in it.

Cork parked on the long circular drive and waded through the snow to the front door. No one answered the bell. He took off his glove and knocked hard. He tried to look through the windows downstairs, but the curtains were drawn and melted snow had turned to ice plastered across the windows. He went back to the Bronco, grabbed a flashlight, and worked his way around to the back of the house. Stepping onto the big terrace, he rubbed a spot clear on the sliding glass door. The curtains were only partially drawn, and through the gap Cork could see a glass of wine sitting on the coffee table in the living room, a little thread of gray smoke curling up from the ashes of the fireplace, but no sign of the judge.

The wind pushed snow across the open ground in a tide that seemed liquid as water. Cork made his way to the garage, cleared a small side window, and poked the flashlight beam through. Both of the judge's vehicles—a black Lincoln Mark IV and a new red Ford pickup—were parked inside. He trudged back toward the front door and kicked around the snow in the big entryway, looking for a paper. Finally he tried the knob. The door was unlocked. He swung it open and stepped in.

"Judge Parrant?" he called. "Judge, it's Corcoran O'Connor!"

He felt uneasy being in the house uninvited. No search warrant. Criminal trespass. Things he still cared about. He knew there was no justification for entering this way. Except a boy who should have been home and wasn't.

"Judge?" he called again, moving into the living room.

There were still embers in the fireplace. The wineglass on the coffee table was less than half full. The upstairs was dark. The only other light came from a room down the hall. Cork headed that way.

The door was well ajar, but gave only a partial view of what looked like the judge's study, a room full of books. Cork pushed the door open all the way. At first he didn't see the judge. He saw the big desk, the map of Minnesota on the wall behind it, and the splatters of blood that ran down the map like red rivers. He put his gloves back on and stepped around the desk. The force of the blast had thrown the judge over in his chair and the shotgun lay fallen beside him. Cork didn't look long at the body. He'd seen men dead this way before, but it was never easy. And the raw smell of so much blood was something you never forgot.

CHAPTER 6

Wally Schanno was an honest man and well thought of in Tamarack County. In his mid-fifties, he was tall and lean, had hollow cheeks, thick pale lips, and a nose like a big ragged chunk of granite shoved into his face. His hands were large. His enormous feet required shoes factory-ordered straight from Red Wing, Minnesota. So far as Cork knew, he had no bad habits. Didn't drink, smoke, or gamble. He was a practicing Lutheran, Missouri Synod. He had a penchant for suspenders—nothing wild, just plain red, or black, or gray—and he almost never sported a tie. He was not a politician by any stretch of the imagination, but he'd managed to get himself elected sheriff after the recall vote that forced Cork from office. Before that Schanno had been chief of police for the village of Green Lake just half a dozen miles southwest of Aurora. He was a decent man, had done his job in Green Lake well for fifteen years. Cork had nothing against Schanno. He'd always had an admiration for the character of the man. But after Schanno replaced him, Cork's admiration took on a grudging edge. To his shame, he found himself looking forward to the day when Wally Schanno would screw up big-time.

Schanno looked at his watch for the third time in five minutes.

"Got a date, Wally?" Cork asked.

"Arletta's home alone," Schanno said.

"Ah," Cork replied.

Arletta was Schanno's wife. She was a woman of rare beauty. Long black hair with flares of brilliant silver, blue-summer-sky eyes, and the most perfect smile Cork had ever seen. She also had Alzheimer's.

"I called her sister. She said she'd try to get over there as fast as she could. I expected to hear from her by now," Schanno said.

"You didn't have to come yourself, Wally," Cork pointed out. "Your men know what they're doing."

"I'm the sheriff," Schanno said, and cast a hard eye on Cork.

Ed Larson, the only man with the rank of captain in the department and the man in charge of the most serious of Tamarack County's crimes, came down the hallway from the judge's study. "I'm finished in there, Wally. But I don't want to bag him until we have a good time of death. Are you sure Sigurd's on the way over?"

"I'm sure. Storm's held him up, most likely."

At the window, Cork watched the wind drive snow against the pane, where it collected in the corners of the mullions, melted, and froze into a thickening glaze.

Schanno hooked his thumb under his black suspenders and ran it up and down thoughtfully for a moment. "Gotta admit, the judge was probably the last man I'd've suspected of suicide. Still, who knows? People fool you all the time."

Cy Borkmann, one of Schanno's deputies, stepped in from the kitchen. "Didn't find any sign of forced entry, Wally, but I dusted all the doorknobs and window casings."

"How about upstairs? See if you can find anything looks broken into."

"I'm on my way."

"Thought you said it was suicide," Cork commented.

"Just making sure. Wouldn't you?" Schanno shoved his huge hands into his pocket and walked around the room a moment, looking things over. "Tell me again about the boy."

"Set off to deliver his papers around two. Never came back. Didn't call. Judge's house was the last stop on the route."

"And no paper here," Schanno said.

"None that I could see."

"You check around outside? Kid may have thrown it in the snow somewhere."

"I looked some. Didn't find anything."

"What about the other customers? They all get papers?"

"South of the tracks. I don't know about out here."

Cork took a cigarette from the pack in his shirt pocket and stuck it in the corner of his mouth. He didn't light it. Although he wanted a smoke pretty bad, he knew better than to take a chance on contaminating the scene.

Schanno said, "You say Darla thinks it's Joe John. What do you think?"

"Maybe." Cork shrugged.

"Joe John used to run off pretty regular when he was drinking. Could be the boy's just taking after him."

"The boy's not like that."

Schanno didn't appear to be as convinced of that as Cork. "Maybe we'll know something more when we talk to the neighbors."

Cork glanced out the window. The porch light was on, but the wind had risen so fiercely and was blowing the snow so hard the only thing illuminated was a blinding curtain of white that hid even the cedars only a dozen yards away. "A brass band could've marched in and out of here this evening without anyone noticing a thing."

The front door opened.

"Our coroner's finally arrived," Schanno said, and headed to the entryway.

The sheriff was wrong. It wasn't Sigurd Nelson.

"Sandy?" Cork heard Schanno say with surprise.

"Where is he?" Sandy Parrant stepped out of the entryway where Cork could see him. The shoulders of his camel-hair coat were dusted with snow. His eyes took in the room, then swung toward the study down the hall. "In there?"

He looked as if he were going to head that way when Schanno moved to block him. "I think you'd better sit down."

Parrant glanced at Cork, and somewhere within all the concern that darkened his face, a mild surprise registered. "Cork?"

"Hello, Sandy," Cork greeted him somberly.

Sandy was a large, powerfully built man, just as the judge had been before the frailty of age had withered him. Both had strong, square faces, huge brown eyes, and long, sharp jawbones. Before the judge's hair had turned white, it had been the same color as Sandy's—a red-blond, like honey mixed with a few drops of blood.

Beyond the physical, similarities in the two men were few. In politics they might as well have been from different planets. Where the judge had been bitterly conservative, Sandy was fiercely liberal. The difference in the men's philosophies might have been explained by Sandy's upbringing in Boston. He'd moved there at age twelve when, following the scandal that killed his father's run for governor, his mother had divorced the judge. More than a dozen years later, he returned to make Aurora his home again. Despite their political differences, he and his father had worked well together in business and had created the Great North Development Company. In an area beset by economic chaos as a result of the closing of the great iron mines of the Mesabi and Vermilion Ranges, the developments financed by the Great North were a godsend.

On the campaign trail during his successful bid for a seat in the U.S. Senate, Sandy Parrant had been indefatigably upbeat and assured. The man standing in the entryway of the judge's home looked pretty well devastated.

"I want to see him," he said.

"No, you don't, Sandy," Schanno advised.

"He's my father. I want to see him."

"He's dead, Sandy. Seeing him like he is now won't do any good."

Parrant stood firm, and for a moment Cork thought he was going to ignore the sheriff's advice, which Cork understood was a veiled order. In other circumstances, a man of Parrant's stature might have prevailed. But Sandy finally nodded, moved to the sofa in the living room, and sat down heavily.

"My god," he said in disbelief. "He was such a tough old bastard."

"I know," Schanno agreed.

"I was afraid of something like this."

"Why?" Schanno asked.

"Cancer. It's everywhere."

"I didn't know," Schanno said.

"He didn't want people to know."

"Prognosis?" Cork asked.

"He didn't have more than six months to live." Parrant shrugged. "Talk to Doc Gunnar."

Schanno wrote something on a notepad he took from his shirt pocket.

"What are you doing here, Cork?" Parrant asked.

"I found your father's body," Cork explained. "I was looking for Paul LeBeau."

"Joe John's boy?"

"He went to deliver newspapers this afternoon and never came back."

"What's my father got to do with that?"

"Last house on the route. It was a long shot," Cork admitted.

"You just walked right in?" Parrant gave him a look of alarm.

"Door was unlocked."

"Nothing unusual about that, Sandy," Schanno pointed out. "Lots of folks in Aurora don't lock their doors. It's that kind of town."

"Or used to be," Cork said.

There was a furious pounding at the front door. Schanno hurried to the entryway. Cork heard the angry voice of Sigurd Nelson. "You got any idea how tough it is getting around out there, Wally?"

"Special case, Sigurd," Cork heard the sheriff reply.

"Special my ass. What's so special it couldn't wait until tomorrow? Old man like the judge dies at home, he probably died of a heart attack or a stroke like most men his age."

"It wasn't a heart attack, Sigurd," Schanno said, bringing the coroner into the living room. "Didn't the office say anything?"

"Just to get out here pronto."

The coroner was a bald man in his late fifties with a comfortable potbelly. A mortician by profession, he'd been the assistant coroner under Dr. Daniel Bergen until Bergen died of a heart attack while fishing the Rainy River. Sigurd Nelson filled in until a special election could be held, then he'd been officially voted into the position. Once or twice a year, he was called to look at someone who'd died unexpectedly. Cork, while he was sheriff, had lobbied the board of commissioners for a change to a medical examiner, someone with some expertise, hired instead of elected, but in that effort he'd been unsuccessful. Judge Robert Parrant had wanted a coroner who was elected. It was another position he could keep under his thumb.

Nelson put down his black bag, removed his heavy black overcoat, and shook it out. He looked around for a place to put it, finally threw it over the back of a chair.

"I can tell you from experience that when a man that old dies suddenly, odds are ten to one it's either a heart attack or a stroke."

"It wasn't a heart attack, Sigurd," Schanno said again.

"No? Well, let's just go and see." He noticed Cork and Sandy Parrant. "Oh. Sandy. I'm sorry."

Parrant lifted his hand in a halfhearted pardon. "That's okay."

"Where is he?" the coroner asked.

"That way," Schanno said, and nodded down the hall.

Sandy Parrant stayed on the sofa, watching them as they moved down the hallway. Sigurd Nelson stepped into the study and stopped dead in his tracks. "Great

God Almighty," he whispered when he saw the blood streaking the map on the wall behind the desk.

"He's all yours, Sigurd," Schanno said.

Thirty minutes later they were back in the living room. As Sigurd Nelson put on his coat, he said, "I'll be able to tell you some more after I work on him tomorrow. But like I said, if it's time of death you're worried about right now, the judge hasn't been dead more than four or five hours."

"Thanks for coming, Sigurd," Schanno told him.

"I'm sorry, Sandy," the coroner said, offering his condolences. "But the judge." He shook his head. "Who would've figured?" He opened the door and pushed into the storm.

Cork began to put on his own coat.

"Where you headed?" Schanno asked.

"Darla LeBeau's."

"Tell her I'll have a man over soon. I'll put a notice about the boy out on the NCIC computer." Schanno took a deep, tired breath and looked at his watch.

"Call home and check on Arletta, Wally," Cork suggested as he pulled on his gloves. "Home ought to be every man's first concern." He glanced at Sandy Parrant, whose face was drawn and colorless and who, for a politician, was unusually quiet. "Want a lift, Sandy?"

Parrant shook his head.

"I'm sorry," Cork said.

"Yeah." Parrant gave him a brief smile of thanks. But he was a man way on the other side of something terrible, and the look in his eyes came from far, far away.

CHAPTER 7

Traditionally the Anishinaabe were a quiet people. Before the whites came, they lived in the silence of great woods and more often than not, the voices they heard were not human. The wind spoke. The water sang. All sound had purpose. When an Anishinaabe approached the wigwam of another, he respectfully made noise to announce his coming. Thunder, therefore, was the respectful way of the storm in announcing its approach. Spirit and purpose in all things. For all creation, respect.

The storm that bent the pine trees and the tamaracks, that drove the snow plows from the roads and froze and snapped the power lines was not an angry spirit. In its passage, it created chaos not because of anger but because it was so vast and powerful and those things it touched, especially those things human, were so small in comparison. In a way, it was like the bear that Cork had once hunted with Sam Winter Moon, huge and oblivious. If the storm, in fact, was responsible for the disappearance of the boy, Cork knew it was not a thing done maliciously. In his experience, only people acted out of pure malice.

When he finally reached Darla's house, the porch light was on and he saw an ancient Kawasaki snowmobile parked near the steps. As he approached the machine, he knew without actually seeing that under the engine oil was staining the snow. He knew it because the machine belonged to Father Tom Griffin and was the oldest of its kind in Tamarack County. It always leaked oil.

He rang the bell, and a moment later Darla opened the door.

"Cork," she said, and gave him a nervous look and stepped back.

The priest was beside her out of sight for a moment, but Cork could see his shadow on the wall, a tall, lanky silhouette. Then Tom Griffin stepped into view, a steadfast smile on his lips and a huge black patch over his left eye.

"Evening, Cork," the priest said, and reached out to shake hands. He had a strong grip that he used gracefully to guide Cork out of the storm and into the house.

Tom Griffin was dressed in black and wearing his cleric's collar, an unusual thing for the man. Except for formal occasions and when performing the formally religious duties of his position, the priest preferred to wear blue jeans and flannel shirts and hiking boots. He had come to Aurora a year and a half earlier to help the aging Father Kelsey manage St. Agnes and to minister to the Catholic parishioners who lived on the Iron Lake Reservation. He was nearing forty, a man of enormous goodwill and energy. In summer he could be seen cutting along the back roads of the reservation on a huge, old Kawasaki motorcycle. In winter, he generally used the Kawasaki snowmobile. As a result, he was affectionately known on the reservation as St. Kawasaki.

"I'm glad you called somebody, Darla," Cork told her.

"You didn't find him," Darla said.

"Maybe you should sit down."

"What is it?"

Cork looked to the priest for help.

"Maybe we should all sit down," Tom Griffin suggested.

He led the way into the living room and sat on the arm of the sofa. Darla sat beside him. Cork settled on the radiator, reluctant to wet the furniture with the drip of the melting snow off his coat.

"Judge Parrant is dead," Cork told them.

"The judge?" the priest said. "How?"

"It looks as if he killed himself. The sheriff's there now. We couldn't find any indication that Paul had been there, so this probably hasn't got a thing to do with him."

"I know that," Darla said.

Cork looked at the priest, then back at Darla. "What's going on?"

"I was out at the reservation this morning. We buried Vernon Blackwater, you know," the priest said.

"So?"

"Word on the reservation is that Joe John is back."

"Has anybody talked to him?" Cork asked.

"Not as far as I know."

"Not even Wanda?"

"I was out there a little while ago. She hasn't seen him or spoken to him, but she's sure he's around."

"He's got Paul?"

"Paul's gone, Joe John's back. I'd say that's hardly coincidence, wouldn't you?"

Cork felt relieved. At least it was Joe John. Not the storm or something worse. "The sheriff will want to know that," he said.

"The sheriff?" Darla looked unhappy.

"He's sending a man over here."

"I don't want any trouble," she said.

"It's Joe John," the priest told Cork. "Can't we do this without the law coming into it?"

"It's out of my hands now," Cork explained. He stood up. "It's late. I'd best get going. I'll stay in touch. And let me know if I can help in any way."

"Thanks, Cork." Darla managed a smile.

"Let me see you out," the priest said.

As he put on his gloves at the door, Cork asked, "Lots of folks at Vernon Blackwater's burial?"

"Most of the reservation. He was an important man."

"He was a son of a bitch," Cork said, drawing his cap out of his coat pocket.

"He was that, too," the priest agreed.

"You were there when he died, weren't you? Gave him last rites?"

"I did."

Cork tugged the cap down over his ears. "Heard his final confession?"

"Yes."

"That's something I would've given my left nut to hear."

"I'd think twice before giving away body parts, Cork," the priest said with a smile and a quick gesture toward the patch over his eye.

Before he reached for the door, Cork asked the priest quietly, "Can I talk with you soon?"

"About what?"

"I haven't been in church in over a year."

"Finally worried about your soul?"

"Please," Cork said.

"Of course we can talk. When?"

"Tomorrow. Late afternoon maybe. Say five o'clock?"

"Make it six," the priest suggested. "My office."

"I'll be there," Cork promised.

In the brief time Cork was inside, his Bronco had become snow-covered again. He started the engine, then stepped out to brush the windows clean. The wind blew so hard the snow came at him levelly out of the darkness and he squinted against the flakes that the wind made bitterly piercing. It was late. The only light he could see came from Darla's house. Across the street was a stand of tall birch and aspen where the wind screamed through and the bare branches rubbed together with a crying sound. Suddenly Cork stopped. Turning, he scanned the darkness at his back and listened to the crying of the trees.

"Who's there?" he yelled.

He got no answer. Near him nothing moved but the snow. He couldn't see a thing in the swaying trees.

"Is anybody there?" he tried again.

No voice answered except the bitter howl of the wind. Cork finished clearing the snow and got into his Bronco. As an afterthought he locked the doors. He waited a moment before driving away, trying one last time to see if anything moved among the trees.

Because he could have sworn someone there had called his name.

CHAPTER 8

Next morning, Cork rose in the dark, stumbled to the kitchen and started coffee dripping in the Mr. Coffee. He showered, shaved, and dressed. Back in the kitchen, he poured himself a cup of coffee and looked out the window. Over the lake, the sky in the east was just turning a faint, powdery blue. He put on his coat, went to the back room, scooped a quarter bucket of corn from the sack, and made his way down to the shore of the lake.

In the night, the storm had moved east beyond Lake Superior and into the Upper Peninsula of Michigan. Its passing left the sky clear and with a few stars still shining. The snow lay smooth and deep, cast in the pale blue-gray light of early morning. The air was so still the white smoke from the chimneys in town rose up straight as birch trunks. Cork loved the painful cold of the morning, the brittle new snow beneath his boots, the breathless clarity of the sky. He loved Aurora deeply in such moments.

The geese were on the water. He was glad to see that they'd made it through the storm. They honked and paddled nearer when they saw him, but they wouldn't come all the way to shore. He kicked a big circle in the snow, clearing it, as he had done with Anne, down to the frozen ground underneath. He shook the grain out of the bucket. After he'd stepped well away, the geese came quickly.

The sun still wasn't up when he left the cabin, but a big bubble of yellow light showed where, in half an hour, it would rise over the bare trees on the far side of the lake.

At Johnny's Pinewood Broiler, Cork found Johnny Pap out front shoveling snow. Johnny was first-generation Greek. His real name was John Papasconstantinou, but his father had shortened it when he arrived in the States. He was fifty, stout, a man of great but nervous energy.

"Winter's here, that's for sure," Johnny observed. "Knew it had to happen."

"Coffee ready yet?" Cork asked.

"Molly's doing it now. Ski'd in from her place. Got here before me even." Johnny leaned on his snow shovel. "Wish Maria was like that," he said, speaking of his wife. "Takes a couple sticks of dynamite to get her out of bed most mornings." He wiped the drip from his nose and eyed Cork man to man. "Wish she was like Molly in a lot of ways, if you know what I mean."

"I'll see you inside," Cork said, and left Johnny to his shoveling.

Except for Molly, the place was empty.

"Well, well." Molly smiled, glancing up from the big stainless steel coffeemaker. "Look what the cat dragged in."

"Anybody ever tell you you look mighty good in the morning?"

"Not for a long time." She leaned across the counter to where Cork sat on a stool. "Thought about you all night," she said.

"Long night?"

"It went on forever."

"Try reading a book next time. It's what I do."

"I knitted. I'm working on a Christmas present for you. Something for cold nights."

"Wool condom?"

Molly laughed, poured him a cup of coffee, and slid it across the counter. Then she turned to the kitchen. She fixed him bacon and eggs and wheat toast. By the time he'd finished eating, the place had begun to fill with men. The Broiler was a popular stopover for people on their way to work. The clientele were regulars, men mostly who ordered the same breakfast every day, said the same things day in and day out. They worked at the brewery or the sawmill or for the highway department. Or they were shop owners killing time before they headed to the task of clearing the walks in front of their stores. Johnny had taken over the cooking. Two other waitresses had arrived, but it was Molly who caught everyone's eye. She moved quickly and efficiently from table to table, booth to booth, slipping easily among men who eyed her just as keenly as Cork did. He liked how she cocked a fist on her hip and said something hard and funny to the ones who made passes, and there were a lot of them. He liked the combination of her plain good looks, her efficiency, and her elusiveness there in a place where men hungered around her in a lot of ways. She was a woman who knew how to take care of herself.

At the register, he spoke to her quietly. "Got it on good authority there's an ex-law enforcement officer heading out your way later. Maybe that civic minded ex-officer could give you a lift."

"Wouldn't accept anything from an ex-officer of the law. But I'm a definite pushover for any man who knows how to flip a burger. Is there a charge for this ride?"

"That's negotiable."

"Then you've got me over a barrel," she admitted with a smile.

Cork lifted his eyebrow. "Now, that sounds interesting."

CHAPTER 9

On the state highway just beyond the limits of Aurora stood a big marquee, a neon bow that shot a neon arrow in the direction of a newly paved road through a stand of white pines. "Chippewa Grand Casino," the marquee proclaimed; "1/4 Mile To A Jackpot Of Good Times And Good Food."

Growing up in Aurora, Cork had often traveled the road through the white pines. The road was gravel then and the pines part of a large county park. At that time the quarter mile led to a ball field and a huge picnic area shaded by maples and a long stretch of beach on the lake. A year ago the land had been sold to the Iron Lake band of Ojibwe so they could build a gambling casino. Under federal law, property purchased by a tribal entity became tribal land, exempt from the prohibition against gaming that constrained non-Native American landholders. Initially there had been a good deal of objection to the sale. Rust River, a good trout stream, ran through the land. Trout fisherman and conservationists questioned whether the stream would be ruined. Construction of the casino was to be bankrolled by a loan from Great North Development, and Sandy Parrant did a bang-up job of assuring everyone that not only the quality of the trout fishing, but the beauty of the land itself would be preserved. He'd kept his promise. The white pines and the stream had been untouched. The ball field had become the casino parking lot. Only the maples of the shaded picnic area were razed and in their place rose the copper dome of the casino.

As Cork drove down the road through the pines, he thought, as he often did, of the lines of a poem whose title he couldn't recall: "In Xanadu did Kubla Khan a stately pleasure-dome decree." The casino was ninety thousand square feet of pure white brick, glass, and glinting copper. It sat in the clearing with a great apron of parking lot in front of it. Behind was a beautifully sculptured landscape where the trout stream ran unspoiled. Through the trees, the broad flat white of the lake was visible. The parking lot had already been plowed and dozens of cars were parked. Snow lay several inches deep on many of them, indicating they'd been there all night. Although it was possible people had been trapped by the storm, it was just as possible they would have been there all night anyway. Gambling, Cork had come to understand, affected some people in an odd way. Not unlike fishing. Fisherman would drive their pickups and four-wheelers out onto thin ice risking their necks just to catch a damn fish. Some gamblers took the same kind of chance at a blackjack table.

Although the casino was well lit inside, it seemed dark compared with the incredible brightness of the snowy morning. There didn't seem to be much action, but the day was young.

Cork caught sight of Ernie Meloux, old Henry Meloux's nephew, crossing the floor between empty blackjack tables, heading toward the Boundary Waters coffee shop. Cork followed and joined him just as Ernie was bending to a cup of coffee at the counter.

"Hey, Ernie, what's up?"

Ernie nodded toward his coffee. "Getting a jump start on the day. How's it going, Cork?"

"No complaints."

Ernie was a small, square man, tightly built, with a mist of gray just beginning to surface through his short black hair. He sipped his coffee and played with a small strip of silver metal the size of an address label that he spun around on the countertop.

"Seen your uncle lately?" Cork asked.

"Last night. Came in here just like he'd stepped off a bus instead of walking through that damn storm. He's a hoot, Uncle Henry is."

"Where is he now?"

"I gave him a ride back to Crow's Point on my snowmobile after I was finished here. You know, I believe he wouldn't've thought anything about hoofing it back."

"I gave him a lift into town. He was talking about seeing a Windigo. He say anything to you about that?"

"Windigo?" Ernie gave the metal strip a spin with his finger. It went round and round like a top. "Didn't say a thing. Just bummed a cigarette and asked where Russell Blackwater was."

"He came all the way here in the middle of that storm just to talk to Russ?"

Ernie shrugged. "I gave up trying to figure that old man a long time ago. Maybe you should talk to Russell." Ernie jabbed a thumb toward the far side of the coffee shop, where Blackwater sat alone reading a newspaper.

"Maybe I will." Cork nodded at the little strip of metal Ernie was fidgeting with. "What've you got there?"

"This?" Ernie picked it up and looked at it with

mock admiration. "This is what I spend most of my time doing. Putting these little doohickeys on all the equipment that comes in."

Cork took it and looked carefully at the word embossed in black across the metal. GameTech. "Why?"

"Got me," Ernie replied. "But they pay me damn near fifteen bucks an hour to do it. A whole sight better'n pumping gas out at the Tomahawk Truck Plaza."

"Fifteen bucks an hour?" Cork whistled. "Need an assistant?"

"To put these things on?" He took back the Game-Tech strip, put it on the counter, and set it spinning again. "Windigo, huh? My uncle really thought he saw one?"

"Seemed to."

"If he says he did, he did." Ernie glanced at his watch, picked up the metal strip, and stood up. "Time to get to work. Got a box of these suckers calling my name. Merry Christmas, Cork."

"Same to you."

When Ernie had gone, Cork considered Russell Blackwater. In his late thirties, tall, powerfully built, Blackwater was a striking man but far from handsome. When Blackwater had been a young militant member of AIM, his nose had been broken during a violent confrontation in the Minneapolis office of the BIA and it had never been set. Consequently, it looked like the nose of an inept prize fighter, squashed and crooked. He also bore a long scar across his left temple, the legacy of a knife fight he never spoke about. But the aspect of Blackwater's appearance that Cork always found least appealing was his eyes. They were dark and calculating, what Sam Winter Moon had once called "hungry hunter's eyes." Russ Blackwater was a man Cork had never trusted.

He was the son of Vernon Blackwater, who, until his recent death, had been chairman of the tribal council, as well as a prosperous businessman on the reservation, operating a lumber mill in Allouette. Russell was one of the few college graduates from the rez. When he returned to help run the lumber mill, he came with his black hair long and braided. He dressed in beaded vests or an old jean jacket with the AIM insignia on the back. He rode a Harley-Davidson chopper. The reservation elders viewed him with caution, watching his hungry hunter's eyes carefully whenever he spoke before the tribal council. But he had a large following among the younger Anishinaabe. He had frequently given Cork a hard time as sheriff, haranguing him for being part of an establishment and a system bent on the continued subjugation of the people of his own blood. Cork had tolerated that, even understood it, and although he never admitted it out loud, he often wrestled with the conflict in his own heritage.

Now that Russell Blackwater was manager of the Chippewa Grand Casino, he kept his hair cut short. Instead of beaded vests, he wore a charcoal suit and wingtips.

Blackwater was eating an omelette while he read the newspaper. He put down his fork and paper as Cork approached. "A little early to be messing around with that slut Lady Luck, isn't it, Cork?"

"I'm not here to gamble, Russ. I understand Henry Meloux was looking for you last night."

"So I heard."

"You didn't talk to him?"

"I wasn't here at all yesterday. My father's funeral," he reminded Cork somberly.

"Any idea what Meloux wanted to see you about?"

"Probably wanted to apologize for not making it

to the funeral. They were old friends, him and my father."

Blackwater went back to eating his breakfast.

"I suppose you've heard about the judge."

"What about him?"

"Dead. Killed himself, looks like."

"The judge?" Blackwater snorted. "I don't believe it."

"Wrapped his mouth around the barrel of a shotgun."

Blackwater paused and considered a forkful of omelette. "How do you know this?"

"I was there after it happened. I saw him."

"What were you doing? You're not the fucking law anymore."

"An accident. I was looking for Paul LeBeau."

"Darla's kid?"

Cork nodded. "He's missing. Word is that Joe John's back."

"Joe John?" Blackwater smiled. "I doubt it."

"Why?"

"Last I heard he was panhandling on Hennepin Avenue in Minneapolis. I don't think he'll ever be sober enough to find his way back here."

"Where'd you hear about the panhandling?"

"I heard." Blackwater shrugged.

"Seen Darla this morning? I wanted to talk to her about Paul and Joe John."

"She called in sick." Blackwater gave Cork a cold grin. "You really like asking questions, don't you? Bet you really miss that uniform, Cork. Just another white man without it."

"You know, Russ, in those clothes you look like just another white man, too. See you around."

CHAPTER 10

Back at Sam's, Cork went to the utility shed—a corrugated aluminum thing Sam Winter Moon had purchased from Sears—and pulled out his old cross-country skis. They were ancient wooden touring skis with hard, hickory edges. Cork took out a scraper, propped the skis against the picnic table in front of Sam's, and began patiently to peel off the layers of old wax.

The snowmobiles were out in force on Iron Lake, zipping about the ice like ants frenzying on a frosted cake. In summer it was motorboats and Jet Skis and sailboats. No matter what the season the lake had little peace.

The Anishinaabe called it Gitchimiskwassab, which meant "big rump." In the myth of the Iron Lake An-ishinaabe, the lake was formed when Naanabozho, the trickster, attempted to steal the tail feathers from an eagle. As Naanabozho grabbed the feathers, the great bird took flight. Higher and higher it flew, and Naanabozho became more and more exhausted at-tempting to hold on. Finally, the trickster let go and fell to earth. Where he landed, a great indentation was made from each of the cheeks of his butt. Naanabozho cried from the pain of his fall and filled the double indentation with his tears. Thus, Gitchimiskwassab.

The Iron Lake Treaty of 1873 placed the northeastern "cheek" of the lake entirely within the reservation of the Iron Lake Anishinaabe. The southwestern "cheek" became public waters. For several generations, the Iron Lake band spearfished and gillnetted their own part of the lake without any trouble. Because the language of the treaty arguably gave the Iron Lake Anishinaabe fishing rights on all the lake, the state of Minnesota had for years paid a small compensation to the band for not exercising those rights. The arrangement had been, at least from a white perspective, reasonable.

Cork scraped the layers of wax from his skis, thinking about the spring a year and a half before, when everything changed.

Several weeks before the first day of spearfishing season—which preceded all other forms of fishing in the state and was limited to Native Americans—Russell Blackwater, speaking on behalf of the Iron Lake band of Ojibwe, declared that The People intended, for the first time in over one hundred years, to spearfish and gillnet all of Iron Lake and its tributaries, not just that portion within reservation boundaries. Speaking for the tribal council, of which he was an elected member, he decried the state's policies of the past that offered the Anishinaabe a pittance in exchange for their treaty rights. He characterized the arrangement as just another in a long line of maneuvers by the white man to take from The People what had been a gift to them from Gitchimanidoo, the Great Spirit.

The resort owners and the white fisherman immediately raised an outcry. A group calling itself SORE, which stood for Save Our Resources and Environment, quickly formed and sought an injunction against the Anishinaabe. As she had so often in the past, Jo O'Connor represented the interests of the Iron Lake band of Ojibwe in an expedited hearing before a federal judge in Minneapolis. The court found in favor of the Anishinaabe.

The next move for SORE was to appeal to the state's department of natural resources, whose responsibility it was to oversee the fish population in all Minnesota waters. SORE's contention was that the level of gill-netting and spearfishing the Iron Lake band proposed would, in conjunction with normal line fishing, result in the depletion of the fish population. The DNR agreed and their own attorneys sought an injunction against the Anishinaabe. Jo O'Connor, on behalf of her clients, argued that while the DNR did, in fact, have the right to enforce limits, they had no right to control how those limits were reached. In essence, the terms of the 1873 treaty gave the Iron Lake Band of Ojibwe the right to take the full limit allowed by the DNR from the lake if they so desired. The court promised a ruling before opening day of spearfishing.

None of the legal maneuvering took place in a vacuum of dry proceedings. Outside the courtroom buildings, SORE members rallied, their numbers swelled by other fishermen who feared the ramifications of the legal decisions handed down in the case of the Iron Lake Ojibwe. Helmuth Hanover, owner and editor of the weekly *Aurora Sentinel*, published a letter from a group calling itself the Minnesota Civilian Brigade warning that if the government didn't stop interfering with rights of American citizens, civil rebellion was the only recourse. As the most visible and outspoken of the Anishinaabe, Russell Blackwater received a number of anonymous threats. In a television interview with a Twin Cities station a week before the fishing was to begin, Blackwater declared that if the whites wanted to wage war, the Anishinaabe were more than ready.

When Cork heard that particular statement, he asked Jo to arrange a meeting with her clients.

"It's just Russell talking," she assured him. "He doesn't mean anything."

"Someone not especially inclined to like Indians in the first place and who is a fisherman in the second won't think of it as just Russell Blackwater's way of talking. I want to speak with your clients."

Jo arranged for the meeting to take place in the old Catholic mission building on the reservation. Since 1953, when Congress passed Public Law 280 transferring jurisdiction on Minnesota reservations from federal hands to the state, it had been the responsibility of Tamarack County to provide law enforcement for the Iron Lake Reservation. Not an easy job considering the distrust that existed among the Ojibwe regarding the white legal system. Before Cork became sheriff, it was rare that a law enforcement officer would even set foot on the reservation. Cork had never sent a deputy there, knowing full well nothing useful would come of it. Reservation affairs he handled himself. More often than not, even he came away feeling that he'd trespassed.

When Cork drove into the meadow where the small white mission building stood, he found the structure surrounded by the cars and trucks of the reservation Anishinaabe. The building had fallen into disrepair from years of neglect, but St. Kawasaki had been working steadily on revamping the structure. Inside, the Anishinaabe were seated on old rough pews, amid the boards and sawhorses that were the evidence of the priest's steady labor.

"You're part Shinnob," Blackwater began the meeting. "What I'd like to know is who the hell's side are you on, anyway?"

"I'm not on a side," Cork explained. "My job is to abide by the law and to see that everyone else in Tamarack County does, too."

"Whose law?" Wanda Manydeeds asked from the back of the room. "The white man's law?"

"The law decided by the court," Cork replied.

"The white man's court," Wanda Manydeeds accused. "What about justice? Most of us here know from experience that justice and the white man's law aren't the same."

A lot of heads nodded in agreement.

"Law is in books," Cork told them. "Justice is a point of view. I can't enforce a point of view."

Blackwater turned to the gathering. "I told you we can't expect any help from this man. Blood of The People may run through his body, but his heart is a white man's heart."

"Please listen to me," Cork said. "If the court says you have the right to fish, I'll do everything I can to guarantee that right. If the court says you have no right, I'll be forced to take action against anyone who tries."

"Action?" Blackwater let a moment of absolute stillness pass, then he said, "What would you do? Shoot us?"

"That will never happen and we both know it, Russell."

"It's happened to The People before."

"It won't happen here. You have my word on it."

"The word of a white man," Blackwater said with disgust.

Sam Winter Moon stood up. "The word of a man we all know to be a good, truthful man."

"Yeah," Joe John LeBeau spoke up. "I've known Cork O'Connor all my life. I believe what he says. Whatever else goes down, I know he'll do his best to see we're treated fair."

"All right," Blackwater said skeptically. "What is it you want from us?"

"I don't want a war," Cork replied. "I don't want any more talk about war. I don't want guns carried around out of fear. The surest way to create an incident is to behave as if it's going to occur. Go on about your business just as you always have and wait for the court to make its decision. And be hopeful. Remember, you have the best attorney in the state working for you." He allowed himself a smile, and was glad to see many of those gathered smiling in return.

Thirty-six hours before opening day of spearfishing, the court handed down its decision. The Anishinaabe had the right under treaty to fish the lake to the full extent of the limit set by the DNR. Cork put all his men on alert and told them they should expect to work extra duty once the fishing began.

The evening before opening day, Cork met with those who were going to spearfish. They gathered in Russell Blackwater's trailer on the reservation. Jo was there. So were half a dozen other Anishinaabe including Joe John LeBeau, Wanda Manydeeds—Joe John's sister—and Sam Winter Moon.

"I promised I'd do everything I can to protect you tomorrow. In order to do that I'm going to need some help from you."

"What help?" Blackwater asked suspiciously.

"I'm most concerned about getting you from your vehicles into the boats and onto the lake. My guess is that we're going to have quite a crowd there to greet you. The faster you get onto the water, the better."

"We're not going to run down there like rabbits," Blackwater said.

"That's not what I'm asking. But the longer you present yourselves as targets to angry people, the greater the chance something can happen. And, Russell, if you saunter down there in front of these folks with some kind of attitude, you're just begging for trouble. That's when someone will get hurt."

"Is that a threat?" Blackwater asked. He glanced at the others in the small room.

"It's a potential." Cork looked around the room himself, pausing briefly to study the Anishinaabe he'd known all his life. "These people don't see the world the same way you do. A lot of the resort owners believe that what you're doing will ruin them. These are desperate people. And what I'm trying to make you understand is that there's real danger in what you're going to do tomorrow. It won't be a cakewalk."

Sam Winter Moon gave a single, slow nod. "There's danger in acting," he said. "There's also danger in sitting still, Cork. The law's finally on the side of The People. If we sit, what have we gained? Seems to me that if trouble comes, it won't be our doing."

"It never was," Cork replied. "But it's always The People who suffer in the end, regardless of right. My own wish is that you'd hold off doing anything until your counsel here has had a chance to negotiate a settlement of some kind with the state. That's what you're after, isn't it, Russell?"

"A settlement with the state will be easier to negotiate if the state knows we're serious in our intent," Blackwater pointed out.

"And if someone has already been hurt," Cork added, looking straight into the hungry hunter's eyes of Russell Blackwater.

"Sounds like another threat to me," Blackwater said.

"Cork," Joe John LeBeau spoke up. "Nobody wants anybody to get hurt. We just want what's ours for a change. Don't you get it? The world's looking on. How can we lose?"

"I can't absolutely guarantee your safety, Joe John. That's my point."

"When did you ever?" Wanda Manydeeds said with a little bitterness.

"Some of your customers will be in the crowd that gathers tomorrow, Joe John," Cork reminded him. "You, too, Sam."

"This isn't about business, Cork." Joe John looked around the room. "I can't ever remember feeling so much like one of The People. That's more important to me, to all of us, than anything else."

"It's not a question anymore of fishing," Sam spoke up. "It's a question of what's right, Cork. We've bent like reeds in a river for generations, bent so far over we've just about forgot how to stand up straight. Look at us now. None of us has ever been so proud of being a Shinnob."

Cork knew that was true. The feeling in the room of Blackwater's trailer was sweeping all of them along toward some inevitability. Russell Blackwater had brought the possibility of power to the reservation, and everyone gathered was ready to follow him anywhere.

"We're going to exercise our rights," Blackwater said. "We expect you to do your job."

"If you get your boats in the water with your gear ready tonight, I'll have a couple of my men watch them to make sure nothing's touched," Cork promised. "When you get to the landing, you can move quickly to the boats and out onto the lake. Would you be willing to do that?"

Blackwater and the others exchanged glances. Sam Winter Moon gave a nod. "We'll do it," Blackwater said.

Jo followed him to his sheriff's car. The sky was overcast, threatening rain. The night was very dark.

"You intend to be there, Counselor?" Cork asked her.

"We've come this far together."

"You don't have to. You're not one of The People."

"I'll be there to make sure their rights are observed."

"I'll be there for that."

She regarded him with the same skepticism Russell Blackwater had. "You're divided. I'm not."

"I have a duty clearly spelled out."

"You have an electorate clearly at odds with you."

"I'll do my duty."

"So will I." She looked back toward the trailer. "It doesn't have to turn ugly."

"Blackwater wants it that way."

"How do you know?"

"I just do."

"He's not everyone."

"It only takes one asshole, Jo."

They stood in the dark under the threatening sky and seemed at a loss for words. Cork reached out to hold her, but it was as if they were too full of the responsibilities they both bore, and there was no comfort in it. "I guess I'll see you in a few hours."

She went back to the trailer. When she opened the door, Cork heard the sound of Wanda Manydeeds, a Midewiwin, singing words he couldn't translate. He saw how they all welcomed Jo among them. Although she had not a drop of the blood of The People in her, she was more one of them at that moment than Cork had ever been.

Morning came gray and drizzly. Well before dawn, Cork had his deputies deployed along the path from the parking area to the boat landing. The small motorboats were tied up and waiting, their nets loaded. Cork was glad he'd talked Blackwater into that at least.

Some of the crowd had been there a good part of the night, but most had begun to gather an hour or so before dawn. A few barrels had been filled with wood and fires started, and people gathered around them warming hands and sipping coffee from thermoses. A couple of equipment trucks from television stations in Duluth and the Twin Cities were parked with their engines running, white exhaust mixing with the gray drizzle. Placards leaned against trees and the barrels, ready to be grabbed up when the moment arrived. There were some children in the crowd; Cork didn't like that at all. He asked the parents to take the children home, but they refused.

At 5:35, he got word over the radio that Helmuth Hanover of the *Aurora Sentinel* had received a call from an anonymous spokesman for the Minnesota Civilian Brigade threatening some form of retaliation if the Indians fished. Cork had no time to consider this development. Less than a minute later, just as the drizzle seemed to let up and the faintest hint of morning light crept across the lake, Deputy Jim Bowdry radioed that the procession of vehicles he was leading from the reservation was only a mile from the landing. Earlier Cork had given instructions to his men to clear a corridor from the parking area to the lake as soon as he gave them the word. He told them now to get started. The crowd, who'd been quiet and had even seemed a little sleepy, came suddenly to life and began chaotically to gather behind the lines formed by the outstretched arms of the deputies. The morning had been still enough to hear the lap of lake water against the shore, but now shouts back and forth across the empty corridor shattered the quiet. Placards rose above the crowd, swinging back and forth like signals at a dangerous railroad crossing. The news teams had crawled out of their trucks and started their cameras rolling.

Cork had a bad feeling in his gut. And for the first time in years, he was so afraid he was shaking.

The procession of five vehicles—the patrol car, two old pickups, a station wagon, and Blackwater's motorcycle—came slowly up the access toward the parking area. Jim Bowdry stopped his patrol car far short of the lot, where some of the crowd were waiting. Cork walked over and asked Blackwater to keep his people there a few moments. Then he hauled a bullhorn from his car, stood on a picnic table, and addressed the crowd.

"This is Sheriff O'Connor! Listen up, everyone!" He waited a moment for a quiet that never quite came. "This is Sheriff O'Connor! I want everyone to stay back of the lines my deputies have formed. I want a clear corridor for these fishermen to walk to their boats. Stay behind the deputies. I repeat, you will stay behind the deputies and keep the corridor clear."

He set the bullhorn on the table, stepped down, and approached Blackwater. "This is what you wanted, Russ. Let's do it."

Cork led the way. Directly behind him, side by side,

came Russell Blackwater and Sam Winter Moon. Jo was back with the others who followed, all of them keeping close together. The big yard light that illuminated the boat landing at the far end of the cleared corridor seemed miles away to Cork. The shouts of the crowd rose angrily on both sides. Cork had ordered his deputies to keep their firearms holstered, that if a situation arose they were to let him handle it. He didn't want an incident. He recognized many of the faces in the crowd, but they were different faces than he'd seen in the shops and the quiet streets of Aurora. They seemed like twisted things, grotesque Halloween masks of anger.

A third of the way to the landing, Cork caught a movement to his left just out of the corner of his eye. He swung around quickly. An empty Pepsi can clattered onto the black asphalt of the corridor and Russell Blackwater kicked it as it rolled across. Cork realized that he was gripping the handle of his holstered revolver. He took a deep breath, turned back toward the landing, and moved on.

They'd come thirty yards safely and had less than a dozen to go to reach the boats. For a moment, Cork finally let himself think it was just about over; they were almost there. He felt how tight he was, all his muscles tensed in a way that suddenly seemed more painful than he could bear, and he let himself relax, just a little. It was only a moment, one brief instant, but it was enough for tragedy.

A small figure stepped into the hard glare beneath the light over the boat landing. He'd come around the end of the crowd, slipped past the last outstretched deputy's arm. He stood at the end of the corridor, dead center. The light above him at his back cast his face in shadow, and Cork couldn't see who it was. The

shadowed mouth didn't utter a word. The arms simply lifted a rifle and pointed it toward Cork.

Forever after, Cork remembered the next few seconds as if it all had happened in slow motion. He
could see every detail. The drizzle-wetted hair plastered to the top of a balding little head. The dark outline of ears sticking out like handles on an urn. A
moment of illumination as the face turned slightly,
looking from side to side behind Cork. And finally
the slow drawing back of the hand that operated the
pump. Cork's own movements seemed like something done underwater, nightmarishly slow. Reaching toward his holster. Fumbling with the strap over
his revolver. Starting to draw the firearm clear. All of
it too slow.

Fire flashed from the rifle barrel. There must
have been a sound, but Cork in all his remembering never heard a sound. He expected to be hit, the
impact to be like a log slammed into his chest, but
he felt nothing and his arm kept moving, clearing
his revolver from its holster. As the figure before
him drew back the pump of the rifle again, Cork
fired. The little man stumbled back. Cork fired again
and again. The rifle discharged once more, but high
this time, uselessly into the dripping sky; the little
man collapsed. Cork followed him with his revolver,
pumping the last of his rounds into the man even as
he lay fallen.

Cork turned back. Behind him Sam Winter Moon
lay sprawled on the wet black asphalt, his chest blown
into a pulpy mess.

No one moved. In the deathly quiet of that moment, in the still Cork always would associate with
terrible tragedy, the lake could be heard again, lap-
ping peacefully against the shore.

The man with the rifle had been Arnold Stanley. All his life he'd held a safe job as an accountant in Chicago. But at fifty he'd risked his whole savings to buy the Bayside Inn, a small resort on a southern inlet of Iron Lake. He was a small, pop-eyed man, nervous. After the shooting, his wife told reporters that he'd been distraught at the prospect of the Indian fishing ruining his business. "He was afraid we'd lose everything," she sobbed on camera. "He wasn't a bad man. He was just so afraid."

People said openly that putting six bullets into a scared little man was excessive. It was a hard statement to disagree with.

Russell Blackwater, speaking for The People, decried Cork's incompetence. The sheriff had promised to protect the unarmed fishermen, who were only exercising their legal right. And once again it was the innocent who suffered when promises were broken.

The day Sam Winter Moon and Arnold Stanley died, the Anishinaabe didn't spearfish or gillnet. Nor did they any other day. A negotiating committee that included Russell Blackwater, Jo O'Connor, Sandy Parrant, and several attorneys for the state of Minnesota convened in St. Paul a few days later. They reached an agreement, pushed quickly through the legislature by Sandy Parrant, requiring the state to pay a much increased annual reimbursement to the Iron Lake band of Ojibwe for not exercising their fishing rights on Iron Lake or any other lake in the state.

The county board of commissioners suspended Cork with full pay pending the findings of an inquest into the shootings. Arnold Stanley was the only man Cork had ever killed. Nervous, popeyed little Stanley, who'd only been scared to death that he was going to lose everything. Cork went over it again and again in his mind, replaying every moment leading to the fatal shooting. Was there something he could have done? Did people have to die?

The inquest proceeded smoothly, evidence showing that Cork had acted reasonably. But the county attorney, Warren Evans, who was a crony of Robert Parrant, asked Cork a question that tilted the whole world of the inquest.

"Why did you shoot six times, Sheriff? Shoot even after the man was down?"

Cork, in the witness stand, looked at his hands and didn't answer right away.

"Did you hear the question?"

"Yes," Cork replied. "I heard."

"Please answer then. Why did you shoot Arnold Stanley six times?"

Although it was midday, midweek, the courtroom was full. Most of the spectators were white, but a number of Iron Lake Ojibwe, including Russell Blackwater, sat near the back off to one side. The quiet in the courtroom at that moment reminded Cork of the quiet at the boat landing after the shooting had stopped.

"Answer the question, Cork," Ed Reilly, the judge, said.

Cork looked out across the waiting faces in the courtroom. He said, "I don't know."

"Is it possible," Warren Evans suggested, "you simply panicked?"

Cork weighed this possibility. "Yes," he admitted, "it's possible I panicked."

———

"I panicked!"

Helmuth Hanover used those fateful words as the headline in the *Sentinel* two days later. And in his editorial, Hanover expressed serious doubts about Corcoran O'Connor's fitness as sheriff, posing the question to the voters of Tamarack County: Wasn't a recall election in order?

In retrospect, Cork thought he might have been able to mount a decent countercampaign, but at that time it hadn't mattered. He felt shattered, broken inside, unsure of everything about himself. Although the recall wasn't a landslide, it was successful. In the special election that followed, Wally Schanno, hand-picked by Judge Robert Parrant, stepped into office.

When he'd cleaned the old wax from the skis, he took a break, lit up a Lucky Strike, and stared across the lake toward the barren trees that lined the shore in front of the casino. In the morning sunlight, the distant copper dome flashed like a flame rising from the snow. Cork understood that, in a way, laying most of the blame for the tragedy on his shoulders had made the casino possible. Sandy Parrant could never have convinced the white population of Tamarack County to approve the land sale if they'd perceived the Anishinaabe to have been responsible for Stanley's death. And Blackwater could never have convinced the tribal council to go forward in the first place if he hadn't also convinced them that it was Cork's incompetence rather than the greed and anger of the whites that had caused the death of Sam Winter Moon. Jo's fortunes had risen with the Anishinaabe's and through her association with Sandy Parrant, whose own political star was well on the rise. Cork tried not to be bitter over it. In the end, prosperity had come to almost everyone in the county—red and white. What was one man's life, or two or three, compared to the welfare of so many?

Not much, he admitted as he flicked his cigarette into the snow. The ember hissed a moment, then died. Not very damn much. Unless it was your own.

CHAPTER 11

In the parking lot of Johnny's Pinewood Broiler, Molly Nurmi clipped on her skis and headed toward the lake three blocks away. Outside the small business district of Aurora, the streets hadn't been touched by a plow blade. Although sidewalks had been cleared or were being cleared, most of the town looked as it had in the early light when Molly came off the lake on her way to work. Drifts sloped against anything upright—fences, hedges, walls. Slender tree limbs wore a thick white layer like icing on a dessert bar. In the sunlight, everything sparkled in a way that thrilled Molly greatly, and when she hit the open flat of the lake, she let herself fly.

Snowmobiles whined across the lake, buzzing like fast small insects, leaving a maze of tracks that reminded Molly of patterns in wormwood. Far out on the ice, a small fleet of four-wheelers had made their way to fishing shanties. There seemed more life on the hard water of Iron Lake than on land.

Molly cut north, following several of the snowmobile tracks toward the small copse of trees that hid the old foundry. Beyond that was Sam's Place, and Cork would be waiting. She loved to push her body, to feel how strong it was, how she could ask so much of it and it would deliver. Her body was the only thing she'd ever known that was so reliable, and she took care of it religiously. In summer she ran the forested, back roads or swam long distances in the lake. Winters, she skiied every chance she got. She fed her body in healthy ways, eschewing caffeine and alcohol especially. There had been a time in her life when she wouldn't have bet money on living past twenty-one. Now she sometimes felt wonderfully invulnerable, as if she could live forever. In a life that had been spent mostly running away from the past, she felt she'd finally come to rest somewhere full of hope.

As she broke from the trees and saw Cork standing near his Bronco watching her approach, she thought it had been a long journey to reach the place she'd come to, nearly thirty years. But she was glad to be there.

"I love this snow!" she exclaimed as she stopped beside the Bronco. She opened her arms in a gesture as if hugging the whole world. "I love winter. I adore everything about it." She leaned to him and kissed him passionately. "And I adore you."

"Let's get those skis on the Bronco," he said.

Molly saw that he had his own skis—old wooden things—already on the rack. "We're going skiing? Together?"

"I'm using your place as a starting point to ski to Meloux's."

"Let's start from here," she suggested.

"Are you kidding? I'd die. Come on, off with those skis. I'll drive you home."

Molly released the toe clips and stepped out. Cork put the skis on the rack and tossed her poles in back with his. He held the door of the Bronco open for her, then got in behind the wheel and pulled away from the Quonset hut. Molly took off her stocking cap and shook out her hair. The heat from her body and the moisture from her sweat steamed the windows and Cork kicked the defrost fan up a couple of notches. Molly watched him closely.

"You've been thinking about Sam Winter Moon and Arnold Stanley," she said.

He was surprised, but tried not to show it. "What makes you think so?"

"I can always tell. Your face gets like a mess of old knotted-up rope." Molly slid across the seat so that she was against him. "I've got an idea. Let's go to my place, do the sauna, roll in the snow, and screw ourselves blind. That'll take the knots right out of you, I guarantee."

"Can't," Cork said.

Molly ran her hand slowly up his thigh. "Not true." She smiled.

"I mean I don't have time right now. Like I said, I'm on my way to see Henry Meloux."

"All right." She shrugged and slid back across the seat. "Your loss."

Although she said it without malice, Cork still felt guilty. "Want to come with me?"

They turned off onto County Road AA, which curved around the north end of the lake toward Molly's place and the thick pines of the Superior National Forest. Meloux's cabin stood on a piece of reservation land just beyond.

"Does Meloux have anything to do with the judge?" she asked as she watched the endless snowbanks sliding past.

"You heard, huh?"

"This isn't exactly New York City, Cork. Death here is big news. Was it awful?"

"I've seen worse."

"Is that supposed to impress me?"

Cork said, "I put Jo through law school by being a cop in the worst part of Chicago. I saw a lot in those days." He drove a little way and, out of the corner of his eye, saw the pinched look of disapproval on Molly's face. "You're right," he admitted. "You never get used to something like that. It was pretty bad."

"It's odd. He was just about the last man I would have suspected of suicide."

"If it was suicide."

"What do you mean?"

"Like you said, he was the last man anybody would suspect. That in itself makes me wonder."

"Did he leave a note or something?"

"Nothing."

"So what, then? Murder?"

"Not my jurisdiction anymore. Ask Wally Schanno."

She reached out and touched his shoulder. "It must be hard sitting on the sidelines."

"I'm getting used to it," he lied. "Here we are."

Molly's lane hadn't been cleared and the plowing of the county road had left a steep snowbank blocking her access. Cork put the Bronco into four-wheel drive and carefully crawled over the bank. He had no trouble in the powdery snow beyond. He stopped in front of Molly's cabin, got out, and pulled the skis from the rack. He changed to his cross-country boots, and as he bent to clip on his skis, Molly asked, "Is Henry expecting you?"

"He has a way of expecting everything," Cork replied.

Meloux's cabin was made of cedar and had been on its small point of the lake—Crow's Point—for as long as anybody could remember. In winter when the other resorts were closed for the season, Meloux was Molly's closest neighbor. Just inside the reservation boundary a mile northeast along the shoreline, Crow's Point was visible from Molly's sauna. As they started out onto the lake, Cork could see smoke from Meloux's tiny cabin rising up calm and straight as you please into the perfectly still air above the pine trees. The shoreline curved away from them in a ragged arc of inlets and small rocky points. Three-quarters of the way across the ice, a long tongue of open water stuck out into the lake. It came from Half Mile Spring, a rush of water that issued from ground so near the lake that it didn't have time to freeze in its journey.

They stayed well clear of the mouth of Half Mile Spring. Crow's Point was rocky and steep, and they had to remove their skis to climb up to the old man's cabin. Meloux opened the door to them even before they knocked, and he stood grinning in welcome. An old yellow dog stood patiently at his side, tongue lolling, tail wagging.

"Corcoran O'Connor," the old man said. "I see you survived the storm." He laughed in a way that sounded as if he were making fun of Cork's concern for him the night before. "And Molly Nurmi. It is always good to see a neighbor's face. Come in, you are both welcome."

He stood aside and let them enter. The cabin was a clean and simple place, one room, with a wood stove, bunk, a rough-hewn table, and two benches. On the walls hung many objects, some from animals— a bearskin, a bow with string made from the skin of a snapping turtle and ornamented with feathers, a deer-prong pipe; some of wood—a birch-bark basket, a small toboggan, snowshoes. On the floor beside the bed lay a mat of woven cedar bark. Not far from the stove hung an old Skelly calendar—1948—with an elaborate cartoon picture of a pretty young lady in revealing shorts, bent to check her makeup in the rearview mirror, much to the delight of an admiring gas station attendant. Cork handed Meloux a pack of Lucky Strikes, which the old man accepted graciously, then Cork sniffed at the air.

"Somebody sick?" he asked. "Smells like you've been burning cedar."

"I purify the air, I purify the spirit," the old man said. "Also, I have been baking. I have baked buttermilk biscuits. Will you eat with me?"

They sat at the table and the old man brought the biscuits and butter and a clay jar of honey. "I have blackberry tea," he told them. He turned to the stove, but before he could move toward it, the blue tea kettle jumped and rattled of its own accord. Molly jerked, startled, and the dog leaped up growling fiercely.

"Go back to sleep, Walleye," the old man said to the dog.

"What was that?" Molly asked breathlessly.

"A Windigo is about," Meloux replied, and went to fetch the tea. Cork explained the myth of the Windigo, the cannibal giant whose heart was ice, and Molly looked with wide eyes at the tea kettle in Meloux's hands.

"Don't worry," Meloux told her. "The Windigo is not hunting you." To put her at ease, the old man entertained them, made them laugh with his stories of all the years in that place. He told stories of Sam Winter Moon and the pranks he used to play as a young man on the Iron Lake Reservation.

"He was hunting once near the edge of the reservation," Meloux said. "A duck fell right out of the sky at his feet. As he picked it up, a white hunter appeared and claimed the duck was his because he'd shot it. Sam Winter Moon pointed out that the duck was on reservation land, and so the hunter had no right to it. The hunter claimed it was his because the duck was not on reservation land when he shot it. Sam Winter Moon looked at the man who was angry and at his rifle and suggested a way to decide. 'We will have a contest,' he said. 'We will kick one another in the nuts and whoever is still standing will get the duck.' The white hunter, who was a very big, mean-looking man, agreed. Sam said he would go first. The white hunter braced himself and Sam Winter Moon gave him a good kick. The man turned red then blue then white. He staggered around holding himself in great pain. After a few minutes he drew himself up and said to Sam Winter Moon, 'Now it is my turn.' But Sam Winter Moon said, 'You win,' handed him the duck, and walked away." Meloux laughed. "He was a good man. He was a warrior. His Anishinaabe name was Animikiikaa, which means 'It thunders.'"

When they rose to leave, Meloux said to Cork, "I have something for you." He went to a basket set in a corner and pulled something out. He returned to Cork and pressed a bit of dried root into his hand.

Cork nodded and turned to Molly. "Could you wait outside for a moment?"

"Sure." Molly left, closing the door behind her.

"I need to ask you something, Henry."

"Ask, then," the old man replied.

"You said you heard the Windigo call a name as it passed overhead. What name?"

The old man shook his head. "With the Windigo, you cannot help, Corcoran O'Connor. I do not think you are the one to fight the Windigo."

"Tell me this. Was the name Judge Parrant?"

The old man laughed. "That is a name I would not mind the Windigo calling, but it was not the name I heard."

"Was it Paul LeBeau?"

"Joe John's boy? No." The old man put his hand on Cork's shoulder. "It will do no good, but I will tell you the name I heard. The name the Windigo called was Harlan Lytton. And that is another name I do not mind the Windigo calling." He walked Cork to the door. "Thank you for visiting. I am grateful for your concern over an old man."

Cork hesitated before leaving.

"What is it?" Meloux asked.

"Sam told me once that a man knows when the Windigo is coming for him. Is that true?"

"A man who listens will hear his name." The old man stared at him a moment. "You heard."

"No." Cork shook his head. "I'm sure it was just a trick of the wind."

"A man knows the difference between the Windigo and the wind."

"Thank you, Henry."

The old man touched Cork's chest with the flat of his hand. *"Mangide'e,"* he said. *Be courageous.*

Molly was waiting for him on the lake. She already had her skis on. As Cork clipped his boots onto his skis, he said, "Come on, I'll race you back."

She beat him by a hundred yards and at the Bronco turned to him scolding, "It's those coffin nails you smoke."

"No," Cork replied as he came up to her. "I just liked the view from behind," and he kissed her. He reached into his pocket and pulled out the small gift Meloux had given him.

"What is that?" Molly asked.

"A little bit of root from a wild pea plant."

"What for?"

"It's supposed to be a lucky charm for a man in a dangerous situation. It's supposed to ensure that everything turns out for the best."

She looked at him carefully. "Cork, are you in some kind of danger?"

"Meloux seems to think so."

"But you don't?"

He put the charm back into his pocket. "If I am, I don't know why."

"The Windigo thing you told me about in there. Is that for real?"

"Just an old myth," Cork said. He released the clips on his skis and stepped out.

"Old myth." She glanced back toward Crow's Point. "Something made that kettle jump."

"Do you know what a *tchissakan* is?" He could tell by her blank expression she didn't. "It's an Anishinaabe magician. It also means *juggler*. It's a person who can juggle the elements of our world and the world of the unseen. Sometimes a *tchissakan* communicates with the dead. Can actually bring forth a voice from the dead. So I'd guess a *tchissakan* is probably a ventriloquist as well."

"Meloux?" she asked.

"There aren't many, and Henry Meloux has never admitted to being one, but I've heard different."

"So it was the trick of a—"

"A *tchissakan*. Probably."

Molly looked unconvinced. She leaned to him and kissed him hard.

"What was that for?" he asked.

"Like the pea root," she replied. "For luck."

CHAPTER 12

Christmas lights twinkled in shop windows along Center Street as Cork pulled into Aurora. With only a week to go until Christmas, the stores would be open late. Cork spotted a woman standing in front of Lenore's Toy and Hobby Shop. Although the temperature was in the teens, she wore only a light sweater. Cork pulled into a parking space, stepped out of the Bronco, climbed over a snowbank, and walked to where the woman stood.

"Christmas shopping, Arletta?" he asked.

Arletta Schanno glanced at him and a frown came to her pretty face. "Wally?"

"Corcoran O'Connor."

"Sheriff O'Connor." She suddenly brightened. "I can't seem to remember if I've bought gifts for the children."

"Here," Cork said. He took off his leather jacket and put it around her shoulders. She was shivering.

"Janie told me she wanted a game this year. Clue, I believe. I think that sounds fine, don't you? Clarissa says she wants a Barbie doll, but she has so many already."

Janie was thirty-five and lived in Baltimore. She worked for the post office there. Clarissa taught high school geography in St. Paul.

"How about a ride home, Arletta," Cork offered. "I just happen to be going that way."

"I don't know," Arletta Schanno said. A distressed and helpless look clouded her face.

"I'll bet Wally would like to help with shopping, don't you?"

"Wally's so busy."

"Not too busy for Christmas shopping. Come on, let's go home."

Cork urged her gently into the Bronco and drove to the Schannos' house. Wally Schanno opened the door, and Cork could tell from the relief that flooded his face he'd been worried sick.

"I found her Christmas shopping," Cork explained.

"Sheriff O'Connor was very kind, dear," Arletta said.

Wally handed Cork back his coat. "Thanks," he said. "You're chilled, Arletta. Why don't you go put on a warmer sweater."

"I think I will." She smiled and walked down the hallway toward the back of the house.

"I called everywhere. The housekeeper had to leave early. It was just a few minutes. Just a few goddamn minutes," Schanno said miserably, "and she was gone."

"Not many places to get lost in Aurora, Wally," Cork said.

Schanno shook his head. "It only gets worse."

"I'm sorry."

"Not your doing," Schanno said, offering his hand to Cork. "Thanks again."

Cork started to turn away.

"By the way," Schanno said, "I called Doc Gunnar this morning. Sandy Parrant was absolutely right. The judge was in bad shape. Riddled with cancer. Gunnar said he only had a few months to live. Guess we've got a motive for suicide."

"Did Sigurd authorize an autopsy?"

"You know how much an autopsy costs, Cork. Sigurd didn't see anything he felt justified an autopsy."

"How about the LeBeau boy? Any word?"

"Darla says she got a call from the boy last night. She says he's with his father. Safe. Maybe it's true, maybe it isn't. It's clear she doesn't want me involved. Unless Darla makes an official complaint, I can't do anything anyway."

Arletta Schanno stepped back into the room wearing a heavy white wool sweater. She came toward Cork smiling warmly.

"Sheriff, what a nice surprise."

Cork glanced at Schanno, who looked down.

Molly had talked him into a sandwich at her place— hummus, sprouts, and tomatoes—that he'd washed down with a beer, so he wasn't hungry. But he still had a while to kill before his meeting with Father Tom Griffin. He drove to Sigurd Nelson's mortuary on Pine Street. The sign on the front door directed him to ring the buzzer in back and Cork complied. In a moment Nelson opened the door, sock-footed and with bread crumbs at the corner of his mouth. He looked surprised to see Cork.

"Sorry to bother you, Sigurd. Wally said you've finished with the body."

"Haven't even started," the coroner said.

"I mean in your official capacity."

"Oh, that. Wasn't much to finish." He stepped back. "Come on in before this house gets full of winter."

They stood in a long hallway at the back of the mortuary. The place was actually a house, a beautiful old two-story affair, one of the nicest in Aurora. The first floor was for business. A showroom up front displaying coffins, to one side a large chapel for memorial services. In back a business office. Over his years in Aurora, Cork had been to the chapel many times. The time he most remembered his father had been there, too, laid out in one of Sigurd Nelson's coffins, a strong, practical man gone to rest in a box lined with satin.

"Who is it, dear?" Grace Nelson called from upstairs. The second floor of the house was the living area for the mortician and his wife.

"Cork O'Connor, Gracie."

"Your dinner's getting cold," she warned him gently.

"I'll be right there," Nelson called back. "What are you doing here, Cork?" he asked impatiently.

"I just wondered why you decided not to autopsy."

"Because I'd have difficulty explaining it to the taxpayers of this county is why. Christ, the man had cancer everywhere. He blew his brains out because he was going to die anyway. What's to autopsy? Open-and-shut case."

"But you looked at the body carefully yourself?"

"Sure I did. And I found just what I expected. He died because he blew his brains out. Period."

"No other marks on his body?"

"Why would there be other marks?"

"Mind if I have a look?"

"Of course I mind. Why are you here, Cork? You're not even the sheriff anymore."

"Come on, Sigurd. Open-and-shut case. You said it yourself. What harm can it do letting me see the body? Just for a minute."

"He's a mess."

"I've seen him before."

Nelson didn't look happy, but he finally turned and led the way.

The basement was divided into several rooms, all with shut doors. Sigurd opened one of the doors, turned on the light, and stepped in. In some ways, the prep room reminded Cork of a scientific laboratory. Red tile floor, off-white walls, cabinets, embalming pump, and flush tank. On a row of pegs along the wall hung Sigurd's blue prep clothing and the plastic face shield he wore when preparing a body. The judge's naked corpse lay on an old white porcelain prep table near the embalming pump.

"He's all yours," Nelson said with a wave toward the table.

The corpse lay on its back. The face was pallid and the features relaxed. Above the eyebrows, the cavity that had at one time held a very bright, but in Cork's opinion very devious, brain was nearly empty. With the top of the skull blown away, the head was crowned by a blood-crusted rim of jagged bone. Cork looked carefully at the neck, the wrists, the ankles, the ribs.

"If you're looking for bruises, you won't find any," the coroner told him. "He wasn't tied up, beat up, or strangled. He just blew his brains out, okay?"

Cork looked closely again at the judge's arms, then at his thighs, and finally his abdomen. "Help me turn him over, Sigurd."

"Why?"

"Just help me, will you?"

Nelson gave a reluctant hand. Cork studied the judge's shoulders, the back of his arms, the small of his back, the cheeks of his buttocks.

"What the hell are you looking for anyway?" Sigurd demanded.

"Nothing. Just looking."

"Just looking?" Nelson grunted as they turned the body onto its back again.

"Chalk it up to idle curiosity, Sigurd," Cork said.

"Idle curiosity? I swear to God—" the coroner said growing red with indignation. "I've got a perfectly good dinner getting cold."

Nelson draped the body with the sheet and flipped off the light switch. He followed Cork upstairs. At the door he warned, "Cork, I got half a mind—" But he didn't finish.

"Thanks," Cork said, and started away.

At his back, Nelson slammed the door.

The coroner had a right to be upset. Cork had no business looking at the body, no business thinking about the case at all. But an Ojibwe boy was missing and Henry Meloux was sure that a Windigo was about, and although Wally Schanno was a good cop, he was one hundred percent white, and neither the boy nor the Windigo would matter as much to him as they did to Cork. Cork sat in the Bronco thinking about the body of the judge. He'd come because he was always suspicious of an easy explanation. Few things were so sure and simple that they could be taken at face value. If he'd believed Sigurd had done a decent job as coroner, he might not have asked to see the body. He was glad he had.

He was running late, but he wanted to stop by Darla LeBeau's house. The place was dark, the sidewalks unshoveled. He rang the front bell anyway. No one answered. He started back to the Bronco, but didn't get in. He studied the woods from which had come the voice Meloux said was the call of the Windigo. The evening was dark and still. Stars dusted the black sky. Cork could see the glimmer of other houses in a small subdivision a hundred yards away, but on the deserted part of the road where he stood, there was no light, no sign of life, no sound but the whisper of his own quiet breathing.

He walked toward the woods, stepped in among the trees. He stood still, listening, watching. The woods felt empty and Cork felt alone.

"Why do you want me?" Cork spoke softly to the stillness. His eyes darted all around. "What have you come for?"

If he expected an answer—and he wasn't certain that he didn't—he was disappointed. He told himself he had imagined the voice in the wind. The Windigo was a myth.

But there was a part of him that knew different. Sam Winter Moon had cautioned him long ago that it was best to believe in all possibilities, that there were more mysteries in the world than a man could ever hope to understand.

CHAPTER 13

The rectory door was opened to him by Ellie Gruber, a stout woman in her late fifties who'd been house-keeper for the ancient Father Kelsey more than a decade. She told him Father Griffin wasn't there yet, but she showed him to the priest's office and brought him coffee. Cork could hear a television in another room. Ellie said the Timberwolves were playing the Bulls. Cork could also hear Father Kelsey mumble and groan and occasionally toss in an unpriestly expletive.

"The Timberwolves must be losing." Cork smiled.

Father Tom Griffin's office was a mess of papers and books covering every flat surface of the room. The furniture consisted of a desk with a telephone and a small brass lamp, three scarred wooden chairs, an ancient green filing cabinet, and, in front of the window, a typing table with an old Olivetti electric. A crucifix hung on one wall; on another were several framed photographs; against the third stood a book-case with every shelf crammed full. Cork gravitated to the photos. He believed a lot could be inferred from the photographs a person chose to display. In Father Tom Griffin's case, Cork saw much of the road the man had traveled to reach that cluttered office. One photo showed a young Tom Griffin, a long and lanky college kid in a Notre Dame baseball uniform with a self-confident and likable grin. Another, taken much later, showed him in his collar standing with the pope. The pope looked small and severe next to the tall priest, who was relaxed and smiling. Several of the other photos seemed to have been taken in Central America. They were village shots, dusty streets or cobblestone, and shy, emaciated mestizo kids smiling for the camera. The last picture was quite recent, taken on the Iron Lake Reservation, and showed Tom Griffin standing beside the mission building he was restoring. With him stood Wanda Manydeeds. It was fitting. The priest and the Midewiwin. Wanda looked serious as ever. The priest, although he had a black eye patch now and he'd let his hair go shaggy, was still smiling just as broadly as the kid in the photo who'd played ball for Notre Dame.

Tom Griffin's eye wasn't the only wounded part of his body. The priest bore other scars, some visible on his hands and arms. Although he had never asked the priest directly, Cork had heard about the long political internment that had ended the cleric's involvement in the church in Central America. This information was always offered in a hushed tone, as if to the conservative parishioners of St. Agnes it was some kind of questionable skeleton in the priest's closet.

Tom Griffin caught Cork by surprise, sweeping into the room suddenly, bringing with him the hard cold that had stiffened his old leather jacket. He wore a stocking cap with the red face mask still pulled down, so that, with only the eye holes and nose hole and mouth, he looked like some kind of demon conjured out of a North Woods black night.

"Sorry I'm late, Cork." He pulled off the stocking cap and mask.

"Didn't hear your snowmobile, Tom," Cork said.

"It died on me out at the mission this afternoon. That's why I'm late. Had to hitch a ride in the back of a pickup." He shrugged off his coat and threw everything on a chair already occupied by a stack of papers. He wore a red plaid flannel shirt, faded jeans, and hiking boots. Rubbing his cold legs vigorously, he smiled at Cork, and said, "I've taken to calling it Lazarus because starting it's like trying to raise the dead.

"I see Mrs. Gruber got you some coffee. Good. I think I might have something a little stronger. Care for a beer? I've also got some Chivas Regal that would spice up that coffee nicely."

"I'm fine, thanks," Cork replied.

"Suit yourself."

The priest stepped over to the file cabinet, opened the top drawer, and took out a bottle. Lifting a plastic cup from the top of the cabinet, he cleaned out something with his little finger and poured in the whiskey. He cleared off a chair and pulled it up next to his desk, motioning for Cork to go ahead and sit. He sipped from his cup, closed his eye, and sighed.

"First chance I've had to sit down all day." The sounds of Father Kelsey's reactions to the game carried into the room. "Timberwolves must be losing tonight." St. Kawasaki smiled and got up to close the door.

"I hear Joe John finally called Darla," Cork said. "Were you there?"

"I was at Darla's most of the night."

"Joe John give any particular reason for taking Paul that way?"

"He missed his son," the priest said with a note of sympathy. "And he was ashamed. He couldn't face Darla. Pretty simple really."

"You talk with him?"

"No."

"Know where he is?"

The priest sipped his Chivas Regal and shook his head. "I was just out at the reservation talking to Wanda. Darla asked me to intercede."

"Did she tell you anything?"

"She says she doesn't know where Joe John is."

"What do you think?"

The priest shrugged. "You know The People, Cork. When they want to, they can say nothing very well."

"And Wanda's saying nothing. That should tell you something."

The priest studied his whiskey a moment. "I have a good feeling about this. Somehow, it's all going to turn out for the best."

"I wish I did," Cork said.

"Maybe that's the difference between the law and religion. I hope for the best, you're prepared for the worst."

"There's another difference," Cork said.

"What's that?"

"Your parishioners can't kick you out."

The priest laughed. Cork took a cigarette from the pack in his shirt pocket. "Mind?" he asked.

"No, go ahead. Can I bum one?"

"I didn't know you smoked," Cork said.

"I gave it up when I was in Central America. Rather involuntarily," he added with a smile.

Cork held out the pack, the priest took a cigarette, and Cork offered his lighter.

"You wanted to talk," the priest said, lighting his cigarette.

"I need some—" Cork thought a moment. "I was going to say advice, but the truth is, I need some guidance, Tom."

"We all do sometimes. It's not always easy to admit."

"I haven't been to church in a long time. Can't remember my last confession."

"Is that what this is?"

"Maybe. At least partly." Cork lit his own cigarette and slipped the lighter in his pocket. "I've been out of the house a long time now. You knew that."

He paused, expecting the priest to say something. But St. Kawasaki appeared content to smoke his cigarette and listen.

"I've started seeing another woman."

The priest didn't seem surprised in the least.

"I didn't think about it at first, where it was going, what ultimately would be involved. I wasn't thinking clearly about a lot of things. But now—" Cork hesitated.

"Now?" the priest encouraged.

"Now every time I see my children, I'm afraid."

"Afraid of what?"

"Hurting them badly. Hurting them forever."

The priest held his cigarette delicately between his thumb and index finger, smoking in a way Cork had always considered continental. He studied the tip of his cigarette a moment, then said, "Children are resilient. But I agree it's a reasonable fear."

"I don't know what to do, Tom. I don't want to lose my family. I don't want my children hurt."

"What I hear you saying is that more than anything you want your family."

The understanding in the priest's voice touched Cork deeply. "Yes," he confessed.

"And this other woman, does she know?"

"She suspects. She hasn't pressed me." Cork felt himself shouldering again a weight that seemed unbearable. "She's a wonderful woman, Tom." He stood up, walked across the cluttered office to the window. He blew smoke against the glass and stared at the empty steps of the church across the yard. "Funny. I remember every detail of the morning Sam Winter Moon and Arnold Stanley died. But the whole next year is a blur. I wasn't much of a husband or a father. I didn't even fight it when Jo asked me to leave. I think about that now and it's like I was someone else. Someone in a bad dream. Or like I was sleepwalking. This woman woke me up, Tom."

"Maybe time did that, Cork."

"Maybe."

"Do you love her?"

"I haven't said that to her, no."

"That's not what I asked."

Cork watched cigarette smoke crawl the window-pane as if it were looking for a way out.

"Yes," he finally admitted. "I do."

"And you love your family."

"Of course."

"Does that include Jo?"

Cork turned back. The priest was watching him with a placid expression.

"Not at the moment. But maybe it could again if we tried. If we had some help."

"From me?"

"Isn't that what priests do?"

"Some."

"Would you?"

"What about Jo? Is this something she wants?"

"She wants a divorce. And one thing about Jo, once she's made up her mind about something, she won't back down."

"Sounds like you're asking me for a miracle."

"It does seem pretty hopeless," Cork said.

"Hopeless." The priest sipped his whiskey and smoked his cigarette and seemed to consider the word. "Let me tell you something, Cork. In all my life I've learned two things." He pointed to the black patch over his eye. "One is never call a small man in a uniform 'Shorty.' The other is that nothing is ever hopeless." He dropped the last of his cigarette into the plastic cup. "I'll talk with Jo. I'll do my best to convince her to join you in some counseling."

"Thanks."

"But, Cork, I need to be sure you're going to end this other relationship. There's nothing that I or anyone else can do if you're not willing to sacrifice everything for your family."

"I know. I'll end it."

St. Kawasaki smiled a little wearily. "The things that ask the most of us are the things most worth having."

Cork left the window and walked to the desk. He tossed his cigarette into St. Kawasaki's cup. "Mind if I use your phone?"

"Go ahead."

He dialed Harlan Lytton's number, waited while the phone at the other end rang eight times. He put the receiver back in the cradle. "Thanks."

"No one home?"

"It's Harlan Lytton. Sometimes he doesn't answer out of sheer orneriness.

"Lytton? The one with the dog they call Jack the Ripper?"

"That's him. I have to go out to see him tonight."

"Mind me asking why you'd want to pay a visit to a man like that?"

"If he answered his phone, I wouldn't have to. But he didn't answer."

"Why go out there at all?"

"Long story. Kind of hard to explain."

The priest grabbed his leather jacket. "I've heard things about this Lytton. I'm not going to let you go there alone. Not at night."

"I used to go out there alone all the time when I was sheriff."

St. Kawasaki put his hand on Cork's shoulder and looked at him seriously with his good eye. "I hate to remind you of this, but you're not the sheriff anymore."

CHAPTER 14

Lytton's cabin lay five miles outside town at the end of a long, narrow cut into two hundred acres of thick brush, bog, balsam pine and tamarack. The lane leading to the cabin was marked by on old hand-painted sign on a cracked gray board nailed to a post: "Taxidermy." A chain strung between two aspen saplings blocked the entry.

Cork eyed the deep snow drifted into the narrow lane. "Long walk in, Tom. I've got skis and snowshoes," he offered.

"The only thing I can handle in the snow is my Kawasaki. I'll walk, thanks."

"Then I'll walk, too."

Cork reached into the glove compartment for a flashlight, then opened the rear door and took his Winchester from its sheath. He pulled several cartridges from his coat pocket and fed them into the rifle.

"What's that for?" the priest asked.

"How much do you know about Jack the Ripper?"

The snow seemed to multiply the light of the moon that was nearly full and the mass of stars that frosted the sky, and even without the flashlight Cork had no trouble seeing the way along the cut through the trees and brush.

"I was out here once just after I first came to Aurora. I brought a big muskie Father Kelsey had caught and wanted mounted. Never made it off my motorcycle. That dog was on me as soon as I pulled up. I gave it full throttle coming back down this lane and the Ripper still nearly caught me. Biggest, fastest, meanest dog I ever saw."

"Lytton lets it run loose," Cork said. "Especially when he's gone, and he's gone a lot. Burglar protection, he claims. I used to warn him about the dog getting off his land, but the Ripper never does. Seems to know his territory. And we're in it right now. I don't want to be caught out here on foot without something to discourage that dog."

The priest shook his head at the rifle. "That thing could discourage a critter to death."

"Lytton's put out word that he's trained the Ripper to attack on command and to go for the kill. Now, that could be just Harlan blowing smoke out his ass, but I'd rather not take that chance."

They passed a tangle of vine thick as a stone wall and covered with snow. The vines blocked Cork's view of much of the woods to his left, and he kept a watchful eye in that direction.

"Why would anyone train a dog to kill?" the priest asked.

"What do you know about Lytton?"

"Only what I've been told. He sounds like a man who could use a good long visit in a confessional."

Cork stopped. The priest stopped, too.

"What is it?" Tom Griffin asked.

"Thought I heard something." Cork looked carefully at the thick vine wall.

"What?"

"Could've been only a clump of snow falling off some branches."

"Or it could be Jack the Ripper circling for a kill." The priest looked carefully around. "I feel like a sitting duck on this road," he whispered.

"Don't ever wander off in these woods, Tom. There's bogs out there could swallow you up without a trace."

Cork listened a little longer, then started walking again, wading through the snow that was nearly knee deep and that would, if they had to run, hold them back like thick molasses. He fed a round into the chamber.

"Lytton's a strange case. He's always been a little different. A loner. His mother used to work for the judge. Housekeeper. After the judge's wife left him and hauled Sandy back east, the judge took a liking to Harlan, treated him in many ways like a son. They did a lot together. Hunting and fishing. That kind of thing. Harlan started getting into a lot of trouble as a teenager. The judge used his influence as much as he could and kept the kid out of jail. Harlan finally joined the marines. Everybody figured him for a lifer, but he came back a few years ago. Word is, less than honorable discharge. Most people just stay out of his way. That's not difficult because mostly he keeps to himself out here."

Tom Griffin said, "I heard he's a bit of a peeping Tom."

"I was never able to catch him at it," Cork replied. "But he's been reported in strange places at strange times. When I was sheriff, the FBI was interested in him. Thought he might be linked to the Minnesota Civilian Brigade."

"The paramilitary group?"

"Yep. I could see it. Typical profile for a member of that kind of group is an unemployed, undereducated white guy. Hell Hanover gives the brigade room in the *Sentinel* once in a while to spout their epithets."

"Hanover certainly doesn't make a secret of the fact that his own sympathies run in that direction." The priest leaned nearer as if someone in the dark might hear. "Just between you and me, with that shaved head and those cold blue eyes, old Hell looks just like a Nazi commandant." As if saying the name of Hell Hanover was like conjuring the devil, the priest looked carefully about. "Why in God's name are you out on a night like this to see a man like Harlan Lytton?"

"Henry Meloux says he heard the Windigo call his name."

"The what?"

"Long story, Tom. Believe me, I wouldn't be out here if Lytton would just answer his damn phone. I've been trying him all day. Either he can't or he's in one of his moods."

"It's important for you to know which?"

"The judge is dead. Harlan and him have a long connection. Now Henry Meloux's heard the Windigo call Harlan's name. I'd just like to check on Harlan."

"Professional curiosity? Isn't that the sheriff's job?"

"The Windigo's not something Wally Schanno's likely to consider seriously."

"And you do?"

Cork thought about telling the priest that he'd heard the Windigo call his own name and that his interest wasn't professional but quite personal and very pressing. But he decided to keep it simple.

"Once I begin to wonder about a thing it's hard for me to let go. There's his cabin," Cork said in a low voice. "He's got lights on. Good sign. Him and the

Ripper enjoying a quiet evening chewing on some-body's bones."

The cabin was small but sturdy, with a shake roof and split shutters, all of cedar. There was a small garage to one side and a shed in back. From what little Cork knew about Lytton, he understood the shed was where the man used to do his taxidermy work. With the Ripper around, very few people brought Lytton that kind of business anymore.

"Lytton!" he called. "Harlan Lytton!"

There was no response from the cabin.

"It's Cork O'Connor! I've got Father Tom Griffin with me!" Cork glanced at the priest. "He was never much impressed with my sheriff's badge. I figure if he's thinking of taking a bead on us, your collar might carry some weight."

"Thanks. He'll shoot me first out of respect."

"Lytton, are you there!" Cork tried again. "Come on, Tom. If he hasn't shot at us by now, he probably won't."

"Don't forget about The Ripper."

Cork started ahead.

From behind the wall of vines to the left came a blur of black against the white of the snow. Cork caught the movement out of the corner of his eye. He swung around as a huge black shape charged through the snow, bounding up and down, moving swiftly as a stone skipping over water.

"Tom!" Cork cried, trying to warn the priest.

St. Kawasaki saw it coming. He lifted his arm to fend off the attack. Cork had the Winchester shouldered, and he fired at the black form as it launched itself at the priest. The Ripper yelped and his body jerked violently in midair. Tom Griffin turned and ducked, taking the impact of the dog with his shoulder. The Ripper slammed into him, then fell and lay still, a great black shape imbedded in the snow at the priest's feet. As they both watched, the dark color of his fur seemed to melt out of its throat, staining the white snow.

"No!" Harlan Lytton screamed, rushing from the cover of the vine wall.

Lytton was a wiry little man with a face always in need of shaving. In the crisp winter air, as Lytton knelt down beside Jack the Ripper, Cork caught the smell of whiskey and the odor of a body long overdue for a bath.

"Jack?" Lytton whispered.

He felt at the dog's throat. The Ripper made a sound, very faint.

"Don't die, Jack," Lytton pleaded. "Don't die, Jackie boy. Don't die on me."

The great dog tried to lift its head. Then it went still and didn't move again.

"I'm sorry, Mr. Lytton," Father Tom Griffin said.

"Fuck you," Lytton sobbed.

"Goddamn it, Harlan!" Cork was flushed with adrenaline and shaking with rage. "I didn't want to shoot your dog. But Jesus! You sicced him on us. What the hell'd you do that for?"

"You were trespassing, you dog-killing son of a bitch!" Lytton lifted his face and Cork could see the line of tears down each of his grizzled cheeks. "You didn't have to shoot him."

"He could've killed somebody," Cork snapped.

"He shoulda killed you!" Lytton leaped to his feet and started at Cork. With surprising speed and strength, the priest grabbed him from behind and restrained him.

"Easy, man," Tom Griffin said. "Just take it easy."

Lytton struggled a moment, swearing at them both. The priest was larger and stronger and held him tightly. Finally Lytton went limp and the only sound he made was a bitter sobbing. The priest let go. Lytton slumped down beside his dog.

"Somebody come sneaking around my place last night," Lytton said in a small voice.

"In the middle of the storm?" Cork said.

"Stood out here calling my name, like you done."

"Did you see who?"

"Fucking coward wouldn't show hisself. I sent Jack after 'im. Scared 'im off."

"We weren't trying to sneak up," the priest said.

But Lytton wasn't listening. He bent and laid his body across his dog.

"Look, Harlan," Cork said. "I'm sorry about Jack."

"I'll get you, O'Connor," he threatened in a choked voice. "I'll make you suffer for killing Jack. I swear to God I will."

Cork looked down, and although he had never liked Harlan Lytton one bit, he felt sorry for him.

"Come on," the priest said, taking Cork by the shoulder. "There's nothing you can do. Leave him be."

Cork followed Tom Griffin back down the lane. They'd gone fifty yards when Cork heard a cry rise behind them, a wail of grief prolonged and primordial.

The priest paused and glanced back. "God be with him," he said. "Because from the looks of it, no one else ever will."

CHAPTER 15

Cork dropped St. Kawasaki off at the rectory. Then he went to Sam's Place. He opened the door, took a step into the dark, and reached for the light switch. His hand never made it.

A blow to his stomach made him double over. Another to his ribs sent him down, breathless and in pain. The weight of a big man settled on his back, pressing him facedown on the cold floor. The icy barrel of a rifle nuzzled his left temple.

"Shut the goddamn door!"

What little light had come into the room with Cork was blotted out as the door slammed shut.

Cork felt hot breath across his cheek and caught the smell of barbecued potato chips. The voice that followed was a rasping whisper.

"Listen up, O'Connor. You got one chance to stay alive. You listening?"

Cork tried to reply, but between the agony of his ribs and the pressure of the man on top of him, all he could do was grunt.

"I said, are you listening?" The rifle barrel cut into his head.

Cork nodded. "Uh-huh."

"Good. Butt out, you understand? You ain't the

fucking law anymore. Just stick to making hamburgers from now on. You got that?"

Cork nodded again.

"He's a fucking redskin, man," another voice near the door argued. "I say just waste him."

"Shut the fuck up."

Cork finally gasped, ". . . hard . . . to . . . breathe . . ."

"You're lucky you can breathe at all." Potato-chip-breath leaned close to his ear. "We're everywhere, O'Connor. We're watching everything you do. You can't take a shit without we don't know about it. One more move we don't like and you're dead. Understand?"

". . . yeah . . ." Cork managed.

The muzzle of the rifle dug into his skull as if drilling for oil. "I can't hear you."

". . . understand . . ."

"Good. And, O'Connor. You know how to keep a secret? Keep this little conversation to yourself. You tell anyone about it, you even talk about it in your sleep, we'll know. If it's one thing we won't tolerate, it's a man who can't keep a secret. Let's go, boys."

Potato-chip-breath pulled away. The weight lifted from Cork's back. The door opened. Before it closed, Cork received a parting kick in his ribs. Then he was in darkness.

It took a minute for him to move. He heard the sound of snowmobiles in the woods where the ruins of the old foundry stood. The sound moved off like a swarm of departing insects. He rose slowly to his knees and touched his ribs. They hurt like hell. He held to the wall and painfully drew himself up. He flipped the light switch.

The sight that greeted him was almost worse than the pain. Sam's Place was in shambles. The window over the kitchen sink was shattered. Cushions lay cut open on the floor. The mattress had been yanked off his bed, sliced apart, and the stuffing pulled out. The cabinets stood open, the contents scattered. There were Christmas presents in the closet, gifts for his children and for Jo and Rose. The wrapping had been ripped off, the gifts torn open. Through the door that led to the burger stand, Cork saw canisters and boxed goods for the summer tourist trade broken apart.

There was another problem. Cork could see his breath. The air inside the cabin felt no warmer than the air outside.

He sat on the cushionless couch for a while, shaking. First from shock, then rage. He wanted to kill someone. Blindly. But he didn't know who.

When he was able to think straight and to move, he cut apart a cardboard box and taped it over the gaping window. The thermostat on the wall was still set for sixty-four degrees, but the room temperature was only three degrees above freezing. The radiators felt like ice. In the basement, he discovered the ancient oil burner was silent as death. He tried the reset button. Nothing happened. He kicked the burner a couple of times, then he went upstairs and called Art Winterbauer, who'd handled the old furnace in the past.

"Did you try the reset?" Winterbauer asked in a tired voice.

"I tried the reset."

"Did you kick 'er a couple of times?"

"I kicked, for Christ sake."

"Don't get mad at me, Cork. I ain't the one with the antique furnace. Look, it could be the thermostat," Winterbauer said. "Won't know till I have a chance to look, and I won't have a chance till Monday at the earliest."

"Monday?"

"Yep. Up to my eyeballs right now. I can give you the names of a couple of other guys you could try, but I doubt you'll have much luck with them either. 'Sides, that old behemoth of yours takes some special doing. If you want to wait till Monday, use a space heater or something. Or drain your water pipes and check into a motel."

He turned off the valve on the main water pipe, put a bucket under the drain valve, and opened it. He emptied the bucket twice in the sink before the flow slowed to an occasional drip. He flushed the toilet and drained the tank. All the while he was considering his options. He could, as Winterbauer suggested, stay in a motel. But he hated motels. Also, it was Christmas and he didn't have that kind of money to throw away. He considered calling Molly, but his promise to the priest quickly turned him from that thought. Finally he went upstairs and dialed the number of the house on Gooseberry Lane. Rose answered.

"Of course you'll stay here," she told him when he explained his predicament. "I'll get the guest room ready."

"I think you should discuss it with Jo," Cork cautioned her.

"If she were here, I would," Rose replied. "But she's not and I'd insist anyway."

"Thanks, Rose," Cork said. "Thanks a lot."

He gathered up a change of clothes and a few toilet articles and put them in a gym bag. He put the gifts into a big box, thinking he would wrap them again at Gooseberry Lane. He took one last item, a rolled bearskin, from a trunk in the cellar behind the old heater. He locked the door, got in the Bronco, and headed . . .

Home.

———

Rose opened the kitchen door. She wore an apron, and the aroma of baking cookies floated out around her. There were traces of flour in her dust-colored hair.

"Christmas baking?" Cork hung his coat on a peg by the door.

"My favorite time of year. I can bake to my heart's content. Would you like some milk and cookies?"

Rose took a half gallon carton of Meadow Gold from the refrigerator. Cork set his gym bag and the box of gifts and the rolled bearskin on the floor and went to the cookie jar on the counter by the sink. The cookie jar was shaped like Ernie from *Sesame Street*. Cork had bought it years before when *Sesame Street* was Jenny's favorite program. Now his daughter admired the darker visions of Sylvia Plath and was considering piercing her nose.

Rose put a glass of milk on the table.

Cork sat down. "So where is everyone?"

Rose bent and peeked through the oven window. "Jo's working late with Sandy Parrant. They're trying to straighten out things with Great North in light of the judge's suicide. Apparently everything's pretty complicated."

"I'll bet," Cork agreed.

"Jenny's on a date."

"Date?" Cork nearly choked. "She's only fourteen."

"They've just gone to a movie."

"Who'd she go with?"

"Chuck Kubiak."

"Don't know him," Cork said with a note of disapproval.

"He's nice, Cork. Really. He'll have her home by eleven-thirty."

The buzzer on the stove went off, and Rose took out a sheet of sugar cookies shaped like Christmas trees.

"Anne's in her room," she went on. "Asleep or reading. And Stevie's been down for hours."

Cork watched his sister-in-law as she tapped colored sprinkles on the cookies. "How did we ever do without you, Rose?"

"You didn't." She laughed.

Which was almost true. She'd come just after Jenny was born, come to help for a few weeks while Jo finished law school. She never left. Although she was heavy then, she was heavier now, and at thirty-five was completely without the prospect of marriage in her own life. There were times when Cork felt sorry for Rose and guilty because all the care she could have given to a family of her own was lavished on his instead.

"I put the guest room in order for you," Rose said as she wiped her forehead with the back of her hand. "That's my last batch tonight. I'm going to bed."

"Any idea when Jo—" Cork began.

The back door opened before he finished speaking, and Jo stepped in. She took in the sight of Cork at the table and his things on the floor.

"A little late for a visit, isn't it, Cork?"

"It's not a visit, Jo."

"What is it, then?" She eyed his gym bag again and the box and bearskin.

"I'd like to stay for a day or two."

"I invited him," Rose jumped in. "His furnace is broken and he has no heat."

Jo went to the cookie jar, lifted Ernie's head, and took out a cookie. She leaned against the counter and considered the situation as she nibbled.

"A day or two?" she said.

"Until Monday," Cork told her. "Art Winterbauer can't come out until Monday at the earliest."

She didn't appear pleased by the prospect.

"It's his house," Rose argued with a note of anger. "For goodness sake, Jo, what harm will a couple of days do?"

Jo sighed and seemed to go a little limp, looking suddenly very tired. "All right," she said.

"I have the guest room ready for him." Rose began to undo her apron.

"I'm tired," Jo said. "It's been a long day. I'm going to bed."

"Shouldn't somebody wait up for Jenny?" Cork asked.

"She's been on dates before." Jo headed toward the living room. "She'll be fine."

Cork picked up his things. "Guess I'm tired, too."

"Go on," Rose said, shooing him with her hands. "I'll lock up."

Cork followed Jo upstairs. He looked in on Stevie, who lay twisted in his blankets. He carefully straightened out the bedding. The door to Anne's room was slightly ajar and he peeked in. The reading lamp was on beside her bed. *The Diary of Anne Frank* lay open at her side, but she was sleeping soundly. Cork put the book on the stand and switched off the light.

Jo watched from the door of her bedroom. She leaned against the doorjamb with her arms folded. Behind her on the bed, her briefcase lay open, files laid out on the side of the bed that used to be Cork's.

"What are you doing here?" she asked.

"I told you. My furnace is on the blink."

Jo looked skeptical. "I mean really. What's this all about?"

"Circumstances beyond my control." He shrugged.

She chewed on the inside of her cheek a moment, a long-standing habit when she was considering saying something against her better judgment. This time she only said, "Don't hope for too much."

"I'm not hoping for anything." He moved past her toward the guest room. Her door closed at his back.

He spent a while in the bathroom tending his ribs, which had turned a sick-looking yellow. He swallowed three ibuprofen tablets, went to the guest room, stripped to his boxers and T-shirt, and crawled under the covers. He could hear Rose moving around in the attic room above him. That room was cozy, with a brass bed, mahogany dresser and vanity, flowered curtains, and a rocker where Rose sat at night for a long time reading. She read mysteries and romance novels and, although she wouldn't admit it, kept a drawer full of *National Enquirers*. Cork lay in his bed listening to the squeak of her rocker as she read in the warm light of her lamp.

He was tired but couldn't sleep. He was puzzled. Too many strange things had happened that didn't seem to make sense. In the way his thinking had been conditioned to work, he was looking for connections.

The judge was dead. Paul LeBeau had vanished— onto the reservation, Cork would bet—with his father. The Windigo had called Lytton's name. And someone had broken into Sam's Place. On the surface, there was nothing, really, to connect any of these things. Still, they were extraordinary in a place like Aurora, and they'd happened within an extraordinarily short time. From what he'd seen examining the judge's body, he believed it was very possible the judge hadn't committed suicide. Whether Paul's disappearance was connected with the judge's death, he couldn't say. It was probably mere coincidence that Joe John had chosen that particular time to spirit his son away. However, coincidence was not something Cork was trained to believe in. The ransacking of his cabin—how did that fit in? And over it all loomed the presence of the Windigo. How much stock should be put in the words of an old Anishinaabe medicine man?

He thought some more about Lytton, wondering why the Windigo would call the man's name. He was a loner, a mean son of a bitch. Even so, Cork found himself feeling sorry for Harlan Lytton. The picture of the man on his knees beside his dog and the terrible sound of his grieving still twisted Cork's insides. Everyone was capable of loving something. Even a man like Lytton, who loved his dog. Now the thing Lytton loved had been taken from him and he was utterly alone. That was something Cork understood.

He couldn't help turning his thinking to Molly. What was she doing now? Knitting? Reading maybe? She was a big reader. Novels, self-discovery, things that when she talked about them seemed interesting and enlightening. She often took classes at Aurora Community College, not with any goal in mind except to learn. She was a woman curious in many ways.

Cork looked out at the darkness beyond the window of the guest room. Sometimes Molly used the sauna at night, then stood outside in the cold and studied the stars while the steam rose off her skin and the chill clamped shut her pores. Was she there now? Like a beautiful white ghost, naked and vaporous?

Whatever she was doing, it would end with her alone in bed. Like Cork. Like Rose. Like Jo.

Finally drowsy, Cork closed his eyes thinking that there was something wrong with a world in which so many people slept alone.

CHAPTER 16

"Daddy!"

They came before Cork was really awake. He heard them scamper across the floor of the guest room, then was jolted wide awake as they leaped onto the bed, driving their knees into his kidneys. He rolled over, felt them warm and wiggly all around him.

"Hey, Anne, Stevie." He grinned.

He wrapped them in his arms and hugged them tightly to him. He felt a stab at his ribs where the blows had hammered him the night before. But the good feel of his children helped him ignore the pain. The kids were still in their rumpled pajamas, their teeth unbrushed, their hair stale and disheveled. Even so, they seemed like heaven to Cork.

"Aunt Rose said you were here." His daughter buried her face against his T-shirt. "Are you staying?"

"For a while," he said.

"Quithmath tree!" Stevie said.

"What?"

"We're going to get our Christmas tree today," Anne explained. "Are you coming?"

Cork rubbed Stevie's hair. "I wouldn't miss it for the world."

Jenny stepped into the open doorway looking tired and grumpy. "What's all the noise?"

Cork lifted his head so that Jenny saw him.

"Oh," she said. "What happened? Break your leg or something?"

"Only my furnace."

She scratched at her purple hair. "Sort of a one-night stand here?"

"Sort of," Cork admitted.

She shrugged and turned to leave.

"We're buying a Christmas tree today," he called after her.

"Ho, ho, ho," she said, her voice trailing dismally down the hall.

Rose had oatmeal ready for them. On top of the steaming cereal in their bowls, Cork and Stevie and Anne made funny faces with raisins. Jo had gone to work long before Cork or the others were up. Jenny finally came down near the end of breakfast.

"Oatmeal, Jen?" Rose offered.

"I'll just make toast," Jenny replied sullenly. "I'm not very hungry." She took a couple of pieces of whole wheat from the bread drawer and dropped them into the toaster. She crossed her arms and waited.

"After breakfast, would you be willing to take a short drive with me?" Cork asked.

"Where?"

"I'm going to visit a couple of hungry friends."

"Some kind of Samaritan visit in keeping with the season? I don't think so, thanks."

"Just for a little while. I'd appreciate it."

"You could order me to go. You're still my father." She was watching the toaster carefully.

"I don't want to do that."

Rose quietly wiped dishes at the sink. Stevie and

Anne had gone to the living room to watch cartoons. The toast popped up. Jenny stared at it a moment.

"I suppose," she finally agreed.

The drive was painfully silent. Cork tried to think exactly what it was he'd meant to say to her, but all the words seemed weak and self-pitying. Jenny stared out the window and sniffed.

"A cold?" Cork finally asked.

"I don't know. Probably."

"How'd your date go last night?"

She shrugged.

"What's his name? Kubiak?"

She didn't seem to think that deserved a response of any kind.

"Go out with him much?"

She waited a few moments, then said, "A couple of times."

"Movies, huh?"

She swung her gaze toward him and gave him a look that made him feel as if a door had just been slammed in his face.

"Just interested," he apologized.

"Yeah," she said. "Sure." She looked away again, as if the all too familiar landscape of Aurora were far more interesting than anything her father could possibly say.

But Cork kept trying. "Still planning on reading Sylvia Plath at the Christmas program?"

"Why wouldn't I?"

"I don't know. I thought maybe you'd talked it over with your teacher. Maybe she'd changed your mind."

"She respects my judgment," Jenny said.

"Good." Cork nodded, trying to generate a show of enthusiasm. "That's great."

He pulled the Bronco up beside Sam's Place.

"What are we doing here?" She gave the Quonset hut a look of disgust.

"Wait and see."

The morning was bright and cold, the sunlight startling. Cork went inside and half-filled the bucket with dried corn.

"Going to try farming now?" Jenny asked when he came back out.

"Follow me."

He led the way down to the open water. The geese glided across the surface, riding their reflections in the still, blue water, leaving gentle creases where they'd moved.

Jenny watched them, unimpressed. "Annie's told me about these two. Dumb if you ask me. Just asking for trouble."

"Spread the grain on the ground for them." Cork pointed to the circle he'd cleared in the snow.

She frowned but did as he'd instructed, then stood expectantly watching the geese on the water.

"Why don't they come? Aren't they hungry?"

"They're wild. They're still more afraid of us than they are hungry. Let's step over this way."

Cork led her some distance away. The geese paddled to the shore and began noisily to eat.

"Why haven't they gone south?" Jenny asked.

"See that one?"

"The male?" Jenny said.

"Good." Cork was surprised she knew. "His wing is injured and he can't fly. They're kind of stuck here now."

"She stays with him?"

"Some geese are like that. They mate for life."

"I'm glad somebody does."

"Could we talk, Jenny?" Cork finally asked. "About your mom and me?"

"What's to talk about?" Jenny kicked at the snow. "You're going to do what you're going to do. That's all there is to it."

"Not quite."

She glanced at him, her eyes full of suspicion. "What's that supposed to mean?"

"I don't think I want to divorce your mom, Jen."

She didn't believe him. The stone look on her face told him that.

"But it's not my decision alone," he explained.

"You mean she wants to divorce you."

"That's kind of how it stands."

"Why? What did you do?"

Cork watched the geese. They'd finished the grain and moved back down to the water. As they entered, they broke the reflection of the sun into a thousand fragments.

"I was gone from her too long."

"You mean since you moved out?"

"Before that. Long before that."

"You want to come back?"

"I miss home."

"I don't believe you," Jenny said. She turned and started for the Bronco.

"I don't blame you," Cork said after her. "In your shoes, I wouldn't believe me either. But, Jen, I've never lied to you. At least not intentionally."

She turned back angrily. "You're saying Mom's responsible for the divorce."

"I'm not trying to turn you against her, sweetheart, really. I hurt her pretty bad, I guess, and maybe all this is exactly what I deserve. I just want you to know that if I could, I'd put it all back together."

For a while Jenny looked at the trampled snow between them, then at the geese. "I thought if you loved someone you were supposed to, like, forgive them. I thought that was what love was supposed to be all about."

Cork shook his head. "Easy to say, harder to do."

"So . . . what are you going to do?" Jenny asked quietly.

Cork risked moving to her. "I'd like to get your mother to talk with me. Tom Griffin—Father Tom—has offered to counsel us. I'm not saying we'll succeed, but I'd like to give it a try. What do you think?"

She looked past him where the ice edged the open water and the signs warned of danger and the safety stations offered the help of ropes and life rings and sturdy sleds. What could he offer her that was as substantial?

"I think I'd like to go now," she said.

They walked back toward the Bronco. Cork saw sunlight glint off a tiny thread of a tear down her cheek. He wanted to reach out, to hold her as he had when she was small and the simplicity of *Sesame Street* had been her world. But he was afraid now. They walked without speaking, and they walked apart.

"Wait here," he told her at the Bronco. "I'll be right back."

He took the bucket back into the Quonset hut. The place was still a mess, but it appeared as if nothing more had been disturbed in his absence. The cardboard was still in place on the kitchen window. The furnace hadn't miraculously repaired itself.

"What happened?"

Jenny stood at the door looking shocked.

"Someone broke in," Cork said.

Jenny took a couple of tentative steps inside. Stevie and Anne had visited Cork there before, but Jenny always found an excuse not to come. This was her first time inside Sam's Place.

"A burglar?" she asked.

"Nothing was taken."

"Why'd they break in?"

"I think they were looking for something they didn't find."

Jenny knelt and picked up a cushion from the floor. "What?"

"If I knew that, I might have a better idea who broke in."

She hugged the pillow to her as she took in the spectacle of the disarray. "It's scary."

"It is a little."

She looked at him suddenly. "What if you'd been here?"

"Maybe they wouldn't have broken in."

"Or maybe they would have hurt you."

Remembering the warning the intruders had painfully delivered, Cork didn't want to say anything more. There was no way Jenny—or any of his family—was going to be involved. "Come on," Cork said brusquely. "Let's go."

The wind rose outside, a sudden body of air that passed over the lake and into the small woods where the old foundry stood. The snow rose and swirled as it passed, as if alive. Cork froze when he heard the voice in the wind.

"Dad, are you okay?" Jenny asked.

He stared at her, wondering if she'd heard. But he could see she hadn't.

"Let's go," he said again, trying not to show how

afraid he was. But Jenny looked at him and he saw that she knew.

"What is it?" she asked, frightened.

"Nothing. It's nothing, Jen." He put his arm around her and led her out into the sunlight, into the winter air that had become still again. He looked toward the trees and, as he'd expected, saw nothing unusual there.

As they drove away, Cork said, "Jenny, promise me something."

"What?"

"Don't say anything about this to anyone. Please."

"Why not?"

"It's hard to explain."

"Is it because you don't want anyone to know you're afraid?"

That seemed as good an explanation as any, so he nodded.

"I understand," Jenny said. And she smiled as if she did. Perfectly.

CHAPTER 17

After lunch, Cork and Rose took the children and headed to the offices of Great North Development Company, where Jo had worked much of the morning with Sandy Parrant. Great North was housed in the old firehouse a block off Center Street. Built in 1897 of charcoal gray granite, the firehouse had been scheduled for demolition, but Sandy Parrant and the judge had bought it and had it remodeled as a home for Great North.

Before he disappeared, Joe John LeBeau had the contract to clean the Great North offices. He'd told Cork the old firehouse was haunted. He claimed that when he cleaned alone late at night, he could hear the boots of the long-dead firefighters clomping across the floor overhead. He swore that once he saw the ghost of Lars Knudsen, who'd become a local hero by giving his life trying to save the children when the old Freemanson orphanage burned in '09. Joe John told Cork these things in the time when he was sober, before he walked away drunk from his truck, abandoning his family and his livelihood, a thing Cork had never understood. But a man who heard ghosts was probably a troubled man to begin with.

Jenny and Rose stayed in the Bronco. Cork took

Anne and Stevie into the old firehouse. Joyce Sandoval, a woman with white hair and half glasses, sat at a reception desk typing into a computer. She looked over the flat top of her glasses at Cork and the kids.

"They pay you a lot for working Saturday, Joyce?"

"They don't pay me a lot, period," she grumbled, but amiably.

"Why aren't you out doing something with Albert?"

Albert Nordberg and Joyce Sandoval had been dating for a quarter of a century. Their courtship was an institution of sorts in Aurora.

Joyce took off her glasses, which were secured by a beaded cord around the back of her neck. "He says he's buying me a Christmas present. He says he doesn't want me to know what it is." She gave Cork a knowing and hopeless look. "He buys me Wind Song cologne. Every year. I made the mistake twenty-five years ago of telling him it was my favorite." She glanced at Anne and winked. "Men, huh?"

"Joyce, would you let Jo know we're here?"

She lifted the receiver of her phone and pushed three buttons. "Cork O'Connor and a couple of elves are here for Jo." She put the receiver down. "They'll be right out. Why don't you have a seat." Joyce Sandoval went back to working on her computer.

Behind the reception desk, the area of the firehouse where the big engine had parked was occupied now by a dozen work spaces, all currently empty. Cork and the children sat on a brown leather sofa in a small waiting area. While they waited, Cork entertained them with ghost stories he'd heard from Joe John LeBeau. By the time the elevator doors opened and Jo and Sandy Parrant stepped out, Stevie's eyes were huge with amazement.

Cork rose and offered his hand in greeting. "Sandy," he said.

"Cork." Sandy gave the children a warm smile. "Hi, kids."

"Hello, Mr. Parrant," Anne said politely.

"Please, it's Sandy," Parrant said.

"Mr. Parrant," Anne began, "I mean, Sandy. When you go to Washington, will you meet the President?"

"I already have, honey," he said. "He's a very nice man."

Stevie picked his nose and looked unimpressed. He was watching the ceiling carefully.

"How's it going?" Cork asked Jo.

"Like a three-legged horse," Parrant replied for her.

Jo zipped the briefcase she carried. "Bob's death complicates Sandy's transition to Washington in a lot of ways."

"Jo tells me you've got a furnace on the blink, Cork," Parrant said, moving abruptly away from the subject of his father's death. "I've got a good man who does a lot of work for Great North. I'd be glad to send him out."

"Thanks, Sandy, but Art Winterbauer is coming on Monday. I'll be fine until then."

Stevie stopped picking his nose and asked suddenly, "Ith it really haunted?"

"Haunted?" Jo looked annoyed. "Who told you that?"

"Daddy."

"I was telling him some of the stories Joe John used to tell me about the things he saw in this place," Cork explained.

"I hate to disappoint you, Stevie"—Sandy Parrant smiled—"but I wouldn't put a lot of stock in the stories of a man like Joe John LeBeau. He'd probably been drinking when he saw those things."

"I think we should be going," Jo said. "Sandy's busy."

Parrant wished them good luck finding a tree and saw them to the door. "Cork, if you change your mind about that furnace, just let me know."

"I've got the situation under control."

"Sure," Parrant said. He watched them until they were all in the Bronco, then he stepped back into the old firehouse.

"He's nice," Anne said.

"Do you think so?" Jo asked.

"And he's met the President," Anne said.

"The President puts his pants on one leg at a time like every other man," Jenny said, dourly unimpressed.

Stevie looked down at his own pants, confused. "I do 'em both together."

The St. Agnes Boy Scouts had been given a corner of the Super Valu parking lot to sell their Christmas trees. Cork's family spread out and called out their finds to one another. Finally they settled on a big white pine with needles soft as cat fur. Cork hauled it to the trailer to pay, and Arne Bjorkson, the scoutmaster, asked if he wanted a new cut on the trunk. Just at that moment, Cork caught sight of Darla LeBeau coming out of the supermarket with a cart full of groceries.

"Go ahead," he said to Arne. "I'll be right back." He jogged away. "Darla!" He called after her.

She was clearly not excited to see him.

"What do you want?" she asked as she unloaded the sacks into her station wagon.

"I just wanted to ask about Paul." He wheezed, trying to catch his breath, swearing silently to quit smoking. "And Joe John. I'm worried."

"I'm Paul's mother. And Joe John's wife. I'll worry." She shoved a sack onto the backseat, pushed the cart away fiercely, and slid into the driver's seat.

"Is something wrong, Darla?" Cork put a hand on her arm. "Is Paul in any danger?"

"I have to go," she said. She pulled her arm away and closed the door.

Cork leaned his face close to the window, so that when he spoke, his breath fogged the glass. "I'm Joe John's friend. I only want to help."

She was intent on jamming the key into the ignition and didn't answer. She started the engine. Her tires spit snow and gravel as she drove away.

Cork stared after her and thought about some of the items he'd seen in the grocery sacks. Cheerios, Pop-Tarts, peanut butter, Fig Newtons, potato chips, Slim Jims. It was possible Darla LeBeau ate these things. But Cork thought they would appeal a great deal more to a hungry teenager.

They moved the sofa into the living room and set the tree in front of the big window that faced the street. Cork hauled the boxes of Christmas decorations up from the basement. Stevie helped him check the lights while Rose and Anne and Jenny put hooks on all the bulbs. Jo sorted through the albums in the record cabinet and pulled out Christmas music and put it on to play.

For a long time Cork had felt lost, but there was something about the tradition of decorating the tree that brought him home. When he unpacked the small box that held the last of the delicate blue bulbs from the first Christmas after he and Jo were married, Jo smiled, and it made him happy. Together they placed the bulbs on the tree, then the children tossed on the icicles. When it was done, they plugged in the lights and stepped back and all of them were silent. The bulbs blinked and the tinsel and garland sparkled, and although it was very much like every tree they'd ever had, this one felt special. Cork moved close to Jo and took a chance. He put his arm about her waist. She seemed a little startled, but didn't stop him. Rose began to sing along with Andy Williams on the stereo, lending her fine soprano to "Joy to the World." Pretty soon they all joined in. It felt like old times, almost as if nothing had ever happened to shatter their happiness.

The telephone rang. Rose answered. "It's for you, Cork," she said.

Cork took the phone. "Yes?" He nodded and said, "Uh-huh," a couple of times; then, "Your office?" He glanced into the living room, where the others had begun to pack up the ornament boxes. "I'll be there," he promised, and hung up. He went back to the living room. "I have to go."

"Will you be back for dinner?" Rose asked.

"I'll call and let you know."

"Do you have to go?" Anne moaned.

Cork put his hand on her red hair. "It's important." He looked once more at the tree. "It's sure a beauty."

Anne smiled and said, "It's the best."

Wally Schanno sat at the desk Cork had occupied for seven years. Cork hadn't set foot in the jail since he'd left office, and he felt strange walking into this room

that had been so much a part of his own life and finding another man so comfortable in his place. Cork
had hung framed prints on the walls, Matisse and
Renoir, reproductions of paintings he'd seen and appreciated in the Art Institute in Chicago. He liked to
think that the law and the rest of a civilized society
were integrated. Schanno had removed the paintings
and put up photographs of himself in a boat and on
a pier proudly holding up big muskies. Among the
items on the three-shelf bookcase behind Schanno
was a simple black Bible. Cork could see from the
tattered corners of the cover that it was often read.
The end of a slender, fabric bookmark, forked like
a serpent's tongue, jutted from the pages near the
middle.

"Thanks for coming, Cork," Schanno said. He
waved toward the chair on the other side of his desk.
"Have a seat."

Cork sat down.

Schanno held a rubber band in his hands and played
with it while he talked. "I heard you were home. That's
why I called there."

"What was so important?" Cork asked.

"Sigurd called me. He said you'd had a look at the
judge's body. Why?"

"Curiosity." Cork sat back and watched Schanno's
fingers fidget with the rubber band.

"Was your curiosity satisfied?"

"I wouldn't say that, no."

Schanno dropped the rubber band. He got up and
went to a big metal thermos sitting on the window-
sill. "Coffee?" he asked.

Cork declined. He watched Schanno pour steaming coffee into the thermos cup. It was like Schanno,
that big thermos. In his suspenders and khakis, he

looked just like the kind of man who'd carry a lunch bucket to work. Schanno took a big gulp of coffee and his throat drew taut against the heat.

"Tell me about it," he said.

"Sigurd does a fine job of making a corpse look good for an open casket, but he doesn't know squat about forensic medicine. Why should he?"

Schanno drank some more coffee and waited.

"Dorsal lividity," Cork explained. "Blood settled along the back of the judge's body after he died. Back of his arms and legs, buttocks. Nothing in front along the ribs, stomach, pelvis. He'd been lying on his back quite a while. But I found him on his stomach."

"You point this out to Sigurd?"

"Sigurd wouldn't have cared. Much simpler for him and everybody if the judge killed himself and that's that."

"Why didn't you call me?"

"Because the truth is, I wouldn't care much either except for what it might mean about the boy."

Schanno traded his coffee cup for the rubber band. He toyed with the band for a while. "What does it mean?"

"I'm not sure. Maybe Paul saw something he shouldn't have, maybe something that scared him. In any case, I think it sent him into hiding."

"He's not hiding. He's with Joe John."

"Where?"

"If I had to make a guess, I'd say somewhere on the reservation. I sent a man out yesterday to talk to Joe John's sister, Wanda Manydeeds. She wouldn't say boo." Schanno lifted his thermos as if to pour himself some more coffee, but he paused and said, "Look, if you're so worried about Paul LeBeau, why don't you have a talk with Wanda? Maybe you can get more out of her than my man could. I'd just as soon be sure about the boy."

"What makes you think she'll talk to me?"

"Your blood," Schanno said honestly. "You got a little Ojibwe running through you. That and the fact you don't wear a badge anymore. What do you say?"

"All right. And maybe you should have a look at the judge's body while I'm out there."

A pinched look crossed Schanno's face, as if his underwear had suddenly shrunk a couple sizes. "Can't."

"Why not?"

"Sigurd already cremated it. Listen, Cork, next time you think you've found something, don't wait to tell me, okay?"

It was his grandmother Dilsey, who'd never been farther from Aurora and the Iron Lake Reservation than the Twin Cities, who had told him the story of how the Anishinaabe came to be a Great Lakes people.

Long ago, the First People (for this was what the word Anishinaabe meant) had lived on the shores of the great salt water far to the east. They were happy there, hunting and fishing and living in peace with their brothers. Gitchie Manitou was good to them and showed his favor by lifting the Megis, a giant seashell, above the water. The rays of the sun reflected off the shiny surface of the shell, giving the Anishinaabe light and health and wisdom.

But one day the shell sank beneath the salt water and a darkness came over the First People. Sickness and death moved among them like hungry animals, and they lived in fear. The Megis rose up again far to the west out of a great river at a place called Mo-ne-aung (Montreal), where the First People built new wigwams and for a long time lived again in the light and warmth of the Megis.

Three more times the Megis disappeared from sight. Three more times it rose up, each time farther west. First on the shore of the great lake called Huron. Next at Bow-e-ting (Sault St. Marie), where the water empties out of Lake Superior. The last time the Megis rose it was at Mo-ning-wuna-kaun-ing (La Pointe Island), where its rays reflected sunlight to even the farthest Anishinaabe villages, blessing them with light, life, and wisdom.

Grandma Dilsey told him a lot of stories, but it wasn't until he took a course in Ojibwe history and culture offered by the fledgling American Indian Studies Department at the University of Minnesota that he learned facts. He was surprised to discover that the Anishinaabe were the largest Native American tribe north of Mexico. They had indeed migrated long ago from the Atlantic coastline, but the death that had descended upon them and forced them west wasn't magic. It was war with the Iroquois nation. The war was old and the hostilities deep. The origin of the word Ojibwe meant "to roast until puckered," for this was the fate that often befell captured enemies.

He learned much about the history of his grandmother's people, including the insidious treaties that had attempted to divide and disenfranchise them. Since their battles with the Iroquois, and later the Dakota, the First People had battled corruption in the BIA, poverty, alcoholism, the cruelty of government schools, and continued attempts by even well-meaning whites to eradicate their culture and their language. The Anishinaabe had survived, and solid populations were spread across Michigan, Wisconsin, Minnesota, North Dakota, and Canada.

But most of Cork's heritage was white, and in his way of living he'd chosen the white man's world. With his reddish hair and fair skin, he looked more Irish than he ever would Ojibwe. And life was difficult enough as it was. To live it as Indian would have made it that much harder.

He headed out to the Iron Lake Reservation in the late afternoon, still buoyed by the warmth of spirit decorating the Christmas tree had given him. The sun was low, nestled into the bare branches of the trees like a fat red rooster.

Iron Lake was not a large reservation. It comprised less than four hundred square miles of woods, lakes, and bogs with its small population of Anishinaabe living in the two villages of Allouette and Brandywine, and in small, isolated houses or shacks or trailers scattered throughout the woods. Except for State Highway 37, which cut through the reservation in a northwest-southeast line, the roads on the reservation were all bumpy, rutted gravel or dirt. Most winters the back roads were impassable for long periods, but as Cork turned off the highway at the gathering of HUD houses and the old government center that was Allouette and headed into the woods toward Nokomis House, he found the snow cleanly plowed right down to the washboard surface of the road.

The casino, he knew.

The Chippewa Grand Casino, owned and operated by the Iron Lake band of Ojibwe, had opened its doors only six months earlier, but already the revenue from the slots and blackjack tables and keno and mega-bingo had surpassed even the most optimistic projections. In those months alone, the casino had reported a gross income of almost six million dollars. The gamblers came by busloads from Milwaukee, Chicago, the Twin Cities, Winnipeg, and even as far as Kansas City on special junkets arranged by travel agencies; or they drove in from small cities and towns and farms for a taste of Vegas in their own backyard. The gambling had paid off big for the Anishinaabe of the reservation. Every household belonging to the Iron Lake band of Ojibwe received a monthly allotment of several thousand dollars from the casino profits. Any Native American wanting a job could find work at the casino. New road maintenance equipment had been purchased. There were plans for paving, for a new tribal council building, and for a school. Cork thought it was no wonder that the Dakota who ran casinos in southern Minnesota called gambling "the new buffalo."

Four miles out of Allouette, still on the washboard gravel road, Cork approached Mission Center. It was only a small clearing with a single, square, one-story building in the middle. The Catholic mission that had once served the reservation had been abandoned for more than a decade before Father Tom Griffin arrived in Aurora and set out almost single-handedly to bring it back to life. He spent a good deal of his free time there, refurbishing the old structure. Although the priest tried to enlist the parishioners of St. Agnes, white and red, Cork had heard that more often than not St. Kawasaki worked alone.

By the time Cork reached Mission Center, the sun had set. Stars were emerging from the amethyst sky of the east. A planet like a small ember glowed above the trees. Mars, the angry god of another religion. Cork was surprised to see smoke rising from the stovepipe on the mission roof although there were no lights visible inside. He stopped and got out. The woods of birch and pine that pressed themselves against the clearing had grown dark. The evening light turned the snow a soft blue, and everything was still except for a slight wind that came out of the trees and across the snow, passing Cork with an icy whisper. He turned his collar up. The front door was locked. He peered in at a window. The first thing Father Tom Griffin had done in refurbishing the old mission was to replace the windows and put up shades, which were now drawn. Cork waded around to the back of the building.

Behind the mission was a cemetery that, unlike the mission, had never been abandoned. It was marked by a black wrought-iron fence, waist high. The Catholics on the reservation had continued to use the cemetery to bury their dead, including most recently Vernon Blackwater, who'd passed away from cancer less than a week before. Many of the Anishinaabe buried in the cemetery had chosen traditional burial houses, small shelters of wood covering the graves. Most of the others were memorialized with a simple stone or a white cross. From what Cork understood, Vernon Blackwater had both. With his feet pointed west along Chebakunah, the Path of Souls, he'd been laid to rest in a grave house marked also by a tall granite cross. It was just like Blackwater to cover all his bases that way. During his illness, he'd been treated not only by the white man's medicines, but also with the charms and the healing songs of Wanda Manydeeds. In the end, as he lay on his deathbed, Blackwater had requested both the priest—Father Tom Griffin—and Wanda Manydeeds to be present. One to give him extreme unction, the other to sing him along the path to the Land of Souls.

Parked near the cemetery gate was St. Kawasaki's old snowmobile, the machine he called Lazarus. The snow behind the mission was stained with black oil spots where Lazarus had leaked. Beside the snowmobile, leaning against the wrought-iron fence around the cemetery, was the priest's motorcycle. As Cork came around the rear corner of the building, the back door opened and St. Kawasaki stepped outside. He was wearing his leather jacket and red-masked stocking cap. He didn't see Cork as he fumbled with the lock.

"Hey, Tom," Cork called.

St. Kawasaki spun. "Jesus, Mary, and Joseph!" he cried hoarsely. He pulled off his stocking cap and mask. His good eye still looked startled. "You scared the piss out of me."

"Sorry, Tom."

"What are you doing here?"

"I'm on my way to see Wanda Manydeeds. I want to talk to her about Joe John and Paul."

The priest scratched his cheek. Cork could hear the scrape of Tom Griffin's fingernails across the grizzle of his five o'clock shadow. "If you think you can get anything out of her, I'd like to hear what she has to say. Mind if I come along?"

"Fine by me. Why don't you come in the Bronco? You can pick up your motorcycle on the way back."

"Sounds good," the priest agreed.

"No luck with Lazarus over there?"

The priest grinned and shook his head hopelessly. "I believe this time it's going to take a real miracle to get it running again."

CHAPTER 18

Like most reservations in Minnesota, the Iron Lake Reservation was a crazy quilt of landholdings. Land held in trust by the tribe, land allotted to tribal members, land that had been sold or leased to non-Indians for such purposes as lumbering and recreation, and land belonging to the county or state or forest service were all patched together within reservation boundaries. Nokomis House stood on land that at one time had been leased out, but had long since reverted to the tribal trust. Large, rustic, and isolated, it had been an old hunting lodge, unused for many years, before Wanda Manydeeds turned it into a shelter for Native American women. The lodge stood at the edge of a small lake called Five Pines because five massive white pines, each ten feet in circumference, stood together along the shoreline near the building. How they'd been missed in the early logging that cleared the area of the great giants long before the turn of the century, Cork didn't know, but there they stood, watching over Nokomis House like a cadre of mute, powerful guardians.

As he drove up, Cork saw Wanda Manydeeds at work in the turnaround that had been plowed beside the lodge. She held a chainsaw and was cutting wood. She wore jeans, hiking boots, and a red down vest over a blue denim shirt. Her son Amik, a small boy bundled heavily in a wool-lined jean jacket, sat on a stump watching.

A yellow Allis-Chalmers bulldozer sat idle and snow-covered beside the turnaround. Behind the bulldozer a quarter acre of trees had been razed, and the ragged ends of uprooted stumps jutted through the snow like the claws of great beasts thrust up from the frozen ground. Even with the soft snow blanketing it all, the scene had a desolate, destroyed look about it. As he parked the Bronco and stepped out, Cork smelled the chainsaw's oily exhaust hanging in the air.

Wanda Manydeeds put down the saw and watched, expressionless, as the two men came toward her.

"Evening, Wanda," Cork said.

The woman tilted her head slightly in a silent greeting.

St. Kawasaki knelt down and, in the language of the Ojibwe, greeted the boy on the stump. "*Anin*, Amik."

The boy smiled shyly. "Anin, Father," he answered quietly.

"What's going on back there?" Cork asked, indicating the area of the razed trees.

"Expansion," Wanda Manydeeds said. "Everything gets bigger now. Courtesy of the casino."

"Don't plan on touching the pines, do you?"

"The pines will be here long after you and I are gone. What do you want?"

"Just to talk a while if I could."

"About what?"

Before Cork could answer, the door of Nokomis House opened and a young woman stepped out. "Amik! *Oondass!*" she called to the boy. Come here.

The boy looked at his mother. Wanda nodded and Amik slipped off the stump and ran to the old lodge. The young woman put her arm protectively around Amik, looked suspiciously at Cork, and ushered the boy inside.

"About your brother," Cork finally replied. "I want to talk about Joe John."

"There's nothing to talk about."

"I heard he's back."

"I heard that, too. Please don't smoke. It's a rule at Nokomis House."

Cork knelt and extinguished his cigarette in the snow. The door to Nokomis House opened again, and a gray-haired woman whom Cork recognized as Tilly Favre, Wanda Manydeeds' aunt, poked her head outside. From within the old lodge came the sound of a baby's incessant crying.

"Makwa!" Tilly Favre called to Wanda. "He's hungry."

Wanda Manydeeds eyed her guests unhappily, but she said, "Come inside."

There was a sitting room just inside the door. A young girl, perhaps twelve, sat on a green sofa with a baby in her arms. As soon as Wanda had hung up her down vest, the girl handed her the baby.

"*Migwech*, Susan," Wanda Manydeeds said.

Although the baby was red-faced, squirming, and crying, the girl seemed sorry to have to give him up. She lingered a moment, as if hoping Wanda would return him to her. As soon as the baby was in his mother's arms, he stopped crying. Wanda nodded toward the doorway and the girl drifted away.

Although Wanda didn't invite him past the sitting room, Cork knew beyond it was a large common room with a huge stone fireplace. The lodge smelled of burning pine, and every once in a while the pop of sap from the next room told Cork there was a good fire going. The second floor of the lodge held bedrooms. Above him, Cork could hear the old boards squeak, shifting under the weight of unseen guests in their wanderings.

Wanda Manydeeds was a tall, stolid woman in her mid-forties, with long black hair parted in the middle so that it lay against her head like the folded wings of a raven. On one wrist was an ornate, beaded bracelet, and beaded earrings swung from her earlobes. As a much younger woman, she'd been part of the takeover of the BIA office in Minneapolis and had been arrested and briefly jailed. More recently, she'd been elected as a member of the tribal council. She had two children and no husband. The boy, Amik, Ojibwe for "beaver," was six. His father, Warren Manydeeds, had been killed in a logging accident just two weeks before Amik was born. Wanda Manydeeds had never remarried. The infant, Makwa, was only four months old, and Wanda had never said a word about the father. Because the priest and Wanda Manydeeds worked closely together, the worst of the rumor mill in Aurora had it that Father Tom Griffin was responsible. Cork didn't believe it for an instant. In their two cultures, they were the guides along the path of upright living, and Cork had never known two people more dedicated to their callings.

Wanda walked to a cane rocker, sat down, and began to rock the squirming baby. "How is the burger business?" she asked.

"In winter, closed," Cork said. "It smells good in here. Bear."

"Yes."

The baby began to whimper.

"Where'd you get bear meat?"

She looked at him as if the question were stupid. "I shot a bear."

"I didn't know you hunted."

"There are lots of things about me you don't know. Why should you? You never lived on the reservation."

The girl who'd held the baby peeked through the doorway. Wanda Manydeeds glanced at her. "Susan, go watch television for a little while."

The girl frowned, but did as she was told.

"Her mother's in the rehab center on the Red Lake rez," Wanda explained. "Susan wants a baby. Someone to love her. She'll make a good mother if I can get her to wait until she's twenty and married." She shifted the fussing baby to her shoulder and patted his back. "You didn't come here to talk about hunting bears. You want to know the same thing the sheriff's man wanted to know. You want to know where Joe John is."

"Yes," Cork said.

"And I'm supposed to tell you? Because you have a little of The People's blood flowing through you? Why do you even care? You're not the sheriff anymore."

"Joe John's my friend."

"Then leave him be."

The baby began to cry in earnest again. Wanda Manydeeds undid the top buttons of her denim blouse, unsnapped her feeding bra. The upper slope of her breast bore an elaborate tattoo that Cork easily recognized as the Wisdom Tree. The Wisdom Tree was an ancient, isolated white cedar—normally a swamp tree—that grew on the very tip of a point of rocky land jutting into Lake Superior. The whites called it the Witch Tree because it grew out of solid rock and had no visible means of sustenance. It was said to be as old as The People themselves and was sacred. Like Henry Meloux, Wanda Manydeeds was of the Cormorant clan, the clan of teachers and the Midewiwin. The baby's mouth clasped Wanda's nipple greedily just below the roots of the tree and the baby settled into quiet sucking.

"Have you seen Joe John?" Cork asked.

"No."

"Is he back?"

"He's around."

"Here on the reservation?"

"In Tamarack County."

"Do you know where?"

Wanda's nipple slipped from the baby's lips. The baby whimpered and she guided the searching mouth back.

"He has Paul?"

She considered a moment before answering. "Paul's safe."

"Why are they hiding?"

"Why does anyone hide?"

"What's Darla afraid of?" Cork pressed. "What's everybody so afraid of? Why won't anyone talk?"

She looked at him, and her almond eyes were hard with contempt. "You look at my silence and Darla's with a man's perception. You believe silence comes only from fear. Silence often comes from strength and from wisdom." She looked down at the baby. "That's all I have to say to you."

The priest, who until that moment had been silent himself, said respectfully, "Thank you, Wanda."

"You're welcome, Tom," she replied without looking up.

The priest turned to leave. Cork stood still and

asked, "Did Joe John have anything to do with the judge's murder?"

Wanda stopped rocking. She glanced up from the baby. Wisdom may have been the reason for her silence, but Cork knew fear was certainly the cause of the look on her face.

"Get out," she said.

"Come on, Cork." The priest put his hand on Cork's shoulder.

Cork said to the woman, "I only want to help."

"Stay out of this, then," she said. "The best thing you can do is just to stay the hell out of this."

The baby began to cry, a rolling wail. Wanda closed up her blouse and stood up, cradling the baby against her. "*Shhh*, Makwa, *shhh*."

Tilly Favre appeared and two other women and the girl. They all shared the same hostile look as they stared at Cork.

"*Migwech*, Wanda," he said. Thanks. He turned and left.

Outside, Cork took one last look at the torn forest next to the lodge. The uprooted trees made him anxious in an inexplicable way. The money from the casino was changing everything, changing it fast and changing it forever. And who could say what change was for the best and what was not?

In the Bronco, the priest said, "What the hell was that about the judge being murdered?"

"I think he may have been," Cork said.

Night had set in fully, and as Cork negotiated the winding road back to the mission, the high beam of his headlights blasted the woods with glare and shadow.

"Murder," the priest said quietly.

"And somehow that boy and his father are involved."

"Do you think Wanda is telling the truth?"

"Yes," Cork said as the mission clearing came into sight. "But she's not telling everything she knows."

Rose was at the kitchen table wrapping presents. She seemed startled when Cork shoved open the back door and stepped in.

"Sorry, Rose," he said. "Didn't mean to scare you." He hung up his coat. "Where is everybody?"

"They went Christmas shopping."

Cork headed to the cookie jar on the counter, lifted Ernie's head, and took out two chocolate chip cookies. He watched Rose, who was intent on making a bow out of a length of gold ribbon. She glanced up at him, seemed about to speak, then looked back down at her ribbon.

"What is it?" Cork asked.

"Nothing."

"Go on."

"It's probably just my imagination."

"What?"

She put the ribbon down. "I think someone's been in the house."

Cork had been leaning against the kitchen counter. He stood up straight. "Why do you think that?"

Rose looked a little uncertain. "It's kind of hard to explain. It's the little things. Like this afternoon. I went to the linen closet for a clean towel. I always put the towels and washcloths in order. Dark blue on the bottom, light blue in the middle, white on top. They were out of order."

"One of the kids," Cork suggested. "Probably looking for hidden Christmas presents."

"Maybe," Rose said.

"Anything else?"

"I took some clothes into Jo's room. Her bed was neatly made but the corner of the spread was up as if it had been lifted so that someone could look under."

"Maybe she just did a lousy job of making her bed this morning."

"You know how neat Jo is."

"Again, it could be kids looking for Christmas presents."

Rose looked unconvinced. "There are other things, all small like that. But it gives me the strangest feeling, and I can't shake it."

"Has anything been taken?"

"Not that I can tell. And I've looked pretty thoroughly."

"When would someone have come in?"

"The only time I can think of is when we were out shopping for the tree."

"Did you lock the door?"

"This is Aurora, Cork. I never lock the door except at night."

The house was dead still. The refrigerator motor clicked on with a deep, startling hum. Rose jerked in her chair.

"I'm sure it's nothing, Rose," Cork said. "But let's start locking the doors just to be sure." He locked the back door. "I'm going upstairs to clean up a little. You okay?"

"Yes." Rose smiled. "I'm sure, like you say, it's nothing." She went back to work on her bow.

Cork locked the front door on his way upstairs. He checked the guest room, Anne's and Jenny's and Stevie's rooms, and finally Jo's. He stood in his wife's bedroom, where on the surface everything looked fine. When he'd lived in the house, he'd had an intimate knowledge of how things should feel, but he'd been gone for months, and he'd lost that feel. Now he stood there a stranger.

Still, he trusted Rose.

First Sam's Place had been violated. Then the house on Gooseberry Lane. Were they looking for something here, too? Or was this just another warning, a subtle indication that his family wasn't safe either? If they were looking for something, what the hell could it be and why did they think he had it?

He went to the basement, took the rolled bearskin from a locked black trunk near the furnace, and brought it to his room. The skin had been left to him by Sam Winter Moon in his will. It had come from the biggest black bear Cork had ever seen, the one he'd hunted with Sam when he was fourteen. Cork undid the ropes. As he rolled out the skin, he uncovered the box he'd put there over a year ago. It was the size of a large dictionary and nearly as heavy. He lifted the lid. Inside was a Smith & Wesson .38 Police Special, a belt and holster, and a box of cartridges. He put them away after he'd killed Arnold Stanley. He'd believed he would never use them again. But like so much about his life, it appeared he might be wrong.

He was tired, so tired he could barely lift his feet to keep walking. The pack on his back felt so heavy he could hardly carry it. Sam Winter Moon moved ahead of him silently, the Winchester held ready in his hands.

They were in an unfamiliar part of the forest, an area torn and desolate. The trees had been razed, the stumps ripped from the ground. Their roots had become claws thrust toward the evening sky. The sun was low and red, and everything in the forest was tinted with an angry hue.

Sam Winter Moon had said the bear was near. Very near. They had to be careful now. Sam moved lightly on the balls of his feet and made no sound. Every step for Cork was labored and broke the silence with a terrible crunching of dry autumn leaves.

They came to the middle of the desolate ground, to a place where stumps and logs and branches had been piled in a heap, the way loggers would leave a mess for burning. The area was full of thistle grown chest high and autumn sumac with leaves gone bloodred along the branches. Sam looked the pile over carefully. In the evening light, it looked like something humped and dying.

Sam Winter Moon chambered a round. He lifted his hand in a sign for Cork to wait, then began to circle the huge pile of debris. In a moment he was lost among the tall thistle and sumac. Cork's heart beat so hard and fast it shook his whole body. The sound of it got louder and louder, so that Cork was sure the noise would startle the bear. He tried to breathe out the fear. He wanted to call to Sam, call him back from the danger, but Sam Winter Moon was already gone, already lost to him.

Then the pile began to stir. The jagged stumps and timber rose up, forming themselves into the great bear standing on its hind legs. It rose above Cork and splayed its claws, long and sharp and white, against the red of the sky. The bear lifted its black muzzle and a deafening roar exploded from its maw. As Cork watched terrified, it came for him.

He gripped the bow in his hands, a bow that had not been there before, and he reached toward his back, toward the quiver that hung where the pack had been. His hands trembled as he drew out an arrow and tried to think where best to shoot for a kill. He glanced at the bowstring and quickly fitted the arrow. When he looked up, the bear had changed. It wasn't the great black animal anymore, but a huge ogre, the Windigo, man-shaped with its skin bloodied and its teeth stained from feeding. Cork raised the bow and sighted on the creature's chest where the heart would be if the Windigo had a heart. But the bow was no longer a bow. It was a .38 Police Special. And as he pulled the trigger, the Windigo was no longer an ogre but was little Arnold Stanley with wet hair and a hopeless look on his face as his chest exploded with splashes of red.

"Cork, are you all right?" It was Jo in the doorway. "You cried out."

Cork sat up in bed, his heart still racing.

"Yes," he said. He breathed deeply, rubbed his eyes with the heels of his hands. "Just a dream."

He pulled off the covers and swung his feet off the bed. He reached to the nightstand for a cigarette. A bit of light came through his window, the reflection of the streetlamp off the snow outside, but his room was mostly dark.

Jo came in, not far. She wore a flannel nightgown and held her arms across her chest as if she were cold. "Want to talk about it?"

"No." He struck a match, lit his cigarette, sighed out a cloud of smoke. "It was just a dream and it's over."

He could smell her, the scent of the Oil of Olay she used at night to soften her skin.

"Putting up the tree today was nice," he said after a while.

"Yes," she answered.

"I'm amazed the blue bulbs have lasted this long," he said.

"We've been careful. About the bulbs at least." She might have smiled. It was hard to see her face clearly. "I'm going back to bed."

"You're cold?" he asked to keep her there.

"Freezing."

"You were always too cold and I was always too warm. You used to pull the blankets off me, remember?"

He heard her take a deep breath. "Good night, Cork." She turned and left.

He finished his cigarette. And then he tried to sleep.

CHAPTER 19

The next morning, after Jo and Rose had taken the children to church, Cork drove to Molly's place. She didn't answer his knock. He checked the shed where she kept her old Saab and found the car still there. He glanced at the sauna by the lake. No smoke from the stovepipe. Ski tracks headed down to the lake, but he couldn't tell how recently they'd been made. He went back to the house and let himself in with the key she hung on a nail under the back steps. She usually kept her skis on a rack on the back porch, but the rack was empty. Cork stepped into the kitchen, took off his hat and gloves and coat, and began to make himself coffee from the can of Hills Brothers Molly kept on hand just for him.

He loved Molly's kitchen. There was always a certain disorder to it that made it feel comfortable. She wasn't slovenly, but she often left a book open on the table, a few dishes sitting by the sink, or her knitting bag sagged on the floor next to a chair. Molly lived in her kitchen and her spirit filled it, so that just standing there, Cork breathed her in.

If he'd believed in prayer, he would have prayed at that moment for a way around what was ahead.

He bent over the sink, feeling weak and sick to his stomach, shaking as if he had a fever.

At least he hadn't told Molly he loved her. Maybe that was a small blessing, something spared them both. The only woman he'd ever been sure he loved and had told so was Jo, and that hadn't exactly turned out well. Was it always that way with love?

He poured himself a cup of coffee, and as he took his first sip, Molly came off the lake and removed her skis. He watched her disappear into the sauna. Smoke began to rise from the stovepipe. She reappeared with a long metal bar with a chiseled end, an ice spud, went ten feet out onto the ice, and began vigorously thrusting the bar downward. It looked as if the heavy metal was going right through the thick ice. But Cork knew there was a hole there Molly would use to plunge into after her sauna. She was simply clearing the thin layer of surface ice that had formed since she'd last taken a dip. When she and Cork did the sauna together, she usually consented to a brief roll in the snow or to just standing in the cold for a time while the icy air cooled them. She did this for Cork, who thought a plunge into the lake in the middle of winter was taking an experience a step too far. She put the ice spud away, took her skis and poles in hand, and started toward the house. When she saw Cork's Bronco, a big smile spread across her pretty face.

"There is a God," she said, sweeping into the kitchen, her cheeks flushed, her clothes carrying the cold that Cork could feel across the room. She pulled off her down jacket and hung it on a wall peg next to Cork's coat. She wore a red sweater that she also pulled off, and under it a white thermal top that hugged her breasts and her flat belly. Her cheeks were deep pink and her eyes full of excitement. "I was out on that gorgeous lake thinking what a treat it would be to come back and sauna with you." She crossed to him exuberantly and kissed him. She stepped back. "What's wrong?"

"Nothing."

"That's not true." She studied him so carefully that Cork had to look away.

He cupped his coffee tightly with both hands. "We've got to talk."

"You never talk. It must be bad."

"Let's sit down."

"I'm okay." She stared at him, and a cold, knowing look seemed to come into her eyes.

"Molly, I've been doing a lot a thinking. About us."

"What about us?"

Cork looked at his coffee. He could see his eyes reflected on the dark surface. They looked worried.

"You've been wonderful, Molly. You've been better than I deserved."

"Don't feed me a lot of crap, Cork. What is it? What's going on?"

"I want to try to put my marriage back together."

"So that's it." She turned away and went to the stove. She took the tea kettle, filled it with water, set it on a burner, and turned on the gas flame. "She asked you back?"

"Not exactly."

"This is your idea, then?"

He stepped nearer. "Molly, it's not about you. You've been wonderful."

"Right."

"The truth is, it's the children. I don't want my kids to hurt anymore. Can you understand? I have a history in that house on Gooseberry Lane. Maybe it's already too late, but I don't want to let go if there's a chance of saving it."

She touched her forehead a moment, as if thinking deeply. "So you'll be moving back in?"

"I already have in a way. I'm staying there now while my furnace gets fixed."

She faced him, and all the freshness that had colored her face when she first came in was gone. "Next you'll tell me you're sleeping with her."

"I want to put my life back together. For better or worse, Jo's part of that."

Molly's eyes narrowed on him for a moment, then she pulled away and went to the cupboard. She grabbed a mug, and swung back toward him. "What do you expect from me? A blessing? Or maybe you think if things don't work out, I'll just throw the door open and you can waltz back in here. Well, you can't, Cork." She tugged at the lid of a canister that held tea. The lid flew off and hit the floor with a tinny clatter. She just stood for a moment, staring at the lid on the floor.

"I'm sorry, Molly."

She shoved the canister back on the countertop. "To hell with the tea." She reached up into the cupboard and took down a bottle of Jack Daniel's.

"You don't drink," Cork told her.

"I do on special occasions." She poured liquor into the mug and drank it down. "What are you waiting for? You've said what you had to."

"I'm just wondering what you ever saw in me anyway. I'm a decade older than you, getting heavy, going bald. I smoke."

"Whatever I thought I saw, I guess I was wrong. It doesn't matter now anyway."

The tea kettle began to whistle. Molly made no move to take it off the flame. Cork left. Outside he could still hear the cry of the tea kettle growing thinner and thinner as he walked away.

After Cork had gone, Molly went down to the sauna. In the changing room she took off her clothes and laid them neatly folded on the wooden bench. She stepped into the sauna itself, sat down in the darkened room, and let the heat draw out of her the anger and the hurt.

She'd almost told him she loved him. So many times, she'd been on the edge of letting the words spill out, but her past had kept her cautious. And now she was glad, very glad, she hadn't. Let him go back to a woman who didn't care. Molly didn't care either. What ran down her cheeks and tasted of salt wasn't tears but good cleansing sweat. It poured from every part of her body. When she finally stood and ran outside, she trailed steam like a thing that had been through fire. As she dropped into the hole she'd cleared of ice, the bitterly cold water of the lake squeezed her hard, wrung her out, and left her wonderfully empty.

CHAPTER 20

After church, Jenny and Anne went with Cork to Sam's Place. While he retrieved his dark suit, the girls spread out the corn for Romeo and Juliet.

"What's that for?" Anne asked when they got back into the Bronco.

"It's what I dress in to say nice things about a bad man."

"Are you going with Mom to the memorial service for Judge Parrant?"

"I am."

"You didn't even like him," Jenny pointed out.

"I like him better now," Cork said.

Jenny smiled, then actually laughed.

At home, Cork put on his suit. While he was slipping on his tie, Anne knocked and came in. She sat on his bed and ran her hands over the bearskin. "Where'd this come from?"

"It belonged to Sam Winter Moon. He left it to me."

"Is it a bearskin?"

"Bingo." Cork leaned near the dresser mirror, took the two ends of his tie in hand and worked on a Windsor knot.

"Why'd he leave it to you?"

"He knew it would mean a lot to me."

"What does it mean to you?"

Cork finished the knot. He sat beside Anne, took the bearskin, and laid it across both their laps. The skin was large and spilled onto the floor.

"It came from the biggest black bear I ever saw. Biggest Sam ever saw, too, and he'd seen plenty. We hunted it together when I was about your sister's age."

"You shot it?"

"Sam did."

"Poor bear," Anne said.

Cork nodded his agreement. "He was a magnificent animal."

"Why'd Sam shoot him?"

"To save my life."

"The bear was after you?" Anne looked up at him, eager for the story.

"In the beginning, *we* were after the bear."

"What happened?"

"We followed him all day, into the Quetico-Superior Wilderness. That's what the Boundary Waters used to be called. We were in a part of the forest not even Sam knew." Cork rubbed the fur of the great skin and remembered. "We camped by a stream and talked late into the night. Next morning we were up early and tracking the bear again. By then Sam had decided not to kill it, but we both wanted to see it. Just to see such a creature."

"You knew it was big?"

"Oh, yes. And smart. We didn't know how smart. We tracked it to rocky ground, to an area full of boulders. After a while it became clear that we'd lost the trail. There wasn't anything to do but turn back. We were both disappointed. Sam, especially, because he prided himself on his ability to track, but the bear had got the best of him."

"If you lost his trail, how'd you kill him?"

"I'm coming to that part. In the late afternoon we came to a clearing, an old logged-over area full of sumac with a huge brush pile in the middle. We'd passed by before when we were tracking the bear, but this time Sam looked at the clearing and it was like he smelled something. He told me to wait and he disappeared into the sumac."

Anne's eyes were huge, staring up into his face. "Then what?"

"I waited like Sam said. I waited a long time. I began to get worried. Then I saw the sumac rustling, and I thought Sam was coming back. But it wasn't Sam."

"It was the bear," Anne jumped in.

"A monster of a bear," Cork said. "It had circled and come back around behind us. I don't know if Sam scared it, or if it had planned to attack, but there it was, charging at me out of the sumac. I was so scared I didn't even think to run. I just stood watching it come at me. When it was as close to me as you are right now, it stood up on its hind legs. Black bears are usually small, but this one towered over me. These claws you see here were ready to rip me apart. I was petrified. Absolutely frozen with fear."

Cork paused, fingering the long, sharp claws that were still the color of pearls.

"What happened?" Anne demanded.

"Sam shot him. I didn't even hear the shots, I was so scared. At first nothing happened. The bear just wavered a little. Then it staggered back and fell. Sam came running out of the sumac. The bear tried again to get up, to defend itself, but it was hopeless. Sam looked sad. He spoke to the bear, said something in Ojibwe that I didn't understand, then he finished it."

Anne was quiet a moment, petting the soft, black fur. "It's sad about the bear," she said. "But I'm glad he didn't kill you."

"Me, too, honey." Cork hugged her.

"Lucky for you Sam was a pretty good shot."

"For you, too, or you wouldn't even be here." He laughed. "Will you help me roll it back up? I think it's time to put it away again."

As they rolled up the skin, Anne said, "I miss Sam."

Cork said, "I miss him, too."

The memorial service for Judge Robert Parrant was held at Reedemer Presbyterian Church. Although the judge hadn't been a man much loved, the church was crowded. The people who packed the pews were powerful—politically and financially. The state caucus was well represented. The Honorable Jim Galsworthy, whom Sandy would replace in the Senate, was there. The governor himself sent a telegram, which Sandy read, praising the life work of Robert Parrant. It was bullshit, Cork knew, but the sombre congregation nodded their collective agreement.

There was a gathering at Sandy Parrant's home afterward. Cork, who'd insisted on driving Jo to the church, insisted on driving her to Parrant's as well.

"Why are you going?" she asked. "You didn't even like Bob."

"Nobody liked the judge. Don't pretend you did."

"He was a business associate," she said. "I have to go to these things."

"Whither thou goest." Cork smiled.

Jo didn't appear at all amused. "Father Tom talked to me today after church."

"Oh?" Cork tried to sound surprised.

"Cork, I really don't see any point in discussing our marriage anymore. With Father Tom or anybody else. I'm trying very hard to make a good end of it. So far it's been amicable, all things considered."

"Amicable is a good beginning."

"This isn't a beginning."

"The last couple of days things have felt nice. Almost normal again."

"Don't set yourself up for a fall." She looked at him with genuine concern. "Don't fool yourself, Cork. Our marriage is over. It really and truly is."

Outside town, Cork turned onto the long, wooded drive that led to Sandy Parrant's place. Parrant lived in a house like none Cork ever would. Surrounded by ten acres of hardwood forest, mostly maple, it stood on a quarter mile of the best shoreline Iron Lake had to offer. It was built on three levels, a little like books stacked slightly askew, and had so much window glass that, were it not for the wall of trees sequestering it, even Sandy Parrant's pissing might not have been a private act. The long asphalt drive through the woods had been cleanly plowed, but a strong wind was blowing out of the northwest. Loose snow swirled across the road and danced up the banks of plowed snow. High clouds had closed overhead, and dark was coming on quickly in that late December afternoon. The house was already full of lights.

"Did you hear me?" she asked.

"I heard," he replied. But he stubbornly held to the priest's advice: Nothing is hopeless.

The inside of Parrant's house was done in cold white—walls, rug, furniture—as if it were winter inside as well as out. A Christmas tree tastefully decorated with a modest number of white bulbs and red lights stood near the fireplace. Two red stockings hung from the mantel. Sandy Parrant wasn't married, and Cork wondered who the second stocking was for.

There were hors d'oeuvres and punch and coffee on a long table, and two caterers keeping a close eye. When Cork's father had died, and again when his mother passed away, neighbors had come with food that filled the house on Gooseberry Lane with the smell of things freshly baked. It hadn't made the grief go away, but Cork remembered how it made him understand that his parents had been loved by a lot of folks besides him, and it made him feel good for his mother and father and for the lives they led. He didn't feel that way at the catered gathering for Judge Robert Parrant. There was something calculated and distant about the carefully arranged platters of cold hors d'oeuvres. But he had to admit they were tasty.

Jo left him as soon as they stepped inside. Cork watched her huddle first with Parrant and several state politicos, then with Parrant and a number of local businessmen. She wore a simple black dress and a single strand of pearls. Her blonde hair was short and finely shaped. She looked beautiful. She stood among the men, not just holding her own, but being asked for advice. She was successful and she wore that success well.

As Cork watched, Sandy Parrant touched her shoulder in a familiar way, leaned to her, and whispered. It wasn't anything, really, but it disturbed him. They looked like a couple, good together.

"How about some fresh air?" Wally Schanno stepped up next to Cork, a cup of coffee in his huge right hand. He was dressed stiffly in a black suit and starched white shirt and dark blue tie. With his tall frame and hollow cheeks and stern gray eyes, he looked like a Bible-thumping minister bent on converting a world of sinners.

Cork asked, "Will Arletta be okay?"

"She's with friends," Schanno said.

Outside on the deck of the house, Cork lit up a Lucky Strike. The deck was a two-level affair. The top level was quite large and had boxes along the railings that held flowers in the summer. The lower level was almost entirely taken up by a redwood hot tub. Cork had heard about that particular hot tub. For a bachelor like Parrant, what Cork had heard was understandable.

The backyard terraced down to the lake, where there was a dock, empty now, and a large boathouse. Beyond that the flat white of the frozen Iron Lake stretched toward the evening sky. West beyond the bare trees of the Parrants' woods, the lights of Aurora sparkled along the shoreline, ending at the tip of North Point. As Cork leaned against the railing of the deck, the wind moved through the bare limbs of the trees with a sound like rushing water. The deck was protected and Cork hardly felt the wind at all.

"I don't think about dying too much," Schanno said, looking away from Cork toward the lake. "Not if I can help it. But, you know, all I've been thinking today is that when I die, I want someone to feel sad about it." Schanno sipped his coffee. "Find out anything from Wanda Manydeeds?"

"She knows more than she's telling. They're afraid of something, Darla and her. Maybe Joe John and Paul, too, and that's why they're hiding."

Schanno leaned against the railing and shook his head. "I still think it's a domestic dispute, Cork. They're Ojibwe. I don't blame 'em one bit for not wanting the law to get involved."

"There's something I haven't told you," Cork said. "Somebody broke into Sam's Place."

Schanno abruptly straightened up. "Burglary?"

"They tore the place up, but nothing seemed to have been taken. Another thing, I think somebody's been in the house on Gooseberry Lane, too."

"Maybe I should send a man over to dust for prints."

"I don't think dusting would turn up anything useful. And I don't want to scare my family."

"What were they after, Cork?"

"If I knew that, I might know who they are."

Schanno sipped his coffee. Cork smoked his cigarette. The wind shifted a little and began to move snow across the deck. Cork was feeling chilled.

"Maybe there's something I ought to tell you," Schanno said.

"I'm listening."

"I had a visit from the ATF recently. Couple of agents stopped by my office. They're interested in the Minnesota Civilian Brigade."

"I covered the same territory with the FBI when I was sheriff. They didn't seem too concerned."

"The ATF is. Seems that somebody's been pumping money into the group. The brigade's better organized than it was before. The ATF's afraid they may be arming themselves pretty heavily."

"Where's the money coming from?"

"That's what the agents wanted to know." Schanno looked at Cork with a curious expression. "You know, Cork, strange things have been going on around here, starting with the judge's death. You were alone in the judge's house a long time before me and my men got there."

"I was there awhile. Why?"

"I'm just wondering if maybe somebody thinks you took something. I'm wondering if they think you've got something that belonged to the judge."

"Are you wondering if I took something, Wally?"

"I didn't say that. But maybe somebody—maybe the brigade, for example—thinks you did. And if what they think you took has anything to do with the judge being dead—" Schanno turned his hard gray eyes on Cork.

The door onto the deck opened, and Arletta Schanno stepped out.

"How do you do," she said politely to Cork, as if he were a stranger.

"Arletta." Cork smiled back.

"Wally, dear, I think we should go home soon. The children."

"The children are all right," Schanno said without a hint of annoyance. "They're not home."

Arletta gave him a distressed look. "Maybe I should call."

"No." Schanno put his arm around her and drew her close to keep her warm. "No, it's time we left anyway." He glanced at Cork. "I'm thinking this is a thing you need to stay way clear of. For your family's sake, you understand? But if you hear anything about Joe John or the boy, you let me know."

Cork nodded. "You look lovely, Arletta. 'Night."

He stayed on the deck awhile, finishing his cigarette. He was just about to head back in when Jo came out.

"Cork, Rose is on the telephone for you."

"What is it?"

"I don't know. She wants to talk to you."

He took the call in the kitchen, where the caterers were working on trays of food.

"What is it, Rose?"

She spoke in a hush. "Harlan Lytton called. He wants you to call him as soon as you can."

"Did he say why?"

"No. But he sounded scary, Cork. And he didn't sound sober."

"Thanks, Rose. Is everything okay there? The kids?"

"Fine. Everything here's fine. I've made sure the doors are locked."

"Good. I'll call Harlan. And, Rose?"

"Yes?"

"Thanks."

Lytton answered right away, as if he'd been watching the phone and waiting to pounce.

"O'Connor. It's about time. Listen, I got something you want to see."

Lytton had a raspy voice. Drunk, it was like splinters.

"What is it?" Cork asked.

"Not over the phone. Get your ass out here."

"It's late, Harlan. Can't it wait until tomorrow?"

"O'Connor, you fuck, get over here. What I got to show you, you'll want to see."

"All right, Harlan. I'll be there in twenty minutes."

Jo and Sandy Parrant were standing together in the living room talking quietly.

"I've got to go," Cork told her.

"Everything's okay at home?" Jo asked.

"Everything's fine. I'm going out to see Harlan Lytton."

"Lytton?" Parrant said. "Why on earth do you want to see him?"

"He says he's got something to show me. I can take you home first, Jo."

"I'm not ready yet," she said.

"I'll see she gets home," Parrant assured Cork.

Cork shook his hand. "Nice memorial for your father."

"He was a good man," Parrant said. "He deserved it."

Sure, Cork thought. And monkeys fly out my butt.

CHAPTER 21

The wind had turned fierce, a bitter southern wind. It made the trees sway and the loose snow rise up, so that occasionally the road was lost in brief ground blizzards. On his way to Lytton's, Cork heard the forecast. More snow. Plunging temperatures.

He parked on the road. Lytton hadn't yet plowed himself out, and the lane leading to his cabin was heavily drifted over. Cork had stopped by the house on Gooseberry Lane to change his clothes and to strap on his belt and holster and his .38. He double-checked the cylinder, snapped it back in place, and got out of the Bronco. What Lytton had in mind, he couldn't even guess at, but things were strange in Aurora these days, and he didn't want to be caught unprepared.

Even in the shelter of the woods, the branches of the trees whipped about wildly. The trunks of the birch and tamarack moaned as they twisted and strained. The wind slapped his face. Little crystals of ice hit him like needles and made his eyes water. The sound of the wind through the trees swallowed every other noise. In the lane, Cork felt vulnerable. But the woods were full of bogs, and he didn't want to leave the certainty of the solid ground. He unbuttoned his coat and reached in to be sure he could get to his revolver quickly. He watched the woods carefully as he crept toward Lytton's cabin.

Three-quarters of the way in, the clear crack of a high powered rifle from the direction of Lytton's place made Cork hit the snow and roll. He scrambled off the open lane and hunkered down under the low branches of a small tamarack and waited.

He breathed hard and thought fast. Would Lytton really try to kill him because of the dog? Was that what this was about? Lytton was a mean son of a bitch and torn up over the death of the Ripper, but was he so stupid—or so confused by grief—that he'd lead a man into an ambush he'd advertised so broadly? Maybe it was exactly what a man would do when he lost what he most loved.

Cork risked a peek around the base of the tree. The ground all around was a tangle of brush and vine clumps. Nothing moved.

A minute had passed. Cork replayed the sound of the shot in his head. It had come from the direction of Lytton's cabin. That didn't mean that Lytton had fired it, or that Cork was the target. He'd been an easy mark on the road, and Lytton was a good shot.

He crouched and stumbled forward to the next tree. He made for the next tree, leaping brush and vines in an open run. Only moments before, he'd been freezing, but as he knelt behind a slender birch and strained to listen, sweat trickled down his temples. He heard nothing but the incessant rush of the wind and the creak and moan of the living woods. Carefully he stepped back out onto the lane and crept toward the cabin.

The lights were on, the cabin door ajar. Cork could see that the front window had been shattered. Wind tore at the curtain inside. He crouched behind the cover of a fallen tree as someone stepped into the doorway. Against the light inside, only the dark outline of the figure and a long rifle barrel were clear. The figure slumped a moment against the doorjamb as if exhausted or maybe wounded, then gathered itself and started around the cabin toward the woods in back.

Cork readied his revolver and hollered into the wind. "Stop! Police!"

The figure turned, scanned the woods, and wildly fired. The tree trunk high above Cork splintered and flakes of bark showered down. The figure turned and ran for the deep woods. Cork sighted, but held off pulling the trigger.

"Stop, goddamn it!"

The warning shot Cork fired into the air didn't make any difference. In a moment the figure was lost in the darkness and the far woods. Cork dashed to the open door of the cabin. Lytton lay on the floor, facedown. His back was a bleeding mess. Cork knelt beside him and found a weak pulse in Lytton's neck. He grabbed the phone that hung on the wall and called the sheriff's office.

Lytton's eyes were open when Cork came back to him. A pool of blood had oozed from beneath him and was slowly spreading across the bare cabin floor. Cork knelt beside him and leaned close to his ear.

"Harlan, this is Cork O'Connor. Hang on. An ambulance is on the way. Harlan, can you hear me?"

Lytton's eyes were yellow-brown, the color of new pine wood. He had a mole on his left cheek that somehow Cork had never noticed before. His ear was small with a long lobe. He smelled raw, smelled of the thick unpleasant odor of blood. Cork felt again at Lytton's neck. This time he found no pulse. He considered pumping Lytton's chest, trying to push his heart back into a rhythm. But the man had a hole in him big as a fist, and Cork was pretty certain anything he tried would be useless.

In the stillness he shared with the dead man, Cork heard the sound of a snowmobile far out in the woods. As he listened, the snowmobile grew distant and then could be heard no more.

He sat beside Lytton, enormously tired. He was no stranger to brutal death. Both as sheriff and as a cop on Chicago's south side, he'd seen his share of dying. Murder, accident, overdose—it happened in many ways, but the end was the same. Something sad and confusing left behind. Only the shape of life, only the empty outline.

He stood up. There was nothing more he could do. The ooze of Lytton's blood had stained his pant leg. The sole of his right boot put a bloody print on the floor. Contaminating the scene. But what was done was done. He wondered what it was Lytton had wanted to show him, wondered if it had anything to do with the man's death. From where he stood, he looked the cabin over. It was small, but efficient. Bunk, table, stove, refrigerator, sink, all in the one room. Lytton wasn't a good housekeeper. A clutter of dirty dishes sat in the sink. The stove was like an erupted volcano with streams of old cooking hardened on the top and sides. Clothes lay wadded on and around the bunk where they'd been carelessly tossed. However, the cabin walls were different. They were carefully decorated with framed photographs, landscapes of the North Woods. The rapids of a small stream, a deer bent to its feeding in an empty meadow, a pond at sunset. Cork was surprised. In the home of Harlan Lytton, he'd expected to see something harsher hanging, something on the order of stuffed animals or mounted heads.

The north end of the cabin had been walled off with plywood into a small second room. Cork took his handkerchief and wiped the blood from his boot, then crossed to the door and opened it. Inside, he pulled a cord to turn on an overhead bulb. It was a darkroom. There was a sink and trays for developing, an enlarger, shelves full of chemical containers and camera equipment. The equipment was sophisticated. Lots of complicated lenses. A few prints hung from a line. Cork took a close look. Winter photos—black and white—of delicate ice formations on the rocks of a small stream. They were surprisingly good. He found other prints sitting on a counter, some in black and white, others in color. They were lovely, and that surprised the hell out of him. He would never have thought it of Harlan Lytton. He opened the drawers under the cabinet. Miscellaneous supplies. A drawer with strips of negatives. Cork lifted a couple of the strips. Wildlife shots. He opened the largest of the drawers, but it was completely empty.

Back in the other room, he wandered the cabin a bit, looking over everything for anything. He checked the small bathroom. There, as everywhere else, Harlan was careless in his cleaning. Cork could hear sirens down on the road approaching Lytton's lane. When he turned back and took a good look at the dead man from another angle, he saw the corner of a manila folder sticking out from under the body. He knelt beside Lytton, trying to avoid the blood. There was something written on the raised corner of the file folder.

The sirens had gone silent, which probably meant they'd reached the lane and were trying to figure how to get to the cabin through the deep snow. He lifted Lytton's body carefully and took the folder off the floor. It was soaked in blood. The scrawl of the handwriting was quite clear, however. In black pen on the label was written Jo O'Connor.

Cork's hands cradled the bloody folder. He opened it. Inside were several black-and-white photographs. They appeared to have been taken at night with some type of night vision lens. In the first photograph Cork clearly recognized the home of Sandy Parrant. It was a view from the lake and showed the dock and boat-house, the long backyard, the house on three levels, the decks. There were two white forms near the hot tub.

Cork could hear the bump and scrape of a plow clearing the lane for the sheriff's cars.

The second photograph was an enlargement of the first with the details enhanced. The enlargement centered on the hot tub. The white forms were two people, clearly naked.

The plow stopped. Cork could hear car doors slamming shut outside the cabin and men shouting to one another.

In the third photograph, a further enlargement with the details grainy but distinct, Cork could see that the two people were making love. The woman was bent slightly forward, leaning on the hot tub for support. The man held her hips, his pelvis shoved against her buttocks, entering her from behind.

Sandy Parrant's grainy face was lifted toward heaven. Jo's eyes were closed, but her mouth was open in what looked to be a little moan of ecstasy.

Cork closed the folder and slid it under his coat a moment before Wally Schanno and his men came through the door.

CHAPTER 22

"And you don't have any idea what it was he wanted to show you," Schanno said, repeating what Cork had already told him.

"If I knew that, Wally, I wouldn't have come all the way out here. He died without saying a word."

Schanno looked down at the dead man, then at Cork. "If the Ripper was alive, the Ripper would've warned him."

"No," Cork said. "The Ripper would've torn the killer apart."

"Lytton's bad luck," Schanno said.

"Yeah," Cork agreed. "Lytton's luck."

"I'm going to have to take your firearm," Schanno said.

"I understand."

"And those clothes. They've got blood all over them." Schanno glanced around and his eyes settled on a young rookie, Jack Wozniak. "Jack, I want you to follow Cork home. Get the clothes he's wearing and bring them back to the office." He eyed Cork again, shook his head in a frustrated way, and said, "I don't want you doing anything else on your own, okay?"

"If I'd known it was going to turn out this way, I'd have invited you." Cork started toward the open door.

"I'll want to talk to you some more tomorrow," Schanno called after him. "You'll be home?"

Home? Cork thought about it. No, he wouldn't be home. He wouldn't be home ever again. "I'll be around," he said.

It was almost midnight when he reached the house on Gooseberry Lane. The back door was locked and all was quiet inside. Cork told Wozniak to wait in the kitchen and asked if he wanted some coffee and cookies. Wozniak said no thanks to the coffee, but he did accept one of Rose's chocolate chip cookies. Cork went upstairs to change. He cleared the bottom drawer of his dresser and put the folder there. The manila was stiff and black with dried blood. He took off his clothes and hung them carefully on hangers. After putting on a robe, he walked the bloody clothing downstairs.

"I'm sorry about this, Cork," the deputy said, looking genuinely guilty about the whole thing.

"Standard procedure. Let it go. Good night, Jack."

Cork checked Jo's room. She wasn't there. He took a shower, put on clean boxer shorts and a clean T-shirt, and went to bed. The wind shook the windows and made the house creak and groan. In a few minutes, he heard the sound of Stevie's footie pajamas shuffling down the hallway. It was only a soft shooshing, but it was a sound that could bring Cork up in an instant even from the deepest sleep. In a minute, Stevie was at his bedside.

"What's up, buddy?" Cork asked.

Stevie clutched his stuffed doll named Peter and stared at his father in the dark. The windowpane shuddered. Stevie glanced toward it and said a single word, whispered in terror. "Monthterth."

"Monsters." Cork nodded gravely. He pushed himself up. "Come on. Let's go have a look."

Stevie pointed to the closet and Cork searched there. Stevie indicated the ultimate blackness beneath his bed and Cork knelt and demanded all monsters come out now. Nothing came, but Stevie grasped his father as if he'd seen a ghost and pointed to the window.

"Outthide," he said.

Together they pressed their noses to the frigid glass. Around the house swirled a white rush—loose snow and wind—and the great elm in the backyard waved its branches as if dreadfully alive. What Cork saw was the awesome power of nature, but for Stevie it was simply the confirmation of his nightmares.

"Only the wind, Steve," Cork explained gently. "It's noisy but it's only wind."

"Monthterth," Stevie insisted with a defiant certainty of some terror to come.

Cork guided him back to bed. "Would you like me to lie down with you awhile?"

In that instant, Stevie's fear vanished. Cork knew it wasn't manipulation, only a son's naive trust in his father's stature. What were monsters, after all, to a man who could touch the ceiling?

Cork lay down beside him. Stevie made himself into a little ball, his breath breaking warm and sweet against Cork's face. In only a minute he was breathing steadily again, sleeping.

It was time for Cork to return to the bed in the guest room. But he lingered beside this son who trusted him, lay awake knowing there were monsters in the wind outside, that his son's fear was not unjustified, and that Stevie would have to face them alone someday. There were people out there so cruel they would wound him for the pleasure of it, dreadful circumstances no man in his worst imaginings could conjure, disappointments so overwhelming they would crush his dreams like eggshells. For a child like Stevie, a child of special graces, there would be such pain that Cork nearly wept in anticipation of it. Against those monsters, a father was powerless. But against the simple terrors of the night, he would do his best.

He heard Jo come in the front door and a moment later the sound of her feet on the stairs. He slid from Stevie's bed and stepped into the hallway. Jo came up the stairs, her hands behind her neck, undoing her pearls. She looked tired.

"Still awake?" she asked. "I thought everybody would be asleep."

"Sandy bring you home?"

"Yes."

She got the pearls off and tried to move by him toward her bedroom, but Cork blocked her way.

"You stayed a long time," he said.

"We were working on business."

"You've been working on business a lot with Sandy."

"I'm his attorney, Cork."

"Is that all you are?"

Jo stepped back. "What are you talking about?"

"I thought it was me," Cork said. He shook his head stupidly. "All along I thought it was my fault. Christ, how blind can a man be?"

Jo watched him closely but said nothing.

"Do you love him?"

Jo didn't answer.

"Are you planning on marrying him as soon as I'm out of the picture?" His voice rose as if Jo's silence was only because she couldn't hear him. "Are you?"

In Anne's room, the bed creaked. "Not here," Jo said.

Cork turned and walked angrily to the guest room. Jo followed and closed the door.

"Well?" Cork said.

Jo stayed by the door, her hands behind her back, gripping the knob.

"You lied to me," Cork accused.

"No. I just didn't tell you."

"Bullshit."

"I didn't want you to know. Sandy's in a vulnerable position. He's a very public figure. And I'm still technically a married woman."

"But that's not your fault, is it? Lord knows, you've done everything you can to hurry this along."

"Cork—"

"How long?"

"What do you mean?"

"How long has it been going on?"

She sighed, closed her eyes. "A while."

"A long while," Cork corrected her.

"Cork, I didn't like not telling you. But how could I? It would've been all over Aurora, and Sandy's standing could have been terribly damaged."

" 'Sandy's standing'?" Cork looked at her, his eyes wide with a kind of horror. "Who are you, Jo? I don't even know you anymore."

"I didn't do it to hurt you. It just happened, Cork."

Everything in him felt drawn taut, ready to snap. He could feel his right temple twitching as if there were something under his skin trying to break out.

"When?" he asked. "When did it just happen? After I was out of your bed? Out of the house? When?"

"Yes."

"Yes what?"

"After you were out of the house."

"You wouldn't lie to me?"

"Why would I lie?"

Cork went to the dresser and pulled out the folder stained with Lytton's blood. He held it out to Jo.

She drew back in revulsion. "What's that?"

"Take it. Open it." He thrust it at her.

She put the pearls on his bed, gingerly took the folder in her hands, and carefully opened it. She studied the photographs. Cork watched her face go pale as her pearls.

"Oh, God," she whispered. "Where did these come from?"

"Does it matter? Look at the lower corner of each of them. There's a time-date stamp. Those pictures were taken the summer after Sam Winter Moon died. I wasn't out then, Jo. Or I guess I was and just didn't know it, huh?"

She looked ill, drained of all her color. "What difference does it make now, Cork?"

He turned away and went to the window. He watched the elm tree in the yard writhe in the wind like a creature in pain.

"What did I do to deserve this, Jo?"

"The world doesn't revolve around you, Cork," she said. Her voice was flat and cold and hard, like frozen ground. "Everything doesn't happen because of you. Some things just happen."

She moved behind him toward the bed. He heard the soft rustle of her dress. He didn't want to look, didn't want to see her at all.

"I've been trying to tell you," she said. "Don't get your hopes up. Didn't I say that? But you wouldn't listen. You didn't want to hear. It's over between us, Cork."

"And Sandy Parrant is the reason."

There was a long stillness, then Jo said, "I suppose."

"Get out."

"Cork—"

"Just get out."

He heard the door open, heard her leave, heard the sound down the hallway of her own door closing. He turned and saw that she'd put the folder on the bed and taken her pearls.

For a long time he stood at the window listening to the howl of the wind outside. If it was true, as Henry Meloux said, that he'd heard the Windigo call his name, he understood why now. Because it felt exactly as if his heart had just been torn out of him and devoured.

CHAPTER 23

Jo lay awake in the black of four a.m. remembering a moment before it all fell apart. She and Cork out at Russell Blackwater's trailer in the hours before the shootings at Burke's Landing. She recalled them holding one another and feeling a terrible numbness where caring should have been. She'd blamed it on the circumstances, the weight of what each of them carried that night, the responsibilities. But it wasn't that. They were holding something dying, maybe already dead, but they were too scared to admit it.

She wondered why the tragedy at Burke's Landing hadn't brought them together. Adversity was supposed to do that, wasn't it? Instead, everything got worse. Cork wasn't just distant. Something in him seemed to have died along with the other deaths that drizzly morning. Nothing mattered. Not his job, his family, her. He called out in the night sometimes, sat bolt upright and grabbed at the air. What was it he was reaching for? The past? Was he trying to pull the dead men back? Trying to pull them all back?

She never knew. He wouldn't talk about it.

Near dawn she heard Cork moving about. She put on her robe, went downstairs to the living room, and sat tensely on the sofa to wait for him. When he came down, she stood up, and clutched the robe around her throat as if she were freezing.

"Cork?" she said.

The living room was dark. He seemed startled by her presence.

"What?" he grumbled.

"Could we talk?"

"I'm on my way out."

"We need to talk."

"What's there to talk about? You made everything clear."

"I don't want us to finish things all bitter and angry."

"What am I supposed to do? Shake your hand and thank you kindly for leaving me for another man?"

"Could we just talk for a while?"

"You said yesterday you didn't want to talk about our marriage anymore. So what's changed?"

"You're hurt. I didn't want that."

"What difference does it make to you?"

"I know you might not believe this, but I care about you."

Cork was a solid darkness within the dark of the living room. Jo could see that he held the gym bag he'd used to bring his clothing from Sam's Place. And he held his rolled-up bearskin.

"Could we talk in my office? Please?"

Cork didn't answer, but he didn't leave. Jo took that as a good sign and led the way. In her office, she closed the door behind them, then switched on the lamp on her desk. They both blinked a moment at the light.

"You look tired," she said.

"I didn't sleep."

"Me either."

"You know what I did, Jo? I lay awake putting it all together, all the signs, signals. I could see it now, in neon. But, you know, what I couldn't put together was where it began."

"I don't think you need to know the details. I don't think that would do anybody any good."

"You wanted to talk. This is what I want to talk about."

Jo leaned against the oak desk thankful for the support of the solid wood. "It was after the shooting at Burke's Landing. When Sandy and I were down in St. Paul together working to negotiate a settlement before any more blood was spilled. Things were intense. It just happened."

"Just happened." Cork shook his head.

"We were drifting already, Cork, don't deny it. There were days we'd come home and not say more than a dozen words to one another, and then it was to talk about money or the kids' school things or the most recent rumor making the rounds in Aurora. I don't know, maybe we thought we knew each other so well we didn't have to talk. If that was it, we were wrong. Because every night it felt as if I was going to bed with a stranger."

"Even when we made love?"

"By then we were just having sex, Cork. I don't even know when we stopped making love."

Cork set his gym bag down and put the bearskin on top of it. He crossed his arms over his chest and leaned back against the door. "And along comes Sandy Parrant with his good looks and his money and just sweeps you off your feet."

"It wasn't his money or his looks. I needed someone, Cork. We're not all as strong and self-contained as you are."

"Oh, yeah, I was real strong after Burke's Landing. Hell, I couldn't even muster the energy to fight the recall petition. I could have used a little support then."

"I tried to reach out, Cork, but you were like something made of ice. It was like everything in you had frozen over. There wasn't any warmth toward me or the kids. Stevie was afraid to go near you, for Christ sake."

"And that's why you asked me to leave. It didn't have anything to do with Sandy Parrant," he said with bitter sarcasm.

Jo looked down. "You're right. It probably had a lot to do with Sandy."

"Christ, Jo, do you know how long I've felt like shit, felt like everything was all my fault?"

"I know, Cork, I know. The truth is," she confessed, "I let you believe it because it made things easier for me."

There was a knock at the door. Rose poked her head in and smiled. "I'm about to start breakfast. Anyone interested?" She glanced down and saw Cork's gym bag and the bearskin, then she looked sadly at the two of them.

"I won't be staying, Rose," Cork told her. "Thanks anyway."

Jenny pushed in behind her, rubbing sleep from her eyes. "Dad, I want to feed the geese." She yawned. "Can you take me to school? We can stop by Sam's Place on the way." She looked carefully at the three adults, then at Cork's things on the floor. She seemed wide awake suddenly. "You're going back?"

"Yeah. But I'll give you a ride so you can feed the geese."

"No, thanks," she said. "It doesn't matter now." She turned and shoved past Rose out the door.

Rose eyed them both again, gave her head a faint shake of disapproval, and stepped out.

"I'm sorry," Jo said.

"Who isn't?" Cork picked up his gym bag, hefted the bearskin, and left.

A dirty van waited outside Sam's Place, the engine running. On the side, barely readable through the crust of grit, was printed "Winterbauer Plumbing and Heating." Art Winterbauer stepped out. He held coffee in a big paper cup from Jeannie's Donuts, and there was a splotch of white cream filling on his upper lip.

"I promised you first thing, Cork. And first thing, here I am. Freeze your butt over the weekend?" He was a short man with a square body and square face. He wore a hat with flaps that hung down the side like the ears of a basset hound. Sliding his van door open, he pulled out a heavy toolbox. He carried his coffee in one hand, his toolbox in the other.

"I took your advice. Stayed somewhere else." Cork unlocked the door.

Winterbauer stepped in and saw the mess. "Christ, what happened in here?"

"You know where everything is," Cork replied without answering.

"Yeah," Winterbauer said, looking at the destruction around him. "But is it still there?"

"I'll be outside if you need me," Cork told him, and left.

He dug into the grain sack and took the bucket of

dried corn out to the lake. A light snow was falling. The flakes settled on the gray open water and disappeared. At first he didn't see Romeo and Juliet. Then he spotted them huddled under a safety station at the edge of the ice. They seemed oddly subdued, quiet and motionless, and didn't appear to be in any hurry to feed.

A maroon Taurus station wagon pulled up beside Winterbauer's van. Helmuth Hanover, editor of the *Aurora Sentinel* stepped out, spotted Cork, and started toward him. Hanover was a tall, slender man in his mid-forties. A veteran of Vietnam, he'd left the lower part of his right leg on a rice paddy dike, courtesy of a claymore mine. He had a prosthetic appendage and walked with a slight limp. He'd begun to bald young, a characteristic he'd chosen to exaggerate by shaving his head clean. With his narrow face, blue unkind eyes, and that shaved head like a cleaned bone, he had an intimidating austerity about him, not unlike a sharply honed knife. Although his byline read "Helm Hanover," he was unaffectionately known as Hell Hanover by anyone who'd been the target of his editorials. And Cork had. During the spearfishing business, Hanover had flayed Cork alive.

Helm exercised a good deal of wisdom and restraint in publishing the *Sentinel*, which was a small town paper devoted to small town news—commissioner's meetings, church bazaars, births, obituaries. He crammed as many names in a story as he possibly could and he was sure to spell them all correctly. In reporting the local news, he generally kept things about as controversial as cottage cheese. But in his editorials and the Letters to the Editor section, he allowed a lot of latitude. Consequently, the *Sentinel* was frequently a voice for all the crackpot philosophies at liberty in Tamarack County. He'd printed odes to the Posse Comitatus, elegies to the Branch Davidians, proclamations of supremacy from the Minnesota Civilian Brigade—all with a nod toward the First Amendment. His own editorials generally carried a sharp, bitter edge, and more often than not, the target of his criticism was government. In any form. Helm Hanover had no use for the distant, inept interference of the federal government, particularly. Cork suspected a lot of this was a deep, burning anger that went all the way back to the flesh and bone Hell had left in Vietnam.

"Morning, Cork," Hanover said. He nodded stiffly in greeting.

"Helm," Cork said. "I don't suppose you're out here hoping for a burger and a shake."

"I've just come from the sheriff's office. I'd like to ask you a few questions." Hanover took a small notebook and pencil from the pocket of the down vest he wore. "About last night."

The geese were slowly making their way to shore, black ripples following in the gray water. Cork watched the geese. He didn't want to look at Hell Hanover. The man always made him angry.

"What exactly did the sheriff tell you?" Cork asked.

"I'd like it to be in your own words," Hanover said.

"My words, Wally's words, what difference does it make? You've got the facts."

Cork set the empty bucket in the snow. Hanover glanced in as if there might be something worth writing about inside it.

"The sheriff said Lytton called you. He wanted to show you something. What was it he wanted to show you?"

"If he hadn't been killed, I might know."

"You haven't got any idea? When he called, he didn't say anything?"

"He only said to come out."

"Why did you feel compelled to go?"

"You wouldn't understand."

"Anything to do with killing his dog?"

Cork glanced over and found Hanover's hard, unkind eyes watching him closely, his sharp pencil poised above his notebook. "Who told you about the dog?"

"Might've been the same person who told me about the Windigo. I heard the Windigo called his name. Is that true?"

Cork looked Hanover in the eye. "You're a newspaperman, Helm. You deal in facts. The Windigo is a myth."

"It wasn't a myth that killed Harlan Lytton."

"My point exactly."

"Did you see the assailant?"

"Just a silhouette."

"Can you describe him?"

"Why do you say 'him,' Helm? There's nothing sexist about murder. Women kill, too."

"Can you describe the assailant?" Hanover corrected.

"You can get my description from the sheriff." Cork bent and lifted the bucket. The geese seemed reluctant to come to shore with Hanover there. Cork turned back toward Sam's Place. Hanover limped after him.

"Funny thing about that dog," Hanover said at his back. "If you hadn't shot him, he might've warned Lytton."

Cork stopped. "What are you getting at, Helm?"

Hanover shrugged innocently. "I'm not getting at anything, Cork. I'm just asking questions. It's my job."

"But it's not mine to answer them. You want to know anything about Lytton's death, talk to Wally Schanno. He's paid for it."

Hanover wrote in his notebook; Cork went on ahead. Hanover caught up with him at the door to Sam's Place.

"Just one more question. When the judge died, you were there. When Lytton died, you were there. If you were on the outside looking in, wouldn't that strike you as a little funny?"

"See you around, Helm." Cork eyed him pointedly until the newspaperman turned and limped back to his wagon. Hanover took out the notebook again and stood in the falling snow, writing. He glanced back at Cork, then slipped into the wagon and drove away.

Cork stood in the doorway. As much as he hated to, he had to agree with Hell. It was a little funny.

By the time Cork reached the old firehouse, the new snow had given a soft, fluffy covering to everything. Parrant's white BMW sat in the parking lot. The windshield was still clear, and Cork figured Parrant hadn't been there long.

Joyce Sandoval glanced up from her computer screen and eyed Cork over her half glasses. "I heard about last night," she said. "It sounds awful."

"I'd like to see Sandy."

"Sure," she said, and reached for the phone. "Just a moment." She punched in three numbers. "Corcoran O'Connor is here to see you." She listened a moment, then hung up. "He'll be with you in a moment. Are you all right?"

"Fine, Joyce," Cork replied, and turned abruptly away. He stood in front of a picture in the hallway, a framed aerial shot of Aurora. Yellow pins that indicated Great North holdings, covered the map like small pustules. The subdivision called Larkin Hills, the Aurora Mall, the Four Seasons Condominiums, the Aurora Office Park. The newest and most expensive of the holdings was also there. The Chippewa Grand Casino. Along the bottom of the enlarged photograph was the inked inscription, "Happy Birthday, Sandy. The Judge."

"He'll see you now," Joyce said.

Parrant stepped out of his office just as Cork reached the top of the stairs. He eyed Cork steadily. "I've been expecting you. I talked with Jo this morning."

"Talked? I didn't think that was what you and Jo did together."

Parrant was dressed for business. Blue suit, white shirt, red silk tie. The fragrance of a fine musk cologne scented the air around him.

"One of the things," he replied calmly.

The door across the hall opened and Parrant's secretary stepped out. "Mr. Parrant—" she began.

"Can it wait, Helen?" Parrant asked. "Cork and I were just about to have a conference in my office."

"Oh, sure," Helen said, and turned away.

"Why don't we step inside to discuss this," Parrant suggested.

Exposed beams ran across the ceiling of Sandy Parrant's office. It had the same effect as a weight lifter showing his biceps. Strength on display. Parrant's desk was very large, very dark, and very shiny. The papers on it were in small neat stacks.

Parrant went to a table near the window and picked up a silver pot. "Coffee?"

"I didn't come on a social call."

Parrant poured coffee into a white porcelain cup. "What are you here for, Cork? Want to take a swing at me?" He stirred in sugar and cream.

"I want to ask a question."

"Only one?" Parrant carefully tasted his coffee.

"Do you intend to marry her?"

Parrant walked casually back to his desk and set the cup down. "I don't see that that's any of your business."

"She comes with baggage," Cork said.

"Baggage? You mean the children." He looked at Cork disdainfully. "I'd never refer to my children as baggage."

"They'll never be your kids. You may get my wife, but you'll never get my kids."

Parrant sat on the edge of his desk, his hands folded calmly in his lap. He had the air of a high school principal sadly disappointed in the behavior of a student.

"Would you use them like weapons, Cork? What kind of father are you that you have to fight me through your children?"

"I don't have to fight through my children."

"I don't think you have it in you to fight any other way."

Cork exploded and lunged at him. Parrant seemed to have anticipated the move and ducked so that he caught Cork full in the chest with the top of his shoulder. They tumbled back. Parrant came up with a hard punch to Cork's ribs that felt like the butt end of a log, then he danced easily away.

"Intramural boxing champ at Harvard." He grinned at Cork.

Cork charged again, wrapping up Parrant in his thick arms. They went down heavily, knocking the phone off Parrant's desk and toppling his chair. Parrant hammered jabs at the place on Cork's ribs where he'd landed the first jarring blow, the same area that had taken a beating a couple of days earlier at Sam's Place. The pain made Cork let go. Parrant rolled away and bounded up, his hands fisted. Cork struggled up, too, just as Parrant's office door opened and his secretary stepped in. She stood a moment looking at the two men.

"Oh," she said when she understood. "I saw your line go on and I thought—"

"That's all right, Helen," Parrant said, dropping his hands. He straightened his red silk tie and brushed his blue suit. "We were just finishing our discussion. I'll be with you in a minute."

The woman nodded, glanced at Cork, and backed quickly out.

Parrant ran his hand through his hair and looked smooth as ever. He moved back to his desk, picked up the phone, and righted the fallen chair.

"Jo said you had photographs. Where'd you get them?"

Cork's ribs hurt every time he took a breath, but he didn't want Parrant to know. "Does it matter?"

"I'd like to know who's so interested in my private life."

"You're a senator now. You haven't got a private life."

"What are you going to do with the photos?"

"I haven't decided."

Parrant sat down and eyed Cork with an unruffled air. "I'm sure you can't hurt me, Cork. But if you try, I'll squash you like a bug."

"I'm shivering in my boots, Sandy."

He turned to leave. As he reached for the door and opened it, Parrant said at his back, "I'm used to winning, Cork. It's what I do best."

Outside Cork got into the Bronco. He undid his shirt and looked at the place where his ribs hurt like hell. The skin was already a brooding purple from the beating he took at Sam's Place. There seemed to be a yellow-green border developing around the bruise. He wondered if Parrant had broken anything. He reached into his shirt pocket for a Lucky Strike, and hauled out a crushed pack. He extracted a bent cigarette, straightened it out, and lit up. After that he sat for a while staring at the windshield that was blanketed with snow.

Eventually he opened the gym bag. He hadn't looked at the pictures since the night before. There was no point in looking again. He knew that. No point except to feed the coldness inside him. In a strange way, that was exactly what he wanted now. He wanted to feed himself to the cold until the cold had consumed him and he didn't care anymore.

He stared at the folder. Manila, old and beaten. Doodles on the outside. Although dried blood obscured some things, others were quite clear. Squares, circles, scribbles. A word here and there. Idle scrawl. But there was something about that scrawl. It was different from the writing on the label that said "Jo O'Connor."

He crushed out his cigarette in the ashtray and stepped from the Bronco. Folder in hand and moving gingerly because of his ribs, he hurried back into the building. He ignored Joyce Sandoval's questioning glance and went straight to the aerial photo hanging on the wall. He studied the handwritten inscription

on the matting. "Happy Birthday, Sandy. The Judge."
The late Judge Robert Parrant had written with a pe-
culiarly grand flourish.

Cork looked at the folder. The doodled words on
the bloody cover were in the same hand.

The folder hadn't originally belonged to Harlan
Lytton. It had belonged to another dead man first.

CHAPTER 24

He'd always loved winter in the North Woods. The clean feel of a new snow. The icy air almost brittle in his nostrils. The way sound carried forever. He could hear Walleye barking a long way off as he parked his Bronco on the frozen lake, climbed the rocky slope of Crow's Point, and made for Henry Meloux's cabin. The world felt empty of everything except that sound.

Meloux stepped out as Cork approached. He was wiping his hands on a rag. Big snowflakes caught in his white hair as he stood waiting.

"Corcoran O'Connor," the old man said with a smile.

Walleye, who was on a rope tied to a metal peg driven into the cabin wall, wagged his tail and nuzzled Cork's crotch.

"You don't seem surprised to see me, Henry," Cork said.

"When you are my age, you will be surprised by little, too." He looked at Cork with concern. "You are moving like a man my age."

"A little accident," Cork said. He gently touched his ribs.

"I have made bean soup," the old man offered.

"We'll eat." He untied the dog, turned, and led the way inside.

The cabin smelled of the soup, a thick, tantalizing aroma. Cork realized he hadn't eaten at all that day, hadn't even been hungry until he smelled the soup. From his coat pocket, he pulled an unopened pack of Lucky Strikes and gave them to the old man. Meloux seemed pleased.

"After we eat"—he nodded—"we can smoke together."

Meloux filled two chipped bowls and brought them to the table. He brought bread in a basket and poured coffee from the blue speckled pot that had jumped by itself the day Molly had been there. Walleye sat patiently on his haunches, watching carefully for anything that might come his way. With the wooden ladle, the old man fished a bone the size of a child's fist from the soup pot and put it on the floor. The dog waited until Meloux called him.

They ate without a word, but not in silence. The old man slurped from his spoon and lapped at the residue of soup along the edges of his lips. In the way of someone used to keeping company with himself, he occasionally mumbled toward his bowl. On the floor, Walleye gnawed greedily on the soup bone. When Meloux was finished, he took the pack of Lucky Strikes Cork had given him and drew out a cigarette. He offered the pack to Cork, then lit his own cigarette with a wooden kitchen match he struck on the underside of his chair. He settled back and seemed quite pleased.

"You make an old man feel pretty good, Corcoran O'Connor," he said. "It is a long hard way here even without snow, but you visit me often now." He gave Cork an ironic smile.

Cork leaned his forearms on the table and bent toward the old man. "Harlan Lytton is dead, Henry."

The old man took a long, slow puff from his cigarette.

"You're not surprised," Cork said.

"Death is no surprise to an old man like me. Being able to take a regular crap, now, there is a surprise."

"Why did you tell me about the Windigo calling his name? Did you think I could do something?"

"Once the Windigo has called a man's name, there's nothing anyone can do."

Cork sat back, eyed the old man, and took a long shot in the dark. "But you told Russell Blackwater the Windigo had called his name."

Something showed in the old man's face, a glimmer of concern, but it passed quickly.

Cork knew he'd hit home and he pressed Meloux. "The night I took you into town you went to the casino, but not to gamble. You wanted to talk with Russell Blackwater. Did you hear the Windigo call his name? Is that why you walked into town in the middle of a blizzard? To warn him?"

The old man took the cigarette from his lips and looked at Cork appreciatively. "The whites were wrong to kick you out as sheriff."

"Did he believe you?"

Meloux shrugged. "It makes no difference if he believes or not. He will still face the Windigo."

"Why warn him and not Lytton?"

"Vernon Blackwater's son is one of The People. Harlan Lytton was not."

"That's why you told me about Harlan? You thought I would warn him?"

"He was white and his heart was probably very

black"—the old man shrugged—"but he was still a man. The Windigo, that is something else."

"You know, Henry, if my grandmother hadn't been one of The People, I'd probably wonder about all this Windigo business."

"If your grandmother hadn't been one of The People, you would probably not be so smart," the old man said with a calm flourish of smoke.

Cork thanked Meloux for the soup and put on his coat to leave.

At the door the old man studied him hard. "This anger in your eyes, is it because you are hunting the Windigo?"

"I don't know what it is I'm hunting, Henry."

Meloux nodded thoughtfully, still looking keenly at Cork. "The Windigo was a man once. His heart was not always ice. What makes a man's heart turn to ice? I would think about that, and I would think about how to fight the Windigo."

"I thought you told me I wasn't the one to fight the Windigo."

Meloux shrugged. "I'm old. I'm not right as much as I used to be."

"Often enough, Henry," Cork replied.

From Meloux's he started across the ice, heading back toward town. A mile to the east he could see the inlet where Molly's sauna stood. He slowed and stopped, then turned in that direction. When she didn't answer his knock, he let himself in with the key on the nail under the steps. The cabin was cool. Molly kept it that way. Lately, whenever they'd crawled into bed, the sheets were cold at first and for the first few minutes they simply held each other while the bedding warmed around them. Cork walked the quiet cabin, taking in the silent disarray of Molly's life. The Sunday paper was folded on the coffee table near the big stone fireplace in the main room. On the floor beside a hand-sewn pillow sat an empty cup with a used tea bag in the saucer and next to it, lying facedown, a book called *The Tao of Loving*. A sweater lay thrown over the back of her rocking chair. He walked up the stairs. In the bathroom her cosmetics were scattered about the counter next to the sink. The lid was still off the Noxzema. Hairbrushes and combs stood together in a small clay pot she'd made herself in an art class at the community college. In the bedroom, the bed had been hastily made. Cork heard the sound of her old Saab coming down the lane. He headed downstairs and stepped into the kitchen as she came in the back door.

Molly glanced at him coldly and hung her coat. "What are you doing here?"

"I let myself in."

She brushed past him and went to the refrigerator. She took out a carton of cherry yogurt and grabbed a spoon from the drawer. She wore the jeans and the taupe sweater she'd waitressed in all morning. There was a spot of mustard on her right sleeve.

"You look good," he said.

"What did you expect? That I'd fall apart?" She gave him a brief appraisal. "You look like a bully just stole your lunch."

"About yesterday," he said cautiously. "I'm sorry. I didn't want to hurt you."

Molly pulled the lid off the yogurt and took a spoonful. "Why are you here?"

Cork shoved his hands into the pockets of his coat and stared at the scarred wooden floor. "I need to talk to someone."

"Find someone else." She turned her back to him and walked to the table.

"There isn't anyone else," he said. "I've lived here almost my whole life and I've got no one to talk to."

She slid a chair out with her foot and sat down heavily. "Try your wife."

"She's in love with someone else."

"I could've told you that."

Cork stared at her, bewildered.

"You know, Cork, for a smart man you're pretty stupid sometimes."

"You knew?"

"I suspected."

Cork felt fuzzy and a little numb, as if something were blocking the flow of blood to his brain. "How?"

"A feeling from the things you told me."

"Christ, I feel like such a fool."

"You're not the first." She considered him a moment, then put down the yogurt. "Would you like some tea?"

"Do you still have that whiskey?"

"Ginseng'll be better for you." She went to the cupboard. "Who is he?"

"Sandy Parrant."

"Is she planning on going with him to Washington?"

"She'd never do that," Cork said. "She'd never take the kids away."

Molly shrugged. "Love makes people do strange things. I ought to know."

Cork turned around and stared out the window. Snow was still falling, still very lightly. It would have been lovely if he hadn't felt so bad.

"I heard about Harlan Lytton," Molly said. She

moved to the stove for the kettle. "It didn't sound pretty."

"It wasn't."

"Any idea who killed him?"

"Not yet." He watched her familiar movements, but she was a distant figure now, on the far side of a chasm he'd created. "I don't think I'll stay for the tea."

"Cork," she said quickly as he turned to the door. "I didn't say anything about Jo because I didn't want you to think I was trying to turn you against her. I didn't want you to think I was just some sort of desperate husband-stealing bitch."

"I would never think that about you. You were the best thing in my life, Molly."

She fisted her hand on her hip and shot back, "Somehow I missed that part in our discussion yesterday."

"Yesterday wasn't about you. I hoped I could save my children from—I don't know—the inevitable."

"Children survive a lot, Cork. You and I both know that."

"I guess we do."

They fell quiet. Cork wanted to say he loved her. He wanted to ask her to forgive him. He wanted to lay his head against her breast and weep into her warm flesh and feel as connected to someone as he'd felt the night the grief passed through him when he hunted the big bear with Sam Winter Moon.

Molly crossed her arms and seemed to read his thoughts. "I told you there wasn't a swinging door here, Cork. I meant it."

"I understand."

"I don't think you do. You hurt me. You were ready to cut me out of your life like I was a rotten spot on an otherwise perfect apple."

He looked at the floor. "I've got no apple now. Only applesauce."

He glanced at her face. If there was a smile anywhere near, she hid it well.

"You've always made me laugh, Cork. That's not what I want now."

"What do you want?"

"To feel needed. To feel that you need me as much as you need air to breathe. I'm worth that." She pointed toward the cold outside. "Go on. Take some time to think about it."

He didn't need any time. Already he couldn't breathe. But he turned the knob anyway, because it was what Molly wanted, and he walked out the door.

CHAPTER 25

In the language of the Anishinaabe, December was called Manidoo-Gizisoons. The month of small spirits.

It was late afternoon by the time he entered the limits of Aurora. December 20. One day away from the shortest, darkest day of the year. The forecast was for continued snow, heavier during the evening, additional accumulations of up to three inches by morning.

Cork wished there were a forecast for his spirit. He felt the dark and the cold penetrating deep in him. He wondered when there would be warmth again, when there would be light. He also wondered if his ribs would ever stop hurting.

He parked in front of Sam's Place and stood a moment looking through falling snow at the geese who were bound to their small world of open water. In a strange way, he figured he knew what that was like. To have the world close down around you. He took his keys and moved to the door. It was already unlocked. He was careful not to look at the windows and wondered if even now he was being watched. He turned away casually, as if he'd changed his mind naturally, and he walked to the side of the Quonset hut; then he edged to the kitchen window that was covered with cardboard. He listened for a minute. Inside, just a couple of feet from his head, a cupboard door squeaked.

They'd looked for something after the judge was killed. Now Lytton was dead. Were they looking this time for something Lytton had? He tried to think of some plan, some way of trapping them. Then he heard glass shatter inside.

The sound of the breaking broke something in Cork. It was like the ripping of a membrane, a thin sheathing that had contained his outrage and his anger. His whole body drew taut and a bitter taste flooded his mouth. His home was being violated again. His whole life was being violated. He headed to the Bronco, took out the tire iron, and stepped to the front door. He took a deep, painful breath, clenched his teeth, kicked open the door, and rushed them.

Jenny crouched in the kitchen near the sink, picking up pieces of a broken glass. She cried out when Cork came at her, and she fell back, holding her arms up to protect herself. Cork stood over her with the tire iron raised.

"What are you doing here?" he asked, hoarse with the rage that still ran in his blood and with the pain that knifed at him from his ribs.

"I . . . I . . ." she stammered. Her eyes were full of terror. "I just wanted to help clean up."

Cork lowered the iron and held his side.

"I'm sorry, sweetheart. I'm sorry I scared you. You had me scared, too."

He glanced around. The place had been picked up. Everything was in order. Dishes sat dripping in the rack by the sink. White suds clung to Jenny's hands.

"Are you all right, Dad?" she asked, seeing how he held himself.

"Fine. Here, let me help you." He knelt carefully

and picked up the last pieces of the broken water glass and dropped them into the garbage can under the sink. "The place looks great. You've been here awhile."

She dried her hands on a dish towel. "I heard about the man who was killed last night. I'm scared for you, Dad."

"There's no reason to be, Jenny."

She stared at him. She had her mother's blue eyes and, normally, her mother's calm, self-assuredness reflected in them. But her eyes were afraid now.

"Somebody killed him," she pointed out. "And shot at you."

That was a point Cork couldn't argue. Still, he smiled reassuringly. "I'm sure I'm safe."

Jenny leaned against the counter, still watching him with her frightened blue eyes. "What's a Windigo?"

"Where'd you hear about that?"

"Around. What is it?"

"A story. That's all it is. Just a story."

Jenny finally looked down, studying her hands that were raw and red from the hot dishwater. "I want to stay here with you."

"Here?" He reached out and held her. "I'm flattered, honey, but I don't think that's such a good idea."

"Why not?"

"For one thing, I'm not the cook your aunt Rose is. I'm used to eating my own bad cooking, but I wouldn't take the chance of poisoning you."

"I'm serious."

"Okay. Let's sit down." He nodded toward the two chairs at the small kitchen table. He saw that Jenny had made a fruit bowl as a centerpiece. Cork had always kept the salt and pepper shakers there. He liked the colorful touch of the fruit. "I'll level with you," he said, taking her hands in his. "I'm concerned about Stevie and Anne. Things are rough enough for them with me gone. They look to you for a lot."

"I don't care."

"I know they're not your responsibility. But I need your help, Jenny. I need you to stay with your mom, to work to keep things together as much as you can. It's probably not a fair thing to ask, but I'm asking."

Her eyes were no longer afraid, but they seemed full of hurt. And their hurt pained him deeply.

"Things won't ever be like they used to, will they?" Jenny searched his face for the truth.

"No." He looked at his hands. Big hands. How useless a man's hands were, he thought, when it came to fixing the important things.

"'Things fall apart,'" she said in a small voice. "'The center will not hold.'"

He gave her a questioning look.

"Yeats," she explained. "W.B."

"'All the king's horses and all the king's men,'" he replied. "Dumpty, H."

Although a tear crawled down one cheek like a small snail, she smiled. "By the way," she said, taking care of the tear with a swipe of her finger, "there's a message on your answering machine."

"You listened?"

She gave him an innocent little shrug.

"What did it say?"

"You can have your gun back."

He dropped Jenny off at home, then stopped by the sheriff's office to retrieve his revolver. While he was there, he used the pay phone to call the casino.

"I'd like to speak with Russell Blackwater, please. Tell him its Corcoran O'Connor." He waited a full minute before Blackwater came on the line.

"What do you want, O'Connor?" Blackwater's tone wasn't civil at all.

"We need to talk."

"About what?"

"Something of concern to us both."

"And what's that?"

"The Windigo," Cork said.

Russell Blackwater's office was decorated with Native American art. On the walls were hung a series of idealized paintings by William Westsky, a Shinnob out of Canada, showing pristine forests and lakes with the faint faces of The People woven into the clouds, watching the land below like good overseers. On Blackwater's desk stood a dark wood sculpture depicting a member of the Grand Medicine Society lifting the pipe in the Pipe Dance of Peace. The desk was big, dark red wood. The surface wore a lustrous shine and the Midewiwin was reflected perfectly below himself, as if offering the pipe to the underworld. Running the length of the back wall of the office was a tinted window overlooking the gambling floor. Blackwater was standing there with his hands in his pockets, looking down at the action. He wore an expensive gray suit, white shirt, blue tie.

"Busy night," Cork observed.

"A good night," Blackwater said.

"For those who win."

"The People win," Blackwater said, turning fully to Cork. "What do you want, O'Connor?"

Cork sat down in a big, brown leather chair. He

settled back and crossed his legs. "Harlan Lytton was killed last night."

"I know. Can't say I'm sorry."

"Did you also know that Henry Meloux heard the Windigo call Lytton's name?"

Blackwater shrugged as if it made no difference one way or the other. "Meloux's an old man. The things old men hear and see can't always be trusted."

"Henry was here the night the judge was killed."

"So?"

"He came to warn you. He heard the Windigo call your name, too."

Blackwater looked unconcerned. "I'm a modern Shinnob. Tell me the legislature is monkeying with the gambling laws and I'll be nervous. But I'm not afraid of an old myth."

Cork stared pointedly at Blackwater, then shook his head in a disappointed way. "I never thought I'd see you looking so much like a businessman, Russell. I remember you wearing deerskin during the Trail of Tears march on Washington."

"I'm still marching," Blackwater insisted. "The clothes don't make any difference."

"I was at Sandy Parrant's house the other day. After the judge's memorial service. Didn't see you there."

"What are you getting at?"

"But I understand Sandy Parrant was at the funeral of your father. What do you make of that? You work with these people. You're making these people rich. You show them respect, but do they reciprocate? As I understand it, Sandy Parrant went out of his way to make sure a lot of people would feel comfortable being at his father's memorial service. But he didn't extend the courtesy to you, did he?"

"Like an invitation?" Blackwater said with sarcasm.

"Whatever."

"What makes you think I'd want to go?"

"I don't know," Cork said. He fingered the sculpture of the Midewiwin on Blackwater's desk, ran his hand casually down the sleek, polished wood. "An invitation at least would be nice. The white man and the red man in enterprise together. You know, hunting the new buffalo like brothers."

Although Russell Blackwater held very still, Cork saw the tendons in his neck go taut. His eyes changed, too, in the way they regarded Cork, watching him closely. His voice was hard, the words tense and spoken carefully.

"Before this casino was built, unemployment on the reservation was seventy percent. Nearly a quarter of our families were below poverty level. Two years ago one Anishinaabe student graduated from Aurora High School. Ten others dropped out. This year four will graduate and no one's dropped out. We have a free health clinic on the drawing board that will be staffed by The People. We'll have a real school soon. We've started looking at a drug-and-alcohol rehabilitation program to be run by us, not by the Public Health Service." He sat up rigidly with his fingers digging into the padded arms of his chair. "That's what I wanted from this enterprise, not an invitation to white men's homes."

Cork nodded and held up his hands in surrender. "Okay by me. Just making a comment. By the way, why don't you unbutton your coat? Looks a little uncomfortable to me."

"My coat's fine."

"You always carry a piece these days?"

Blackwater tugged at his suit coat, straightening the way it fell over his chest and the shoulder holster he was wearing. "When I'm working. It's licensed."

"Not thinking of shooting an old myth, are you?" Cork got up and headed for the door. "By the way, the sheriff's probably going to want to know where you were when Lytton was shot."

"Why?"

"Because I intend to tell him to ask. 'Night, Russell."

CHAPTER 26

The judge's estate occupied the whole tip of North Point. The property was shaped roughly like a fingernail, and along the shoreline grew a wall of tall pines. Cork guided the Bronco off the ice through a gap between the boathouse and the trees and parked where the vehicle couldn't be seen. He got out and waded up the steep slope of the grounds toward the house. In the stillness he could hear the steady whine of a snowmobile cutting across the ice, heading back toward Aurora from one of the many ice huts on the lake. He looked back, but the darkness and the gentle snowfall kept him from seeing anything.

The patio doors were locked, but Cork was surprised to discover that a small pane in the mullioned window of the kitchen door had been broken and the door was unlocked. Carefully he pushed it open. From inside came a startling clatter. He stepped hurriedly into the kitchen and found that he'd knocked over a brown paper bag full of empty aluminum cans that appeared to have been saved for recycling.

The kitchen smelled of garbage souring somewhere out of sight. In the living room, the curtains were open, letting in a pale white light from the snow outside. The house was absolutely still and very cool.

He had only a vague idea of what he was looking for. The judge hadn't been a tremendously charismatic or beloved man, but he had nonetheless been a powerful political figure in the Iron Range. Power had many sources besides charisma. Money was one. Although Robert Parrant had been a wealthy man, Cork figured it would have taken a hell of a lot more than even the judge had to maintain his hold on a population as independent as that of the Iron Range. Power also came from leverage. The bloody folder with the judge's doodling all over the cover, the folder that held such graphic evidence of Jo's infidelity, that was one kind of leverage, and was certainly in keeping with the character of the judge. It was entirely possible that the judge's death had something to do with that kind of leverage.

Cork crept down the short hallway to the study. The curtains were closed and the room quite dark. He made his way to the desk and fumbled to turn on the lamp. When the light came on, he heard a discreet cough behind him. He turned quickly and found himself staring across the room at Wally Schanno, who stood in front of a wall lined with bookshelves.

"Evening, Cork," Schanno said. In one hand he held a flashlight. In the other was a gun pointed directly at Cork. Stacks of books pulled from the shelves lay on the floor at Schanno's feet.

"Library closed?" Cork asked.

Schanno glanced down at the books, but didn't smile.

Cork jabbed his thumb over his shoulder in the direction of the kitchen. "Window's broken. Wasn't me."

"I know," Schanno said.

"You don't seem surprised to see me."

"It's been a tough week. Not much surprises me now."

"What are you doing here, Wally?"

"Police quarantine. I'm allowed here. The real question is what are you doing here?"

Cork glanced around the room. "Lights off. Bookshelves ransacked. And you even have a thermos of coffee. What's going on, Wally?"

Schanno narrowed his eyes severely. "I look at things on the surface and what I see is you, Cork. The judge is dead and there you are. Lytton's killed and there you are again. On the surface, looks like I ought to suspect you like hell."

"Do you really think I killed those men?"

"Doesn't matter what I think. A man can always be wrong in his thinking. I try to look at the facts." He holstered his gun. "I sent Ed out this afternoon to check on your story about Henry Meloux and that—what did you call it?"

"Windigo."

"Yeah, that. Old Meloux told Ed he didn't know what the hell you were talking about."

Cork relaxed against the judge's big desk. "That doesn't surprise me. Ed's white."

"The old man lied?"

"Sure. If you were crazy enough to indict me, he'd tell the truth. In the meantime, there's no reason. He knows you'd just look at him like he was goofy."

"Or like maybe he had something to do with killing Lytton," Schanno suggested.

"I'd consider a lot of other people before I'd consider him," Cork replied.

Schanno took a deep breath, then reached down toward the floor for his steel thermos and poured himself some hot coffee. "You told me a lot of stories without much of anything to back them up. The break-in at your place. The condition of the judge's body. Somebody shooting at you out at Lytton's."

"They weren't stories, Wally."

Schanno took a sip of his coffee, drawing his throat tight against the heat. "You're a hard man to disbelieve." He nodded in the direction of the kitchen. "I came here the night after the judge died to look things over for myself, see if I could find anything we missed. I surprised somebody coming in the side door. Don't know who. They got away. I've been here a lot since then, checking to make sure things stay secure, and still looking for anything that might support your claim about the judge's body being moved."

Cork looked down at the books pulled from the shelves. "Find anything there?"

Schanno set his coffee on an empty shelf and walked to the big desk. The mess of the judge's death hadn't been cleaned away. The Minnesota map on the wall was still splattered with blood and bits of what once had been a complex—and devious—brain. Traces of blood streaked the wall toward a pooling on the floor. It had all gone brown now, clotted over. Schanno stepped carefully. He slid open and then shut drawer after drawer in frustration.

"I'm just about down to checking the cobwebs in the corners. Nothing, Cork. Not a goll darn thing anywhere. If someone moved the judge, they did a pretty good job of covering up after themselves and covering up the reason why." He arched his back, stretching in a tired way. "I got my hands so full at the moment, I can't sleep at all. I've posted Cy Borkmann over to Harlan Lytton's cabin nights to make sure nothing's disturbed there. He's pissed about that. Arletta's staying with her sister. She's got it in her head I've deserted her and taken the kids somewhere. Hell Hanover's on my ass. Says I'm just another example of incompetent, interfering law enforcement.

It strikes me that man just doesn't like cops. Cork, I know there's something going on in Aurora. I just can't get a handle on what it is." Wally Schanno looked straight at him with his honest gray eyes that were sunk deep with exhaustion. "And you still haven't told me what you're doing here."

Cork heard the sound of a snowmobile again, closer this time, cutting along the ice around North Point. It sounded small and distant, like a pesky mosquito. He thought about the folder with Jo's name on it, the one that had first belonged to the judge, and didn't know how to tell a man—Schanno or anybody else—what was in it. He couldn't even be sure there was any significance in the folder having been in the judge's hands at one time. Finally, he said, "Pretty much the same reason you are, Wally. To see about the judge's body being moved."

"You're sure that's it?"

"As sure as I am of anything."

Schanno grunted unhappily. "You'd best leave this to me. I'm the one on the payroll."

Cork left the study and headed down the hallway with Schanno following. At the staircase, Schanno halted and said, "Better go out the front. Sounds like you already made a mess of the kitchen back there. Close the door on your way out. Me, I've got to take a good long piss."

Cork took in the empty house, where the feel of death was as real as any of the furnishings. "Be careful, Wally," he cautioned.

"Nothing to it. I been pissing all my life." Schanno managed a grin.

Cork stepped out the front door. The snow was falling harder, and he could barely see beyond the hedges that edged the front of the estate. Slowly he made his way around the house down the slope of the grounds to the Bronco, but he didn't get in right away. The air was still, the snow tumbling straight down in huge beautiful flakes. He lit a cigarette and turned his face upward so that the snow settled cold on his forehead and cheeks and melted there.

He smoked and thought about truth.

He'd learned early not to invest a lot of emotion in thinking about the truth in a crime. As a cop, he'd gathered evidence that had been used to guess at the truth, but in the end responsibility for assembling the pieces and nailing truth to the wall was in the hands of others—lawyers, judges, and juries. Truth became a democratic process, the will of twelve. He'd been burned when he cared too deeply. As a result, he'd trained himself to remain a little distant in his emotional involvement on a case. In the end, the outcome was out of his hands, and to allow himself to believe too strongly in the absoluteness of a thing he couldn't control was useless. He felt different now. Desperate in a way. This time he had to hold the truth in his own hands like a beating heart.

In the stillness, two gunshots came from the house, two clear pops like kernels of corn. Cork threw down his cigarette, reached into the glove box of his Bronco, and drew out the revolver he'd picked up earlier at the sheriff's office. He started around the boathouse and up the backyard at a dead run, stumbling in the deep snow. When he reached the door to the kitchen, he stopped. It was wide open. He hesitated before plunging into the dark of the house and he listened.

Deep inside, someone swore painfully.

"Wally?" he called.

"Damn it, Cork!" Schanno hollered.

Cork ran in, knocking cans across the kitchen floor.

Schanno sat at the bottom of the stairs holding his right thigh with both hands. Cork could see the dark blood welling up, spilling between Schanno's fingers.

"Bastard sneaked up," Schanno said through clenched teeth.

"I'll call you in." Cork turned quickly to the phone on the stand beside the banister.

"No! Go after him! I'll call myself in. Go on before he's away clean."

Cork hesitated a moment.

"Go on, damn you, I'm not dying!"

Cork dashed back out the kitchen door. Tracks in the snow led toward the row of pine trees that lined the northern shore of the estate. Before he could follow, the rough cough of a snowmobile engine trying to turn over came from beyond the trees. Cork ran for the Bronco. As he opened the door, he heard the engine of the snowmobile leap into a steady whine. He didn't have much time. If the snowmobile headed north across the lake toward national forest land, he'd probably lose it. It would have too great a headstart and once it hit the trails in the woods, he wouldn't be able to follow anyway.

But he was lucky. Just as he turned the key in the Bronco, the dark shape of the little machine shot past on the ice behind the boathouse, heading toward Aurora.

The snowmobile was running with its headlights on, but Cork drove the Bronco dark. The snowmobile headed straight for town with Cork less than fifty yards behind and gaining. If his luck held, he could close the gap completely before the driver of the snowmobile was even aware he was being followed.

His luck didn't hold. When he was within thirty yards, the headlights of the little machine went dark and the snowmobile suddenly tunneled into the snowy night and was lost to him. He switched on his own headlights, but it was too late. The snowmobile was nowhere to be seen. He braked and the Bronco spun on the ice. It did a full 360 degrees before it came to a stop. Cork rolled his window down and listened. He heard the whine of the snowmobile cutting east, heading toward the reservation, the nearest forest land, where thick woods would swallow it quickly. Cork turned the Bronco in that direction.

He kicked his lights up to high beam. The flurry of snowflakes flew at him like a swarm of white moths. He wanted to floor the accelerator, but he was heading into a section of the lake popular with ice fisherman and he didn't want to risk a collision with a shanty. He kept his window rolled down and leaned his head out. Although the wind rushed at him with a dull roar, he could still hear ahead of him the persistent high pitch of the snowmobile feverishly speeding away.

Then he heard something else. The sound of impact. Splintering wood followed by the thumping of heavy metal, and finally silence. He slowed and listened. The night on the lake had become still again, deceptively peaceful.

He crept the Bronco ahead. Within a minute his lights picked up the wreckage of a small shanty that lay on its side amid fragments of splintered boards. One wall was caved in, a ragged hole torn open. Cork couldn't see the snowmobile, but from the line of scattered debris, he could guess the trajectory it must have taken after glancing off the shanty. He turned the Bronco slowly until the headlights swung onto the snowmobile. It was standing upright, as if it had simply been parked. Vehicular accidents were like that sometimes. A car could flip two or three times and come to rest on its wheels as if nothing had happened. The driver of the snowmobile was nowhere to be seen.

Cork gripped the .38 and stepped out. He looked carefully around, saw no one, listened, and heard only the distant, steady thrum behind him of a freight train moving slowly through Aurora. He'd taken a few cautious steps toward the snowmobile when a figure in goggles and a green parka popped up from behind the machine, laid an arm across the hood, and pulled off two rounds before Cork could move. The headlight beside him exploded and he felt a numbing blow to his right hand. He hit the snow and rolled under the Bronco. His hand had no feeling and it no longer held the revolver. The green parka let loose another round. Cork heard the bullet chisel into the ice near the rear tire. He reached out and swept through the snow with his left hand, desperately searching for the gun.

Illuminated in the beam of the remaining headlight, the green parka straddled the snowmobile again. The engine kicked over twice, then caught. The machine swung out of the light, following an arc into the darkness that would take it back toward Aurora.

Cork scrambled from under the Bronco. He wanted to find his gun, but knew it would take precious time. He jumped back in behind the wheel and cried out when he wrapped his right hand around the knob of the gear shift. In the glow from his dashboard lights, he could see something protruding from the glove on his hand between his thumb and index finger. He gave a quick, agonizing jerk and pulled out a jagged piece of glass two inches long. He hadn't been hit by the round, but by a chunk of the shattered headlight. Although his glove was soaked with blood, he found he could manage with the glass fragment out. Using the heel of his hand he pushed the Bronco into gear, swung the vehicle around and headed in pursuit of the green parka.

In the chaos of the chase Cork had lost a feel for exactly where on the lake he was. The snow curtained the shoreline and he had nothing from which to get his bearings. He knew he was headed in the direction of Aurora, but he had only a general sense of distance. Although he wanted desperately to catch the snowmobile, he resisted the temptation to bear down on the accelerator. The near disaster with the ice hut had been a resounding caution against blind speed. Also, his luck had returned in a way. In the collision, the snowmobile had sprung an oil leak and was leaving a clear, black trail for Cork to follow across the lake.

He was intent on the trail of oil when out of the corner of his eye he caught a flash of orange at the far right fringe of his headlight beam. He realized it was one of the signs warning of open water ahead, and he pumped his brakes, fighting to keep from sliding into an uncontrolled spin as he attempted to turn the Bronco. He felt the wheels drift over the ice as the vehicle slid sideways. A brief, panicked vision came to him of the Bronco gliding unchecked off the ice and plunging into the black depths of Iron Lake. He eased the wheel into the spin and managed to regain control. From behind the curtain of falling snow ahead, the blackness of the open water came at him like a gaping mouth. He continued to slow and to bring the Bronco around. Then he heard the ice groan and crack beneath him. Steadily he pushed down on the accelerator, running parallel for a moment to the open water, trying to keep the weight of the Bronco moving ahead of the breaking ice. His right hand ached, but he held tight and carefully brought the wheel around until he was moving back to safety. He made a wide full circle. When he came across the black train of oil, he centered it in the beam of the headlight, illuminating the stretch of ice between him and the open water. He killed the engine and got out. He could hear wild flailing in the water ahead. From the glove compartment he grabbed a flashlight.

He stopped well back from the edge of the ice. Using the flashlight, he located the snowmobile that appeared to have skipped twenty yards over the surface of the water before it stopped and began to sink. The hood was still above water, the green parka clinging to it desperately. Cork spun around and began to run, cutting the darkness right and left with the beam of his flashlight. He found what he was looking for, a safety station. He pulled the white life ring loose and the loops of yellow rope, then he ran back. The green parka was still holding to the hood of the snowmobile, although there was not much left above water. Cork unlooped the rope. He tried grasping the ring with his right hand, but the wound from the glass chunk hurt too much. He switched it to his left, brought it back, and heaved it. This time the pain was in his ribs. The ring fell several yards short and to the right.

"Swim for it!" Cork yelled.

The green parka started for the ring but stopped inexplicably and grabbed again for the snowmobile.

Cork hauled in the rope. He held the ring in his right hand this time and chucked it underhand, crying out as the pain knifed into him. The ring arched and fell within easy reach of the figure in the water. The green parka grabbed the ring just as the snowmobile slid from sight.

Cork began to draw in the rope hand over hand. But something was wrong. Although it hurt like hell to pull, he shouldn't have felt much resistance. Yet tug as he might, he couldn't budge the green parka from the spot where the snowmobile had gone under. Then to his shock, he felt the line slipping from his grasp. Despite his tortured ribs, he looped the rope around his own body. The pull at the other end began to drag him toward the water. He was confused. The life ring should have come easily, but it was as if Cork were in a battle with something that wanted the green parka more than he did. Vainly he dug at the ice with his heels. When he looked up, he saw that the green parka was grasping the ring desperately, beating at the water, and was still being dragged inexorably under. Cork strained against the rope as he was inched nearer and nearer the edge. He heard the thin ice crack under his weight and knew that in a moment the water would have him, too.

He let go. The green parka slid from sight, swallowed by the lake as if by a hungry giant. The rope continued to jerk for another minute, and then it was still.

Cork's right hand throbbed. His ribs hurt so much that he could barely breathe. He realized he was shivering, although he wasn't cold. He could hear the wail of sirens somewhere off to his right. Wally Schanno was getting help. He stared at the black water. White flakes of snow drifted down onto the surface and melted. The lake looked so calm, so peaceful, as if swallowing a man was nothing.

The flashing lights brought out a lot of spectators from town. They gathered along the shoreline and watched as if it were an event. Cork spotted Sandy Parrant speaking with some of the deputies and nodding authoritatively as they gestured toward the open water. Their eyes met briefly, coldly, then Parrant left. Cork refused to leave until the divers from the fire department had brought the body up. Near midnight, they hauled it dripping onto the ice and laid it in the glare of the floodlights that had been set up a safe distance from the perimeter of the water. The divers said they had to cut a shoe free; the lace had become entangled in the track of the snowmobile. Although the body had been in the water more than an hour, standard procedure required the paramedics to attempt revival. They pumped on his chest and tried administering oxygen, but even a blind man could see that their efforts were useless.

The face of the man in the green parka was a lighter color than Cork had ever believed it could be. And maybe more peaceful. Russell Blackwater, the man with the hungry hunter's eyes, would hunt the earth no more.

CHAPTER 27

He slept late, slept through the ringing of the telephone, thought he heard a knocking at the door and slept through that, too. It was cold in the Quonset hut but warm under his blanket, and he didn't want to leave that very small place where he curled for safety. Finally the deep, ceaseless throbbing of his hand forced him to get up. He took a couple of the extra-strength ibuprofen the resident on duty at the community hospital emergency ward had given him when he stitched up his hand. The doctor had also x-rayed the place along Cork's ribs where his skin had turned a deep brooding purple. Nothing broken. In the bathroom, he studied himself in the mirror. He looked old, a decade older than a week before. His eyes were dark circled, his face puffy. There seemed to be a brutish aspect in his appearance that he'd never recognized before, and he felt a cold, abiding despair sunk all the way to his bones. Who was this man staring at him? What was he becoming?

It was late morning when he stepped outside. Snow no longer fell, but the sky was heavily overcast. A wind blew across the lake, harsh and steady, and tore at the edges of a note he found tacked to his door. "Call me." It was signed by Father Tom Griffin. Cork checked the headlight that had been shattered by the bullet from Blackwater's gun. It would have to be fixed, but he wasn't in any hurry. He went to the storage shed and hauled out his auger and ice spud. He loaded them in the back of the Bronco, and he put his fishing gear there, too. He went once more into Sam's Place to fill a bucket with grain, and then he headed down to the lake. The geese were gone. After last night, that didn't surprise him. He stood a moment, looking across the choppy, gray water. There'd been something welcoming about it when the geese were there. Now the open water seemed only menacing. He emptied the bucket and left it in the snow.

He hated hospitals. He couldn't get beyond the idea of them representing death. In his experience, people went to the hospital to die. His father had died in a hospital with Cork helpless beside him. He hated the sinister cleanliness of their look and smell, the hush of them as if holding a big insidious secret. In so many ways, the scent of burning cedar and sage and the chant of the Midewiwin seemed more real and hopeful.

Wally Schanno was no longer in the Aurora Community Hospital. Cork spoke with the resident, a young man named Dr. Ferman, the same one who'd stitched up Cork's hand and who'd been on duty since early morning. He looked even more tired than Cork. Schanno had checked himself out several hours ago against the doctor's advice. The gunshot wound was clean, no bone or artery hit, but Dr. Ferman would have liked a day or so for observation anyway. The doctor said that a little before noon Sigurd Nelson visited Schanno, and a short time later the sheriff told the station nurse he was leaving. Dr. Ferman had come down and argued with him.

"He's a grown man. He can make his own decisions." The exhausted resident shrugged. "He signed the waiver. My hands are clean."

Cork called the sheriff's office from a hospital pay phone. Schanno was there.

"Get over here," the sheriff said, sounding tired but pretty excited for a man with a hole recently torn through his leg. "I've got something you'll want to see."

Sandy Parrant sat in a chair near Schanno's desk. He looked at Cork with a blank expression. Cork returned the look in kind.

"Hope you don't mind if I don't get up, Cork," Schanno said with a big grin and a nod toward his leg, which was hidden by the desk. Leaning against the wall directly behind him was a pair of crutches. "Come on in. Hang up your coat."

"How's the leg feel?" Cork asked.

"I'm on painkiller right now, so not so bad. The doctor said I'd have a couple of scars, but nothing to worry about."

"Voters like scars on their lawmen," Cork said.

Schanno gave an appreciative laugh.

Cork said, "Those painkillers sure seem to help your humor, Wally."

"It's not the painkillers. I think I'm just about ready to close the book on what's been going on around here. It's pretty simple in the end."

Cork sat in an old wooden chair near the window. He crossed his legs and looked at the two men. He saw Schanno's eyes shift for the briefest instant toward a small, white three-drawer filing cabinet sitting on the floor near Parrant. It was out of place with the tall green cabinets in which the sheriff kept the regular files.

"Any of your people find my thirty-eight last night out where Blackwater collided with the ice hut?" Cork asked.

"I don't know. Check with the desk officer on your way out." Schanno seemed irritated that Cork had jumped to a different track suddenly, but the pleased look came back to him as he went on. "I found something very interesting this morning. A folder Harlan Lytton had that I think explains everything."

"One file," Cork considered. "And it explains everything?"

"Have a look for yourself," Schanno said.

He picked up a manila folder in front of him and offered it to Cork. The typewritten name on the folder, read "Blackwater, R." Inside were several pages of computer printout with figures and money amounts arranged under headings and columns that clearly dealt with the Chippewa Grand Casino. In several places the figures in the columns had been highlighted with a yellow marker.

Midway through the pages, Cork glanced up, questioningly.

"I know. They don't look like much," Schanno admitted. "I wasn't sure about them either. So I asked Sandy here to take a look, considering his association with the casino."

Cork swung his gaze over to Parrant.

"It doesn't take a genius," Parrant said, "to see that the figures have been juggled. A good accountant would spot it eventually. Or someone who knows the casino operation well. Like Dad or me."

"Embezzlement?" Cork asked.

Parrant nodded. "From just the cursory look I took, I'd say at least a hundred thousand. A complete audit will probably turn up a lot more."

"How did he expect to get away with it?" Cork asked. "If you saw it right off?"

"Regulations regarding Indian-run casinos are extremely lax. An audit wouldn't necessarily take place for years. We tried to negotiate a contract with the Iron Lake band that would give management responsibility to Great North, because we have all the business expertise they need. They chose to manage it themselves, with Russell Blackwater at the helm. This is the result." Parrant shook his head disdainfully.

"How'd Lytton get hold of this report?"

Parrant shrugged. "Paid off someone in the business office. It wouldn't be that hard."

Schanno sat back in his chair, looking pleased. "I told you the ATF was interested in Lytton and the Minnesota Civilian Brigade. They believed money had become suddenly available to finance arms. I figure Lytton was blackmailing Blackwater. Sure would be a good way to come by lots of untraceable income."

"So you think Blackwater killed Lytton to end the blackmail," Cork said.

"I think once Jack the Ripper was out of the way, it looked like a piece of cake to Blackwater. If the Ripper had still been alive, maybe Lytton would be, too."

The accusation in Schanno's words wasn't wasted on Cork.

"I'm taking Cy Borkmann off his surveillance of Lytton's cabin," Schanno went on. "He'll be happy he can sleep at home nights. Maybe I can sleep now, too."

Parrant stood up and put on his coat. "If you don't

need me anymore, I'd like to get back to the office. I think I've done what I can in all this."

"Thanks for your help, Sandy. I'll be in touch."

Parrant offered Cork a cool nod in parting.

"Crazy world, Cork," Wally Schanno observed after Parrant was gone. He swiveled in his chair, grimaced a little and held his leg a moment. Cork saw the distortion under his pants that was the thick rounding of bandages about his thigh. "Crazy world," Schanno went on, "but it makes a lot more sense to me now than it did yesterday."

"Seems that way," Cork said.

"Seems?" Schanno shot him an unpleasant look. "What do you mean by that?"

"Where'd you get this folder, Wally?"

"Like I said, Lytton had it."

"Where?"

"Does that matter?"

"It might. Did Sigurd bring you the file?"

"Sigurd?"

"They told me at the hospital our coroner visited you this morning. You left right after. Did he bring you the file?"

"In a manner of speaking." He reached into his desk drawer and brought out a key that he handed to Cork. "He brought me that."

The key was silver with "Aurora U-Store" engraved on the head along with the number 213.

"He found it on Lytton when he took a look at the body in his official capacity. My men must've missed it."

"So you went over and found the shed that fit the key."

"Exactly. The file was there."

"All by itself? Just waiting for you to pick it up?"

"No. I had to do some digging. Lytton had a lot of equipment in the shed. A slew of eavesdropping equipment, fancy camera apparatus."

"And that?" Cork pointed toward the white filing cabinet he'd noticed earlier.

"And that," Schanno admitted.

"Mind if I look at it?"

The sheriff considered it a moment. "I don't see why not. Maybe it'll help you understand my dilemma."

Cork opened the top drawer. It was full of folders like the one on Russell Blackwater. He recognized many of the names on the folder labels.

"Try the middle drawer, midway back," Schanno suggested.

Cork checked the drawer, found a folder marked "O'Connor, C." He pulled it out. It was thin. Inside were a couple of photographs, enlarged. Of Molly and him embracing naked on the shore by her sauna. Like the photos of Jo and Parrant, they'd been taken from somewhere out on the lake at night.

Schanno rocked back carefully. "You know the equipment in Lytton's unit at the Aurora U-Store was pretty sophisticated stuff. A lot of those files have photographs more or less like those. I'm sure they were shot by Harlan Lytton. All of the subjects have been caught in some indiscretion, things the folks here in Aurora would love to chew on for a while, but nothing really criminal, so far as I've been able to see. Blackwater's file was different."

"You think Lytton was blackmailing all these people?"

"Was he blackmailing you?"

"No."

"Then he probably wasn't. Kept it limited to where

he could make the most with the least difficulty. Black-water got a lot from his embezzling. Enough to share easily with Harlan Lytton."

"You really think Lytton was smart enough to figure out the thing with Blackwater and the casino?"

"Look at those files, Cork. The man was used to nosing through other people's crap. Man like that probably knows where to look for the worst."

Cork had to agree. Lytton was just that kind of man. "What do you think about Blackwater? What was he doing at the judge's?"

Schanno's hand instinctively sought out his bandaged leg and felt it gently. "I read your statement this morning. You told Blackwater last night at the casino that you were going to have me check out his whereabouts on the night Lytton was killed. I think Blackwater followed you. I think he planned to kill you to keep from putting me onto him. He saw you go in the side door. He just didn't see you go out the front. Bastard shot me by mistake."

"I suppose I ought to thank you, then," Cork said. "You probably saved my life."

Schanno waved it off. "Getting things back to normal around here is all I want."

Cork closed the folder but didn't return it to the drawer. "Will things ever be back to normal, Wally? Seems to me when you found this file cabinet, you latched onto a real Pandora's box. Now that you've opened it, can you close it again?"

Schanno looked uneasy. "I don't know. I figure the worst is over. I'm not sure what purpose would be served by bringing all this to light. Seems like it would only lead to a lot of decent folks getting hurt. So far as I know, only you and me know what's in there. I'd just as soon keep it that way." He nodded toward the cabinet. "Whyn't you put the folder back, Cork."

Cork slipped it in where he'd found it, then spotted a folder not far behind with the name "Parrant, S." He pulled the folder out.

"Cork!" Schanno hollered.

Cork ignored Schanno and opened the folder.

"Goddamn you, Cork, get outta there!" Schanno was struggling to stand, grabbing at the crutches that leaned against the wall behind him.

There were several photographs inside. Shots like those he'd seen before. Of trysting around Parrant's hot tub. Although several different women were involved, none of them was Jo. Cork recognized a couple. Parrant's secretary, Helen Barnes. Sue Jacobson, the chancellor of Aurora Community College. Unlike Jo, they were not married. Cork noted quickly the time date at the bottom of each photo. They'd all been taken before Parrant began his affair with Jo. From the looks of it, the man had been faithful. In his way. That there were no pictures of Jo surprised Cork. But he was also relieved since Schanno had undoubtedly already looked at the folder.

Schanno grabbed the folder angrily from Cork's hands. His face was contorted with outrage and pain.

"That was uncalled for, damn you, Cork! I ought to have your sorry carcass thrown in jail."

Schanno shoved the pictures back into Parrant's folder and sat on the file cabinet. He squeezed his eyes shut a moment and held his leg. He breathed deeply, easing out the pain. When he opened his eyes again and looked at Cork, all the euphoria was gone. "Get outta here before I have you arrested."

Cork took his leather jacket from the coat tree and reached for the doorknob.

"Cork?" Schanno's voice was ragged with irritation and pain. He'd moved himself onto his crutches and was leaning on them heavily. "What would you do if you were me?"

"I'd be tempted to burn them," Cork answered honestly. "Save myself the worry over whose lives are ruined by what might come to light. But then, I'm not the sheriff, Wally, so I'm not even going to think about that."

He left Schanno's office and checked with the desk officer on his way out. No one had found his revolver.

CHAPTER 28

Maiden Cove was on reservation land just west of the state forest. Formed by a rugged arm of dark gray rock that nearly cut off the small inlet from the rest of the lake, accessible only by water and an unmarked inland trail, the cove was nearly invisible to those who did not know where to look. It had always been a special place in Cork's thinking. Before his father was killed, they had often canoed in with Sam Winter Moon and camped there. Cork loved to jump off the gray rock that jutted up a dozen feet above the water. The cove was surprisingly deep. He had wonderful memories of the cool, still water in summer and of swimming deep among the big rocks on the bottom, where the refracted sunlight turned everything a rich green-gold. Life seemed simple then—the quiet of the woods and lake, a welcoming campfire, and the two men he loved most still alive.

That's what Cork wanted. Everything simple again.

With an ice spud he chipped a hole eight inches wide through ice that was more than half a foot thick. He cleared the ice chunks from the water with a plastic skimmer, then dropped a little vegetable oil onto the surface to keep the water from refreezing quickly. On a small Russian spoon, he put a grub, then sank it with a two-pound test line. He settled himself on a folding canvas chair. Holding his jigging rod in one hand, he reached into the deep pocket of his coat and brought out a bottle of peppermint schnapps.

He opened the bottle, but before he had a chance to take a drink, the grind of a snowmobile engine came from a long way off. He hoped it would move on, pass the cove by. In a few minutes, all the rocks and trees rattled with the incessant whine of the little engine. Cork watched the snowmobile shoot through the narrow opening, swing toward him, and come to a stop a few yards away. It was an old machine. The oldest Cork knew of in Tamarack County. St. Kawasaki dismounted, lifted his goggles, and walked toward Cork.

"What are you doing here?" Cork asked, not in a friendly way.

"I thought you might need someone to talk to." He adjusted the black patch over his right eye.

"How'd you find me?"

"Jo told me this was your favorite spot. I took a chance."

Cork glanced behind him at the old Kawasaki. "I thought that machine was dead."

The priest smiled and shrugged. "That's why I call it Lazarus." He saw the bottle in Cork's hand. "Mind if I take a shot of that? It's a long, cold way out here."

Cork handed him the schnapps. The priest took a swallow and gave the bottle back.

"Nice place," Tom Griffin said, surveying the cove. "I wasn't sure if I could find it. Are they biting?"

"Not yet." Cork jigged the line, drawing the baited spoon upward several times, then he let it settle back.

"What are you fishing for?" the priest asked.

"What are you?" Cork replied.

St. Kawasaki smiled. "I thought you might need to talk."

"Nothing to talk about. It's all settled. Bullets and lawyers, between them they've got a monopoly on the resolution of conflict." Cork took a long drink of schnapps, then handed the bottle back to the priest.

"If everything's settled, what harm can a little talking do?"

"What good can it do?" Cork pulled out his Lucky Strikes, took off his gloves, and lit a cigarette. "Let me ask you a question."

"Shoot."

"Do you believe in God?"

St. Kawasaki looked amused. "Hell of a question to ask a priest."

Cork carefully watched the end of his rod, a spring device that acted as a bobber. It hadn't moved at all in the time he'd been there. "I'm asking because I've been a cop most of my life, but I don't believe in justice anymore. I just wondered if the same was true in your work."

"Why wouldn't it be? Priests are only human. We question, doubt, even grow a little despondent at times because what the world shoves at us doesn't seem to bear much mark of the divine." The priest held the bottle toward the gray sky and squinted his one eye, as if making some kind of judgment about the schnapps. "But in the end I always come back to believing."

"Why? Why believe in something that continues to let you down?"

"Like justice, eh?" The priest drank and made a satisfied sound. "Sure hits the spot, Cork." He looked down where Cork sat on the folding canvas chair. "Everything disappoints us sometimes. Everybody disappoints us. Men let women down, women let men down, ideals don't hold water. And God doesn't seem to give a damn. I can't speak for God, Cork, but I'll tell you what I think. I think we expect too much. Simple as that. And the only thing that lets us down is our own expectation. I used to pray to God for an easy life. Now I pray to be a strong person."

"I'm glad you found a prayer that works," Cork said. "Think you can find your way back to town?"

"Cork," the priest went on in a frank tone, "I don't know if anybody's told you this, but you look like hell."

"I don't care, okay? Look, why don't you just jump back on Lazarus there and leave me the hell alone."

"In my experience, only dead men don't care."

"Then shake the hand of a ghost, Father."

Cork shoved his hand up at the priest, who merely put the bottle of schnapps in it.

"I won't try to argue you out of this pit you've climbed into, Cork. But if you want to talk to someone—when you need to talk to someone—I'm willing to listen."

"I'll keep it in mind." Cork turned back toward the hole in the ice.

The priest returned to Lazarus, kicked the old machine over, and guided it out of the cove. Cork listened until the sound of it was finally lost in the direction of Aurora.

He finished his cigarette and threw the butt in the snow. He considered finishing the schnapps. Instead, he heaved the bottle as far as he could.

Think, he told himself. Think like you've trained yourself to think. Think like a goddamn cop.

Wally Schanno was satisfied. Russell Blackwater had done it all. Embezzled. Killed Lytton. Then tried to kill him and Cork, too. It worked. It was a safe assumption. But Cork felt it was wrong. It was too easy an answer, had come right out of the blue, handed over by Sigurd Nelson in the form of a small, silver key that had been conveniently overlooked the night Lytton died.

He hauled up his line. Not even a nibble. Well, some days were like that. He threw his gear into the back of the Bronco. As he came around to the driver's side, he saw a huge black oil stain in the snow where the priest had parked the snowmobile.

Lazarus was running again, but as always, running on borrowed time.

CHAPTER 29

Cork called the casino from Sam's Place.

"Give me Darla LeBeau," he said.

After half a minute, Darla's voice, with a forced cheerleader sweetness, floated over the line. "This is Darla. How may I help you?"

"Corcoran O'Connor, Darla. How are you?"

There was a pause that Cork interpreted as a wary silence. Then Darla replied, "I'm fine."

"I called to find out how Paul's doing."

"I haven't seen Paul since he disappeared last Thursday."

Cork thought about the groceries he'd seen her buy and was certain she was lying.

"What about Joe John? Hear anything from him?"

"No."

Simple answer. Nothing more offered than what he'd asked. How much was she hiding? Cork wondered, and why? Why now?

"How are things there at the casino? I mean, considering Russell and all."

"Confusing," Darla said. "I have to go."

"Sure. I understand. I was just concerned."

Darla hung up without thanking him for his concern. Although he couldn't see her, he'd have been willing to bet she dropped that phone as if it were a scorpion about to sting.

"Cork?"

Wally Schanno looked surprised. He tried to get up from his desk chair, but Cork waved him back down.

"Answer me a question, Wally. Those files, did you dust them for prints?"

"Why?"

"To see if anyone besides Lytton might have handled them."

"What difference would it make? I have what I need."

Cork glanced around the office. The white filing cabinet was no longer there.

"You didn't do it, Wally. You didn't really burn them."

"There's nothing left but ashes in the incinerator out back." Schanno sat back, looking satisfied with himself.

"Jesus Christ. I don't believe it."

"It was your idea," he reminded Cork. "Like you said, a Pandora's box. The things in there could have hurt a lot of good people if they ever came to light." He lifted a manila folder from his desk and waved it at Cork. "I have everything I need right here. Blackwater's file. Why hold onto anything else? Burn it. You said so yourself."

"Christ, Wally, I can say anything I goddamn well please. I'm not the sheriff. Great police work."

"I suppose you'd have done it differently," Schanno said angrily.

"Goddamn right I would."

"If you're so goddamn good at it," Schanno shouted, "why am I the one doing the job?"

Cork planted his hands on Schanno's desk and leaned close to Schanno's red face. "Did you have a file in there, Wally? Is that the real reason you were so quick to torch everything?"

Schanno started to reply, but the words died on his lips and he looked down.

"I guess I have my answer," Cork said, and turned away.

Ellie Gruber escorted Cork back to the office of Father Tom Griffin. The office door was closed and she knocked lightly. A moment later, the priest opened the door.

"Cork." He smiled. "Come in, come in. Thank you, Mrs. Gruber." He ushered Cork in and cleared a chair. "Have a seat." The priest sat on the edge of his cluttered desk. "So, change your mind about wanting to talk?"

"Not about what you think. But I do want to talk."

"Fire away."

"You're a priest."

"Glad you noticed." Tom Griffin grinned.

"People—a lot of people—would trust you with something they couldn't confide to anyone else."

"I suppose so."

"Have you talked with Darla LeBeau lately?"

"Sure."

"And she's concerned about her son?"

The priest gave Cork a slightly bewildered look. "Of course. Wouldn't you be?"

"But Paul's with Joe John, isn't he? And Joe John loves him."

"I don't understand what you're getting at."

Cork pulled out his cigarettes. "Want one?"

The priest declined with a shake of his head. He glanced at his desk and offered Cork a heavy ceramic mug as an ashtray. Cork lit up. He inhaled deeply and felt a stab of pain from his bruised ribs.

"You okay?" Tom Griffin asked.

"Got any aspirin?"

"Sure."

The priest opened his desk drawer and took out a half-full bottle of aspirin. He tossed the bottle to Cork. "Let me get some water."

"Don't bother." Cork tapped out a couple tablets and swallowed them.

"What about Paul LeBeau?" the priest pressed him.

"Darla knows where he is," Cork said.

"That seems like a huge assumption."

"Is it? You talk with her every day. You tell me. Is she afraid?"

"Yes," the priest admitted.

"Do you know why?"

"Her son." The priest shrugged as if it were obvious.

"Let me ask you something else. Have you seen Joe John?"

The priest gave a definite shake of his head. "No."

"Do you know where he is?"

"If I knew that, wouldn't I know where Paul is? Look, Cork, playing twenty questions won't get you far. What is it you really want from me?"

"I want you to do me a favor. I want you to tell Darla I'm interested in what she's afraid of, what the boy's afraid of. Hell, what Joe John and everybody else is afraid of, too, for that matter. I'm not a cop anymore, so nothing I'm told is official."

There was a knock at the door, soft, the light tap of Mrs. Gruber.

"Just a moment!" the priest called. His good eye bored into Cork. "Why should they trust you?"

"Because that boy can't hide forever. And sooner or later they're going to have to trust somebody who knows how to protect him."

"From what?"

"You tell me." Cork ground his cigarette out in the bottom of the mug. He stood up to leave and handed the mug back to the priest. "Talk to them, then let me know. I can help, believe me."

The priest walked him to the door and opened it. Ellie Gruber stood in the hallway with Wanda Manydeeds.

"I'm sorry to disturb you, Father," Mrs. Gruber said, "but she said it was urgent."

Wanda Manydeed's dark eyes shot past the priest to where Cork stood at his back. "What's he doing here?"

"It's all right," Father Tom Griffin assured her. "We were just finishing."

In all the years Cork had known Wanda Manydeeds, he'd seldom seen those hard chestnut eyes clear of suspicion. Wanda looked at the world with chronic distrust. It was as if she'd been born without innocence, and although she had suffered much in her life, she'd never suffered from a mistake caused by naïveté.

"Going to discuss a joint service for Russell Blackwater?"

"That's right." The priest spoke for them both.

"Too bad Russell didn't have the forewarning his father did. You both could have been there to expedite his passage over. But come to think of it, he did.

He knew the Windigo had called his name. He just didn't believe it."

Wanda Manydeeds finally addressed Cork. "Word is you heard the Windigo, too."

"I did." He smiled coldly. "The difference is I'm ready for the son of a bitch." He nodded to them both in parting. " 'Night."

CHAPTER 30

The geese weren't there. Cork looked across the dark, empty water and listened in vain. The grain lay in the snow by the bucket, untouched. He figured they were gone for good.

In the cabin, there was a message on his answering machine. Molly. "Call me," she said.

He kicked the heat up and reminded himself that tomorrow he'd get the window fixed. His ribs felt like hell, but his stitched hand seemed okay. He opened a can of Hormel chili, heated it up, grated a little cheese over it, ate the chili with saltines. After he'd cleared the dishes, he made a pot of coffee and sat down at the old table Sam Winter Moon had made from birch. He set Jo's folder in front of him. For a long time he simply sipped his coffee and stared at the blood-crusted, unopened folder. He wanted to believe that what the photographs captured didn't matter now. Old infidelity. But it did. The pictures chronicled more than Jo's unfaithfulness. They were a testament to the ridiculous nature of the trust people placed in one another. Marriage was only one example. There were others. Elections. The ministry. Medicine. The bottom line was that people who leaned too heavily on someone else were setting themselves up for a terrible fall, and they had no one to blame in the end but themselves for the hurt they suffered. Cork had learned the hard way. And he vowed it would not happen again.

He considered the closed folder. He wasn't sure that studying what it contained would do any good. But he didn't have any other ideas.

The first photograph wasn't so hard. A distance shot. It framed the bow of Parrant's sailboat tied up to the dock. The name *"Thor's Hammer"* was clear on the side. Beyond the dock was the long dark of the backyard. And beyond that the whole rear of Parrant's house rising up and filling the photo. There was firelight in the living room, the soft glow visible through the sliding doors of the upper deck, and two slivers of light lower down where the hot tub was, illuminating what appeared to be a single large white shape. Cork put the photograph on the table to his left.

The next photo was an enlargement of the first, centered on the hot tub. Two candles burned on the rim of the tub, and in their soft light the large white shape clearly defined itself as two naked bodies pressed together. The faces weren't yet clear. The dark-haired male arching from behind could have been almost anybody. But to someone who knew what to look for, the woman bent forward was plainly Jo. She'd worn her hair longer then and crimped.

Despite his resolve to look carefully at all the photographs, Cork turned away. He fished around in his pocket for his cigarettes, and as he lit up, he saw that his hands were shaking. His stomach was like a ball of wet clay, and he realized he was breathing fast. He got up, walked away from the table, and leaned back against the kitchen counter. The draft through the cardboard chilled the back of his neck.

What had he hoped to see? What could those photographs possibly tell him about the deaths, about whether Paul LeBeau had really gone into hiding, and Joe John, too, and what, if anything, they had to do with all of this? The photos couldn't tell him any more than he already knew—that Jo didn't love him and hadn't for longer than he cared to consider. It was a sobering realization, but not one that particularly advanced his understanding of the recent events in Aurora. Jo, like Cork and so many others, had simply been captured by Lytton's lens in a selfish, potentially damaging act.

Cork tapped the ash of his cigarette into the sink and found himself wondering about Lytton. Had the man enjoyed the show? Had he taken the film back to his isolated cabin, developed it, and got some kicks from seeing Jo fucked like a dog?

He threw his cigarette in the sink, stomped to the table, and slapped the folder closed. He wanted to burn the damn thing. Schanno had probably been right. The best place for such trash was an ash heap.

In the dead of night from a dead sleep, Cork snapped wide awake, threw off the covers, and began to pace the room. The air was chilly, but he felt strangely warm and excited. He barely noticed the cold floorboards under his bare feet. He stopped at the bedroom window and stared outside. In the snowy darkness, the world was reduced to black and white.

He knew. Son of a bitch, he knew.

It was like this sometimes. Sometimes a thing was right in front of him, so simple. Yet it wasn't until he closed his eyes and shut down his thinking that what was simple became clear.

The key was the folder itself.

Cork went into the other room, flipped on the light,

and looked at the manila folder that had Jo's name on it. Like most office folders, it had several additional creases just to the right of the center fold. The creases were there so that the folder could be accordioned outward as the contents increased. In Jo's case, although the folder was old, the additional creases had never been used. His own folder in the white file cabinet in Schanno's office had been like that as well. But Cork would have sworn the folder on Sandy Parrant had been different. The creases were worn as if the folder had been enlarged to contain a great deal more than the photographs of the indiscretions around the hot tub. At one time there had been something else in the file.

What was it that had been removed? And who had removed it? Sigurd Nelson, the coroner, before he delivered the small silver key to Wally Schanno? Schanno himself? Or was it possible Sandy Parrant had somehow managed to get to the folder and remove the worst of what it contained?

His feet were getting cold, but he didn't want to break his thinking and he went on pacing the room.

Was there a way to find out what had been in Parrant's file? Was there a way around the blundering of Schanno?

He looked down at the old folder with Jo's name. There hadn't been a file for her next to his in the white filing cabinet. Yet here was what such a file might have held. If there had been a folder, Cork figured it hadn't been this one. The bloody folder didn't have a typed label as all the others had, only Lytton's own handwritten labeling. Had Jo's been pulled? If so and if it was Lytton who'd taken it, why had he transferred the photographs to another folder? It didn't make sense.

And then again, maybe it did.

Lytton probably did all his own film developing. If he wanted to produce photographs of Jo and Parrant that would hurt and humiliate Cork, he didn't need to pull them from the file cabinet in his rented Aurora U-Store shed. He had the negatives. All he had to do was make prints. And put them in something, any old thing. An old folder lying around. And if that was true, then where were the negatives? Cork wondered how thoroughly Lytton's place had been gone through. Was it possible all the negatives were still hidden there somewhere?

His feet were going numb from the cold. He decided that in the morning he would go to Harlan Lytton's place and have a look. These days things had a way of happening around him. Although events seemed chaotic, Cork was beginning to suspect they weren't at all. Sam Winter Moon used to say that sometimes the only way a man learns the true spirit of a rock is to stub his toe on it.

Cork turned out the lights and headed back to bed.

Even if he didn't find what he was looking for in the morning, he had a strong sense that something would find him.

CHAPTER 31

Well before dawn, Jo left the bed where she'd barely slept a wink, dressed, and, in the cold black when the rest of Aurora still slept, drove to the home of Sandy Parrant.

She took a key from her purse, unlocked the front door, and stepped inside.

The house was deathly quiet. She made her way to the living room and stood a moment sunk in the thick white carpet. Sandy's place was perfectly decorated in shades of white and was always kept in perfect order. Even though Rose was an excellent housekeeper, the rooms of the house on Gooseberry Lane usually carried evidence of the lives they contained, especially the thoughtless disarray of children. Sandy's home always felt a little unreal to Jo, deliciously extravagant, like an excellent hotel.

Dawn was showing itself through the big sliding glass panes that overlooked the lake; a rat-gray light crawled the face of the eastern sky.

Jo walked down the long hallway to Sandy's bedroom and pushed open the door. Sandy lay on his side in his big bed, the covers over him barely disturbed.

Jo envied him his peaceful sleep. She felt tired and afraid and dreaded what she was there for. She crossed silently to his bed and studied him in the dim, gray light. He was handsome, with a strong, resolute line to his jaw, a head of red-blond hair thick as a lion's mane. When they were open, his eyes were alert and intelligent, but often Sandy hid their shrewdness behind a beguilling smile. There was an irresistible recklessness about him. Also a ruthlessness of purpose once he'd set his mind on something, and that was appealing, too, in a disturbing sort of way. In his lovemaking, he'd been adventurous and attentive. Although they'd made love dozens of times, she never felt he took it for granted. She was infatuated; there was no doubt about it. But she'd never let herself use the word "love" even in her thinking. Sandy Parrant was a man headed somewhere else, and Jo knew she was a woman bound by circumstance to Aurora.

She removed her gloves and touched the satin shoulder of his pajamas. He stirred. She sat carefully on the bed, ran her hand along his fine jawline, swept her palm lightly over the heavy stubble there. She'd never slept with him, never awakened beside him, never seen his hair tousled from sleep or smelled the stale breath of morning slip from his lips. For some reason, he seemed more real to her in that vulnerable moment before waking, while his face was still slack and his eyelids trembled with dreaming, and she felt something break inside her. Before she knew it, she was crying.

"What is it?" Sandy was instantly awake. He sat up and reached for the light beside the bed.

"No, don't," Jo said, stopping his hand.

"Are you all right? What are you doing here?"

She stood up and stepped away from the bed. "I didn't sleep at all last night. I've been thinking."

"Terrible thoughts, it sounds like."

"Sandy, maybe we shouldn't see each other anymore."

"Why?"

"There's no future in it. We've both known from the beginning."

"No. We agreed not to talk about a future together. That's different."

"Because we knew it couldn't be," she insisted. She walked to the window. The sky had turned an empty white, still sunless. "My life is here. My family is here. In a couple of weeks you're gone for good."

"You can join me. After you take care of the divorce."

"You make it sound easy."

"It's not as hard as you think."

"What is it you see in me?" She turned and faced him. "I'm not young. I have children."

"I see you beside me in the White House."

"I'm serious."

"So am I." Sandy threw aside the covers and stood up. He wore blue satin pajamas and with his red-brown hair a little ruffled looked like an exotic bird. "Jo, no one in Aurora would blame you for leaving Cork. He's a man disgraced, falling apart. He hasn't been a fit husband or father for a long time. You've said so yourself. And have you taken a good look at him lately?"

"He's been terribly hurt."

"You don't have to defend him."

"It's the children I'm worried about."

"My parents divorced and I survived. Your mother raised you alone and you turned out beautifully. Children are resilient."

The long night felt heavy on her. She sighed. "Why does everything have to be so complicated?"

"It doesn't, believe me." He stepped toward her and took her hand. "Look, Jo, I have one more exhibit to offer in evidence. Something that might make everything easier for you. Come with me."

Sandy led her from the bedroom to his office. He switched on his desk lamp, opened a drawer, and took out a large photo, eight by ten.

"I recently came into possession of this. I wasn't sure if I should show you, but I think it's for the best now."

"What is it?"

"Something Dad gave me. He was trying to be helpful."

Sandy handed it over. Jo took a good look. The photograph showed Cork naked, embracing another woman. They were outside somewhere. Near a small building by a lake.

"Who is she?" Jo asked.

"Molly Nurmi."

"Nurmi?" Jo was surprised and stung. Molly Nurmi? She was only a waitress. A woman with a reputation. A girl everyone knew had broken her father's heart. Was that the kind of woman Cork wanted?

"From what I gather, they've been at it quite a while. He's playing you for a sucker, Jo. Acting the victim while he commits the crime."

"That son of a bitch," Jo said. Anger climbed inside her like fire up a dry tree. It flared in her brain, brilliant and blinding. "Making me feel like some kind of coldhearted snake. And all the time he's the snake." She flung the photograph away. "God, he was good. He had me convinced."

"Jo, this is going to sound strange, I know," Sandy said calmly. "But give him a break. He's a man after all. You didn't expect him to stay celibate forever."

"He's not a man!" she hissed. "He's a—a—worm."

"Jo—"

"What!" she snapped.

He looked at her appreciatively, undaunted by her anger. "Have I told you lately what a beautiful woman you are?"

She felt suddenly free. From the shoulders of her weary conscience a great burden simply vanished. She felt weightless, rising into an atmosphere where every breath made her feel wonderfully ruthless and wild. She stepped to Sandy, put her arms around him, and kissed him long and hard.

"Let's go to my bedroom," Sandy murmured.

"Bedroom, hell," Jo said, and she drew him down with her to the floor.

An hour later she lay sprawled on Sandy's bed, the covers pulled loosely over her. She'd made love ferociously and now she felt exhausted, ready to sleep.

Sandy came in wearing his robe. "I called my housekeeper, told her to take the day off. We can sleep as long as we like."

He threw off the robe and crawled into bed, naked beside her.

"Grand," Jo said. She pushed herself against him and closed her eyes. In a moment she was deeply asleep, carrying with her into her dreaming the musky smell of the freshman Senator from Minnesota.

CHAPTER 32

Cork was up and out of Sam's Place early. The sun was still below the trees, the sky clear, a cold bright day at hand. He paused at Hardee's to pick up a drive-through breakfast—a biscuit sandwich with sausage and egg, and a cup of steaming black coffee. Then he headed east out of Aurora, past the casino and, a mile farther, the turnoff to Sandy Parrant's. Three miles beyond that he took a right, moving away from the lake along County Road 16. The road wove through marshland and a long stretch of hayfield, then Cork could see the big stand of balsam, birch, and tamarack that marked Harlan Lytton's land. He turned up the narrow lane, which was streaked with red-orange sunlight and shadows.

It was dead quiet when he got out of the Bronco. He stood a moment, his breath clouding the air as he looked the cabin over. The shattered window had been boarded up. Across the doorway, Wally's men had put the yellow-and-black tape warning "Crime Scene Do Not Cross." Cork walked around the cabin. In back was a garage housing Lytton's pickup and snowmobile. Just beyond that stood a large shed. Cork glanced into one of the dirty windows of the shed and could see it was where Lytton did his taxidermy work. Outside, a cord of split wood had been laid up neatly against one wall. The only other structure was an ancient outhouse, the boards gray, the nails loose, the whole thing leaning like a tired old drunk.

A bird fluttered onto a branch of a birch at the edge of the clearing where the cabin and other buildings stood. It caught Cork's eye mostly because of the flash of color on its breast. A robin. Middle of winter and there was a robin still about, apparently plump and healthy.

Because of the stories of The People told him by his grandma Dilsey, Cork knew the robin was created in rather a sad way. A young man wandered from his tribe one spring to undergo *giigwishimowin*, the fasting that would bring him visions to guide him into manhood. After several days, the young man's father came and urged his son to persist in the fasting. The young man obeyed. Several more days passed, and the father returned again to urge his son to continue the fast. Although the young man had seen all the visions he needed to prepare himself for his life as a man, he obeyed his father's request. After a time, the father once more visited his son and found him painted red and lying at the foot of a tree, dying. The young man chastised his father for urging him to fast beyond his time. As the father watched, his son slowly rose upward, changing in the air with a flutter of feathers, and perched on a branch of the tree, having become a robin. To his father he said, "Whenever danger threatens any of the Anishinaabe, I will alert them with this call . . . *nin-don-wan-chee-gay*, I am warning."

The robin was a good spirit, *manidoo*, that warned of danger or the nearness of enemies or of the approach of a *maji-manidoo*, evil spirit. Cork looked at the robin, out of place in that bitter winter landscape, and returned to the Bronco. He lifted his Winchester from the backseat, took several shells from the box of cartridges in his glove box, and loaded the rifle.

The front door of the cabin was locked. Cork walked around to the rear and found the back door locked as well. Using the butt of his rifle, he broke a pane in the bathroom window, undid the latch, and slid the window up. He put the rifle in first, then struggled through himself. Inside, everything was quiet. Outside, the robin had stopped its calling.

He stepped into the main room. He knew it had been thoroughly searched by Schanno's men already, and he wasn't exactly certain what he was looking for. He held the Winchester loosely in his left hand and walked carefully around the room. The boards over the window blocked much of the light, and the place was dark and had a lonely feel to it. Cork stood a moment staring down at the crusted blood on the floor where Lytton had died.

He walked the room slowly, tapping the boards on the wall and the floor with the butt of his rifle, listening for a hollow sound. He checked the Ben Franklin stove, the kindling box, all around the sink and the few appliances. He looked under the mattress on the bunk, then felt all over the mattress itself. He opened the door to the back room that Lytton had used as a darkroom. As nearly as he could tell, all the equipment was still there—cameras, enlarger, developing trays, chemicals. He opened the drawers, found odds and ends he'd seen when he was there before. The drawer that had held wildlife negatives was empty. Wally Schanno had probably taken them. Cork wondered if there'd been other kinds of negatives, more sinister than wildlife, mixed in. He looked in the big-

gest drawer, which had been completely empty the
night Lytton was killed. At first, it still looked just
as empty. But as he was about to shove it closed, he
noticed the black edge of a negative pinched between
the bottom and the back of the drawer. He tried to
pull it free, but the negative was stuck. He took the
drawer out and hit the bottom loose with his fist. The
negative fell to the floor. It was actually a strip of
negatives from photographs shot in a series. Cork
held the strip up to the bulb and studied it carefully.

"I'll be damned," he whispered.

The negatives showed a man undressing in front
of another man, who, in the final frame, embraced
him. Who they were, Cork couldn't tell from the
negatives. But he was certain now that what he was
looking for did exist.

The last room he checked was the bathroom; he
found nothing there. He stood by the open window
trying to think. The drawer had been empty the night
Lytton died. He thought about the figure who'd shot
at him and then run into the night. As clearly as he
could recall, the silhouette had held nothing but a rifle
in its arms. So it was probably Lytton who'd moved
the negatives, maybe in response to the judge's murder. And where would a man like Lytton hide them?

The stillness and Cork's thinking were both disturbed by the sudden calling of the robin. Instinctively, Cork stepped away from the open window. He
knelt and carefully peered through the frame, studying the clearing and the woods. Nothing moved. The
bird left the birch tree with a startling flap of its
wings and headed east toward the low morning sun.
Cork listened in the quiet after the bird's leaving, but
there was nothing more to hear.

As he looked out the window, his eyes fell on the

old outhouse. He suddenly thought, with a grim smile, that the kind of shit Lytton had hid belonged down an outhouse hole. He didn't credit Lytton with enough sense of irony to have put the negatives there for that reason, but it might follow that he'd put them in a place where most people would be reluctant to look. Cork crawled out the window and walked to the outhouse.

The door hung by a single rusted hinge. Snow had drifted against it, so that he couldn't swing the door open. He leaned his rifle against the side of the outhouse, took the door in his gloved hands, and easily tore it from the remaining hinge. Snow had sifted through the cracks between the old gray boards and had accumulated a foot deep in the small square of the floor. There was a piece of rotting plywood over the hole in the seat and on top of that an old Sears catalog with the pages wrinkled and stuck together and chewed on by rodents. Cork knocked the catalog off and slid the board away. The darkness inside the hole yielded nothing. If Lytton had put something down there, he would have attached it in some way to be easily retrieved, but there was nothing like that. The maze of worm tunnels in the outline of the plywood indicated that the old board had been undisturbed for a good long time. Cork left the outhouse and stood a moment considering the two remaining structures—the garage and the taxidermy shed.

He walked to the shed, where the cord of split balsam lay stacked neatly against the wall. There was a strong padlock on the door. Cork went to the Bronco and brought back his ice spud. Although the padlock was good, the wood on the doorframe of the shed was cracked and weathered. In only a couple of minutes, he had the plate of the lock fixture pried loose, screws and all. Inside, the smell was confusing, like a combination meat locker and paint store, the raw odor of blood and flesh mingled with the harsh smell of shellac and turpentine. The glass eyes of a stuffed red fox studied Cork from one of the shelves on the walls. The pelt of an otter had been stretched on a tanning board. A big tin labeled "Arsenic" sat on the floor.

On a worktable beneath a pegboard full of cutting tools lay Lytton's dog, Jack the Ripper. Cork stepped closer and looked the dog over. Blood crusted the raw wounds in its neck torn open by the bullet from Cork's Winchester. The dog's eyes were closed, the limbs stiff from the hard cold inside the shed. Cork felt an unaccountable sadness as he considered the possibility that Lytton had brought the dog there with the idea of stuffing Jack, of keeping company with his sole friend forever.

He looked through the drawers and cupboards of the shed. He opened the tin of arsenic but didn't find the kind of poison he was looking for there. Outside, the robin had returned to the birch tree and for such a small bird was raising quite a ruckus. The smell in the shed, the residual odors of chronic death, had begun to get to Cork. He felt a little ill. He was just about to leave when he took a last look at Jack the Ripper and noticed something that he'd overlooked before. In the gray fur of the dog's underside, a faint but definite line ran from the chest to the genitals. Cork stepped closer and smoothed away the fur. An incision had been made in the dog's flesh and carefully sewn back together. Cork reached for a hacksaw that hung on the pegboard and began to saw across the belly of the carcass. It was a little like cutting into green, unkilned wood. The blade had penetrated an inch or so when it snagged. Cork tugged hard and the teeth came out full of soft black threads. From the pegboard, Cork took a knife with a six-inch serrated blade and began to cut along the original incision perpendicular to the cut he'd made with the hacksaw, so that in a few minutes he was able to pull back four flaps of frozen flesh. All of the internal organs had been removed—heart, lungs, liver, stomach, intestines—and a black canvas bag had been shoved into the cavity that remained. The bag was stuck to the inside of the carcass, glued to the rib cage by frozen blood. Cork carefully worked the bag away from the body and lifted it free. He stepped outside the shed into the bright morning light, set the bag in the snow, and opened it. Inside was a second bag, large and made of clear plastic. And inside the plastic were strips of negatives jumbled together like a nest of black snakes.

The crunch of a boot on snow made him turn. He stared into two eyes glaring from behind a ski mask, then the morning exploded.

For a moment the light in his right eye seemed as bright and hot as if he were staring at the sun. The searing heat was followed by sparks of fiery color, and Cork was dreaming about the bear in the flaming red sumac and he heard gunshots and thought Sam Winter Moon must be firing at the bear, and then his eyes were open and he was staring at the piercing blue sky and his head hurt like hell. He rolled to his side. A pair of legs in old denim rose above him. He reached out, but the legs slipped away and began to run. The black bag was still beside him along with a slender balsam log stained with blood. Cork felt his forehead above his right eye. The lump was huge and his hand came away bloody. He struggled to his feet, stumbled into the shed, and grabbed his Winchester. Outside again, he hefted the black bag over his shoulder and began to lope after the figure who'd already disappeared into the woods. The tracks were easy to follow in the snow. Cork tried to push himself to run faster, but his breath was coming short and an iron fist was pounding at his brain. Every few moments the light flashed across his eyes in a way that made him afraid he was going to faint.

He swung around a thicket and saw the figure seventy yards ahead struggling in a clump of vines. Cork's eyes were still too unfocused to make out details, but it appeared that whoever it was had become entangled in blackberry brambles. Cork dropped to one knee and let the bag fall to the snow. He worked the lever of the Winchester and put a round into the breech. As, he lifted the rifle to his shoulder and tried to sight, the light flashed across his vision. He rubbed his right eye with his knuckle and took aim again dead center in the back of the struggling figure. A moment before he squeezed off the round, he shifted his sight to the trunk of a tamarack a few yards to the left of the blackberry brambles. The tamarack exploded in a shower of bark. The figure jerked free of the thorns and scrambled away. Cork stayed on his knee a minute, leaning on the Winchester for support. He couldn't have picked himself up to give chase even if he'd wanted to. Further away through the trees, he heard a snowmobile kick over and scoot off. Slowly he got up and moved to the blackberry brambles. A rifle lay fallen deep in the snarl of thorny vines. He left it there for a moment, intending to fish it out on his way back. With the bag and his own rifle in hand, he followed the footprints until he came to a place where clearly the snowmobile had circled and headed away.

Cork sat down feeling heavy and tired and so tortured by his body that he could barely think. But he didn't have to think to know whose snowmobile it was that had been there. A big black oil stain marked the spot where the machine had been parked. Only one machine he knew of leaked oil that badly. It was called Lazarus.

CHAPTER 33

Cork let himself into Molly's cabin with the key under the back steps. After he hung his coat by the back door, he went upstairs and took four Advil from the container in the bathroom cabinet. He hurt all over. There was a large, blood-oozing, purple lump on his forehead and a headache that made him see white. His ribs felt as if Parrant had just given them another healthy beating. He'd torn the stitches in his hand.

He wanted to look carefully through the contents of the black bag, but he knew in his present condition he wouldn't be able to concentrate. He had to lie down for a while. He looked for a place to hide the bag and finally made room under the logs in the woodbox next to the fireplace. Then he made his way upstairs and lay down on Molly's bed and promptly went to sleep.

When he woke, he smelled wood smoke. He sat up, pleased to find that the headache was gone although the lump on his head was still tender and so were his ribs. There was blood on the sheets from his hand and the ooze from the lump on his forehead had stained the pillowcase, but he was no longer bleeding. Outside Molly's bedroom window, the sky was nearly dark. Cork realized he'd slept for hours.

Downstairs he found Molly sitting in the main room, reading. A blaze in the fireplace made the corners of the room flicker with shadow. Cork hesitated near the kitchen door, where the tantalizing aroma of potato soup was strong. Molly sat in her easy chair, in the small circle of lamplight. She wore jeans and a red wool sweater and red wool socks. Her red hair was done in a long braid that hung loosely over her shoulder. She glanced up and eyed Cork, who stood uncertainly in the quivering light on the far side of the room.

"Smells good," he said.

Molly closed her book, marking her place with a playing card, the ace of spades. Cork saw she was reading *The Road Less Traveled*. She folded her hands on the book and waited for an explanation.

"I need you," he said. "I haven't been able to breathe since I left you. I need you, Molly. As much as I need air."

"Cork," she whispered, and rose from the chair.

He stepped toward her, into the stronger light of the lamp.

When she saw his forehead, her face mirrored his hurt. "Oh, Cork, what happened?"

"A log. I don't for the life of me know why they call fir a softwood."

Molly reached up and touched the lump.

"Ouch!"

"I'm sorry."

"That's okay."

"It's not bleeding, but I think I should put something on it. Maybe ice."

"It's fine." He looked down uneasily at the braided rug under his stockinged feet. "I'm sorry, Molly. I'm sorry for everything."

"I know." She touched his cheek. "Let's talk about that later. Right now I'll get some hot soup into you."

Cork put his arms around her waist. "I don't deserve you," he said. "I never did."

"You've got a lot of time to work on it," she answered.

After they'd eaten, Molly went out to lay a fire in the sauna.

"It's a beautiful night out there," she said when she swept back in. "Let's go, Cork."

The moon was rising, turning the vast flat of the lake a ghostly blue-white. A few isolated pinpoints of light marked the far shore, but Cork felt as if the night belonged to Molly and him alone. They stepped into the small dressing room of the sauna. Molly had lighted a Coleman lantern and turned it low. The heat from the stove just beyond the inner door made the temperature in the room pleasant. Molly eased off his coat, then removed her own. She undid the buttons of his shirt and kissed his chest.

"I've missed you," she said.

Cork lifted the bottom of her sweater, and she raised her arms to let him slide it off her. She wore no bra. He gently touched her breasts with his palms, then bent and kissed them. Her skin was moist and smelled faintly of the smoke from laying the fire. Cork appreciated the scent.

"I've missed you, too," he said.

He kissed her fingers, every one. She pulled her hands away and moved them to the brass button of her jeans. Cork watched her hands as they opened the jeans with a soft sizzle of the zipper. She eased the jeans past her hips, her thighs, her calves, until they were a puddle of denim at her feet. She pulled them off and kicked them free. Reaching back, she undid her braid, and shook out her red hair. The room seemed terribly warm to Cork.

"I don't deserve this," he said.

"What life gives us, good or bad, we seldom deserve." She took a blanket that had been folded on a bench behind her and arranged it on the floor. She knelt on it and watched as he undressed to his red-plaid flannel boxers. She laughed. "New?"

"They're warm." He shrugged.

Then Molly saw something that made her give a little cry.

He looked down at the deep bruising over his ribs. "It's nothing."

"Nothing? Come here."

He stepped near her on the blanket. She put her lips to the bruise. "Better?" she asked.

"Much," he said.

She stood and pressed her breasts against him and gave him a long kiss. Then she slipped her fingers into the elastic of his flannel boxers and began to draw them down. Looking at him through a wisp of her red hair, she promised, "I'll be gentle."

"Not too," he replied hoarsely.

"You didn't see who hit you?" Molly asked.

Cork shook his head. "It happened too fast."

"I don't understand. If they were after the bag, why didn't they just take it?"

"That's something I don't understand either," Cork said.

Molly stepped down from the high seat in the sauna, took a dipper from a bucket, and threw water over the hot stones. The water hissed and steam shot up into the air, and Cork felt the sweat pour from him. It felt good to sweat so freely. Cleansing. Molly sat back down beside him.

"Unless," she said.

"Unless what?"

"Unless they managed to take what they wanted while you were unconscious."

"I suppose that's possible," Cork said.

"How long were you out?"

"I don't know. Not long, I think." He wiped his face with his hands, then ran his fingers through his hair, which was as wet as if he were in the shower. "There's something else, though. When I was out, I dreamed I heard a couple of gunshots. And when I found the rifle in the blackberry bramble, I could tell it had just been fired."

"At you?"

Cork made a show of feeling himself. "No new holes."

"Shooting at who, then?"

"I don't know. It doesn't make much sense. Maybe it'll all be clearer once I've had a look in that bag."

"Do you think the oil stain in the snow means it's Tom Griffin?"

"I'll definitely have a talk with St. Kawasaki."

"But you don't really want it to be him, do you?"

Cork glanced at her. Her face ran with sweat. Her red hair clung to her flushed cheeks.

"You want it to be Sandy Parrant," she said.

"Yes," Cork admitted. "I want it to be Parrant."

"I'm worried," she told him, and touched his shoulder. "I wonder what knowing the kinds of secrets that are in that bag might do to a person. Not just you. Anyone. I wonder if Wally Schanno didn't have the right idea."

"Schanno destroyed evidence," Cork said.

"And maybe he saved a lot of good people needless pain."

"Was that his motive?" Cork asked her pointedly. "Look, I don't know how to get to the truth without going through that bag. If you have a better idea, I'm willing to listen."

Molly stared into the grating of the stove, where the fire blazed with a searing red-orange flame.

"You see?" Cork said.

"Where's the bag?" Molly asked.

"Hidden."

"Here?"

"In the woodbox. It was just a precaution. Probably not even necessary. Even so, I don't want to stay here with it. After I've had chance to look through it, I'll take that bag somewhere else."

"No," Molly said. "If you're off somewhere in the night, I'll worry. As long as we're together, I'm not afraid for you."

He listened to the crackle of the fire as it heated the stove, the rocks, the air all around him. He glanced at Molly. It was weak of him, he knew, but he didn't want to leave.

"All right," he agreed. "As long as we're together."

She leaned to him and kissed him. "Time to cool off. I cleared the hole in the ice. The water will feel wonderful. Here." She handed him socks she'd laid out earlier so that his wet feet wouldn't stick to the ice.

They ran together out of the sauna. The deck was slippery with ice, and Cork had to catch himself on the railing to keep from falling. Molly ran ahead, surefooted and graceful, and dropped into the hole with a frigid splash. She came up quickly and Cork helped her out.

"Your turn." She laughed, steaming in the moonlight.

CHAPTER 34

The blood from Jack the Ripper's carcass was no longer frozen on the bag. It had thawed, making an unpleasant mess of the canvas. Molly eyed the bag grimly as Cork lifted it from the woodbox and carried it to the kitchen.

"Here," she said. She took some newspapers from a stack by the kitchen door and laid them out on the floor.

Cork set the messy canvas on the papers, opened it, and took out the plastic bag inside.

"Can I get rid of that?" Molly asked nodding at the canvas.

"I'll toss it," Cork said.

He carried the canvas bag wrapped in newspaper outside to the garbage bin, a lidded wooden crate that held two metal garbage cans. There was a latch on the crate lid to discourage raccoons. Cork dropped the bloody canvas into one of the cans and returned to the kitchen.

"Want some help?" Molly asked without enthusiasm.

"Do you really want to?"

"No. Do you mind?"

Cork was almost certain the truth was there among the contents in the plastic bag. Or at least the guideposts that would lead him to the truth. But Molly was probably right. There was sure to be more in the bag than he needed to know, than anyone needed to know.

"I'd best do it alone," he answered.

"I'll make you some coffee." And she did. Then she walked to him and kissed the top of his head where his hair was thinning. "I'll be upstairs in bed if you need me. Should I wait up?"

He shook his head. "This will take a while."

She stood at his back, her arms around his neck. "I've never told you, Cork, but I love you."

She didn't wait for a reply. She went through the kitchen door, and Cork heard her creak up the old stairs.

When Cork was a boy and still believed in God and the Church and heaven, the ringing of the morning Angelus had always had a strange effect on him. It was a sound that filled him with hope, no matter what his mood. Molly's words—"I love you"—had the same effect, dropping hope into a hopeless place. Cork wanted to hold on to the feeling, to believe in the possibility of some other greater power that would make all things right.

But he looked down at the black jumble of negatives bound up in plastic, and he knew it was never so simple.

Onto Molly's kitchen table, he dumped the contents of the bag, a mess of dozens of strips of black-and-white negatives mixed with several audiocassette tapes. He checked the tapes first. Each was identified only by number, nothing else. He took a strip of negatives at random, lifted it toward the ceiling light, and saw immediately that unraveling any secrets they held would be far more difficult than he'd expected.

Looking at a print was simple. A print was a reflection, more or less, of what the eye naturally saw. Trying to decipher the inverted lighting of a negative in which shadow is light and light is shadow was going to be no easy task. The small size of the negative was another stumbling block.

Cork squinted at the images on the strip in his hand. The first photograph, like the one of Jo and Parrant, had been shot at night. Lytton seemed fond of night shots, of using the night vision lens, an apparatus that could magnify small sources of light hundreds of times to illuminate night images. But then, night was the best time for activities people preferred kept secret. The photograph appeared to have been shot from a distance. Several people sat around a table in a room that looked to be on the upper floor of a building. A telescopic lens brought the next photos much closer. The room itself had a picture on the wall, much too small for Cork to make out details, and a bookcase. But that was really all he could tell. He turned the strip over, hoping that a reversed view might help. It didn't. Who they were, where they were, and why Harlan Lytton saw fit to capture them on film remained a mystery.

It was clear to him that he would need to enlarge the image. He looked in the drawers of Molly's kitchen for a magnifying glass, but found nothing. He trudged upstairs, where Molly lay reading in bed. She took off her glasses and gave him a smile.

"Done so soon? Or is it just that you couldn't resist the temptation of my bed?"

"No and yes," Cork said, crossing to her. "No, not done by a long sight, and yes, the temptation of your bed is mighty." He sat beside her, leaned where she lay propped on her pillow, and kissed her. "I need something that will magnify the negatives. Do you have a magnifying glass or a loupe hidden away somewhere?"

She thought a moment. "I don't think so. The only time I need to magnify anything is when I read." She looked down at the glasses she'd set on the bed. "Will these help?"

Cork took them and experimented with enlarging the print in the book Molly had been reading. "Not perfect, but they'll do. Sure you don't mind?"

"If they'll bring you to bed sooner, you have my blessing."

"One more thing. Do you have a tape player?"

"You mean like for cassettes?"

"Yes."

She shook her head regretfully. "I'm a CD person, Cork. What about the tape player in your Bronco?"

"Broken."

"Is it important?"

"It'll keep until tomorrow."

She gave him a kiss before he rose and headed to the door.

On his way to the kitchen he took a small lamp from the living room. He set it by the jumble of negatives on the table, plugged it in, and removed the shade. He held the strip of negatives to the bare bulb and, using Molly's glasses to enlarge the image, studied each negative in the strip carefully. After five minutes his head had begun to ache, and he still had no clue who the people were or why Lytton had photographed them.

One after another he studied the strips of negatives, but he found nothing he understood. He was beginning to feel discouraged when he picked up a strip and recognized immediately a familiar structure. The mission building on the rez. The first shot showed the mission from a distance. The next was much closer and centered on St. Kawasaki's old motorcycle, which was parked near the cemetery fence. The subsequent shots in the series seemed to have been taken through a crack between the bottom of a window shade and the sill. Two bodies by candlelight, a man and woman in a naked embrace. They were standing amid the disarray of construction—sawhorses and two-by-fours. Who they were was unclear because the shade cut off their heads. The middle shots in the sequence were unusual, close-ups of a rib cage. Looking closely, Cork could discern long scars across the ribs. The final photograph focused on a hand caressing a breast. Spilling out on the skin beneath the hand was an image—a tattoo of the Wisdom Tree.

Cork's head throbbed. This wasn't what he wanted, expected. Still, it did explain why Tom Griffin might have attacked him at Harlan Lytton's cabin. And although St. Kawasaki didn't seem like a man given to that kind of violence, God alone knew the true limits of desperate people.

He kept at it, and a few minutes later came across another strip that was different from the others. They weren't photographs of people but of documents. Cork adjusted the right lens of Molly's glasses until he could just make out the words of the letterhead that appeared on each document: GameTech. He sat back a moment, thinking. GameTech. Where had he heard that name before? He looked at the negatives again. Everything with the exception of the bold name on the letterhead was too small to make out. GameTech. It sounded so familiar. He got up, walked to Molly's cupboard, took down a cup, and filled it from the faucet at the kitchen sink. GameTech. He took a sip, then put the cup down, turned the faucet back on, and splashed a little water on his face. He dabbed it off with a hand towel and looked out the dark window over the sink. GameTech.

And it came to him. That was the logo Ernie Meloux had been twirling on the countertop when Cork spoke with him at the casino the day after the judge died. He didn't know what the connection was, but he put the strip aside.

A few strips later he came upon a figure easy to identify even in the reverse world of a negative. Hell Hanover. His white bald head was like a black carbuncle grown up from his shoulders. He was dressed in clothing with an odd pattern. Cork finally realized they were army fatigues. In the first negative, Hanover stood alone, framed by a large American flag that hung between two trees behind him. The second shot, still set against the background of the flag, captured him shaking hands with another man. They were turned to the camera. Posed. Cork adjusted Molly's glasses and looked closely. Then he smiled.

"Shake hands with the devil," he whispered.

For the man who'd joined Hell Hanover was none other than Judge Robert Parrant.

The other shots showed the two men reviewing several lines of what appeared to be armed soldiers in fatigues. Although the clothing bore no identifying insignia, even an idiot could guess that the photographs documented a gathering of the Minnesota Civilian Brigade.

Cork kept digging. As midnight approached, he was dog tired. He'd found nothing more that seemed significant. Mostly a lot of people caught in the act of things better left between them and their own consciences. Infidelity, recreational drugs, homosexuality. In a city these were things as ordinary as catching a bus. In Aurora, they could obliterate a life.

His back hurt. His neck and shoulders were tied in knots. His head was pounding. He'd developed a tick in one eye that was beginning to drive him crazy. He was about to call it a night when he pulled out a strip of negatives that made him feel suddenly empty and afraid.

He held them to the bulb and looked over each negative carefully. In the first, a man stood with a rifle cradled in his arms, his foot atop an animal that had been killed. A trophy shot.

Looking closer, Cork realized that the animal was human.

The next shot, a close-up, showed a face wearing what looked like a black-and-white mask. In the inverted world of the negative, Cork knew the black was skin. And the white? That had to be blood. So much of it the face was all but obliterated. But there was an unusual aspect of the hair that was quite clear. It was braided.

The other shots were more of the same, as if an artist were documenting his work from several angles. Cork still couldn't be sure who'd been killed or who'd done the killing. What he needed was a print. Or, better yet, an enlargement.

Molly stirred, waking slowly as he sat on the bed.

"I've got to leave for a while," he told her.

She was instantly awake. "What time is it?"

"Going on midnight."

"Where are you heading at this time of night?" She slid upright, her back against the headboard.

"Harlan Lytton's."

"Why in heaven's name would you want to go back there?"

"I need to use his equipment."

"Can't it wait until morning?"

"No. There are things I have to know."

"Bad things?"

"Yes."

She threw the covers off. "I'm coming with you."

Molly dressed quickly while Cork selected the negatives he wanted to take. He separated the others into two piles—those he'd already looked at and the larger jumble that still remained. He put the negatives he hadn't yet scanned and the cassette tapes in the plastic bag, then put everything into a large paper sack, and placed it all carefully back under the logs in the woodbox.

On the way to Lytton's, he told Molly she'd been right. Most of what he'd seen he was probably better off not knowing.

"You said what you found was bad. How bad?"

Cork told her about the photo that looked like a trophy shot. He told her about the man with braided hair and a mask of blood.

"Do you have any idea who they are?"

"Pretty sure."

She waited. "Well?"

"I believe Harlan Lytton was the man who did the killing."

"And the man he killed."

"I think that was Joe John LeBeau."

CHAPTER 35

Molly scrambled through the window of the bathroom in Lytton's cabin, then turned and took the Winchester that was passed up to her. Cork climbed in after her, pulled a flashlight from his coat, and took back his rifle.

They moved to the big room. The beam of the flashlight showed nothing different from his earlier visit. He played the light along the walls, the furnishings, the floor with its big stain.

"Is that what I think it is?" Molly asked.

"This way." Cork led her to Lytton's darkroom, giving a wide berth to the crusty stain on the floor.

In the dark, he found the light string and switched on the bare, overhead bulb. He could see his breath.

"I've got to get some heat in here. I don't know if the chemicals will work this cold. You can stay here."

"Are you kidding? I'm not letting you out of my sight."

She followed him into the big room. There were electric baseboard heaters set just warm enough to keep the cabin pipes from freezing. Cork turned them to high. Then he took logs and kindling from the woodbox next to the Ben Franklin stove and had a fire going in no time.

While the cabin warmed, Cork checked Lytton's

equipment and supplies. He found plenty of developer, paper, and wash. He tested the safelight and the enlarger.

"Where'd you learn this?" Molly asked.

"A buddy of mine was a police photographer when I was on the force in Chicago. I just hope I remember enough."

When the cabin had warmed sufficiently, Cork laid out trays of developer, stop bath, fixer, and water. He took out the negatives and inserted the strip with the dead man into the negative carrier of the enlarger. He turned on the safelight and turned off the bare bulb. He focused the image from the enlarger until the negative that was like a trophy shot was clear on the bare easel, then he opened a package of photo paper and inserted a piece.

"Here goes."

He switched on the enlarger lamp for fifteen seconds, took the print through the developer, stop bath, fixer, and wash. Using a squeegee, he wiped the excess water off the print and held it up carefully for a good look.

"You were right," Molly said, a little hoarsely. "Harlan Lytton killed Joe John."

In the enlargement, the satisfied look was quite clear on Harlan Lytton's face as he stood with his foot on the body of Joe John LeBeau.

Cork repeated the process with the close-ups of Joe John. They were grisly images. From left. Right. Above. The head and body had been adjusted slightly with each shot.

"God." Molly grimaced. "What was he doing?"

"I think Harlan was attempting art."

A sharp snap from the other room made them both freeze. Cork picked up the Winchester from where Molly had propped it against the wall. He held a finger to his lips and stepped to the closed door of the darkroom. He gestured for Molly to switch off the safelight, then he carefully opened the door.

The darkness inside the cabin was profound. Cork crouched with the Winchester readied while he probed the dark with his eyes. Nothing moved. He could hear Molly's shallow breathing directly at his back. Then he heard the crack of the floorboards near the potbelly stove as they expanded with the heat. He stood up.

"I think we should leave," Molly suggested. "This place gives me the creeps."

"I agree. But I want to make a few more prints first."

Cork made enlargements of all the photos of Joe John's murdered body. Then he did the same with the negatives of Hell Hanover, the judge, and the Minnesota Civilian Brigade. The brigade photos appeared to have been taken in a clearing somewhere surrounded by unbroken pine forest. Cork recognized a number of faces among the three or four dozen men in the ranks. Any of them were capable of breaking into Sam's Place and working him over. Most were probably capable of murder as well. He'd been lucky to have come away with only bruised ribs. Luckier than Joe John had been.

Finally he slipped the negatives of the GameTech documents into the enlarger and took a look.

"Consultant contract?" Molly asked, peeking over his shoulder at the first image.

"It appears so. For Stu Grantham's services as a property consultant."

"But he's head of the county board of commissioners."

"That he is. And look who signed for GameTech,"

Cork said, pointing to the flamboyant signature of Robert Parrant.

Cork scanned the other documents, all contracts for consulting services from various individuals in Tamarack County, including—for consulting on the issues of security—Wally Schanno. He made a print of Schanno's contract, then he said, "Let's get out of here. The smell of this stuff is making me sick."

They were quiet a long time on the way back to Molly's cabin. It was late and the roads were empty.

"Why?" Molly finally asked.

"I don't know."

"I thought Joe John was back. But he couldn't have been, could he?"

"I'm pretty sure those pictures were taken months ago when Joe John disappeared. My guess is Harlan dumped the body somewhere. Probably in one of the bogs on his land. Nobody would go snooping there with Jack the Ripper roaming around loose. Then he crashed the truck somewhere else so there'd be no evidence of the murder."

"Which brings us back to why."

"I'm so tired right now I can't think straight." He pulled into Molly's lane and parked in front of the cabin. "I need a cigarette and a beer. And I need a good night's sleep. Tomorrow I'll see what I can figure in the why department."

"Where do you plan on sleeping?"

"Right now, I'd take a bed of nails if it were offered."

"How about the left side of my mattress? It's not a bed of nails, but it is a little lumpy."

Cork smiled wearily. "Best offer I've had in ages."

CHAPTER 36

He woke with her arm over him, her cheek against his back, and the warm morning smell of her all around him. He'd never slept with Molly before. Before, the bed had been a place of brief coming together and of leaving. It felt good to lie beside her with the early sun beyond the window and the cabin full of quiet. It was peaceful and healing to be with her and not be cut apart by guilt.

He lay very still, reluctant to move even the least bit, to do anything that would wake her. There was something protective in the way her arm lay over him, the way her breath warmed his back. Then he felt the light, deliberate touch of her lips on his shoulder.

"You awake?" she asked softly.

"Still dreaming," he answered. "The sun's up. I thought you had to be at the Pinewood Broiler early."

She brushed a kiss across his back. "I called Johnny and told him I'd be late."

"When?"

"An hour ago."

"I didn't feel you leave."

"You were sleeping soundly."

He kissed her hand. She made a pleased sound in her throat and snuggled more firmly against him.

"Let's stay in bed, Cork. Let's stay here the whole day."

"What'll Johnny say?"

"Screw him. I've never once missed a day. I've never even been late."

"Tempting," Cork admitted.

"But?"

He didn't reply. She drew away just a little.

"You're going to stick your nose into things, aren't you?" she said.

"Know what I'd like?" he said, trying to hold onto the brightness. "I'd like to take a shower with you, then fix you breakfast. It's been a long time since I made breakfast for anyone but myself."

"Cork, promise me something."

"What?"

"You won't do anything that'll get you hurt."

"I'm not what you'd call a brave man," he assured her.

She sighed, her breath making the hair at the back of his neck shiver. "Maybe not, but you're stubborn, and that's just as bad."

After they'd showered, Cork bounced downstairs ahead of Molly and made two telephone calls. He was just hanging up when she came down the stairs.

"Who're you calling?" she asked.

"First I called the number on the GameTech letterhead."

"And?"

"A recording. Leave your name and number and we'll get back to you. So I called Ed Larson at the sheriff's office. Asked him to track down an address for that number. He owes me a favor or two." Cork stepped into the kitchen and opened the refrigerator door. "Perfect," he said, taking out three leftover boiled potatoes. "Hash browns à la O'Connor. How's that sound?"

"Delicious. I'll get the coffee going." Molly headed to the coffeemaker. "So what are you going to do?"

"Fry up a few potatoes, cut up some onion and green pepper, throw on a little—"

"I mean about Joe John."

Cork pulled out the cutting board and a knife and began dicing the potatoes, skin and all. "I've been thinking about it. The only thing that makes sense is he was killed because he knew something about the brigade or about the casino or both. He cleaned the offices of Great North every night, so maybe he saw or heard or stumbled onto something he shouldn't have. I'd guess, given what I know about the judge and Lytton, that the judge arranged to have Lytton take care of things." Cork shrugged. "It's all speculation. But one thing seems sure. Joe John was killed in cold blood."

Cork took a small green pepper and an onion from the crisper and set them on the cutting board.

When the coffeemaker stopped dripping, Molly got a mug from the cupboard and filled it for Cork.

"Thanks," he said. "Aren't you going to have some?"

"I'll fix a little herbal tea later." She leaned her hip against the counter, crossed her arms, and looked sad. "It's hard to believe. All of this is hard to believe in Aurora."

"Happens everywhere," Cork said. "Nature of the beast. *Ouch!*"

"What?"

"Cut myself." He jammed his finger into his mouth and sucked.

"Bad?"

"No."

"Wash it off in the sink. I'll finish cutting."

Molly took the knife. Cork ran water over his finger and saw a small clean slice near his nail. He pressed it with his thumb and in a moment the bleeding had stopped.

"I'll live." He smiled. "But I could sure use a cigarette. Mind?"

"Go ahead."

He plucked the pack from his shirt pocket. "You know," he said apologetically, "you put up with a lot from me. Why?"

"I thought I made that clear last night." She tossed him a smile over her shoulder.

Cork looked at the cigarettes. Impulsively he crumpled the pack and dropped it in the wastebasket under the sink.

Molly paused with the knife in her hand. "Is that for real?"

"There are a lot of things that will be different about me from now on. I promise."

He moved behind her, and as he held her, his face against her hair that was still damp from the shower, he gazed out the window above the sink. He could see the cabins that lined the way down to the lake. They were old cabins, but sturdy. Molly's father had built them himself not long after Molly was born and only a short time before his wife ran off and left him to raise the baby girl alone. Cork supposed the old man had done his best as a parent. But he had a reputation as a drinker, and the girl he raised had had a reputation for wildness.

"Do you ever think of fixing up the cabins, opening up this place again as a resort?" Cork asked.

"Almost never," she said. "I like the solitude. And besides, it's something I'd never want to tackle alone."

"Maybe I could help," Cork said.

She turned in his arms, turned to face him, and she looked up seriously into his eyes. "I wouldn't want to run the place alone either."

Cork gathered himself together and came as near as he'd ever come to saying he loved her. He said, "Maybe you wouldn't have to."

Molly kissed him and held him for a long time in the sunlight through her window.

"You know, you don't have a Christmas tree yet," he pointed out.

"I never get a tree," she said, pulling away gently and turning back to the cutting board.

"Why not?"

"When I was a kid my father used to promise all kinds of things at Christmas. He never came through with anything. Christmas means mostly disappointment to me."

"Let me finish those potatoes," Cork said.

"Finish your coffee," Molly told him. "I can see the general direction you were taking."

Cork sipped from his mug. "Would you get a tree if we went together?"

"I'd consider it." She looked out the window a moment. "But only if we made our own decorations. You know, popcorn and cranberries on strings, paper chains, that kind of thing. I don't want all the commercial crap. Blinking lights and shiny ornaments and that stringy, glittery stuff."

"Icicles?"

"Yeah, those."

"Whatever you want," he said. "Let's get it today."

"When?"

"As soon as you're off work."

"All right," she agreed. "And tonight we'll make decorations."

The telephone rang. Cork answered. He listened a minute, said thanks, and hung up.

"So?" Molly asked. She placed the cast iron skillet on the stove over a medium flame and dropped in a bit of butter.

Cork sat back and sipped his coffee. It was black and strong and good. A cigarette would have made it perfect.

"Ed says the address is the judge's house," Cork told her. "Makes sense. The judge signed all the documents, and I don't imagine, given the probable nature of the enterprise, that he operated out of his Great North offices. Too much chance of someone stumbling onto something."

"But I thought you said his house had been searched thoroughly by Schanno and his men."

"Maybe they missed something," Cork said hopefully. "I don't know if there's a connection between this GameTech business and Joe John's murder, but it might go a long way toward explaining the odd behavior of a certain county sheriff lately. Sometimes an investigation's like pulling on the loose threads of a sweater. Grab the right one and the whole thing unravels."

"Will you talk to Schanno?"

"If I don't find anything at the judge's house, I may have to fall back on the direct approach—with Wally or one of the other consultants."

"What about St. Kawasaki and—what did you call it?—Lazarus?"

"I intend absolutely to have a talk with him. He's got a lot to explain. Also, I need to pick up a cassette player so I can hear what those tapes have to tell me."

"Busy day," she noted. "Sure you'll have time to hunt down a Christmas tree with me?"

Cork watched her at the counter in her red robe, with her damp red hair. He watched her carry the cutting board to the stove and he smiled at the way her thick red wool socks had bunched around her ankles. As she spilled the diced vegetables and potatoes into the hot skillet, he said to her, "I love you, Molly."

But the sizzle from the skillet was loud and she didn't seem to hear.

CHAPTER 37

Cork made his way through the snow, up the long slope of the judge's estate. The broken pane on the side door had been covered with a bit of plywood that Cork easily pried loose. He reached in, unlocked the door, stepped inside. The cans he'd knocked over the night Russell Blackwater died still lay strewn across the kitchen floor. The smell of rotting garbage had grown worse. Cork made his way back to the judge's study, where all the evidence of what the shotgun had done to the judge's head still remained splattered on the map behind the desk, brownish now, more like mud than rivers of red. Cork started with the desk. He checked the telephone, a complicated thing with lots of buttons. Beside two of the buttons numbers were listed, one of which belonged to GameTech. He checked the drawers but found nothing that seemed relevant. He went through the judge's mahogany secretary and came up blank there, too. He removed the books from the shelves, as Schanno had done, and, probably like Schanno, found nothing.

Including the bathroom, there were seven rooms on the first floor. Cork went through them all. If the judge kept any GameTech-related documents at his home, they weren't downstairs. Cork headed up to the second floor. As he reached the top of the landing, he heard the front door open and quietly close. A shadow passed through a bar of sunlight across the floor, but he couldn't see the figure who'd cast it. Carefully, he descended the stairway. From the kitchen came the squeak of a hinge like that of a little mouse. Cork crossed the bare wood floor, hoping the complaint of an old board wouldn't give him away. He hadn't thought to bring his Winchester, so he picked up a black metal sculpture of a perched hawk and cradled the heavy piece in his hand as he edged toward the kitchen doorway.

Hannah Mueller screamed as she stepped from the kitchen and saw Cork with the heavy black hawk drawn back ready to strike.

"Christ, Hannah, I'm sorry." Cork let his hand drop immediately.

"Sheriff O'Connor!" the woman said breathlessly. Her eyes were huge with fright.

"It's all right, Hannah. I didn't know it was you."

Hannah Mueller was a woman about forty, small, heavy, with dull gray-blonde hair pulled back in a ponytail and bound with a rubber band. She had a plain face, and in her blue eyes was an innocence much younger than her forty years, for Hannah was mildly retarded. She wore blue jeans and a blue work shirt and sneakers. She carried a mop and a bucket.

"I came to clean," she said, as if she needed to defend her presence. "Mr. Parrant called me and said it was okay for me to clean. I didn't clean my regular days."

"That's fine, Hannah," Cork assured her. "That's just fine."

Hannah looked at him, her gaze full of question.

"I'm investigating, Hannah."

"Oh," Hannah said, as if that explained it just fine.

She looked past Cork toward the hallway that led to the judge's study. "I heard it's bad."

"It's not pleasant," Cork acknowledged. "Hannah, what are your regular days?"

"Monday, Wednesday, and Friday. Sometimes I clean on Sunday if the judge has a party or something. He leaves me a note."

"He doesn't speak with you?"

"I don't ever see him. He's always gone."

Cork looked at his watch. "You always come at nine?"

"Nine." Hannah nodded. "Always at nine."

"And the judge is always gone."

"Always gone." Hannah nodded.

"What if you needed to talk to him? Could you call him?"

"Yes."

"Where?"

"At the numbers."

"What numbers?"

Hannah reached into her back pocket and drew out an old leather wallet with a nicely tooled design. She extracted a worn piece of paper and handed it to Cork. Two telephone numbers were written on the paper. Beside one Hannah had noted "Monday & Friday." Beside the other she'd written, "Wensday." The "Wensday" number was preceded by the digit 1. Long distance, same area code as Aurora.

"Wait just a minute, Hannah." Cork put the hawk back on its stand, stepped to the phone near the stairs, and dialed the Monday/Friday number.

"Good morning. Great North. How may I direct your call?"

Cork smiled. "Joyce. Cork O'Connor."

"Yes, Cork. Hi."

"Could I ask you a question?"

"You can. Doesn't mean I can answer it."

"Did the judge work at Great North on Wednesdays?"

"No. For the last year or so Wednesday has been his day off."

"Thanks, Joyce. You're wonderful."

"Tell Albert that."

Cork hung up. He tried the Wednesday number. The phone rang and rang, but no one answered. He called Ed Larson and asked for one last favor. Could he track down a long distance number?

"I have to wait for someone to call me back," he explained to Hannah, who'd stood patiently, mop and bucket in hand, while he called.

"Sure, okay," she shrugged. She looked again, not with great enthusiasm, toward the back hallway.

"You don't have to do that, Hannah," Cork said.

"It's Christmas," she explained. "The money."

"Then let me do it," Cork offered.

"No." She shook her head vigorously, her dull ponytail swishing across her blue collar. "It wouldn't be right. Mr. Parrant said he'd pay me."

"Mr. Parrant doesn't have to know."

"It wouldn't be right," she insisted. She looked at Cork gratefully. "But it's sure nice of you to offer, Sheriff."

"At least let me help."

"No. It's my job."

The phone rang. Cork picked it up. He listened. "Just a minute. Let me write this down." There was a notepad by the phone but nothing to write with. Cork checked his pockets for a pen, then glanced at Hannah, who'd put down her bucket and was holding out to him a stubby pencil that looked as if the point had been sharpened with a knife. Cork smiled gratefully. He wrote down the address, thanked Ed, and hung up.

"Thanks, Hannah."

"You're welcome." She picked up her bucket, took a deep breath, and started toward the back room.

It seemed to Cork the good people were always cleaning up the messes.

Not surprisingly, the address of the Wednesday number was in Duluth. It fit. As Cork made the two-hour drive to the port city on Lake Superior, he thought about the judge making the same trip once a week, retrieving GameTech mail from the post office box, and sitting in an anonymous office somewhere taking care of business. Cork wasn't exactly sure what the business was, but the more he'd learned the more certain he was that it was a less than honorable enterprise.

He found the address near the harbor bridge. A small office building—square, red brick—that had probably once been busy when the ore ships ran regularly, but it looked as if it was mostly abandoned now. A big sign in one of the first-floor windows advertised office space for rent. Parked in front was a white van that had "Mosely Remodeling" printed on the sides. The directory just inside the front door had as many gaps as a Minnesota street had potholes. GameTech didn't appear at all.

From somewhere above came the whine of a power saw. It lasted a few seconds, then stopped, but was repeated as Cork started up the stairway. The stairs were gritty from the sand and dirt tracked in on the bottom of snowy shoes and boots. Cork climbed to the second floor and walked down the hallway, which was uncarpeted brown tile long in need of a good waxing. Only a few of the office doors carried logos on their translucent glass, and fewer still seemed currently occupied. Cork heard a phone ring in an office somewhere ahead and the laughter of a woman involved in one side of the conversation that followed.

The address Ed Larson had given him was Suite 214. There was nothing on the door to indicate that it was the office of GameTech. The light was off inside, the door locked.

From above him the sudden cry of the saw came again. It drowned the sound of the woman on the phone for a couple of seconds, then stopped. Something— a severed board?—clunked onto the floor almost directly over Cork's head. A few moments later the pounding of a hammer began.

Cork considered the locked door. The phone rang again down the hallway. The woman's voice and laughter followed. She sounded as if she enjoyed her job. The hammering stopped. The saw took up its drowning whine.

Cork went back outside to his Bronco parked behind the van on the street, hauled out the ice spud, returned to Suite 214, and the next time the saw blade howled, punched out a chunk of glass from a corner of the window in the door. He reached inside and undid the lock.

The room was dark and he opened the blinds. The office had a nice view of the northeast. Beyond the bridge and the harbor opening, the ice of Lake Superior stretched away under the morning sun like the great salt flats of Utah. Cork took a good look at the office. It was small, one room, not a suite at all. The walls were bare. The carpet was beige, and either new or so little used as to still look new. There was a desk near the windows, an L-shaped affair with a computer and printer on the long part of the L. A white three-drawer filing cabinet sat in one corner, exactly the same kind of cabinet that had been in Schanno's office.

Cork checked the filing cabinet. The top drawer was marked "GameTech" and held a number of hanging files: Budget, Finance, Lease Agreements, Personnel, Taxes. He lifted Personnel. Inside he found folders labeled with many familiar names and containing the originals of the documents that had appeared among the negatives he'd found at Lytton's. Next he pulled Lease Agreements. The file contained contracts signed by Russell Blackwater for the lease on a monthly basis of gaming equipment. He set the file on the desk beside the other.

The middle drawer was labeled "Vendors," and each hanging file was designated with the name of a company. Cork pulled the file for a company called Polaris Gaming and found invoices for the purchase of a variety of gaming equipment. He began checking the invoices against the prices on the lease agreements signed by Blackwater. After Polaris Gaming, he checked the files of two other vendors.

The last drawer, unmarked, held a single file: Partnership Agreement. The document had been prepared by the judge, and although it was long and involved, as Cork scanned it, he understood exactly what it was about.

As he stood hunched over the partnership document, the saw cut out above him, and in the abrupt stillness that followed, Cork heard a slight rustle at his back. He turned and found himself confronting the cold determination in Hell Hanover's pale blue eyes.

Flanking Hanover on either side were Al Lamarck and Bo Peterson, two men Cork recognized from the pictures of the ranks of the Minnesota Civilian Brigade.

"I don't suppose you're here to invite me to go Christmas caroling," Cork said.

Hanover carefully drew off his black stocking cap. In the light from the window, his bald head shone like an ivory doorknob. The left corner of his mouth twitched as if a smile had been stillborn.

"When you first started sticking your nose into all this, O'Connor," Hanover said, "I told the men to discourage you. It didn't work."

Cork glanced at Lamarck and Peterson. They'd unzipped their leather coats. Both wore .45s, military issue, holstered on their hips. Cork wondered if either of them had been present at Sam's Place the night he'd been jumped.

Hanover limped forward on his artificial leg and studied the documents Cork had spread out on the desk. "When you persisted," he went on, "I decided to let you go ahead, figuring that at worst you'd hit the same dead ends we had. On the other hand, it was possible you just might lead us to where we all wanted to be."

"And let me guess where that is," Cork offered. "At the source for funding the weapons stockpile for the brigade."

Hanover moved around the desk to the computer and turned it on. He studied the screen and said, "What is it you think we're all about, O'Connor?"

"I could guess all day, Helm. Why don't you save us both a lot of time and just lay it out for me."

Hanover hit the keys as he talked. "Do you remember your American history? Remember why the farmers took up rifles at Lexington and Concord? They were fed up being governed by a distant tyranny, living under laws made by men who had no idea or interest in what those farmers' lives were all about." He grew quiet a moment as he studied something he'd found on the computer. "Here in America, we're right back where we started. You think those fat bastards in Washington, those lawyers, have any idea what it's like to lose your job to an Indian because of affirmative action?"

"Or lose your business because some damn owl lives in the trees you got a lease to cut," Bo Peterson added angrily.

"The government governs," Hanover went on, "with the consent of the people. But what happens, O'Connor, when the people no longer give consent? And what happens when those in power refuse to acknowledge the people's dissent?"

"The Minnesota Civilian Brigade," Cork guessed.

"And the Viper Militia and the Freeman and the Posse Comitatus. All this is only a beginning. A prelude. We're in touch with others like us all across the country. It's coming. Lexington and Concord all over again. And we're going to be ready."

Hanover stepped away from the computer and looked more carefully at the documents on the desk.

"If you'd like, I'll explain everything to you, Helm," Cork offered.

"It would be interesting," Hanover replied, "to find out just how much you know."

Cork moved, and Lamarck and Peterson tensed, ready to spring. He held his hands up to show he meant no harm.

"Most of it's pretty simple. GameTech supplies the Chippewa Grand Casino with all of its gaming equipment. GameTech purchases the equipment from a number of companies, then leases to the casino. If you compare the cost of leasing with the outright purchase price, you'll see that within a very short time the casino has paid out far more to GameTech than the machines would ever be worth. Over several years, it could amount to millions. Quite a carrot to dangle in front of you wasn't it, Helm?"

"What do you mean?"

"The judge was a son of a bitch. Power hungry. When he cut his own political throat, he started looking for other avenues. My guess is that Harlan Lytton was his connection with the brigade, and he offered you a partnership in GameTech, a continuing source of substantial income to finance arms for the brigade. In return, he wanted to wear a uniform and be saluted by men like Bo and Al, here."

"Like we'd ever salute that old prick," Lamarck scoffed.

"He wanted to share command, Helm?" Cork guessed. "That was part of the bargain?"

"Share?" Hell Hanover nearly spit. "The bastard wanted it all. He was a pain in the ass."

"So you eliminated him."

Hanover appeared to be truly confounded. "What are you talking about?"

"What I don't understand," Cork went on, "is why you killed him before you knew where he kept all the paperwork."

"Are you crazy, O'Connor? What the hell are you talking about, killed the judge? He killed himself. The old shit was riddled with cancer. Everybody knows that." Hanover stared at him, still looking puzzled.

From the hallway beyond the door came the thud of boots.

"Set'er up there, Roy," a man said. "We can pull down those ceiling tiles and get to the ducts from here. Blueprints say there's a junction up above."

Hanover exchanged a look of concern with his men. His blue eyes shot to the broken glass on the door.

"Let me ask you a question, Helm," Cork ventured, speaking quietly, as if for the benefit of the men of the brigade. "Were you thinking of killing me?"

"I'm still thinking of it," Helm said.

"I wouldn't if I were you."

"Why? If you were me."

"Those men out there, for one thing. Witnesses. Loose ends. Unless you intend to kill a lot of innocent people, too."

"Sometimes innocent people have to die," Hanover said.

"There's no reason to kill me. Or them. Especially if it's true you didn't kill the judge."

"I wouldn't have minded killing him, but I didn't."

"What I'm saying is that on paper you've committed no crime. The partnership agreement seems valid enough. So do the equipment leases. It looks like the judge took care of taxes and anything else that might have brought GameTech under too much scrutiny. So far everything's legal. Except for the military hardware hanging on the hips of your honor guard there."

Lamarck and Peterson automatically glanced down at their weapons.

"Why don't you call it a day, Helm," Cork suggested.

Hanover's mouth was thin and tight, as if a razor had been drawn across his face in a bloodless cut. "We'll lose GameTech. You'll see to that."

"You were going to lose it anyway. The judge's un-

timely death did that, not me. Too many people looking too closely at things. If it hadn't been me, it would
have been somebody else. Cut your losses, Helm.
This isn't Lexington and Concord yet."

From the hallway came the snap of a stepladder
locking into place, followed by the scrape of its aluminum legs on tile. "Get Luther on the walkie-talkie,
tell him we'll be down here a while. We'll let him
know when we hit the junction."

"What're we gonna do?" Lamarck asked.

"Leave now, Helm. There'll be other battles for
the brigade," Cork offered judiciously.

Peterson said, "We gotta do something, Helm."

Hanover's eyes were frozen on Cork. His bare
scalp glistened. Finally he nodded, once. "Another
day, O'Connor." He settled the black stocking cap on
his head and moved from the desk limping toward
the door. "Come on, let's go."

When the men had gone, Cork gathered the documents from the desk. As he took a last look at the
GameTech office, he noticed an indentation in the
carpeting next to the file cabinet. He knelt and looked
at it carefully. It was just the right size and shape
for the cabinet that had held the files Wally Schanno
burned.

Wally and Arletta Schanno lived just outside Aurora in a nice one-story rambler painted blue with
gray shutters on the windows. The back of the lot ran
along the east side of a small pond surrounded by
red pines. In the front yard stood a couple of crab
apple trees that were beautiful in the spring when the
branches were full of blossoms. Arletta Schanno was
famous in Tamarack County for her crab apple jelly.

Arletta answered the door, greeting Cork with a warm smile. "Sheriff O'Connor. What a nice surprise. Won't you come in?"

"Thanks, Arletta." Cork stepped in, tugging off his heavy gloves. "Is your husband home?"

"In here, Cork." Schanno's voice came from the living room.

"Let me take your coat," Arletta said. "And could I offer you coffee?"

"Thanks, no," Cork replied.

He handed her his coat and she hung it carefully in the closet of the entryway.

"Come on in, Cork," Schanno called to him.

Cork walked to the living room. It was a pleasant room with a flowered sofa and matching love seat and a big leather easy chair, where Schanno sat in a robe with his bandaged leg up on an ottoman. A glass-topped coffee table was situated between the sofa and love seat, a small white vase full of silk daisies in the center and several issues of *Smithsonian* magazine fanned out carefully beside it. Proudly displayed on the mantel above a pale brick fireplace were framed high-school graduation photographs of the Schannos' two daughters. Between the photos sat a beautiful old Seth Thomas clock. A decorated Christmas tree—a big Scotch pine—took up one corner of the room. A large console occupied another, but the television in it was off. Schanno took off his glasses and closed a book on his lap. Cork saw he'd been reading from the Bible. Revised Standard Version.

"Taking good care of him?" Cork asked Arletta, who'd followed him in.

"He's difficult." She smiled and shook her head hopelessly. "Could I offer you coffee?"

"You already did," Schanno reminded her gently.

For a moment a look of distress and then sadness came over Arletta's pretty face.

"That's a nice tree you have there," Cork put in quickly.

She brightened immediately. "The girls like them big. Do you have children, Sheriff?"

"Three," Cork replied. She'd taught two of them, Jenny and Annie, when they passed through her third grade class at Aurora Elementary. He'd sat in conferences with Arletta many times.

"Then you know. Christmas is such an important time for children."

"I wonder if I could speak with your husband alone, Arletta."

"Why, certainly. I've got things to do myself." She started away, but turned back suddenly. "May I get you a cup of coffee or anything before I go?"

"No thank you," Cork said.

Arletta left, humming softly to herself.

"Have a seat," Schanno said.

Cork sat on the flowered sofa.

"This a friendly visit or official?" Schanno asked.

"They told me at the department that you were home, nursing that leg," Cork said. "I've got to have some answers, Wally."

Schanno settled back. "Sounds official."

Cork leaned toward him. "Tell me about GameTech."

"GameTech?" Schanno gave him a blank look.

"You heard me. GameTech."

Schanno shrugged. "There's nothing to tell."

"What is GameTech?"

Arletta passed in the hallway, heading from the kitchen toward the back of the house. She was singing softly in a fine voice, "Sleigh bells ring, are you listening . . ."

"Just a company I do some security consulting for."

"Security consulting? What exactly does that involve?"

Schanno gave him a hard, impatient look. "What the hell do you think it involves?"

"Building security?" Cork offered. "Personnel checks. That kind of thing?"

"Yes, that kind of thing."

"Who hired you?"

"What's all this about, Cork?"

"Who hired you, Wally?" Cork pressed him.

"How do you know about GameTech?" Schanno countered angrily.

"You didn't answer my question."

"I'm not going to play games with you."

"Not a game, Wally. People are dead." Cork kept his voice low because of Arletta, but there was an explosive tension in his words. "You're a security consultant for GameTech. Stu Grantham, head of the board of supervisors, is a real estate consultant. Mark Hawras, the BIA man out of this district, is consultant on Indian affairs. And Sigurd Nelson, of all people, is a personnel consultant. I could go on. It's a long list. If you were me, what would you think? Wally, did you burn those files to cover your ass, or maybe to cover somebody else's?"

Schanno's long hands gripped the arms of his chair, making deep indentations in the leather. "There was nothing in those files that had to do with GameTech. I give you my word."

"Hell, Wally, right now your word carries about as

much weight with me as a rabbit turd. What's Game-Tech all about?"

"GameTech is perfectly legal," Schanno insisted.

"Then why are you so jumpy? Why won't you tell me who hired you? What is it that's making you so nervous if everything's so legal? Come on, Wally, what's going on with GameTech? Is GameTech why all these men are dead?"

Wally's right fist came down on the arm of his chair. "I told you, GameTech's got nothing to do with anything that's happened!"

"You keep talking, Wally, but I don't hear any answers. What are you hiding? What are you so afraid of?"

Schanno gave Cork a fierce glare with his hard gray eyes. His long jaw worked, but he didn't say a word. He breathed through his nose, deep and fast, and the air moved in and out in angry little whistles.

"All right," Cork told him coolly, "I'll tell you what I know, then I'll tell you what I suspect. Then if I don't get something more out of you, I'll give a call to a reporter I know on the *St. Paul Pioneer Press*. We'll see how you like it with your name in headlines."

Cork stood up and walked to the Christmas tree. It was nicely done. Lots of colored bulbs. Garlands. Icicles. Ornaments that looked old and probably conjured memories for the Schannos of Christmases past. More pleasant Christmases than this one, for sure.

"I checked out the GameTech office in Duluth," Cork told him. "Checked it out this morning. A one-room office in an old building, Wally. No warehouse. No machines, no parts. Just one room. You were doing building security for a company that has one room. And personnel checks? As near as I could tell the only personnel on the GameTech payroll are all consultants like you, paid pretty well for doing nothing. Am I right?"

Schanno looked down at his bandaged leg and didn't appear to have anything to say yet.

"Ernie Meloux adds the GameTech logo to all the gaming equipment at the casino. He doesn't know why. Just does what he's told. The judge bought gaming equipment and leased it to the casino through GameTech. Didn't even bother to launder the process much. Had the companies ship the equipment straight to the casino, where Ernie added the logo. The lease agreements I saw and the invoices for the equipment made it pretty clear that GameTech's making a fortune off the arrangement. A nice pool of money for the judge to draw on. And what for? I'd guess that if he didn't have dirt on somebody, he simply bought them. You and Sigurd Nelson and Stu Grantham and the others. And no one really gets hurt in the end, right? Sure, a little money's siphoned from all that cash the Indians are raking in. But with so much, who's to miss it? And the beauty of it is that it's all perfectly legal. Am I right, Wally? Your hands are clean, aren't they?"

Schanno's anger had drained away. His already gaunt face seemed to have caved in. He closed his eyes.

Cork walked to him and leaned close. "But the judge had you by the balls, didn't he, Wally? You and the others. Maybe you wouldn't go to jail over it, but if people knew about you and GameTech, an otherwise sterling reputation would be sorely tarnished. A hard way for a man to end his career, eh, Wally?" Cork stood upright. "The night Blackwater shot you, he wasn't after me. He was after that file you showed me. He was at the judge's because it was the judge who had been blackmailing him, Wally. And you were there for the same reason, weren't you? Looking for anything that might implicate you in all this. It didn't have anything to do with trying to get the truth. Why in God's name would you ever let yourself get into that kind of bind?"

Schanno turned his head, following the music of Arletta's singing in the back room. "She'll only get worse," he said quietly. "Eventually she'll require constant care. On a sheriff's salary, all I could afford is some damn nursing home or institution. I figured the money would let me keep her here somehow, where she's been happy. Where we've been happy." He listened a minute more, then looked back at Cork. "I couldn't stand the thought of her somewhere where no one really cared. Do you understand?"

Sure, he understood. But people were dead. And that made a difference. He walked back to the Christmas tree.

"Did the judge ever ask anything of you?" Cork said.

"What do you mean?"

"Anything you thought about twice, anything that ran against your grain?"

"You mean illegal?" Schanno sounded incensed at the idea.

"For God's sake, Wally, the man was giving you money under the table. He wasn't Santa Claus."

"No," Wally said, anger again putting a hard edge to his voice.

"What about Joe John LeBeau?"

"What about him?"

"How carefully did you investigate his disappearance?"

"Joe John was a man with a history of drinking

and running off. His truck reeked of whiskey. I didn't spend much time on it at all. Would you?" His eyes narrowed on Cork. "Why?"

Cork went to his coat hanging in the closet. He took out the prints he'd made at Lytton's. "Take a look at these."

Schanno lifted his reading glasses from where he'd set them on the gold-leafed Bible in his lap and slipped them on. He spent a couple of minutes looking carefully at the photographs. Finally he turned his face up toward Cork. He looked broken. "I didn't know. I swear to you, Cork, I didn't know."

"I'll ask again, Wally. Those files you burned. Did you do it to cover your own ass? Did you do it to cover for someone else?"

"No," Schanno insisted earnestly. "I did it because what was in those files would only bring shame to a lot of decent people. God as my witness, nothing I burned was anything like this." He nodded toward the photos. "I guess you found the negatives. I'd've looked for them myself except for this bum leg. Where in heaven's name did you find them?"

"About as far from heaven as you can get, Wally." He reached for the prints; Schanno seemed reluctant to give them over.

"I should keep them," he said.

"What for?"

"I'll need to reopen Joe John's case."

"Maybe. Maybe not." Cork pulled the prints away.

"What are you going to do, Cork?"

"I'll know that when I've finally dug down to the bottom of this whole pile of shit."

"Maybe it all went down just like it seems," Schanno said with faint hope. "Blackwater really did kill the judge and Lytton because of blackmail."

"That theory almost ties everything together nicely, but not quite."

"What's left?"

"Two things. First, the judge had a partner. Hell Hanover. I'm pretty sure GameTech is the source of the money the brigade's been getting. I've got documents and photographs I'll turn over to you later. I don't care about you and GameTech, Wally. But I want the brigade taken care of."

"And the other thing?"

"The boy," Cork said. "Paul LeBeau. He saw something at the judge's house that scared him into hiding. I want to know what."

"You'll have to find him first. I couldn't."

"I think I know who can." Cork stood a moment, looking down at Schanno who seemed to have shriveled in just the few minutes that Cork had been there.

"Did I really do anything so wrong?" Schanno asked, his face sunk deep into hopelessness.

"You stopped looking for the truth, Wally. But I'd guess that's a sin we've all been guilty of." He turned toward the entryway. "I'll be in touch."

He paused at the front door before leaving. He listened to Arletta still singing somewhere in a back room. There was a joyfulness in her voice that carried beautifully the feel of what the season was supposed to be all about. Cork opened the door and stepped outside wondering if Arletta had any idea what awaited her beyond that season.

CHAPTER 38

Molly stepped out the back door of the Pinewood Broiler. Her skis and poles stood propped against the wall beside the Dumpster. She lifted them, cradled the skis on her shoulder, and hiked three blocks to the lake.

Sunlight exploded out of a sky as blue as she'd ever seen. The lake was empty, not even a snowmobile breaking the stillness. Far out stood the ice shanties, clustered here and there like isolated little communities. They reminded her of the deserted towns in westerns when all the cowardly citizens hid themselves just before the outlaws rode in.

She skied north, skirting the open water behind the brewery, where Russell Blackwater had drowned after trying to shoot Cork. Thank you, she found herself saying, with a little upward cast of her eyes, for keeping Cork safe. She passed North Point, where the judge had been found dead and Sheriff Wally Schanno had been wounded. She knew that somehow it was all tied to the killing of Joe John LeBeau. Terrible events, for sure, but on that glorious afternoon, with the sun at her back and the vast pure white of the lake all her own, she didn't want to dwell on tragedy. She felt no guilt about that at all. In fact, she wasn't sure if she'd ever felt better.

Halfway home she stopped and turned back. Leaning on her poles, she stared toward Aurora, which was mostly a distant feathering of chimney smoke. She had never loved the town, never felt a sense of belonging there. Years before when she'd run away, she'd left nothing behind her. After her father died, she'd returned only to take care of business, with the idea of selling the old resort, which she put immediately on the market. No one made an offer. The big cabin was run-down and the smaller ones fallen into even greater ruin. She took the job at the Pinewood Broiler and began to fix up the big cabin, at first with no greater intention than to ensure the plumbing worked reliably and she could eat a meal at the kitchen table without a chair leg snapping under her. She worked alone, learning as she went. The more she accomplished, the more she planned. She refinished the kitchen table. She tuck-pointed the fireplace chimney and repaired the mantel. She replaced the copper tubing to all the faucets so the water flowed hard and fast.

In her second summer, she received an offer. An architect from the Twin Cities wanted to buy the big cabin, gut it, and fashion it to his own taste. The offer was good money. But in the end she turned it down and took the place off the market.

She smiled as she looked back at Aurora. It wasn't heaven, not by a long stretch, but she had something there that no other place offered her. She had history, which some people might call roots, and she had a future now.

She stopped at the sauna and started a fire in the stove. She was hoping that Cork might have finished his business and come back already, but when she reached the cabin, Cork's Bronco wasn't there.

She leaned her skis and poles beside the back door and stepped into the kitchen. The cabin felt empty. She shook off her disappointment and decided to go ahead and sauna alone. After that, she'd come back and clear a space for the Christmas tree.

While the sauna heated, she cut herself a slice of dark bread and ate it with butter and honey. She poured a big glass of juice. As she drank it, she made a decision definitely to take the next day off. She'd spend it with Cork somehow, the whole day. Maybe get him on his skis over on the North Arm trails. Or maybe just lounge in bed all day. It would be a first, whatever they did, because at the end of it, he wouldn't have to leave.

She went to the wall phone by the refrigerator, intending to call the Pinewood. The phone was dead. That wasn't too unusual. Ice on the lines sometimes brought them down. Or a tree that fell in the wind. She'd take care of it later.

She rinsed out the juice glass, put away the butter and honey, and wiped the bread crumbs from the cutting board. She was just about to step outside and head down to the sauna when she heard the groan of an old plank on the stairway.

"Cork?" she called, startled. "Is that you?"

Stepping into the main room, she looked toward the stairs and listened. On impulse, she checked the woodbox. The paper sack that held the plastic bag full of negatives was still hidden under the logs. She walked to the stairs and stood looking up toward the second floor. Not a sound anywhere. The old place often gave a groan here or there, and she never took notice. But the bag was in the cabin now, and that made a difference.

A single knock at the back door brought her around

suddenly. She made her way cautiously to the kitchen. She couldn't see anyone waiting on the back steps, and she debated opening the door. Why only one knock? she asked herself. And who would knock once and then leave? Finally she reached for the knob and opened the door.

A ski fell in. She jumped back startled, then laughed at herself. It was a ski that had come knocking. One of her skis that had fallen against the door. She laughed at herself. All this cloak-and-dagger stuff was getting to her.

She went upstairs and took a fresh fluffy towel from the bathroom and a pair of white socks from her bedroom dresser, then headed down to the sauna. In the dressing room, she took her clothes off and laid them carefully on the bench. Between the heat from the stove and the sunlight streaming through the windows, the room felt warm and inviting. She took the pair of white socks to wear when she ran onto the ice and she stepped into the sauna. Except for the firelight through the grating of the stove, the small room was dark. She dipped water from a bucket and threw it on the heated stones and an explosion of steam rose up. She sat on the highest bench. In a few minutes she was sweating profusely.

Closing her eyes, she began to let herself dream. Not sleep dreaming, but dreaming of how her life might be. It was a thing she didn't often do. In her experience, good things came with great difficulty and were too easily snatched away. She'd long ago learned to accept what she had at any given moment and try to be happy with only that. She could think about the future, plan even, but not expect. It was the expectation that was the trap.

But there she was, dripping in the sauna, expecting

great things of her future with Cork. It was foolish, she knew, but she let herself indulge, just this once. She was happy, happier than she could ever remember.

The door toward the lake swung open and blinding sunlight invaded her dark. She blinked at it, saw a big silhouette fill the doorway.

"Cork?" she asked, shielding her eyes, trying to see.

The silhouetted figure took a step toward her, coming in with the cold. "Guess again."

CHAPTER 39

"He's not here," Ellie Gruber told Cork at the rectory door. "Father Griffin left this morning before I got here and hasn't been back."

"Did he tell Father Kelsey where he was going?"

"He never says where he's going," she said with exasperation. "And I mean to tell you it's got Father Kelsey more than a little upset."

"Did he take his motorcycle or his snowmobile?" Cork asked.

"Why that old snowmobile went kaput nearly a week ago. He's left it out at the mission, I believe. So he took that old monster of a motorcycle, must be."

"Lazarus is still at the mission? Are you sure?"

She thought a moment. "I suppose I am."

The reservation road curved between solid pines, then dipped into a long flat area of marsh populated by swamp alder, tamarack, and gnarled oak. Cork came to a turnoff in the marsh half a mile shy of the old mission. The turnoff was a road that had been started into the marsh so long ago Cork couldn't even remember why. There was nothing to log, and the ground was too swampy to support buildings of any kind. Construction hadn't progressed well, evidenced by an old bulldozer that lay sunk in the marsh near the road, only one rust-crusted corner of the blade left above the snow. Work had been abandoned before the road had gone even a quarter of a mile. The dead end turnoff was blocked now by a bank of plowed snow. Cork put the Bronco into four-wheel drive and cleared the snowbank. He drove a hundred yards into the trees until he was out of sight of the main road and he parked.

He fed a few shells into his Winchester. Then he took off his coat and his red flannel shirt, which left him dressed in his jeans—the denim had been washed so many times they were nearly white as ice—his white wool thermal top, white Nikes, and a light gray stocking cap. In the pale winter colors, he was less likely to be seen, but he was also likely to freeze if he had to spend a lot of time dressed that way. He hoped he wouldn't.

The mission stood in the middle of a meadow beyond a hill at the end of the marsh. Cork approached the top of the rise in a crouch, keeping to the gray shadow of the snowbank. A hundred and fifty yards ahead, rising white from the white of the snow in the meadow, stood the old mission building. Smoke feathered up from the stovepipe toward the high blue-white of the sky. He knelt and watched the mission for a while. In the wide flat of the meadow and along the dark wall of pine trees and bare birch that surrounded it, nothing moved. He was to the north of the building and a little east. It was nearing two o'clock and the sun was low and bright. Staring into the glare off the field of snow made his eyes water. Finally he had to look away. The images behind him seemed darker then. The tamaracks, the swamp alders, the bare oaks. A shadow flickered over the road and a large crow alighted on a branch of a young tamarack near Cork. It cocked a yellow eye at him, but seemed content to be quietly curious. To the Anishinaabe, the crow was a symbol of wisdom. As he crouched shivering from the cold, Cork hoped the bird was a good sign that he'd find some answers before he froze to death.

He glanced again at the mission and immediately hunkered lower.

Someone stood outside the back door. He couldn't tell if it was a man or a woman. Whoever it was stood very still and seemed to be looking across the meadow to Cork's right where a white-tail doe and her two yearlings had come out of the woods. They stepped carefully in the deep snowdrifts. The yearlings had to leap to keep up. The doe would take a few steps and pause, her body poised in an alert stance, her ears flickering left and right as she watched and listened. Each time she stopped the yearlings took the opportunity to bound to her side. All three were coming straight at Cork. If he didn't move, the deer would lead the eyes of the watching figure right to him. If he did move, the deer would bolt. In either event, he stood a good chance of giving himself away. He sat frozen in place, watching the deer approach.

From behind him came the sound of a vehicle on the reservation road. Cork glanced back. He couldn't see anything yet, but in only a few moments the vehicle would round the curve and drop down into the flat of the marsh and whoever it was that was coming would clearly see him. But there was no way to move without being seen from the mission. He was trapped.

It was the crow who saved him. The black bird sud-

denly let out three shrill caws that broke like thunder-
bolts through the stillness of the meadow. The doe's
eyes darted toward Cork and she lurched away with
the two yearlings leaping wildly after her. The figure
at the mission watched the deer intently as they fled.
In the moment before the animals disappeared again
into the woods, when the eyes of the watcher were
turned farthest from Cork, he threw himself and the
Winchester over the snowbank and sunk facedown
into the soft snow on the far side. He lay unmoving as the vehicle—an old truck, he guessed from
the deep sound of the engine and the rattle of the
undercarriage—followed the road into the low-lying
marsh area, came up the rise, and passed on the other
side of the snowbank. He heard it pull to a stop at the
mission and heard the sound of its old doors squeak-
ing open and slamming shut. He heard voices briefly,
but didn't want to look for fear of being seen.

Several minutes passed before he finally risked a
peek. There was no one to be seen at the mission.
The vehicle that had come along the road had parked
on the far side of the building and wasn't visible to
him. He grabbed the Winchester, made a dive over
the snowbank, and rolled onto the road. Crawling to
the shelter of the snowbank's shadow, he crouched,
shivering violently. He was wet from lying in the
snow, and he knew he had to do something quickly.
He could head for the Bronco and warm up, but if he
did he might miss a chance at uncovering something
important at the mission.

He moved toward the building, staying below the
snowbank and in its shadow as much as possible. As
he approached the mission, he saw that both Lazarus
and Father Tom Griffin's old Kawasaki motorcycle
were parked behind it. Cork dashed to the side of the

building, where he stood in a thigh-deep drift and pressed himself against the old white wood planking. The shades over all the windows had been pulled. He leaned near the glass of a front window and listened.

Inside, someone whimpered as if being hurt.

CHAPTER 40

Cork crept to the back of the mission building and peered around the corner. A half cord of split wood lay stacked near the back door. The snow behind the building was hard packed by a lot of comings and goings. The deep snow off to the sides of the back entrance was stained yellow where someone had done a good deal of urinating. He edged his way to the door. Leaning close, he listened again for the whimper. This time the only sound he heard was the click of the latch as the door was thrown open and the long blue barrel of a rifle came at him out of the dark inside.

"You alone?"

"Alone." Cork nodded. He slowly lowered the Winchester and leaned it against the side of the mission.

Wanda Manydeeds motioned him back with the rifle and risked a glance out the door, right then left. She jerked her head toward the room behind her. "Inside."

She moved back to let Cork through, then closed the door behind him. Only a dim light filtered through the drawn shades into the mission's single room. Cork's pupils were still contracted from the sunlight outside and he felt blind, as if he'd stepped into a dark cave. He stumbled over something soft, but caught himself before he fell. Near one of the windows he identified the black, bulky silhouette of a potbelly stove, the source of the warmth in the room. Not far to his left, stacked against a wall under a window, lay a clutter of two-by-fours along with a couple of sawhorses, evidence of St. Kawasaki's continuing efforts to refurbish the old structure. Directly ahead, worn gray benches marched away in rows toward the far, as yet impenetrable, dark at the front of the mission. From that dark came a whimper.

"*Shhhh*, Makwa. *Shhhh*," a soft voice cooed.

Another voice suggested firmly, "Put the rifle down, Wanda."

The old floorboards squeaked and groaned as St. Kawasaki came forward out of the dark. He was followed by Darla LeBeau. Someone else came a few steps behind Darla. It was Paul LeBeau. He carried a squirming bundle of blanket in his arms.

"*Poo-wah*," Paul said, speaking in Ojibwe slang. It stinks. "He needs his diapers changed, Aunt Wanda," he said in English.

Wanda Manydeeds set the rifle against the wall and took the baby.

The priest was grinning. "Here Darla and I spent all morning trying to find you, and it was you who found us. How'd you know to come here?"

"I was looking for Lazarus," Cork replied. "It keeps rising from the dead." Cork glanced at the stove. "I'm freezing, Tom. Mind if I warm up?"

"Go ahead. By all means."

Heat rolled off the stove, and Cork stood turning first one side of his body then the other to the hot cast iron.

"You saw me coming?" he asked.

"Paul saw someone," Tom Griffin replied. "We didn't know it was you."

"You've been here the whole time?" he asked the boy.

Paul looked to the priest, who gave him an almost imperceptible nod. "Mostly," Paul answered. "Father Tom thought it was the safest place."

Cork, whose eyes had just about adjusted to the faint light inside the mission, noticed the sleeping bag rolled and tied on the floor. That was the soft obstacle he'd stumbled over on entering the mission. He also saw several sacks of groceries lined up on one of the benches.

"Safe from what?" he asked.

No one answered his question. He studied the boy—hardly a boy anymore. Paul stood nearly as tall as he. If he kept growing, he'd easily reach his father's height.

"Someone drove Lazarus out to Harlan Lytton's place yesterday," Cork went on. "Was it you, Tom?"

"No." The priest looked puzzled and glanced at the boy.

"I was there," Paul admitted.

"In the ski mask?" Cork asked.

The boy shook his head. "I fired a couple shots at the ski mask and scared him away."

"Fired a couple of shots?" the priest said with surprise. "Wait a minute. Paul, put some more wood in that stove. Crank up the heat for our friend. Cork, we'll tell you everything, but it's going to take a while." He glanced at Paul. "Maybe even longer than I thought. How about putting some hot water on the stove, Darla? I could use some coffee. Even if it's instant."

Paul and Darla did as the priest directed. Wanda Manydeeds finished changing Makwa's diapers.

"Cork, help me haul this pew nearer the stove," the priest said. "Give you a warm place to sit."

When the backless old pew was settled, the water hot, and the instant coffee stirred into foam plastic cups that had been pulled from the grocery bags, the priest said, "Okay, let's talk. But before we do, I want to remind you of a couple of things, Cork. First of all, you're not the sheriff anymore. That's one reason we've all decided to trust you. Also you told me not long ago that you don't believe there is such a thing as justice. These people feel the same way."

Cork sat on the pew near Wanda Manydeeds, who rocked Mawka. Darla and Paul stood near the back door. Tom Griffin moved about freely with his coffee in his hand, gesturing toward those present.

"What we discuss here goes no further," the priest said.

"Then why tell me at all?"

"Because I think you'll keep digging until you know the truth anyway. We'd just as soon try to deal with it now."

Cork considered them all a moment. "All right. But first there's something I have to tell you." He looked at Darla and Paul LeBeau. "You might want to sit down."

Darla moved to her son and put her arm protectively around him, although he was a full head taller than she. "We're fine," she said.

He plunged in, telling it bluntly because there seemed no other way. "Joe John's dead. I believe he was murdered."

He'd delivered tragic news before. It had been part of the job, but he'd never become immune to the effect tragedy had on those who had to hear of it, and he'd never become used to his own feeling of helplessness in those situations. But the LeBeaus surprised him. Their faces didn't change in the least.

"They know, Cork," St. Kawasaki informed him quietly. "I already told them."

"You knew?" Cork asked the priest.

"I've known since Vernon Blackwater passed away." He gestured toward Wanda. "We both have known."

"How?"

Wanda spoke while she rocked Makwa next to her breast. "When Vernon was dying, he asked us both to come. Tom for the part of him that was Catholic, me because I am a Midewiwin. We were alone in the room with him. When he made a last confession to Tom, I overheard."

"He confessed to helping kill Joe John?" Cork asked the priest.

Tom Griffin stood near a window looking uncomfortable. "Why don't you talk to Wanda about what she overheard. It probably doesn't matter now, but I still don't feel right about sharing with you what was told to me in confession."

"You shared it with Darla and Paul," Cork pointed out.

"That was different. I had no choice."

"Why?"

The priest pulled the shade away from the window just a crack and looked out at the road. A streak of afternoon sunlight cut across his face like yellow war paint. "Because I had to explain to Paul why the judge was dead."

Cork felt as if his brain were stuffed with cotton. He squinted at St. Kawasaki and asked dumbly, "Was it you who killed the judge?"

The priest let the shade fall back into place and shook his head. "No."

Wanda said, "I did."

Makwa began to whimper again. Wanda stood up and walked slowly about the room, cooing softly to her baby. She didn't seem in any hurry to tell Cork any more.

"Was it an accident, Wanda?" Cork asked hopefully.

"No. I meant to kill him."

"Here," Darla said to Wanda when the baby went on fussing, "let me take him awhile."

Wanda gave Makwa over to her sister-in-law and turned back to Cork. Her long black hair was braided and hung over her shoulder like a length of rope. Her face was the color of sandstone and no less hard.

"Vernon confessed to watching Harlan Lytton kill my brother. He said the judge set it up. He wouldn't say why, only that Joe John was murdered and the judge and Lytton were responsible. Vernon didn't want to die with that secret weighing on him as he walked the Path of Souls."

Cork glanced at the priest. "Did you ask him why?"

St. Kawasaki shook his head. "He was barely able to speak as it was. I just listened."

"You should have asked," Wanda said with an accusing tone.

"I was his confessor, Wanda, not his inquisitor," the priest reminded her gently. "We've speculated it probably had something to do with Russell embezzling."

"You know about that?" Cork was surprised.

"Everybody knows about that now," Wanda said.

"Small town," the priest added.

"So what happened between you and the judge?" he asked Wanda.

"I went there that afternoon to talk to him. Tom

wanted me to wait until we could figure a way to do something about it. I didn't want to wait. I couldn't. It was like having a wild animal inside me eating me up."

"So you confronted the judge," Cork said.

"Yes."

"And I'll bet he just laughed at you."

Wanda gave Cork a look that said he was right on the money.

"He said I had no proof of anything. 'Hearsay,' is what he called it. I told him I didn't need any proof. I'd just tell what I'd heard. People would listen."

"You threatened the judge? I would like to have been there. What did he do?"

Wanda, who'd looked directly at Cork until that moment, looked away.

"He threatened her back, Cork," St. Kawasaki said. "He had some . . . information." The priest hesitated, and it seemed as if he and Wanda spoke silently to one another with their eyes.

Cork said, "It's all right. I know about the judge and his pieces of information. You're not the only one he dealt with that way, Wanda. What happened then?"

"He told me to get out," Wanda went on bitterly. "He turned away to go to the front door. I grabbed the poker from the fireplace and I hit him. I didn't even think about it. I just hit him, right in the back of the head." She put her hand on her own head to show Cork.

"Then you put the shotgun into his mouth to make it look like suicide," Cork finished for her.

"No." The priest folded his arms and leaned against the mission wall. "That was my doing," he said.

"You?"

"Wanda called me from the judge's place. I went

over on Lazarus, cut across the lake as fast as I could. He was dead when I got there."

"And you figured in a white courtroom, under white law, Wanda stood a snowball's chance in hell of getting justice. So you faked the suicide."

"That's about the size of it, Cork. It wasn't pleasant, but it was workable. I've seen worse things in my life, believe me."

Cork did. He rubbed his forehead a moment, wishing like hell he had a cigarette. He glanced at Paul. "So you must have stumbled onto all this, is that it?"

"Yeah," Paul said.

"About where did you come in?"

"When I delivered the paper, I heard the shotgun go off."

"And you went inside to check on the judge. But you found Father Tom and your Aunt Wanda instead."

The boy nodded.

The priest broke in, "I brought him out here so I could explain to him carefully what he saw. Then I went to Darla's to get her so she wouldn't be worried. When you came and told us the sheriff wanted to speak to Paul about the judge, I thought it would be best to keep him out here awhile. We let out that Joe John was around, hoping to create a little smoke."

"What about Harlan Lytton, Tom? Whose doing was that?"

The silence of the room reminded Cork of how it was to be underwater, making your way to the surface in a thick, unbreathable stillness. Everyone looked at everyone else and all of them looked unhappy he'd asked.

It was Paul, drawing himself up to his full height, who said, "I killed him. And I'd do it again."

If he'd sounded like a boy before, the youthful

sound was gone from his voice now. Cork looked at him and saw the hard face of a man.

"No, he wouldn't," Darla said, putting her arms around her son.

Paul shrugged away from her. "He killed my father and I killed him and I'd do it again without thinking twice."

"Cork," the priest interjected. "It wasn't entirely his fault. I left him Lazarus in case he needed transportation. And Wanda—well, Wanda—"

"I left him my rifle," she said evenly. "I didn't think he'd use it that way. But I don't blame him at all."

Cork studied the young man, who didn't flinch under his gaze. "And it was you on Lazarus at Lytton's place yesterday."

"Yes."

"What were you doing there?"

"I was there to kill another man," the boy said almost proudly.

"Paul!" His mother looked horrified.

"You don't mean that," St. Kawasaki told him.

"It's the truth," the boy said. "I thought we were supposed to be telling the truth."

"No, Paul," Darla pleaded.

"Let him tell it, Darla," St. Kawasaki said. "He's right. The truth is what we're here for. We've come this far."

"What man were you going to kill?" Cork asked young LeBeau.

"The last man who had a part in murdering my father," Paul said.

"Who was that?"

"Mr. Parrant."

"Mr. Parrant? You mean Sandy?"

"Yeah, him."

Darla put her hands to her mouth. "No," she whispered.

"Why do you think he had something to do with your father's death, Paul?" Cork asked.

"Well." Paul stopped a moment and seemed for the first time a little uncertain. He glanced at the priest and Wanda Manydeeds and his mother. "They said it."

"What did you say?" Cork asked them generally.

It was Darla who finally spoke. "Sandy Parrant said Joe John showed up drunk for work at Great North the night he disappeared. He said they had words and he fired him. I believed it then. Because of the way Joe John had been. God help me, I believed it. But Joe John was murdered. He didn't desert us. Sandy Parrant must have been lying."

"And why would he lie except to cover up?" the priest finished.

Cork looked back at the boy. "How did you know he was at Harlan Lytton's?"

"I went to his house yesterday," Paul said. "I was on Lazarus. I had Aunt Wanda's rifle. I was going to kill him."

"No, he wasn't," Darla insisted. "My son's not a killer."

"We all are under the right circumstances, Darla," Cork said. "Go on, Paul."

"I came across the lake, through his woods. But he was just leaving. I saw his car heading down the drive."

"What kind of car was it?"

"White." Paul shrugged.

"Just white?"

"I saw it through the trees."

"The man has a white vehicle of some kind," St. Kawasaki said.

"A lot of people have white vehicles," Cork pointed out. "Go on, Paul."

"I tried to follow him, running Lazarus down in the ditch beside the road. When I saw him turn off onto County 16, I figured he must be headed for the Lytton place. It's just about the only thing down that road. I caught the Glacier Trail. You know it cuts back of the Lytton property. So I got there ahead of him and hid in the trees. Only I didn't see him. It was you I saw. I watched and waited and when you came out of that shed, I saw him hit you with a club or something. I thought he was going to kill you. I shot at him. But," he added with a note of shame, "I missed."

"He got away, and it was you I almost took a shot at," Cork concluded. "I'm sorry, Paul."

The young man shrugged and managed a slight grin. "S'okay."

"You're sure it was Parrant?"

"It had to be."

"Did you see his face?"

"He was wearing a ski mask."

"The white vehicle. Did you see it at Lytton's?"

Paul shook his head, but said definitely, "It had to be him."

"Had to be?" Cork let his voice go very hard. "Would you swear to that in court? Would you swear absolutely beyond a shadow of a doubt it was Sandy Parrant who hit me?"

"Well—" Paul seemed confused by the sudden harshness in Cork's voice. He looked at the floor a moment.

"Swear to it beyond a shadow of a doubt." Cork pressed him.

"I guess I couldn't," Paul admitted.

"Cork, you're saying you don't think it was him?" Wanda asked, as if she couldn't believe what she'd heard.

"We have no real proof of anything. Nothing that involves Parrant directly," Cork replied. "It's all pretty circumstantial at this point."

"What about Vernon Blackwater's confession?" Wanda demanded.

"Did he mention Parrant at all?"

"No, but the man had to know."

"Isn't it possible," Cork offered, "that Joe John was drunk? Who knows why? And that Sandy did fire him and it had nothing to do with Joe John's murder?"

"Cork—"

"Do you have any proof of anything that involves Sandy Parrant?" He waited. "I take it your silence means no. So, you'd condemn a man to death on the basis of speculation, is that it?"

"We didn't condemn—" Wanda began.

"Your speculation put that rifle in Paul's hands yesterday. For all we know, he might have ended up killing an innocent man."

"I don't believe that for a minute," Wanda said. "Do you?"

"What I know is that we can fool ourselves into believing almost anything." Cork turned to Paul. "You killed Harlan Lytton. How did that feel?"

"If you want me to say I'm sorry, I won't," Paul told him stubbornly.

"That's not what I asked. How did it feel to kill a man?"

"Cork, please don't," Darla pleaded.

"Let him answer," the priest said.

Cork went on, "I saw the man on the floor of his cabin. His heart was shattered, blown apart, but he was still alive. He was still alive when you were in the cabin, too, wasn't he?"

The boy's face was stone.

Cork stood up and crossed to the boy. He leaned close. "He was alive. There was a hole in his chest and blood everywhere and you couldn't believe he could still be alive, but he was, wasn't he? Did he look at you? Did he try to talk to you? Was his voice all choked with the sound of him dying? How was it, Paul? How was it watching the man you killed die?"

The corners of his mouth twitched. His lips trembled. "I . . . He . . ."

"Did it feel good with the rifle in your hand and a man dying right there at your feet? Tell me how good it felt, Paul. Tell us all what a great feeling it was."

A wounded look entered Paul LeBeau's eyes. His face began to change. The hardness of the man melted like a wax mask, revealing the face of a child in great pain.

Cork pressed Paul harshly, "Go on. Tell us. Tell us all how good and honorable it felt."

Tears appeared along his lower lids and in a moment began to trickle down his cheeks. "He looked at . . . me . . ."

Darla tried to put herself between Paul and Cork. "Don't," she begged.

Cork took Paul harshly by the shoulders and pulled him away from his mother. Darla grabbed for him, but the priest held her back. Cork made the boy look at him. "Did it make you feel like a man to see him die? Did it?"

The boy couldn't speak. His voice was choked with sobbing. Finally he managed to say, "I'm sorry."

"Look at me," Cork ordered.

The boy raised his head.

"Once someone's dead, being sorry doesn't cut it. If you hit a man, you can apologize. If you destroy his property, you can pay him back. But if you take his life, there's nothing you can ever do to make that right. Do you understand?"

"Paul—" Darla tried to break free of the priest, who held her tightly.

"Do you understand, Paul?"

The boy wept so much he couldn't reply.

"You were ready to kill another man. A man who may be innocent. Could you live with that the rest of your life? Could you!"

The mission was filled with the sound of the boy's weeping.

"Answer me!" Cork demanded.

"No," the boy finally sobbed.

Cork, who'd kept Paul firmly at arm's length, drew him close. He put his arms around him and held him tightly while the boy wept. "No," Cork agreed gently. "And thank God for that."

After a while, Paul pulled away and Cork let him return to his mother. The priest said quietly, "I guess that's the truth of everything, Cork."

"What are you going to do?" Wanda asked.

Cork looked them over and sighed heavily. "I'm not the sheriff anymore." He said to Darla, "Keep Paul here a while longer, until this business is done for good." To the priest he said, "How about a ride to my Bronco."

"Cork." Wanda touched his arm. "*Migwech.*" Thanks.

St. Kawasaki stepped outside with Cork. The sun had dropped below the treeline and the snow across the meadow was a soft blue-white. The air was turning colder.

"I didn't know about Paul at Lytton's place yesterday," the priest said. "I feel responsible."

"Paul's responsible for his own actions. He knows it." Cork picked up his rifle from where it leaned against the mission wall. "Thanks," he said to Tom Griffin.

"For what?"

"Holding Darla. Letting me work with Paul."

"It was hard, but easier on him than the legal system. He's a fine young man." The priest took a deep breath. "So, what now?"

"Now I get what I need to put a real son of a bitch in his place."

"You have something on Parrant?"

"I think I probably do."

"And you'll be able to keep all this out of it?"

"Whatever happens, they're safe," he said, nodding toward the mission. He opened the door of Wanda Manydeeds's old truck. "I feel exhausted. Is this what you feel like after hearing a confession?"

"Usually," St. Kawasaki said, "I feel like a drink."

CHAPTER 41

Molly looked down on the water from a great height. The surface was perfectly blue and so still it looked like a cloudless sky. Lake Tahoe? she wondered. Tahoe was like that. Blue. Still. Cold. Freezing cold. So cold when she swam in it sometimes she hurt all over as if she were being squeezed by a great blue hand.

Like now, she thought suddenly. And she realized she was not above the water, but in it.

She shivered in the grip of that perfectly still water, in the terrible grip of the blue water cold as ice.

The sun burned her eyes. She should look away, she knew. If she looked at the sun too long, she would turn into a sunflower. She'd heard that when she was small from a lady at her father's cabin. The lady was fat and laughed a lot and gave her Baby Ruth and Oh Henry candy bars and smelled like flowers. Gardenias.

The fat lady pointed a plump finger at her and warned her laughing, you'll turn into a sunflower. Her father told her different, told her she'd go blind. Her father was probably right. Maybe that's why her head hurt so much. She was going blind from staring at the sun. He'd told her the truth. About that and many things. Told her she came from bad blood. Told her her mother was a tramp. Told her she would end up one, too. Told her men would be after her like devils, and if she let them have her, she would burn. Was that it? Was that the burning in her head? Was she burning like he said she would? Then why was the rest of her so cold?

She tried to lift her hand, to shield her eyes and block the fire that burned them. But she could not feel her hand, could not tell where it was, if it moved at all.

Am I dying? she wondered. Then why am I not afraid?

Cork's hands were full of flowers. Brilliant yellow petals around a black center. Sunflowers. He held them gently, held them out as if offering them. He stood on the still blue water with fire at his back, all alone with the sunflowers in his hands. She tried to call to him, but she had no voice. He let the flowers drop one by one onto the water. They landed without a ripple and floated toward her, formed a circle, and the circle was warm. That made her happy. To be warm again. She lay in the warm circle of sunflowers thinking how tired she was and how good it would feel to sleep. To sleep and sleep while she waited for Cork to lie down, too.

She was afraid.

. . . Did I tell him? . . .

The fire burned in the blue water around her, in the blue that was all that was left of her vision. The blue and the fire. And then the cloud, black as smoke, moved above her. In the shadow of the black cloud she could see no more.

. . . Did I tell him . . .

Yes.

The voice came from the cloud.

Yes, you told me.

. . . No . . . not you . . . did I tell Cork . . .

Tell him what?

But her eyes were too heavy, and she was too tired to talk. Molly fell back, fell into the dark, into the vast warm dark with one last question trailing her like a broken rope.

. . . Did I tell Cork . . . Did I tell him . . . did I tell him I love him . . .

CHAPTER 42

In the fading blue of the late afternoon light, Cork drove toward Aurora. He felt satisfied in a grim way. Things had fallen into place. Most things anyway. The judge. Lytton. Joe John LeBeau's incomprehensible abandonment of his family. All these things made sense and, in some way, had been reckoned with. There was, however, still one open loop to the maze of tragic events that had befallen Aurora, and down that last convoluted passage hid Sandy Parrant. Did he know he was being pursued? Cork wondered. If not, he soon would. The canvas bag was his undoing. With the evidence Cork was sure the bloody bag had held, he would nail Parrant's coffin shut. Bam!

It was going on four o'clock when Cork pulled into the parking lot of Johnny's Pinewood Broiler. He thought he'd surprise Molly with a lift home, but she wasn't there.

Johnny was hunched at the register, doing some figures with a pencil on the back of a menu. He looked slightly amused when Cork asked about Molly.

"She left two, three hours ago, big hurry. Said she had to go home to clear a space for a Christmas tree. Christmas tree." Johnny hooted. "No woman hustles that hard for a Christmas tree. It was a guy, I'll lay you odds." Johnny paused a moment, set his pencil down, and looked Cork over keenly. A broad grin spread across his face. "Well, knock me over with a feather."

Cork thanked him and headed toward the door.

"Christmas tree!" Johnny laughed at his back. "O, Tannenbaum," he called.

As Cork started back to his Bronco, a car braked hard on the street, hard enough to skid, and when he looked up, he saw Jo's blue Toyota back up, whip into the lot, and slide to a stop a few feet from where he stood. Jo leaped out, drilling him with an angry glare as she came. She glanced at the Pinewood, tugged off her gloves, and seemed for a moment on the verge of giving Cork a hard slap across the face.

"You know, you really had me fooled," she said bitterly.

"What do you mean?"

"I really believed you were serious about wanting to put things back together."

"I was."

"My ass," she snapped.

"Look, what's this all about, Jo?"

"Guilt, shame, remorse, you name it, I was feeding on it. What kind of horrible woman was I to have done that kind of thing to such a nice guy like you. Good father. Faithful husband. Oh, you were good."

Cork leaned against the hood of the Bronco. Jo's voice was carrying, and people on the sidewalk looked at them in passing.

"I don't have the slightest idea what you're talking about," he said.

"I'm talking about you and that slut Molly Nurmi." She jabbed a finger toward the Pinewood Broiler.

"What?"

"Don't look surprised. How long's it been going on, Cork? *Hmmm?* How long has she been giving you more than coffee at the Broiler?"

Cork took a step away from the Bronco and nearer Jo. The cloud of his breathing broke over her face. "Who told you about Molly?"

"What difference does it make?"

Cork grasped her shoulders. "Who told you?"

"Let go of me or I swear I'll have you arrested for assault. Don't think I won't." Cork let go and she smoothed her coat where his hands had gripped. "I'm not the only one who was caught with my pants down."

Cork studied the satisfaction on her face a moment, then understood. "Someone showed you the photographs."

"Good close shots, Cork. No mistake. A little sauna, a little skinny dip, a little—"

"Who showed you those pictures?"

Jo smiled enigmatically and didn't reply.

"Was it Sandy Parrant? It was Parrant, wasn't it?"

"I went to tell him it would be best not to see one another for a while. I was thinking maybe you and I ought to try to work through things, maybe with counseling this time. Foolish me."

"And he showed you the pictures?"

"Yes!" she threw at him, then shook her head with mock amazement. "You really had me going. You almost had me convinced."

Cork walked quickly past her toward the Broiler.

"Where are you going? I haven't finished," Jo called after him.

Cork pushed through the door of the Pinewood and went to the pay phone on the wall. He dug in his pocket for a quarter, but couldn't find one.

"Johnny," he called, "loan me a quarter for a phone call."

Johnny, who was still at the register, popped the cash drawer, slipped out a quarter, and tossed it to Cork. "There'll be interest." He laughed.

Jo stepped through the door and stood watching Cork. Johnny took a look at Jo, then at Cork, and said quietly, "Uh-oh."

Cork dialed Molly's number. All he got was a busy signal. He slammed the receiver down and hurried out the door.

"My quarter!" Johnny called.

But Cork was outside already, with Jo right behind him.

"What are you doing?" she asked.

"Parrant knows about me and Molly. I've got to get out there before he does." Cork broke into a run.

"Why?" Jo slipped on a patch of ice, caught herself, and rushed to catch up. "What would he want with her?"

"Not her. What she has."

Cork jumped into the Bronco. Jo got into the passenger side.

"What do you think you're doing?" Cork growled.

"I want to make sure it's not Sandy you're after. I don't want you doing anything stupid."

"Hold on," Cork said, too worried about Molly to argue.

He shot the Bronco in reverse, nearly sliding into the Dumpster in back of the Broiler. Then he skidded onto the street and headed toward Molly's.

On the way, he told Jo everything he knew. About the judge and Lytton and Joe John's murder. About

GameTech and the brigade. He told her his suspicions about Sandy Parrant. Jo sat with her arms crossed, looking out the window as if she weren't hearing a thing.

"It's lies," she said. "I don't believe a word of it."

He pulled out the prints of Lytton and Joe John LeBeau and gave them to her. Jo looked at them one by one.

"Christ," she said. Then, "He didn't know anything about it."

Cork turned into the lane to Molly's place.

"This would never stand up in court," she insisted. "It doesn't prove anything about Sandy."

"Come on, Jo, how could he not have known?"

He stopped in Molly's yard and saw her skis propped by the back door. It was growing dark, yet there was no light on in the big cabin. Cork ran to the back door and into the kitchen.

"Molly!" he called toward the stairs.

He lifted the lid on the woodbox, yanked out the top logs, and saw that the bag of negatives was no longer there. He ran to the stairs and bounded up them calling, "Molly!" as he went.

She wasn't upstairs. When Cork hurried down, he found Jo standing in the kitchen looking irritated. "Well?" she said.

"Something's wrong. She should be here. Somewhere."

Cork pushed past Jo and rushed outside to the shed where Molly kept her old Saab. The Saab was still there.

"See?" Jo said. "No one. Not your precious Molly. Not Sandy. Just no one."

"The bag's gone," Cork said darkly.

"What bag?"

"It had negatives of photographs like the ones I showed you and Sandy showed you. Pictures the judge used for blackmail."

"If there is such a bag, maybe Molly took it," Jo said. "Maybe she had reason."

"It wasn't Molly."

He looked toward the sauna by the frozen lake. Jo grabbed his arm.

"Cork, you can't spread these vicious lies about Sandy. Not now, just as he's about to head to Washington. If you do, if you say one word that casts a shadow over his going, I swear to God I'll help him slap a slander suit on you so fast your head'll swim."

Cork pulled loose and started for the sauna. Jo was at his heels.

"Is this about us?" she said, nearly shouting. "Do you want to hurt Sandy because of me?"

"Don't flatter yourself," Cork replied. "And what makes you think Parrant's so goddamned innocent?"

"Because I'd know," Jo told him earnestly. "He couldn't lie to me."

"Jesus, Jo, after everything we've been through you believe that? People lie all the time and they do a pretty damn good job of it."

"Not Sandy."

"Fuck Sandy," Cork said, and broke into a run.

He pushed open the door to the changing room of the sauna. It was nearly dark inside, but Cork could see clothing piled neatly on a bench. He lifted the sweater, checking its color, wondering with a note of desperation, was this what Molly had worn this morning? He shoved through the door into the sauna that was still warm. He waited a minute for his eyes to adjust to the deeper dark inside the windowless room, and he confirmed that Molly wasn't there. He stood a moment trying to figure. Where could she be? Had she run? Been taken?

"I'm tired of this, Cork," Jo said from the changing room. "I want to go home. You can come back and wait for your girlfriend without me."

Cork looked at the other door, the closed door that opened onto the lake.

"Face the facts, Cork. You're just trying to hurt Sandy because he hurt you. All these accusations—"

"Are true," Cork said.

He reached for the door.

"Then prove them, goddamn it. Show me the proof."

Cork opened the door. Framed in the threshold lay the snow-covered lake, a pale, peaceful blue in the twilight. A sky, pure as springwater, ran above it to the far shoreline. Ten yards from the door was the hole in the ice that Molly and Cork had dipped in when they'd finished their sauna the night before. And between that hole and the door where Cork dumbly stood, Molly lay naked on the ice.

His legs would not move. They barely held him up. His throat went dry and he couldn't swallow, could hardly even breathe. Yet his senses took in everything about her. Her eyes were open and the look on her face was calm. Her white skin had gone blue, nearly the same soft color the twilight gave the snow. Her long red hair stuck to her shoulders and to the ice, the matted strands stiff as broom straw. Her right arm was outstretched, her hand fisted as if it held to something fiercely.

He felt as if he'd stood there forever, though in truth it was but a moment. Jo whispered behind him, "Oh, God, Cork."

He moved then, moved although he knew with a

cold, empty certainty that it was useless. He knelt at her side, felt at her throat for a pulse in her carotid artery. Her skin was encased in a thin sheathing of ice and seemed almost brittle to his fingertips. He finally took his hand away and looked at Jo.

"Call the sheriff's office," he said quietly.

Jo backed away and turned without a word toward the cabin.

"And bring a blanket," he asked her.

He tried to lift Molly's head, to cradle her in his lap, but her hair, frozen solid, held her prisoner to the ice.

"The phone's not working."

Jo handed him the blanket.

He covered Molly, except her face. Then he dug into his pocket and brought out the keys to the Bronco.

"Find a phone," he said.

She took the keys but didn't move.

"Cork." She touched his shoulder. "I'm sorry."

"Yeah."

She stepped back, turned, and left. Cork heard the Bronco start up, the gears grind as Jo struggled to find reverse, then she was gone and he was alone with Molly.

The sun had fallen behind the trees, and an orange glow, as if from a distant fire, spread out from the west across the whole sky. The evening star glimmered brilliantly above the dark eastern horizon. Not a sound, not even the faintest breath of wind disturbed the silence.

Molly's gray-green eyes looked to the sky and Cork looked there, too, into a distance no man could measure.

"Please, God," he whispered, praying for the first time in years, "take care of her."

He bent his head and he wept, and although he didn't see, where the tears fell onto Molly's soft blue cheek, for just a moment, the ice there melted.

CHAPTER 43

Wally Schanno looked about as bad as Jo had ever seen a man look. Hobbling on his crutches, a grimace of pain at every step, he made his way up from the lake to Molly Nurmi's cabin. The whole way he kept a few yards behind the men who bore the covered stretcher to the ambulance. Although he was a tall man and not particularly old, he seemed small and ancient, bent under the weight of the work of that evening.

In contrast, Cork was like some hard piece of wood, carved into the shape of a man. Nothing showed on his face. He sat at the table in Molly Nurmi's kitchen and he had not moved since he'd placed himself there shortly after the sheriff's arrival. Jo had fixed coffee, fumbling in the kitchen cabinets and drawers for filters and a coffee tin and measuring spoon. Cork hadn't said a word. He'd barely spoken at all in response to the questioning of Captain Ed Larson, into whose hands Schanno had placed the investigation, while he leaned on his crutches and listened. Sigurd Nelson came, waddling down to the ice in his heavy coat, voicing his displeasure at having to be called yet again to do the work of his elected—and underpaid—office. Under the spotlights Schanno's people had set up, Sigurd pointed out the blue lips, as in carbon dioxide poisoning, the effect of prolonged decreased oxygen flow in hypothermia. The limbs were rigid as well, and the skin hard as ice from deep frostbite, all definite indications of death by hypothermia. She probably fell on her way from the sauna, he speculated, hit her head on the ice, and froze to death. Jo waited, expecting Cork to scream out his protest, to alter that hasty judgment, but he didn't say a thing as Molly Nurmi's body was worked loose from the ice, warm water carefully used to melt the link between her frozen skin and the frozen lake water. There was no blood, no sign of a struggle. Nothing to indicate anything other than what it appeared to be—a terrible, terrible accident.

"Go on up to the cabin," Schanno suggested to Cork as the woman's body was being freed. "Wait for me there. We'll talk."

Now Cork sat rigid, the coffee Jo had poured for him untouched on the table. Jo stood at the sink, watching the mobile spotlights go off down at the lake as the last of Schanno's people packed it up and the silent column made its way into the bright yard light behind the cabin where their vehicles were parked.

"They're taking her to the ambulance," Jo said, thinking it might be something Cork would want to know.

He didn't respond, although he flinched at the muffled thump-thump of the ambulance doors closing.

"Where's Wally?" Cork finally asked.

"Talking with Ed Larson. They're looking at some papers. Ed's going now. Here comes Wally."

Schanno came in on his crutches. He moved to the table where Cork sat, slipped the crutches from under his arms, leaned them against the table, and sat down in a chair so suddenly and heavily it looked as if the pull of gravity had just increased on him tenfold.

"Coffee, Sheriff?" Jo asked.

Schanno waved it off. He pulled off his gloves, grunting from the effort. He looked at Cork, then at Jo, and thought for a moment before he spoke.

"Her clothes were folded neatly on the bench in the changing room. The sauna was still warm. No sign of a struggle. The ice down that ramp is treacherous. I nearly lost two men there myself. So, is there any reason I ought to think this wasn't just a terrible accident?"

Jo waited. She figured if Cork was going to say anything about the bag and Sandy, this was it. But Cork finally said, "No."

"Ah." Schanno nodded, but didn't look convinced. "You told Ed you were both out here to help her get a Christmas tree. That right?"

"You were down there, Wally. You heard me say it," Cork told him. Cork was staring down at his untouched coffee. "She didn't have a tree. Take a look." He made a brief motion with his head toward the main room through the kitchen door.

The sheriff considered this awhile, eyeing Jo most of the time. She returned his gaze steadily.

"The two of you. Together. You were both going to help?" Schanno asked.

"Yes," Jo replied. She turned away from Schanno's skeptical look, went to the coffeemaker, and topped off the coffee in her cup.

"Word is you're working on a divorce. But here you are together way out here just to help this girl get a tree."

Cork said, "Christmas is like that."

"Jo," Wally finally said, "mind if I speak with your husband alone for a few minutes?"

"Forgive me for asking, Sheriff, but is it something he might want an attorney present for?"

Schanno swung his tired eyes to Cork. "You want an attorney here while we talk?"

"No," Cork said quietly.

Jo put on her coat. "I'll wait outside, then."

When she was gone, Schanno said sincerely, "I'm sorry, Cork."

"Yes."

"Cork . . ." Schanno faltered. "Cork, I got to ask. Does Jo know about you and Molly Nurmi?"

"Why?" Cork stared at him, hollow-eyed. "Oh, Christ, Wally, Jo didn't have anything to do with this."

"Then you tell me what is going on."

"What's it look like is going on?"

"It looks like that poor girl had a bad accident. But you and I both know that looks don't count for much around here anymore." The sheriff sat back and ran his hand through his thin gray hair. "Hell's bells, I remember a time when I thought I knew this town pretty well. I look at people now, people I've known most of my life, and I wonder what they're hiding. It's like that, isn't it, Cork? You stuff your own closet full of skeletons and you wonder what kind of bones everyone else has stuffed away." He looked at Cork. His eyes were baggy with exhaustion and full of hesitation. "Was it an accident?"

Cork said, "I haven't got any evidence to the contrary."

"You didn't answer my question. Let me rephrase it. Does what happened here tonight have any connection to everything else that's gone on lately?"

"Wally," Cork said, leaning earnestly toward the man with the bum leg. "Go home. Go home to Arletta. Go home and hold her while you still can. There's nothing more to find out here tonight."

Schanno stared at Cork and finally seemed to accept that he would get nowhere. He closed his eyes. His lids were spiderwebbed with red veins. "I'm so tired my brain feels like it's swimming around in molasses." He rubbed his face and sighed through his hands. "I'll want to talk with you some more tomorrow."

"I'm sure you will," Cork said. He stood up, gathered Schanno's crutches, and handed them to the man. "Good night, Wally."

The sheriff tugged his gloves on and slipped the crutches under his armpits, leaning on them heavily. "Everything's getting away, Cork. Everything's falling apart, and I can't seem to do a thing about it."

"Not your fault, Wally," Cork said.

Schanno grunted, then headed for the door. Outside he said something to Jo that Cork couldn't hear. Then he hobbled to his car, where a deputy was waiting to drive him back to town. The car pulled away. Except for Jo, the yard was empty. She turned and came back into the cabin. Cork was standing at the sink, looking out the window.

"What now?" Jo asked.

"Now comes justice," Cork said. He walked to the coffeemaker and hit the off switch. He turned out the lamp in the main room. "Let's go," he said.

"To Sandy's? Is that why you kept quiet? So you could—what?—kill him?"

"I said let's go."

"No."

Cork thought it over a second. "All right. Stay. You

can't go anywhere. Phone's dead, so you can't warn him."

He started toward the back door. Jo moved to block his way.

"You don't have any proof, Cork," she argued. "If you've made a mistake in your thinking and you do something terrible, where will you be? Everything you've told me about Sandy, everything you know is circumstantial. For Christ sake think like a lawman. Don't be stupid."

"Stupid?" Cork leveled his cold, determined eyes on her. "I'll tell you what stupid is, Jo. It's thinking that the law could ever take care of anything, thinking that the law matters at all. Out of my way, Jo."

He shoved her roughly away and went outside to the Bronco. He took the cartridges he'd ejected from his Winchester after he left the mission and fed them back into the rifle. He slid behind the steering wheel as Jo climbed into the passenger side.

"Get out," he ordered.

"Or what?" she challenged him with an angry look. "You'll shoot me?"

Cork fixed her with his own angry eyes. "Get in my way and I might."

CHAPTER 44

After they'd driven several minutes in cold, bitter silence, Jo said, "I'll help you. But you have to promise me one thing."

"I don't need your help," Cork told her.

They were nearing Aurora. The long corrugated fence of Johannsen's Auto Salvage flashed by on their right at the edge of the headlight beam. Ahead on the left, red Christmas bells hung from the yellow marquee of the Iron Lake Inn. Across the road in a halogen glare stood the twelve pumps of the brand-new Food-N-Fuel. It was all bland, familiar territory to Jo, but she felt frighteningly disoriented, as if it were all dangerous, unknown ground, and there was no help no matter where she turned.

"What are you going to do," she argued. "Go in there with that rifle blazing? What if he does have the bag, but he's hidden it? If you do something rash, you might never find it."

Cork drove through town, past the Pinewood Broiler with its neon flame still burning, past the open shops on Oak Street, where the display windows were hung with garland and tinsel and strings of lights, past the turnoff onto Gooseberry Lane. Jo glanced down the street, saw her own house with the lights blinking around the front door and framing the picture window. She wished she were home with Rose and the kids and that she didn't know what she knew and wasn't scared for them all the way she was.

Cork finally said, "I'm listening."

"When we get to Sandy's, I want you to leave the rifle in the car. It can only lead to trouble."

"Go on," he said, not sounding exactly convinced.

"Let me do the questioning. It's what I'm good at."

"You?" Cork nearly drove off the road. "You love the son of a bitch."

"And you hate his guts," she pressed on. "Look at you. You're so upset you can hardly talk. If you don't like what I'm asking or how I'm asking it, you can interject whatever you want. If he's done these things you claim—and I'm not saying for one minute that I believe he has—I want to know as much as you do."

"No, you don't." Cork gave her a withering look not lost on her in the dark.

"I'm sorry. You're right. But it's something I need to know."

They passed the city limits of Aurora and the road to the casino. Another couple of minutes and Cork turned onto the long drive that led through the trees to Sandy's big house.

"You haven't responded to my proposal," Jo pointed out.

"No, I haven't," Cork said.

He parked in front of the double garage that was built below the main section of the house. He turned off the engine and nodded once.

"All right," he said.

"You agree?"

"I'll let you do the questioning. But I take the rifle as incentive for him to answer." He reached over the seat and grabbed the Winchester.

"He won't," she insisted. "Because he knows, and I know, that you wouldn't use it. Cork, you know it, too. In a negotiation, never make a threat you don't intend to carry out."

"I'd blow his fucking heart out in a minute."

"If he gave you cause, maybe. He won't. Cork, leave it. Just leave it."

Cork held the rifle in both hands, studying its long, sleek lines. He pumped the cartridges out of the chamber and put them on the seat.

"The rifle still goes," he said. "I like the way it looks in my hands. Parrant will appreciate that, too."

Lights were on inside. Jo rang the bell, but no one answered. Cork knocked hard and got no better response. He stepped back, looked the house over, then returned to the garage. There was a digital opener affixed to the frame of the door. He looked at Jo.

"Do you know the code?"

She stepped up, lifted the cover, and punched in four numbers. The door slid upward. Cork saw Sandy Parrant's two vehicles parked inside, the white BMW and a black Jeep Grand Cherokee. He opened the door of the BMW, reached under the dash, and popped the hood. He laid his hand on the engine.

"What are you doing?" Jo asked.

"Checking to see if the engine's warm. I want to know if your friend's been out lately."

"Well?"

"This one's cold," he said.

He did the same with the Cherokee. He looked puzzled. "Cold, too."

"Satisfied? Can we go now?"

"Does he own a snowmobile?"

"No. He thinks they're a travesty in the quiet of

the woods." She could tell he was disappointed, but he didn't look at all ready to quit.

"I want to talk to the son of a bitch."

"I think I know where he'll be," Jo said.

She pushed the button on the garage door mechanism that lowered the door behind them, and she started to the left around the house. A wide roadway had been plowed there, angling off the drive toward the boathouse and the lake.

"He takes the Cherokee down this way when he wants to go ice fishing," Jo explained.

"You know a hell of a lot about him," Cork noted bitterly.

Jo didn't bother to reply. At the back side of the house, she left the plowed area and waded into the snow of the backyard. She made her way to the steps that led up to the decks. Cork heard the sound of water surging in the hot tub on the first level of the deck. When they reached the landing, they found Sandy Parrant lying back in the big redwood hot tub, steaming water swirling around him, his eyes open toward the sky as if hypnotized. A glass of wine sat on the rim of the tub, along with an ashtray that held a lit cigar. He didn't seem to notice their approach.

"Sandy," Jo said quietly.

"Jo," he greeted her in a relaxed way. Then he saw Cork and looked amused. "Cork? I hope you'll forgive me if I don't rise to greet you. I'm not wearing anything. I wasn't expecting visitors." He waved a dripping hand toward the sky. "I was just admiring the northern lights."

Jo glanced across the lake and saw that Sandy was right. A display had begun, a shifting curtain of red and green with yellow streaks shooting through like searchlights.

"It's only just starting," Parrant said. "It will get better." He sat up, sloshing water over the rim of the tub. The water splashed onto the deck, steaming as it hit ice that had formed on the wood planking from previous spills. The overhang of the roof above him was thick with frost where the water vapor rose up and froze. "You're welcome to join me, if you'd like."

"You bastard," Cork said, "you know why we're here."

"Cork!" Jo snapped, stepping between them.

Parrant looked at the rifle gripped in Cork's hands. "Maybe I should change my position on gun control." He reached for his wineglass and took a sip. "I assume you're here so that we can finally sit down and discuss like adults the situation between me and Jo. I'm guessing she told you about the photographs I shared with her."

"Sandy, where'd you get those photographs?" Jo asked. "You told me Bob gave them to you."

"He did."

"You're a liar," Cork accused. "You got them from a file cabinet you moved to Harlan Lytton's shed at the Aurora U-Store."

"I don't have the slightest idea what you're talking about."

"GameTech. Your father. The Minnesota Civilian Brigade. Murder, you son of a bitch. I'm talking about murder."

"That's enough, Cork." Jo turned to him and looked at him steadily until he backed away. She faced Parrant again and explained what Cork had found at the office in Duluth.

Sandy Parrant looked stunned. "I don't believe it."

"Cork has proof."

Parrant shook his head slowly. "Dad could be a hard bastard sometimes. But I don't believe for a minute he'd be party to what you're accusing him of. Let me see your proof."

Cork took out the photographs he'd stuffed in his coat pocket. Parrant held them carefully in his wet hands.

"My father was extreme in many ways," he finally said. "And not perfect by a long shot. Toward the end his judgment wasn't always good. So this brigade thing I can see. But murder? I don't think so, Cork. Nothing here makes me accept that." He put the photos on the edge of the tub and Cork snatched them back.

"There's more," Cork said. "Negatives Molly had."

"Molly?" Parrant looked to Jo.

Jo said, "We've just come from Molly Nurmi's place."

"Confronting the other woman, Jo? I wouldn't have thought it mattered much at this point."

"She's dead, Sandy," Jo informed him.

"Dead? How did it happen?"

"It looks like an accident. It appears that she hit her head on the ice."

"Looks? Appears?" Parrant studied both their faces. "Sounds as if you think otherwise. And do you think that I'm somehow connected?" He nodded toward the Winchester in Cork's right hand. "I guess that explains the hardware there."

"Where were you between noon and three o'clock this afternoon?" Jo asked.

"Here. I was here all day, in fact, working at the computer in my office drafting my maiden address to the Senate."

"Can you prove that?"

"I can show you the speech on my computer."

"I don't think that would prove anything, Sandy," she pointed out. "You could have drafted that speech any time."

Parrant lifted his wineglass again and thought a moment. "Talk to Ruth Becker, my housekeeper. She'd know if I was gone at all today."

"Is she here?" Jo asked.

"Ruth goes home at five. You know that, Jo. You've spent enough evenings here."

She felt rather than saw the look Cork threw at her. "Do you mind if we call her?"

"Be my guest. The kitchen phone is probably the most convenient. If you need it, there's a phone book in the first drawer to the right of the refrigerator."

"Go ahead, Cork," Jo said.

"I'd rather stay here with him," Cork replied.

"I'd rather you called."

Reluctantly, he gave in and headed up the stairs to the deck level that led onto the main floor of the house. He vanished through the sliding doors.

"Jo, you don't really think I had anything to do with that young woman's death, do you?" Sandy asked. "Why would I?"

"Cork believes she had evidence that would have ruined you. He believes you killed her to get it."

"Do you believe that?"

The northern lights had grown more intense. Jo found it odd that she wasn't more overwhelmed by the spectacle. At the moment, she was using it simply as a means to divert her gaze from Sandy.

"Jo, do you believe I'd do that?" Sandy pressed her.

Without looking at him she replied, "You're ambitious, and I've seen a ruthlessness in you sometimes when you want something very badly."

"I'm ambitious, I admit. And as for that ruthlessness, all I can say is that no one ever accomplished great things without being ruthless at times. But I'm not a murderer." He reached out and took her gloved hand. "Jo, I've held you in my arms, made love to you. Haven't you seen that part of me as well? A man's many things. To isolate one part of him and judge him on that alone is to do him an injustice, don't you think?"

The doors slid open on the upper deck and Cork stepped from the house. Jo drew back her hand.

"Well?" Sandy asked coldly as Cork descended the stairs.

"She says that you were here all day, locked in your office. She says that she never saw you leave."

"There you have it," Sandy concluded.

"She also says," Cork went on, "that she never saw you at all after you went into your office. You didn't respond when she knocked to tell you she was leaving."

"That's not unusual. If you'd asked her, she would have told you that."

"It's true, Cork," Jo interjected. "He often locks himself away for hours and no one can reach him."

"It's when I do my best work," Sandy said.

"Ruth said she left lunch for you on a tray outside your door about one o'clock. She said you didn't touch it. She picked up the tray at three."

"When I'm concentrating, as I was on this speech, I tune everything out. Jo?" He turned to her for verification.

"True again, Cork."

"Any more questions?" Sandy asked with a note of impatience.

Cork closed his eyes a moment, thinking. Jo saw

how his shoulders had fallen, how the anger was draining out of him. But when he eyed Sandy again, there was still determination in his look.

"Yesterday morning," he said, "I was attacked at Harlan Lytton's place. Someone saw you head out that way on County Sixteen shortly before it happened."

"Someone?"

"A reliable source."

Parrant glanced at Jo.

"He couldn't have, Cork," Jo informed him quietly.

"Why not?"

"He was with me. We were here together."

"Here?" Cork looked from one to the other. "All morning?"

"Yes."

"And not working," he guessed.

"Not exactly," Parrant said.

Cork's eyes seemed hollow and desperate, and Jo was glad he'd emptied the rifle of cartridges.

Parrant leaned forward in the tub, speaking reasonably. "Look, Cork, I know this woman's death must hurt you. I can understand, given the relationship between Jo and me, that I would be an easy target for your anger. But I'm the wrong target, I swear."

"He's right, Cork," Jo said softly.

Cork looked down at the useless rifle in his hand. When he lifted his face, Jo saw how tired he was.

"I'm beat," he whispered. "I'm absolutely beat."

He turned away and started down the stairs.

"Cork, I'll come—" Jo began.

"No," he said without turning. "I'd rather be alone."

He waded through the snow and disappeared around the corner of the house.

"I feel so sorry for him," Jo said. "He's lost so much

in the last couple of years. He's a good man, Sandy. He really is."

"You're not still thinking of trying to work on your marriage." Irritation rang in his words like the sour note of a cracked bell.

"I don't love Cork," Jo assured him. "But I'll always care. I feel so sad for him, that's all. Right at this moment, I just feel like crying."

"Join me in here," Sandy suggested, sweeping his hand over the surface of the water. "I guarantee you can't cry in a hot tub. It's one of those unusual laws of physics."

"I don't think so, thanks."

"Then let me give you your Christmas present."

"It's not Christmas yet."

"I've never been good at waiting, especially when I want to cheer up a sad lady. Just let me get dressed."

He rose, naked and steaming, from the tub.

CHAPTER 45

By the time Sandy was dressed, the northern lights had intensified, grown so bright that the flat of the lake beyond the boathouse was awash in color, exploding with red and green and brief flashes of yellow. In all her years, Jo had never seen anything like it.

"It's your Christmas present from the cosmos," Sandy told her as they walked the plowed lane toward the lake. "The whole universe," he said, indicating the brilliant heavens with a sweep of his arm, "is trying to cheer you up."

"You don't seem worried about what Cork's uncovered about Bob," she noted.

"Sins of the father. I suppose some people might try to hold me responsible, but I think I can distance myself enough. And I have a long time ahead of me to prove myself. I'll worry about it all tomorrow. Right now there's something I want to show you."

He wouldn't tell her why they were headed to the boathouse, only that it had to do with her gift. Jo would have preferred waiting. All the terrible events of the day—the sight of Molly Nurmi frozen to the ice, Cork's angry accusations, her own unforgivable questioning of Sandy—rattled around inside her like disconnected nuts and bolts. She wished for a little

time to herself to put all of it together and understand it. But Sandy was insistent, and although his
efforts were a little misguided, his heart was in the
right place. She let herself be led.

At the boathouse, Sandy said, "Close your eyes."

She heard him roll back the big sliding door and
heard the click of the light switch.

"Step carefully," he said and guided her in.

The boathouse smelled of canvas and rope and
gasoline. Even with her eyes closed she knew what
was there. A large enclosure with shelving and lock-
ers for gear, with life jackets, preservers, and water
skis hung on the walls, and at the center of it all, rest-
ing on its trailer, Sandy's big motor launch. However,
when Sandy said, "Open your eyes," Jo found herself
surprised.

Instead of the motor launch, she gazed upon a new
white Mercedes-Benz sedan.

"Merry Christmas, Jo."

"For me?"

"Who else?"

"Sandy, I can't—"

"You can and you will. I'm tired of seeing you
drive around town in that old Toyota."

"And how do I explain this to people?"

"You don't have to explain it." He took off his
gloves, then removed hers so that she could feel the
warmth of his hands. "Jo, I'm in. I've been elected.
You're divorcing Cork. I expect that within the year
we can marry."

"Marry? This is Minnesota, Sandy, not California
or New York. Divorce is an issue here."

"If Cork decides to go public with those photos of
you and me, the best defense is love and marriage.
Six years from now when I'm up for reelection, peo-

ple will have forgotten that you were ever married to someone else." He squeezed her hands gently but earnestly. "Jo, I need someone beside me when I make a bid for the White House."

In anyone else, she might have thought a statement like that was presumptuous, an idle boast. But she knew that if Sandy Parrant had his heart set on a run at the presidency, he would do it.

"You'd look wonderful beside me in the Rose Garden," he went on. "We're compatible, you and me. We make a good team. We think alike."

She made herself withdraw her hands. "I can't even think about this right now. I'm sorry, Sandy."

"Don't think, then," he urged her. "Just feel." He took her right hand and placed it on the cold, sleek side of the white Mercedes. "Feel the elegance. This is a lifestyle to which I can accustom you. No more worry about how to pay the orthodontist. And a shot at being First Lady to boot. Tell me you don't want that." He guided her like a partner in a formal dance toward the car door, which he opened with a graceful motion. "Here. Sit." He patted the seat.

"Sandy—" She made a weak attempt at protesting, but he took her by the shoulders and gently made her sit. He put her hands on the wheel.

"Now, doesn't that feel just like heaven?"

"Maybe not 'just like,'"—she laughed—"but pretty damn close."

He opened the hood. "Come and have a look at the engine. That's really the heart of a machine."

She didn't have the slightest idea what she was looking at, but it was nothing like the engine under the hood of her Toyota. The Toyota engine was caked with oil and dirt, the hoses brittle-looking, the belts cracked. The engine of the Mercedes was as clean as a medical instrument and looked powerful enough to launch rockets.

"This is an E-four-twenty. Eight cylinder, thirty-two valve, two hundred fifty-six cubic inches," Sandy said, touching the top of the engine with admiration. "Two hundred seventy-five horsepower, it'll go zero to sixty in six point six seconds."

"That's good?" she asked.

"Very good," he replied.

She put out her hand to touch the heart of the magnificent machine. In an instant, all her euphoria vanished.

"Does it drive as good as it looks?" she asked, drawing back her hand.

"Every bit. It handles like a dream."

"You've driven it quite a bit, then?"

"Only a road test."

"You didn't drive it today?"

"No. Why would I?" He closed the hood. "I meant to put a bow on it before you saw it."

"You didn't drive it at all?"

"Today?" He gave her a puzzled look. "No, I just told you."

"Someone did," she said. "There's a faint trace of warmth in the engine. The radiator hose, too."

"Oh, that. I ran it for a few minutes, just to keep the fluids flowing. It's not good to let a car sit idle for a long time in the cold, especially one as delicate as this."

Jo walked slowly around the car until she arrived at the trunk. "Could you open it?"

"The trunk?" Sandy came and stood beside her. "It's just a trunk. Not nearly as exciting as the engine, believe me." He smiled.

"I'd like to see everything."

"I don't have the key with me." He shrugged.

"I believe I saw a lock release on the driver's side."

The excitement melted from his face. "The trunk," he said. "Whatever."

He opened the car door, bent down, and the trunk sprung open a crack. Jo hesitated, suddenly reluctant to go any further, afraid to see if the trunk held a bag full of negatives.

"Go on," Sandy told her. "I thought you wanted to see."

Still she held back. What could the truth do now but ruin everything?

"Let me, then," Sandy said.

He reached out. Jo braced herself. Sandy raised the lid. The trunk was empty.

Jo felt weak with relief. She turned to Sandy and threw her arms around him.

"It's the most beautiful trunk I've ever seen."

"I'm glad you like it." He laughed. "The rest of the car is usually what sells people. Would you like to go for a spin?"

"I should be getting home."

"Just a quick one. I'll go up to the house and get the keys. What do you say?"

She debated a millisecond. "Okay."

Sandy gave her a brief kiss; she held him back for a longer one, then let him go. After he'd gone, she sat in the driver's seat with her hands on the wheel. How could she ever have doubted him? It was true, what she'd said, that he was ruthless at times, but it was an understandable thing in a man who reached for greatness. And Sandy had great things ahead of him, she had no doubt.

"First Lady," she said giddily.

She ran her hand over the dash. The feel of the car

was something extraordinary. She touched the seat beside her, felt the luxurious softness of the leather. The tip of her index finger caught on a sharp, unexpected edge. Something was lodged in the shadowy crevice between cushion and seat back. Something with a square, paper-thin, black corner.

When Sandy stepped back into the boathouse, Jo was leaning against the car, holding the strip of negative gingerly away from her with two fingers, as if it were a piece of rotting filth she'd rather not have had to touch.

"What's that?" Sandy asked innocently.

"You know what it is."

"I didn't kill her," he said. "I swear to you, Jo, I didn't kill her."

"A few minutes ago you hadn't even been to see her."

"Look," he explained, approaching slowly, "I got a call this afternoon. A woman. She said she had something I'd want to buy. She mentioned the things Cork talked about. Evidence about my father. She said she had the negatives. She gave me directions. I followed them."

"It was Molly Nurmi?"

"I can't say for sure it was."

"Your housekeeper said you didn't leave."

"She works with headphones on. She doesn't hear a thing. I slipped out and took the Mercedes. She never knew."

"You saw Molly Nurmi?"

"Not at first. I knocked on the door. No one answered. I saw smoke coming from the sauna and went down there. The bag was in the changing room, negatives all over the place. It looked as if someone had gone through them wildly."

"And Molly Nurmi?"

"I checked the sauna. She wasn't there. Then I looked outside. She was dead, Jo. There wasn't anything I could do to help her."

"And you ran."

"Yes." He looked down, ashamed.

"How do you know she was dead?"

"She was frozen to the ice, for God's sake. Jo, I panicked. I saw everything I've worked for slipping through my hands. I'm not proud that I ran. But better a coward than a murderer."

"You took the negatives?"

"Not exactly. I hid them out there. At the Nurmi place. I didn't want them found; you can understand that. And for obvious reasons I didn't want them in my possession." He looked at her, deep concern eroding the handsome features of his face. "You don't believe me."

"No, I don't."

"What kind of monster do you think I am?"

"I'm beginning to wonder."

He stood up straight and looked at her squarely. There was hurt in his eyes, but he spoke evenly. "What do you want me to do? Tell me and I'll do it. Whatever I have to do to prove to you who I am, I'll do it."

"Turn the negatives over to Cork," she said without a moment's hesitation. "And tell Wally Schanno everything that happened."

He took a deep breath and nodded his agreement. "I suspect that in that bag are things that will tear this county—hell, maybe this state—apart," he warned her. "But I'll give the bag to Cork, if that's what you want."

"That's what I want."

"And you'll believe the things I've said? You'll believe I really love you?"

"I'll believe you about everything."

"Then I'll do it. You're the most important thing in my life, Jo. I'll do anything to keep you in it."

He reached out his hand. She took it.

"Let's go up to the house," he suggested. "You can call Cork from there. Tell him to meet us at the Nurmi woman's place. I'll give him the bag."

She held back a moment. "This will mean the end of all your dreams."

Somehow he managed a faint smile. "No. It just means I'll never be president." He kissed her hand gently. "But I'll always have you."

CHAPTER 46

He had one picture of Molly. Only one. It was a Polaroid he'd taken with her camera in the summer just moments after she stepped onto the shore from a dip in the lake near the sauna. She wore a black one-piece and had a good tan. She was bent a little awkwardly, torn between reaching down for her beach towel and trying to say "Cheese" for the camera. Her red hair clung to her back and shoulders and hung over her face in long, wet strands. She was laughing.

He'd kept the picture in a collection of poems by Robert Frost, hidden from the eyes of anyone who might, in idle curiosity, have stumbled onto it in a drawer. He always slipped it in with the poem "Stopping by Woods on a Snowy Evening." Cork didn't know much more about poetry than the next guy, but he understood well how it felt to have miles to go before he slept.

Now he lay on his bunk, one arm pillowing his head, studying the one and only picture he'd allowed himself of Molly. She looked exactly the way he wanted to remember her, full of life, laughing. That was Molly to him. Not the pale blue iced-over body with its sightless eyes set on heaven. Molly deserved to be remembered differently. She deserved a lot of things life never offered her, not the least of which was someone who told her often he loved her. Why hadn't he? Why had he been so afraid? He couldn't think of anything so important now that it should have kept him from telling Molly how he felt.

And now it was too late. Too late forever.

Sam's Place had never felt so empty. He suspected the emptiness was not in the old Quonset hut; it was in him. There was nothing in him now, nothing but the great emptiness of death, which he seemed to carry with him like a virus. People died around him, but he was immune. There was no justice. He should have died long ago. Maybe if he had, Molly would still be alive. And Sam Winter Moon and Arnold Stanley, and God only knew who else. He remembered a line he'd heard once, from an ancient text it seemed. "I am become death . . ." That was him.

The phone rang. He didn't want to talk to anyone, but he'd neglected to turn on his answering machine and on the tenth ring he lifted the receiver.

"Cork, it's Jo."

"Yeah," he grunted.

"I know where the negatives are."

He sat up, instantly alert. "Where?"

"Meet me at Molly Nurmi's." She paused, covered the mouthpiece, and mumbled something faintly to someone else. "In half an hour," she concluded.

"At Molly's?"

"Yes."

"Jo, did you know all along?"

"No."

"Sandy," he guessed.

"Meet me, Cork. Let me explain." She hung up without waiting for him to answer.

Cork walked calmly to the front door. He put on his coat and his stocking cap. He grasped his Winchester and fed in the shells he'd stuffed in his pockets at Parrant's.

"Mr. Senator," he said as he worked the lever, feeding the first cartridge into the chamber.

"He'll be there?" Sandy asked as Jo hung up the kitchen phone.

"He'll be there."

"Well," he said somberly, "let's get it over with."

She touched his arm. "It will be good to get clear. Whatever happens, whatever those negatives hold, at least we won't be looking over our shoulders for the rest of our lives waiting for the worst to catch up with us."

"You're right. As usual."

They headed downstairs, through the basement recreation room and Sandy's tool room, to the garage.

"Let's take the Cherokee," Sandy suggested.

Jo walked past the BMW.

"*Oops.* Just a minute," Sandy said, tapping his forehead as if he'd just remembered something. "I'll be right back." He returned to the tool room and came out with a roll of silver duct tape. "Almost forgot." He laughed as he neared her.

"What's that for?" she asked.

Sandy lunged for her, catching her completely by surprise. He spun her, threw her against the hood of the Cherokee, grasped her arms, and pinned them behind her. She began to struggle, but it was too late. Her wrists were tightly bound together with the tape.

"You're hurting me, Sandy."

"And you don't think you're hurting me?" he replied, cold and fierce. "Asking me to give up everything. Christ!" He opened the door of the Cherokee. "Get in," he ordered her.

Jo backed away. He grabbed her arm, yanked her to the open door, and shoved her in. Roughly he settled her in a sitting position, then knelt and began to tape her ankles. She brought her knees up swiftly, striking him squarely in the nose. He fell back, blood streaming from his nostrils, and he sat on the concrete floor, stunned. Jo tried to free her legs so she could run, but Sandy had managed to get one loop of tape around her ankles and she couldn't break loose. He touched his nose and carefully studied the blood on his fingertips.

"I deserved that," he concluded in a tone that sounded quite rational. He took a handkerchief from his back pocket and dabbed at his bloody nose. "Let me ask you something, Jo. If I told you I'd killed the Nurmi woman, could you let it go? Could you live with me and work with me and love me like you have?"

"My God," Jo said, breathless as the horrific truth uncoiled before her. "You did murder her."

"In its own way, it was an accident." He stood up and used the side mirror of the BMW to assess the damage to his nose. "I didn't go there meaning to kill her. I did what I had to do to protect myself. You see, we're not just talking about the end of my political career. What's in that bag could land me in jail for a good long time. The political thing I could live with, I suppose. There are other challenges. But I couldn't live in prison. You might as well shoot me."

"Are you going to kill me? And Cork?"

"What would you do if you were me?"

"You said you loved me."

Sandy leaned against the BMW and crossed his

legs casually as if he were posing for an ad layout. "The truth about love is that you can find it around any corner. Love's easy. Now a shot at the White House, that's rare."

"I can't believe this," Jo said.

"I'll tell you what I think defines greatness. The ability and willingness to perform in extraordinary ways. That's me, Jo. I've always known that I was destined for great things." He approached her again. "I'm going to tape your ankles now. If you insist on trying to kick me again, I'll hit you. Very hard. I'd rather not do that, but I will. Okay?"

She gave no sign that she heard or that she agreed at all to his terms. He kept away a little, reaching far out this time to grasp her legs. She lifted her feet suddenly and swung them at his face. He moved fast, dipped his shoulder and tilted his head in the way of a fighter trained to dodge a glove. Her feet struck the door uselessly. Almost immediately, she felt the blow he'd promised, hard to her head, and she saw fireworks. When the light show faded, she was left with a ringing in her right ear and a terrible throbbing in her jaw. Sandy had bound her ankles tightly. He was already backing the Cherokee out of the garage and was saying something about being truly sorry it had to be this way.

He drove down the plowed lane toward the lake. Beside the boathouse he stopped and turned off the engine.

"I'll be right back," he promised, and patted her knee. He stepped inside the boathouse and flipped on the light.

Sandy had strapped her in tightly with the seat belt. Even so, she was able to lean forward almost to the dash. With her hands still taped behind her, she struggled to reach the door handle. She made it, wrapped her fingers around the cool metal, and tested to make certain she could, if she had the chance, open the door. Satisfied, she sat back as the light went out in the boathouse.

He came back carrying a clear plastic bag full of negatives, which he set on the floor of the rear seat. He slipped behind the wheel and started the Cherokee again. "It was in the footlocker where I keep the ropes. And this"—he held up his right gloved hand in which he gripped a revolver—"a thirty-eight Police Special, registered to Corcoran O'Connor." He headed out onto the ice and started across the lake toward Molly Nurmi's. "You see," he explained in the self-satisfied tone that until that moment Jo had always forgiven, "while everyone else was looking for Russell Blackwater's body in the lake, I was looking for Cork's gun. I had a sense that, with all his prying, I might have to implicate him at some point. In life, as in politics, foresight is all."

Sandy drove without headlights, but he had no trouble seeing the way. The northern lights made the snow ahead of them dance with color, and the moon was just rising as well. The lights of Aurora drifted past far to their left, thinning out gradually until there was nothing paralleling the Cherokee in its journey but the dark, forested shore.

"I thought I might have to use it on the Nurmi woman," he said after a while. "But I only had to threaten her with it to get her into the water. I figured a few minutes in the lake and she would be ready to tell me anything. She turned out to be tougher than I imagined. But no one can last forever in cold like that. A tap on the head after she got out and it looked exactly like a terrible accident." He glanced at her, his face a kaleidoscope of shifting colors that changed with the lights from the sky. "I honestly thought you'd be good beside me in Washington," he said, clearly disappointed. "I thought we had the same dream, Jo. Greatness. I guess I was wrong."

"You'll never be anything, Sandy," Jo said. "Look how you've got what you have. Lies, bribery, extortion."

"That's politics." He shrugged.

"And murder?"

"I'm not the first. I suspect I won't be the last."

"How could I have loved you?" she asked bitterly.

"How could you not? Once I decided I wanted you, it was all over. I always get what I want, Jo. That's part of my attraction, isn't it?"

They drove in silence after that. The moon went on rising, bright enough in its part of the sky to wash out the colors of the northern lights. Moonlight defined more clearly the details of the lake and shoreline. Shadows below the rims of small drifts curled across the moonlit snow like black snakes. The evergreens on the shore looked dark and ragged. Jo tried to think what was out this way besides Molly Nurmi's cabin. If she could slip away somehow, was there a place to run to? She eyed the big pines for a break, a light, a sign of hope, but she saw nothing.

"Yesterday," Jo said, "it was you who tried to kill Cork at Harlan Lytton's."

"You were sleeping so soundly." He smiled. "I was gone and back and you never left the safe territory of your dreams. But I wouldn't have killed Cork. I only wanted the negatives. Same for the Nurmi woman, actually. You see, I'm only dangerous if you get in my way." He laughed to himself. "Not like my father. There was a real son of a bitch. After he died, I found keys and other things that led me to his office in Duluth and to that shed of Lytton's. Cork was right about everything. The old bastard had documented every evil a town can generate. He even kept files on me. I think he had an idea he was going to keep me in line in Washington, make me dance to his tune. If he hadn't killed himself, I might have done it for him eventually. Here," he said, pulling a cassette from his coat pocket. "Maybe this will help you understand. For the last year or two, the tricky son of a bitch taped every conversation that took place in his office. The Richard Nixon of the Iron Range."

He put the cassette into the tape player in the dash, pushed the fast-forward button a few moments, then let up.

". . . in the middle of a campaign, goddamn it," Sandy's voice declared angrily on the tape.

Sandy fast-forwarded again.

". . . don't understand why, Russell." Sandy's voice again. Still angry. "You had a good thing going. Why fuck it up with something like this?"

"Listen, rich boy—" Russell Blackwater tried to cut in.

"No, you listen. I don't intend to lose this election because of your larceny."

"What do you suggest, Sandy?" It was the judge's voice. Calm. And, it seemed, slightly amused.

"Christ, I don't know. Vernon, why the hell didn't you keep your boy in line?"

"He is a man," Vernon Blackwater replied indignantly. "Not a boy."

"What he pulled with the casino sure as hell makes me wonder."

A doorbell rang in the background.

"I have a suggestion," the judge interjected. "I

asked Joe John here. I thought we might all talk this out reasonably. Sandy, would you get the door?"

Sandy Parrant reached out and fast-forwarded the tape again.

". . . you want, Joe John?" Sandy's voice.

"The People deserve better," Joe John replied. He sounded proud and incensed. "I thought you would understand and help."

"I do understand," Sandy insisted on the tape. "And I want to help."

"I don't think so. I think mostly you're worried about your own ass."

"Sit down, Joe John," the judge ordered. After a pause, he requested, "Please, sit down. I have one final negotiation to offer."

Silence. In the Cherokee, Jo leaned forward struggling to hear. Then a chair creaked on the tape as a body sat down heavily.

"Thank you," the judge went on. "It's been my own opinion since you first stumbled onto all this that the usual inducements we might offer would be ineffective. I've watched you carefully, Joe John. From a drunk to a man with good reason to have a lot of self-respect. I've thought all along you wouldn't give up that hard-earned self-respect easily. Not for money, certainly. You've more than proven that this evening. And I just want to add how much I appreciate your promise to refrain from making all this public until we've had a chance to work things out. Now, the fact of the matter is that my son can't lose this election. And for many reasons, Russell Blackwater should continue to manage the casino. What I've done, therefore, is invite an outside negotiator to help us reach a resolution. I believe he is, as the saying goes, prepared to make you an offer, Joe John, that you can't refuse. Harlan?"

A door opened.

"What the—" Joe John began.

Three shots. Very close together. Loud on the tape. In the Cherokee, Jo jerked, startled.

"My God!" Sandy Parrant's taped voice cried.

Behind the steering wheel, the real Parrant mouthed the words as if he'd listened to the tape a hundred times and knew it by heart.

"Jesus," Russell Blackwater gasped.

"And that, gentlemen," concluded the judge, "solves everything."

Sandy stopped the tape.

"It was over so quickly I couldn't do anything," he explained.

"And then you had a choice, didn't you?" Jo guessed bitterly. "Expose everything and probably lose the election. Or stay silent."

His face in the dark was intense, fired. "I was born to greatness. I've known that all my life. Even when things started going bad, it was like I was favored by the gods. Fate smiled and everyone who could incriminate me was eliminated. My father, Lytton, the Blackwaters. I was clear of it all. No one was even looking in my direction except for that fucking husband of yours." Sandy peered intently through the windshield and slowed the Cherokee to a crawl. "There it is."

Jo could see the sauna, square and black, and farther up among the trees the light from inside the cabin. Cork had turned all the lights off when they left earlier. That meant he was there now, waiting innocently for them to arrive. Her fault! God, how could she have been so stupid, so blind?

Sandy stopped the Cherokee behind the sauna, out of sight of the cabin. He slipped the key from the ignition and shoved it into the pocket of his jeans. "This shouldn't take long." He lifted the revolver from his lap.

"You're not—" she began.

"Going to shoot him? In cold blood? If I have to. But I don't think I will. Not yet."

He took the roll of duct tape from his pocket, tore off a strip, and pressed it over her mouth. He reached into the glove compartment and drew out a flashlight. Stepping from the Cherokee, he came around to Jo's side and opened the door. He took out his jackknife and snapped out the blade.

"I'm only going to cut your feet loose so you can walk. I'm not going to hurt you. But if you try something, I will."

Slowly he knelt. He reached out carefully with the knife and cut the tape from her ankles.

"In here," he said, leading her to the sauna door.

He switched on the flashlight. There were three tiers of seats in the sauna, hard, bare cedar planks. Sandy guided her up to the top, forced her to sit, and bound her ankles again with tape.

"I'm just going to have a peek and make sure Cork's not planning any surprises of his own. I'll be right back."

He stepped down, clicked off the flashlight, and left her in total darkness. The boards creaked on the small deck outside as he crept around to the side of the building and headed toward the cabin. She waited a few moments after the creaking had stopped, then she rolled to her side and bumped down the tiers of cedar planks. She felt a jolting pain in her right shoulder as she hit the floor. She scooted toward the door, which opened inward. Pushing herself against the wall, she managed to slide to a standing position. With her hands bound behind her, she groped in the dark for the knob, finally found it, and opened the door a crack, just enough to wedge her body through. She tumbled onto the deck outside.

Like an inchworm, she coiled and uncoiled herself, crawling along the deck toward the edge. She came to the end, a sudden drop-off with the ice three feet below. She brought her body around until she lay parallel with the edge of the deck, then she rolled off. The wind had blown the snow on the ice into uneven depths; where she hit there was almost nothing to cushion the blow on her head. For the second time that night, she was stunned to the point of seeing lights. Her head felt thick and burning as if full of some scorching liquid. Vital seconds passed, a fact she was aware of even through the haze that clouded her thinking. On her side, her injured shoulder taking the brunt of the struggle, she began to move away from the sauna toward a pine tree backed by a small thicket just beyond the shoreline a dozen yards away. She dug at the ice, propelling herself with the side of her boot. Her jacket was a down-filled nylon shell, and the slick material helped her slide easily over the ice, the only piece of luck she'd had all night.

Five feet. Ten. She struggled against fainting. Goddamn it, no! She fed her pain to her anger. She wouldn't give in. She wouldn't give Sandy the satisfaction. The pine and the thicket seemed an enormous distance away. If she couldn't make it there, she'd find another way. Desperately she scanned the area around her, looking for a drift against the shore that might be deep enough to burrow into, to cover herself with snow. Could he find her then? Could he follow a worm's trail in the night? She was wearing dark clothing, a mistake she regretted now as bitterly as she regretted loving Sandy. She was too easy to see, especially in the unnatural brightness from the northern lights and the rising moon. Her best hope still was to make the thicket before Sandy came back.

She breathed heavily, pushing hard, turning inches into feet, feet into yards. The tree was almost within her reach. She glanced back at the snow-draped thicket just beyond. If she could reach it, nestle in, he might never find her. She hoped he wouldn't kill one of them unless he was sure he could kill them both.

Ignoring the pounding in her head, the burning in her shoulder, she redoubled her efforts. A moment later she bumped into something hard. The trunk of the pine, she thought with relief. She looked back to gauge the distance left to the thicket and found that the pine tree had not stopped her. It was Sandy Parrant's left leg.

"I would have been disappointed in you if you hadn't tried," he said. "One of the things I've always found most attractive is your tenacity." He took out his jackknife, knelt, and whispered, "You're also one hell of a piece of ass." He cut her ankles free and lifted her brusquely.

"Let's go," he said. "Our pigeon is roosting."

CHAPTER 47

Cork sat at the kitchen table facing the back door. He wore his coat and his stocking cap, but he'd taken off his gloves and they lay crumpled in front of him on the table. It was warm in the cabin, but that wasn't why he'd removed his gloves.

The back door swung open and Parrant brought Jo in. Cork looked at her bound wrists, the tape across her mouth, and the familiar revolver in Parrant's hand.

"Going to kill the whole county?" he asked.

"If I have to."

"Starting with us," Cork concluded.

"That depends," Sandy replied.

"We both know it doesn't." He addressed Jo, "You okay?" She nodded.

"We have a lot of talking to do before I decide on anything," Parrant said.

"Bullshit. You've already decided."

Parrant put the revolver to Jo's temple. "I want to know one thing. Does anyone else know about the negatives?"

"Yes."

"Who?"

"You expect me to answer that? It would be like signing a death warrant."

"Not necessarily," Parrant said. "Some people can be bought. Most people in fact. Or they can be scared easily enough. Who else knows?"

"I lied," Cork told him. "No one else knows."

"I don't believe you." Parrant rubbed at his nose, thinking. "Tell you what I'm going to do. From now on, every time I get an answer I don't believe—" He put his arm around Jo to hold her and he pointed the barrel of the .38 at her foot. "—I'll put a bullet through one of Jo's extremities."

"You'd really do that?"

"Maybe. Maybe I'm lying. But think about it. What have I got to lose? A man who aspires to the White House ought to be able to be ruthless if the situation demands. So, what do you think? Will I really do it?"

Parrant's eyes were quite clear and unblinking as a snake's. "Let's begin again," he said. "Did you tell anyone else about the negatives."

"No."

"Did you talk to anyone else about your suspicions of me?"

"No."

The sound of the gunshot made Cork jerk as if he'd been struck by the bullet. Jo tried to yank free, almost separating from Parrant as she screamed into the duct tape. From under the table, where it had lain cradled on his lap, Cork swung the Winchester. The safety was off, a cartridge chambered. For the briefest instant he had a shot at Parrant. Not a clear shot, however, for Parrant was struggling to pull Jo back. Cork hesitated. That was all Sandy Parrant needed.

"Drop it!" he shouted at Cork, jamming the revolver into the back of Jo's head. "She's not hit. But I'll kill her, I swear to God."

Cork saw that although Jo stood tottering, she was unharmed. He lowered the rifle to the floor.

"Brinkmanship, O'Connor," Parrant explained with a galling note of triumph. "A game I'm rather good at. John Kennedy was a fucking amateur." Parrant resettled his grasp on Jo, wrapped his arm around her, and once again aimed the gun at her foot. "Next time, I promise you, I won't miss. Once more, did you tell anyone about the negatives?"

"Schanno."

"When?"

"I saw him today. We discussed GameTech."

"Schanno." Parrant considered this and didn't appear too upset. "I've got things on him. I can get to him."

"I think you underestimate the man," Cork said.

"No one else knows about the negatives?"

"No one."

"Did you discuss your suspicions about me with anyone?"

"The priest."

"Tom Griffin? In confession?"

"I haven't made a confession in years."

Parrant took a deep breath and thought that one over.

"He's free to talk," Cork reminded him. "Maybe he already has. You may end up having to kill all of Aurora, Sandy."

"But he doesn't know about the negatives?"

"Like I said, no one besides Schanno knows."

Parrant glanced down as if preparing to fire at Jo's foot. "I think you're lying."

"How can I prove I'm not?" Cork asked quickly. "Look, I've already put two men's lives in danger. What will satisfy you?"

Parrant reached into the pocket of his coat and

brought out a jackknife. He carefully extended the blade and moved it toward Jo's back.

"Christ no, Sandy!" Cork half rose from his chair.

Parrant cut Jo's wrists free. "Take the tape off," he told her.

She obeyed and let the pieces from her wrists and mouth drop to the floor. "I'm sorry," she told Cork.

"It's okay."

"Over there beside him," Sandy said. He shoved her toward Cork, then bent and picked up the loose pieces of tape and put them in his pocket. He took out the roll of duct tape and tossed it to Cork. "Tape her wrists," he ordered.

Jo looked confused, then understood. "Fingerprints. You want Cork's fingerprints on the tape."

"So it looks like I bound and killed you," Cork finished.

"You'd have to be distraught," Jo went on. "But distraught over what?"

Parrant reached inside his coat and brought out folded photographs. He tossed them onto the table. "Pick them up," he instructed Cork.

Cork lifted the pictures. They were photos of Molly and him embracing by the sauna. They'd been taken at night with a night vision lens from somewhere out on the water. Harlan Lytton's handiwork for sure.

"These are the ones he showed you?" Cork asked Jo.

"Yes."

"And now they're covered with your fingerprints, too," Parrant said with satisfaction.

"My gun, my fingerprints on the tape and the pictures." Cork nodded as if he admired the thoroughness. "We argue over my dead lover. I freak, kill Jo, and then what, Sandy? I commit suicide? Or do I just disappear like Joe John LeBeau?"

"Just tape her," Parrant said.

"What do we do, Cork?" Jo asked.

"You do what I say," Parrant threatened.

"Or what?" Cork asked. "You're going to kill us anyway."

The tea kettle on Molly's stove suddenly jumped and skittered across the burner. Startled, Parrant swung the revolver that way and let off a round that buried itself in the wall. "What the hell?"

"Windigo," Cork said. "You know what a Windigo is, don't you, Sandy?"

"A fucking fairy tale."

"It wasn't a fairy tale made that pot jump around," Cork said.

The wind rose outside. The windowpane over the sink rattled. From the dark of the night surrounding the cabin came a long low howl that was not the wind but was wrapped within it. And buried somewhere within the howling was the name of Sandy Parrant.

"The Windigo's calling you, Sandy. Do you know what that means?"

Parrant eyed the window angrily. "It means there's a joker out there who's going to die with you."

"Can't kill the Windigo with that gun," Cork told him. "The Windigo called the names of Russell Blackwater and Harlan Lytton, too. Blackwater knew it and carried a gun and it didn't matter."

"I don't believe that crap."

"Sam Winter Moon once told me there's more in these woods than a man can ever see. More than he can ever hope to understand."

"Shut up!"

Parrant pointed the revolver at Jo's heart as if to fire, to finally end it all. But the light in the kitchen went out suddenly. Cork pushed Jo to the side and threw himself in the other direction. Parrant fired wildly. In the blindness after the loss of the light, Cork spread his arms wide and charged the place where Parrant had been standing. He caught the man in his arms and they tumbled down. Cork heard the scrape of the .38 as it slid loose across the floorboards.

Parrant squirmed from Cork's grasp and was back on his feet instantly, kicking hard at Cork's ribs. Cork rolled away and brought himself up. Parrant was at him, throwing punches out of the dark, landing blow after blow to his torso. Cork stumbled back, retreating across the kitchen until he was pinned against the sink. Hunched and grunting, he tried vainly to protect himself as Parrant hammered at his sides and head.

A shattering of crockery and Parrant stopped abruptly. Moonlight streamed through the window over the sink. Parrant, in milky white, staggered back, holding his head. Cork tried to move, to attack, but the pain in his ribs paralyzed him.

Jo's hand was on his arm and her voice urged him, "Cork, quick!" She pushed him through the kitchen door and into the cold night. Tugging, she pulled him toward the sanctuary of the woods.

They'd barely reached the first of the trees when the crack of Cork's revolver came from the cabin. Jo ran hard, weaving among the trees and thickets, fighting her way desperately through the deep snow and drifts. She ran until she was nearly breathless, then she risked a glance back. Cork was nowhere to be seen. She stopped and turned, frantically searching among the trees for any sign of him. A black form separated itself from a nearby tree trunk and stepped toward her. Jo almost screamed. Then she recognized the old man Henry Meloux.

"Here," Meloux whispered, and pointed toward a cedar with its branches bent low under the weight of snow.

"Cork—" Jo tried to explain.

The old man ignored her. "In there quick," and he held aside a cedar bough showing a hollow in the snow, a little sanctuary. He urged her in, surprising her with his strength. "The man is almost here," he whispered.

In less than a minute, Sandy approached through the trees, the beam of a flashlight scanning the snow in front of him as he came. Jo realized he was following her tracks. In a few more seconds he would be at the place where Meloux had met her and the tracks would lead him to their hiding place. Meloux's face showed no fear, only an intense concentration.

Cork's cry from the direction of the cabin brought Parrant to a sharp stop. He turned and began a hard run back.

"Cork!" she whispered, afraid.

"I will find him," Meloux said. "Stay here."

"Like hell I will."

The old man's strong hand restrained her. "You have children. Think of them."

Meloux was gone in an instant, leaving Jo alone in the safe hollow under the cedar boughs.

CHAPTER 48

A dozen yards into the woods, Cork knew he couldn't keep up with Jo. Adrenaline couldn't mask all his pain, couldn't undo the shortness of breath that was the legacy of tobacco. As Jo had moved farther ahead, Cork looked for a place to hide. He spotted a humping of snow-covered vines, and with all the strength he could muster, he'd leaped the thicket. The deep snow on the far side cushioned his landing and he crawled to cover only seconds before Parrant rushed by pursuing Jo.

He had no idea how far ahead Jo had been able to run, but he wanted to give her the best chance he could to make it safely away. He crawled from the safety of the thicket. When the beam of flashlight was forty or fifty yards beyond him, he let out a cry. He'd meant it to be a cry of challenge, but the stabbing in his ribs turned it to a howl of pain. Still, it did the trick. Parrant turned for him and Cork ran for his life.

He skirted the cabin, not even trying to make it inside to find the rifle. It would be too great a gamble fumbling around, hoping to find the Winchester before Parrant reached him. He made instead for the vast, unbroken wilderness of the Superior National Forest a mile northeast.

He ran numbly through drifts above his knees. Awkwardly he vaulted a fallen log and came down in a snag of branches on the other side. His foot became entangled. While he worked himself free, he checked the woods behind him. Nothing. No movement. Only sound. Above him the wind raced through the tops of the pines, its passage marked by the scrape and groan of branches. From farther east came a deeper sound, a throaty grumble that Cork recognized as the tumble of fast water in a stream. Half Mile Spring. The flow gushed out of high ground and rushed down a deep ravine to the lake. As its name implied, the spring didn't have a long run from its source to its ending, and even in the coldest winter the water never froze.

He became aware of something else, the smell of wood smoke in the wind. Meloux's cabin! The place wasn't far beyond the spring. Cork tried to think if Meloux owned a firearm. The old man had been a hunter once, a great one it was said, but did he own a working firearm?

Cork knew he should be moving again. Two things held him there at the log. He wanted to be certain Parrant was still following him. If Parrant was after him, it meant that Jo had a good chance of getting away. The other thing was the simple fact that he couldn't move. The adrenaline had washed out of him, and what had seeped in to take its place was searing pain. The beating his ribs had sustained was too much. He couldn't straighten up, could barely take a breath. Even the slightest movement drove a spike of pain right through his chest.

He'd left his gloves on Molly's kitchen table. His hands, vulnerable to the bitter, single-digit temperature of the night, ached from the cold. He tried to blow on them for warmth, but the stabbing of his ribs gave him almost no breath for it.

The flashlight beam shot like an arrow through the trees. Cork tried to rise but grabbed at his ribs and doubled over with a moan. The flashlight swung his way. He crouched behind the log as the light played past him. He thought about the ravine at his back. Even if he could escape Parrant somehow, the deep, rugged walls of the ravine and the rush of Half Mile Spring would stop him. His best hope would be to turn to the lake, cut across the ice, and make for Meloux's cabin. But first he would have to elude Parrant, a possibility that became less likely with each step Parrant took.

The .38 fired unexpectedly. Cork jerked although nothing hit near him. Parrant shot another round. Cork risked a glance over the log. The light swung back and forth, scanning the woods to the left. What had he fired at? Jo? Christ, no! Cork braced himself to rise, to call out, to draw Parrant's fire, but a hand on his shoulder restrained him.

Meloux crouched beside him. He beckoned to Cork and began to crawl on all fours toward the ravine. Cork followed his example, snow up to his chin. After a short distance, the old man rose and loped ahead, graceful despite his age. Cork did the same, although much less gracefully and a good deal slower.

He glanced back once. The beam of the flashlight had vanished.

Jo cursed the old man. Cursed him because he'd made her afraid.

In Molly Nurmi's kitchen, she had been angry. She'd been trapped in something she didn't see any

way out of and she'd been blind with rage. Rage at
Sandy for what he was, what he'd been able to hide
from her so well, and rage at herself for her stupidity
and blindness. The sanctuary the old man offered her
had changed things. She wasn't backed into a corner
anymore. She had hope. But something unexpected
had accompanied the hope. Fear. Fear so overpower-
ing it made her tremble violently as if she were bitterly cold. She'd never been so afraid. She knew what
it was now to be paralyzed by cowardice, because she
didn't think she could move.

She'd done as Meloux had suggested. She'd thought
about the children. What would happen if both Cork
and she were killed? She tried to remember exactly
the language of their will. She wanted Rose to be the
children's guardian. She'd made that clear. Of course,
it didn't necessarily mean the court had to comply, but
there was no one to contest that request. No close rel-
atives left alive. Jo realized more clearly than she ever
had how alone they all were in the world. God, they
should have held together. They should have found a
way.

She looked at herself, cowering in the dark little
hollow, and she felt full of disgust. Cork's cry had
saved her from being discovered by Sandy. And the
old man had put himself in danger, too, even though
this trouble had nothing to do with him.

But here I am, she thought coldly, pulling herself
together around a small fire of anger and self-loathing.
Hiding like a damn rabbit.

The next shots, two of them, came from some distance away, beyond the cabin it seemed. If she were
ever going to move, if she were ever going to do anything, now was the time.

She shoved aside the bough and crawled out. At

her back, miles down the lake, was the safety of Aurora. She could make it. Keeping to the trees, moving carefully, she could make it. That would leave Cork and the old man to deal with Sandy alone. If Cork and the old man were still alive. If they weren't, she was all that remained of the complications for Sandy to clear up. And he would do his best to kill her. When he wanted something, he always did his best.

She looked south toward Aurora, looked with an ache of longing toward where her children were safe with Rose. Then she turned back toward the cabin and she began to run.

She paused at the edge of the clearing, studying the dark cabin. The last shots had come from far enough away that she didn't believe Sandy could have returned already, but she waited, watching carefully. Moonlight and the northern lights made the clearing and the cabin easy to see. The wind that had risen lifted snow off the pine trees and cabin roof, and swirls of white danced ghostlike before her. Nothing human moved, and Jo finally made a rush at the door, quietly opened it, and slipped inside. In the moonlit kitchen, she knelt and searched the floor for the rifle Cork had dropped. She found it kicked against a baseboard, and she took it in her hands.

From the window above the kitchen sink, she studied the clearing and the lane that ran between the small cabins all the way down to the lake. All around her the big cabin groaned in the wind. Sprays of loose snow gusted across the clearing. Her legs quaked and her whole body shivered with terrible anticipation. She thought about shooting Sandy Parrant. Less than fifteen minutes before, she would have done it without a second thought. Now she stood wondering. Could she pull the trigger if she had to? Could she really kill him? It might be a moot point anyway since she wasn't sure she could hold the rifle steady enough to shoot ducks in a barrel. Even so, she understood the wisdom of old Henry Meloux. If she'd charged out of her little sanctuary full of blind rage, the only thing she would have done was get herself killed. Now at least she had a chance.

A figure emerged from the trees, loping into the clearing. She raised the rifle and sighted through the windowpane. She had no idea if she could hit a moving target, and she wasn't sure who the target was. Her hands ached from their desperate grip on the rifle. She shook violently as if she were freezing cold. The figure turned down the lane and headed for the lake. Only then did Jo see clearly that it was Sandy, and then it was too late. He was too far away. She watched him trot past the old cabins and vanish behind the sauna. Jo felt a rush of relief that he hadn't come her way, that she hadn't had to shoot.

But what was Sandy up to?

She cracked open the back door. Above the sound of the wind rushing through the treetops, she heard the engine of the Cherokee turn over. A moment later, the black shape of it headed away slowly across the ice.

Where was he going?

Then she remembered the two shots. With a plummeting of hope she thought, He's going after their bodies.

At the ravine, the sound of Half Mile Spring grew to a small roar. Meloux turned back and searched the woods behind them for any sign of Parrant.

"Jo?" Cork croaked as soon as he reached Meloux.

He stood holding his ribs, bent so far over that he had to raise his eyes to look into the old man's creased face.

"Safe," Meloux replied.

"Thank God," Cork wheezed. He coughed several times and groaned as the pain hit him, echoing every blow Parrant had slammed into him.

"Your hands," Meloux said, ignoring Cork's attention to his ribs. He gestured for Cork to show him his hands.

They were clumsy things, bare and without feeling. The old man took off his knitted mittens. He wrapped his own wrinkled hands around Cork's, but Cork couldn't even feel their touch let alone any heat from them. The old man blew his warm breath over them and rubbed them gently, all the while scanning the woods for Parrant. Cork smelled sage rising off the old man's clothing and skin and hair.

In a while Cork began to feel tingling in the tips of his fingers. He knew he'd probably suffered frostbite, but the tingling, which was rapidly becoming a painful stinging, was a relief.

"Here." Meloux slipped his mittens onto Cork's hands. Cork started to protest, but the old man hushed him. He motioned for Cork to follow again and started along the ravine toward the lake.

Jo was safe. But where? And for how long?

They reached a cliff overlooking Iron Lake where Half Mile Spring fed in. Black, open water lay along the base of the rock twenty feet below, and a slender black tongue of open water extended a couple of dozen yards out into the ice. Meloux moved along the cliff until he came to a tall solitary pine, then he began a careful descent. Cork would never have seen the path even with the bright moon and the northern lights. He realized Meloux must know every inch of that part of the lake, and he followed the old man with blind trust.

On the ice, a safe distance from the open water, Henry Meloux waited. The wind blew snow off the cliff so that it drifted down around him like sparkling magic powder. In the moonlight, he cast a huge shadow on the ice. Cork saw the old man suddenly in a kind of vision, as if beholding in the long black shadow the real Meloux, a great hunter spirit, silent and powerful. Cork was very grateful to have the old man on his side.

He figured they would probably skirt the thin ice around the open water, then head toward the safety of Meloux's cabin on Crow's Point. But the old man surprised him. He started back toward Molly's.

"Henry?" Cork reached out and grabbed his arm.

"We have been rabbits," Meloux explained. "It's time to become a more dangerous animal. There is a vehicle parked on the ice near Molly Nurmi's sauna. He will go there soon enough."

Meloux lifted the bottom of his plaid mackinaw. A sheath hung from his belt. The old man slid out a hunting knife. Its six-inch blade caught the moonlight with a cold glint and Cork saw that the edge had been honed razor sharp. Meloux held the knife out to him.

"To kill the Windigo," the old hunter advised somberly, "a man must become a Windigo, too. He must have a heart of ice. There must be no hesitation."

Meloux began at an easy lope along the shoreline. Cork grasped the knife tightly, trying to put from his mind the knifelike stabbing at his own ribs.

It's time to become a more dangerous animal.

He thought about the bear hunt decades ago with

Sam Winter Moon, recalling how the great creature had lost them and doubled back, how surprised he had been when the bear charged at him out of the sumac. It had been a cunning tactic. But there was one problem. They'd killed the bear.

Jo hustled down to the lake and looked where Sandy and the Cherokee had gone. The wind blew hard across the ice and shoved such a bitter cold at her face that her eyes watered immediately. She could just make out the black shape of the Cherokee cautiously moving over the ice along the shoreline. The sound of the engine carried to her faintly on the wind. She didn't know the lake well, but she knew that somewhere in that direction was a little spring and beyond the spring was Crow's Point, where Cork visited Henry Meloux.

Did Sandy know about the old man's cabin? If he did, he probably knew Cork would head in that direction. If that was the case, it probably meant two things. That Cork and the old man were still alive. And that Sandy Parrant intended to cut them off before they reached the cabin.

She started across the ice just as the brake lights of the Cherokee flashed, red as the eyes of a night demon, then went dark. Jo paused and considered Sandy's move. Why stop? If they were headed toward the old man's cabin, wouldn't Sandy still be moving? Maybe they weren't headed to Meloux's. Maybe they were coming back across the ice, doubling back. Coming straight toward Sandy.

She began to run.

The shoreline between the ravine and Molly's place curved in a ragged, inward arc that was punctuated by several tiny inlets and small rocky peninsulas covered with stunted pines. The two men made straight for the sauna, a line that took them away from the arc of the shoreline, far from cover. Cork knew it was a bold and dangerous move, but it would allow them to reach more quickly the vehicle Meloux had spotted.

They hadn't gone far when Meloux stopped.

"Listen," he said.

Cork cocked his ear toward Molly's, but all he heard was the rush of the wind at his back.

"There." Meloux pointed toward a dark point of land ahead and to the right.

Cork saw nothing.

"Off the ice!" Meloux said, turning suddenly for the shoreline. "Quick!" The old man began to run, not a lope this time but a full-blown retreat.

Cork followed blindly. A moment later, he understood.

Headlights came on at the tip of the point, as if a beast had opened its eyes. Parrant's Cherokee started for them. They were only fifty yards from shore, but they might as well have been a mile. Cork knew they'd never make it. Whatever well of adrenaline had pumped his muscles and numbed his pain was empty, and he couldn't make himself run the way he knew he had to. And Meloux, for all his amazing ability, was still an old man. Parrant would run them down long before they reached safety.

Cork split off suddenly, moving away from Meloux and toward the cliffs at Half Mile Spring. When he looked back, Parrant had slowed the Cherokee almost to a stop, as if confused. Cork stopped, too, and turned to show himself clearly in the headlights.

"I'm here, you son of a bitch! I'm the one you want!"

Cork stood dead still on the lake. The urgency of fleeing had vanished. In its place was a deep calm, and around that calm, like an aureola around the dark center of an eclipse, blazed a fierce resolve to be done with it.

To kill the Windigo, Meloux had said, you must become a Windigo, too.

A man was never just a man. A man was endless possibility waiting to become.

In the hoary glare of the headlights, Cork changed. He grew. Past the pain of his body. Past the fear of dying. Past the concerns of conscience that kept a man small. He stood huge and full of an icy determination to see Sandy Parrant dead. To kill him with his own hands. He felt no pain in the fingers that gripped Meloux's knife. He felt no pain in his ribs as he drew himself upright. He felt only a depthless, pitiless cold that froze his heart.

He even smiled as the Cherokee came for him.

The vehicle launched itself across the lake. Cork heard the sizzle of the tires spinning on the ice as Parrant accelerated toward a killing speed. The sound was like the whine of a hungry animal. Death was coming and Cork opened his arms to embrace it, to bring it to him so that he could feed on it. Welling up from a dark place inside him he'd never known rose a cry he didn't recognize or understand, the howl of a hungry beast. He stood with the knife in his hand, howling beneath the moon as the Cherokee bore down on him. He crouched to meet it.

He didn't hear the shots. But he heard the shatter of glass and saw the vehicle swerve at the last instant. The Cherokee missed him by several feet, drifting into a lazy spin as Parrant fought to bring it under control. He never did. The end seemed to take a long time. Cork watched it all with a dispassionate appreciation for the beauty of circumstance.

As the Cherokee approached the open water from Half Mile Spring, the thin ice at the edge gave with a crack, as if the earth had split. The jeep tilted, its tires touching water. It rolled to its side, then flipped onto its top. It narrowly missed the open water, and like a new Christmas sled skated across the frozen lake on the bare metal of its roof, hardly slowing at all before it slammed into the base of the cliff on the far side of Half Mile Spring.

A moment of absolute quiet followed. The night caught its breath. Then the gas tank exploded.

Fire washed the cliff and the lake all around with a fearsome, wavering orange. The snow and ice melted on the rock wall and ran like black tears down the face of the cliff. Where he stood, Cork felt the heat reaching out toward him. He watched flames engulf the vehicle and listened to glass exploding from the intense heat.

"Cork!" Jo came out of the dark, the Winchester in her hand. "Are you all right?"

Cork looked at the rifle. "Thanks to you, I guess."

Meloux materialized beside them. He also noted the Winchester and nodded to Jo. "I thought for sure this old man would not be getting any older. I thank you."

The Winchester suddenly seemed too heavy for Jo to hold. She handed it to Cork. She felt empty and a little weak and she sat down abruptly on the ice. Meloux sat down cross-legged beside her.

Cork asked, "Back at the cabin, Henry. The Windigo calling. Was that you?"

In the quivering light that came off the burning Cherokee, Cork saw a perturbed look cross the old man's face, as if he'd been asked a rather stupid question. A glittering dust of snow blew over them and Meloux glanced up at the sky. The northern lights were fading, but the moon was high, looking bright and new as if it had only just been created.

"Whatever it was brought the Windigo here to feed is gone," Meloux declared.

He closed his eyes and began to sing, words Cork didn't understand. But he knew what it was about. The song of the dead. Henry Meloux was singing his fallen enemy onto the Path of Souls.

CHAPTER 49

Snow fell on Christmas morning, small flakes, which meant the snowfall would last a long time. It paved the streets and sidewalks of Aurora in trackless white and gave a fresh cover to the dirty snowbanks, like a clean comforter on an old bed. It came down straight and landed soft as dreaming. And Cork, as he turned onto the road to Molly's, thought it was one of the loveliest snowfalls he'd ever seen.

The big cabin was empty and unlit. The small shabby cabins that lined the lane to the lake stood in two dark rows like silent mourners. Cork walked between them one last time down to the sauna and looked over the lake from the place Molly had hated so much and then loved so well. Crow's Point was only a squat gray finger pointing toward something in the distance, something lost in the falling snow. All the signs on the ice that would have marked the desperate struggles there were covered now. The lake wore a face of immense serenity.

He returned to the Bronco and took from the backseat a small Christmas tree in a green metal stand. He'd strung popcorn and cranberries and made paper chains. At the very top, he'd placed an angel he'd constructed from pipe cleaners and a bit of white lace. He didn't want to go into the cabin—without Molly it would be the emptiest of places. So he set the tree in the snow outside.

"I didn't do such a good job with the decorations," he explained as if she could hear, and he held up his bandaged, frostbitten hands to show the reason for his clumsiness. "Even so, I think it looks all right."

The snow muffled every sound, reminding Cork of the way it used to be in church when he believed in God and felt reverence in the very silence of St. Agnes.

"Jenny was supposed to read a poem at her Christmas program yesterday. I think I told you. She was going to read Sylvia Plath, but she changed her mind. She read Frost instead. 'Stopping by Woods on a Snowy Evening.' You know, 'miles to go before I sleep.' Jo says she changed it for me. A good sign, I guess."

He looked down, a little embarrassed by his rambling, although talking made him feel less alone. He saw tracks in the snow near the back door, small hand prints almost human. Raccoons.

"The geese are back. You remember, Romeo and Juliet. It's nice having them around. Like a couple of old friends."

Small flakes settled on his face and melted into drops that ran down his cheeks like tears. But he wasn't crying. He'd cried himself dry already. And if Molly could see him—who knew?—he wanted her, on this morning, to see him smile.

So he did. He smiled upward into all that fell from heaven.

"Merry Christmas, Molly."

As snow gathered on the branches of the Christmas tree and in the loops of the paper chain and settled lightly on the shoulders of the angel he'd made, Cork turned and walked away.

ACKNOWLEDGMENTS

I'm not sure anyone writes a book alone. I didn't. A lot of good people deserve my thanks for the help they've given me along the way.

First and foremost, thanks to the members of Crème de la Crime who never let an easy answer slide: Carl Brookins, Betty James, Michael Kac, Joan Loshek, Jean Miriam Paul, Betsey Rhame, Susan Runholt, and Anne B. Webb. A better group of writers, critics, and friends of the genre would be hard to find.

Thanks also to two very special people who shared with me their insights on the Anishinaabe people: Barbara Briseno of the Mille Lacs Band of Ojibwe, who offered not only her knowledge but also her astute editorial eye; and Alex Ghebregzi, a "Southern Shinnob," whose knowledge of the Ojibwe language and culture has been invaluable, and whose fierce passion for justice for all indigenous peoples of the world has been inspiring.

I owe much to those who've chronicled the Anishinaabe culture, past and present: William Warren and Francis Densmore, early ethnographers; Gerald Vizenor, whose own writing is as beautiful as the Ojibwe tales he relates; and Basil Johnson for his reverential rendering of the ceremonies of the Anishinaabe. The language of the Ojibwe is one of the most difficult on earth. In most cases, I have relied on *An Ojibwe Word Resource Book*, edited by John Nichols and Earl Nyholm, as the authority for spellings and meanings.

To those unselfish friends who helped bring this manuscript into the computer age, I owe an abiding debt of gratitude: LuJean Huffman-Nordberg, Debra McDonald, Kaye O'Geay, and Cheryl Madsen. A special thanks to Wendy McCormick who understands the rhythm of words better than anyone I know, and to Cheryl Gfrerer whose help in trimming the fat was invaluable.

Thanks to my agent Jane Jordan Browne and to her associates Katy Holmgren and Danielle Egan-Miller for their advice and guidance in so many ways. Thanks also to my editor Dave Stern whose enthusiasm has been a blessing.

Finally, I would like to thank Jimmy Theros and the entire staff of the St. Clair Broiler where most of this manuscript was written. A good place for coffee, a great place to write.

Dear Reader,

The following short story took a circuitous route to get into your hands.

Every year, the Mystery Writers of America puts out a call for submissions for its annual anthology of short stories. There are always an enormous number of submissions from which only a very few are chosen for inclusion. Shortly after my first novel, *Iron Lake*, was released, my editor encouraged me to submit a story to MWA featuring Cork O'Connor. "Corpus Delicti" was the result. I was delighted when I received word that my story was among those chosen for the anthology, which would be edited by Mary Higgins Clark and titled *The Night Awakens*.

Here's where it gets weird. Although I was paid for "Corpus Delicti," it never appeared in the printed anthology. Why? To this day, I have no idea. But it was included in the audio version of the anthology. Over time, my own hard copy and digital copy of the story were lost. A few years later, a very nice guy named John Frantzen, who is a fan of my work, told me he had access to the audio version and offered to transcribe the story. A publisher named Jim Seels heard about the generous offer and gave this story its first ever life in print in a deluxe limited-edition anthology.

Now, twenty years after it was written, and on the twentieth anniversary of the first Cork O'Connor novel, "Corpus Delicti" is finally in print for anyone who wants to read it. I hope you will enjoy the very first Cork O'Connor short story.

Sincerely,
William Kent Krueger

CORPUS DELICTI

It was dark by the time they found the red Mustang. Since noon, the temperature had dropped another twenty degrees. The wind was from the northwest, coming straight out of Canada hard as a fist. The windchill hovered around sixty below. The driver's door was wide open, the keys still in the ignition. Snow had drifted inside, settling deep enough to bury the woman's body, if she'd stayed with the car; she hadn't. Sheriff Corcoran O'Connor sifted through the drifted snow and came up with a nearly empty Tanqueray bottle. The last two fingers of gin had turned to slush. He told McDougal to radio the office and swing all available deputies to Cedar Lake Road to help search for Louise Esterville.

Snow had fallen for almost two days straight. When it finally stopped, a bitter cold descended and the wind swept in, creating blizzard conditions. Schools and most businesses hadn't bothered opening. Even the plows had been taken off the roads. The wind undid their work within an hour or two of passing, filling the trenches they'd cut, leveling the snow as if the plow blades had never been there. The front end of the Mustang sat nudged against a big red pine at a curve in the road. Cork O'Connor dug away the drift covering the hood and bumper; not much damage. Louise hadn't hit the tree at great velocity. With his flashlight, he checked more carefully inside the car. On the windshield, just above the steering wheel, he found a smudge of frozen blood. The Mustang was a vintage 1965 convertible, no air bag. Cork guessed Louise hadn't been wearing her seat belt and the impact of the collision with the pine had launched her into the glass, not hard enough to damage the windshield, but it appeared to have damaged Louise Esterville.

Cork stood with the hood of his parka cinched so that only his eyes were exposed. They felt frozen in their sockets. Every few moments, swirls of snow gusted off the lake, whipping out of the dark into the slender beam of his flashlight. Other than that, there was nothing to be seen along the narrow road that divided the pines except Louise Esterville's red Mustang and the Land Cruiser he and McDougal had come in. He opened the hood of his parka just enough to clear his lips.

"Louise," he shouted. The word was snatched up by the wind and carried away as if it were a mouse in the grasp of a hungry hawk. Cork climbed into the Land Cruiser, grateful for the warmth inside.

"They're rounding up whoever they can," McDougal reported. "Porter and Ollie are over to the lumber mill. 'Fire in the stacks,' they said."

"Christ, how can anything burn when it's this cold? Get back on the air. Tell them to come by snowmobile and stay off the road itself. If Louise is under a drift somewhere, I don't want her run over. And for God's sake, tell them not to let a plow come this way." Cork took off his gloves and blew in his hands. "Any more word from Oren? Any chance she made it back home?"

"No."

"Tell them to check the hospital, see if anybody brought Louise in."

"You think somebody picked her up on this road? There's nobody out here but the Estervilles."

"I want to be sure."

McDougal reached for the radio. "A sober man dressed for it would have a tough time in this cold, Cork. At these temperatures, bare skin freezes in a few minutes. You know we're not going to find her alive."

The Land Cruiser shook in the wind. Cork watched the snow move off the lake and engulf them as if it were a living thing.

"Somebody ought to call Kaplan," McDougal said.

Cork didn't want to, but he knew he should. "Tell them to do it."

The deputies huddled in the lee of the Land Cruiser while Cork briefed them. Oren Esterville had called the sheriff's office at 4:43 p.m. to report his wife missing. According to Esterville, she'd left several hours earlier, headed to the truck stop at Sand River Crossing, the nearest location where she could purchase cigarettes. Esterville called the truck stop, but no one had seen his wife come in. She hadn't returned home. Cork and McDougal found her red Mustang at 5:50.

"So, I guess we're looking for her body," Chip Ledbetter said over the wind.

"If she's out here," Cork said, "then yes, we're most likely looking for her body."

Cork spread them a few feet apart and started up the road toward Sand River Crossing, kicking at the deep snow as they went. They proceeded almost a mile before turning back. They squeezed into the Land Cruiser to warm themselves. After fifteen minutes, they followed the same procedure heading toward the Esterville place.

Kaplan was at the Mustang when they came back. He had one of his dogs with him, a big Saint Bernard that was already sniffing at the inside of the car. The deputies scrambled into the Land Cruiser. Cork went to Kaplan.

"You haven't found her?" Kaplan asked. He wore a red woolen mask that covered his face except for his eyes. Over those, he wore clear goggles. He held a flashlight in one thick-gloved hand and the dog's leash in the other.

"No, George, I'm sorry."

"Maybe somebody picked her up," Kaplan said. His words were muffled through the mask and battered by the wind, but Cork caught the drift.

"Maybe," he allowed.

Kaplan said, "It looks like she might have hit her head on the windshield." He swung the flashlight beam toward the smeared glass.

"Looks that way," Cork said. His eyes were tearing in the wind, so he turned his back to the lake. "Look, George, if she's still out there—"

"I know," Kaplan cut him off.

"Can the dog find her, in snow?"

"Jude's my best." He looked around him at the snow blowing out of the darkness. "But with all this drifting . . ." He let it drop.

Cork was iced to the bone, so stiff with cold it hurt to move. He went to the Land Cruiser and shoved in with the others to warm up.

"He brought that dog with him on his snowmobile?" Ledbetter asked.

McDougal eyed them through the window. "Poor son of a bitch," he said quietly.

"Which one, the dog or the man?" Ledbetter laughed.

Cork said, "I'm taking one of the snowmobiles and heading down to talk to Esterville. Give Kaplan whatever he needs."

"What he needs at this point," McDougal said, "is a fucking miracle."

All the land on that side of the lake was Esterville land. The big log home at the end of Cedar Lake Road had been built for Louise as a wedding present by her father in the days when his open-pit mine near Hibbing supplied a good share of the iron pellets transported by the great ore boats out of Duluth. The old man had been dead a decade and a half. His iron mine was filled with water the color of weak tea. The ore boats didn't run anymore, but the woman Oren Esterville had married was still very rich.

Half a mile from the house, Cork came upon a black Ford Ranger buried in a drift. The vanity plate read EVILLE. A couple of minutes more and he was climbing off the snowmobile and up the front steps to the big log home. Esterville opened the door looking white as the snow that had ghosted in after Cork.

"Any word, Sheriff?"

Cork had known Oren Esterville a long time. They'd never been on good terms. Esterville had thrown a lot of money into the effort to keep Cork from being elected sheriff. Partly, this was politics. Esterville was an important man in the state Independent Republican party, and Cork was a Democrat. But even more, it was the bias of a rich white man. Cork was one-quarter Anishinaabe. His wife, Jo, was an attorney who often represented the Anishinaabe of the Iron Lake Reservation in their efforts to keep men like Esterville from stealing what little they had left. Although Corcoran O'Connor didn't look especially Indian—he had green-blue eyes and the reddish hair of his Irish lineage—Esterville called him a breed behind his back. To his face, however, he was Sheriff O'Connor. With a smile.

"I was hoping you might have heard something," Cork said.

"Nothing." Esterville rubbed his forehead hard as if he were trying to erase a mistake that had been written there. "I can't believe this is happening."

"Her car's up against a tree about a mile and a half down the road. She's not in it, Oren. It looks like she was hurt and maybe tried to walk out. I've got men going over the road now. I wish I could say things didn't look bad."

Esterville turned to a window that rattled in the wind. "She wasn't dressed for this."

"I saw your Ranger a ways back."

"When I got worried, I headed out to look for her. Didn't get far before I got stuck myself. That's when I came back and called your office."

"It's bad out there," Cork agreed. But McDougal and I made it, he thought to himself. "I found a gin bottle in the car, almost empty."

Esterville sucked in heavy breath. "She started drinking again."

"When you called the office, you said she'd left to get cigarettes."

"She had to have a smoke. Her and her bad habits. She had a lot of them. I told her they'd kill her someday." He looked at Cork and seemed ready to cry.

"We'll find her, Oren." It was a standard thing to

say at this uncertain juncture. The funny thing was, it came out more as a challenge than a comfort, and Esterville looked at him strangely. "Mind if I use your bathroom? Sorry to ask, but it always happens to me when I come in from the cold."

The bathroom on the main floor was done in peach hues and was scented to match. Cork stood at the toilet relieving himself and studying a framed photograph that hung on the wall. It was a picture of Esterville and Louise together on their sailboat on Cedar Lake. Louise was not a beautiful woman. She had flat brown hair that stood up stiffly in the wind, a long, thin face, large teeth, and an awkward boniness that made her seem more like a wooden marionette than a woman of flesh. The day looked bright and sunny, and Esterville looked full of robust confidence. Louise wasn't smiling so much as squinting into the sun. Cork tried to recall a time when he'd ever seen her looking happy. She'd grown up in the house of a tyrant, a man who'd raped the Iron Range for its ore, and she'd moved through her life as she must have moved through her father's house, quietly and with her eyes averted.

Oren Esterville had been a husband handpicked by her old man. He was ambitious, had good business sense, and was willing to marry a plain woman. In his marriage, Oren Esterville had been as faithful as an alley cat. Louise seldom ventured from the house. As far as anyone could tell, she did very little but keep company with a bottle of gin. Still, they showed up arm in arm every Sunday at Mt. Zion Lutheran Church, and they'd been together so long in their way that they'd ceased to be an item of interest in the gossip of Aurora. Cork finished and zipped up. As he reached for the handle to flush, he thought how Oren Esterville, in the conversation they'd just had, used the past tense exclusively when speaking of his wife. It was a small thing, but Cork decided to hold on to it.

He told the deputies to take the snowmobiles and head back to Sand River. They needed hot food and hot coffee, and he needed to decide what to do next.

"Where's Kaplan?" he asked McDougal.

"Took off into the woods a while ago. Him and the dog's been all over the place. He's crazy, Cork. He's going to kill that animal or himself."

"We'll wait for him. He's going with us."

McDougal shook his head. "He won't like it."

"Who likes any of this?" Cork turned up the radio. Only static. "Any word? She show up at a neighbor's?"

"What neighbors?" McDougal said.

Kaplan wasn't happy with Cork's orders, but it was clear he was dead tired and the dog was limping. He gave in and after he'd warmed up some, climbed on his snowmobile with his dog and followed the Land Cruiser back to the café at Sand River Crossing. McDougal joined the other deputies, who had spread out in a booth of the twenty-four-hour truck stop. Cork and Kaplan sat across the room. A few truckers trapped by the storm were hunched at the counter, dividing their attention between the sudden invasion of law enforcement officers and the pretty, dark-haired waitress who was pouring coffee. The place smelled of the hot griddle. The music that came from the radio in back of the counter was some lively Garth Brooks. Cork felt very glad to be out of the cold.

Kaplan had removed his goggles when he stepped into the café and pulled off his red wool mask. The face he'd revealed was almost as red as the mask and as carefully constructed. George Kaplan had been a Marine assigned to the barracks in Beirut when a terrorist on a suicide mission destroyed the structure with a truck bomb. Unlike a lot of his buddies, Kaplan survived. The blast, however, demolished his face. He'd been through a dozen operations, reconstructions, grafts. All the features were in place, identifiable, but the result was mostly a suggestion of humanity. Kaplan's face was the mottled red of a Lake Superior agate. The grafted pieces of skin came together as distinctly as ragged continents. One eye sat at an angle in its socket, so that whenever Kaplan addressed anyone, they had the uncomfortable impression he was speaking to someone at their side. Cork knew Kaplan well, and the man's appearance didn't startle him anymore. Because a lot of people in Aurora, Minnesota, weren't like Cork, Kaplan seldom came into town.

"George," Cork said, "I can't tell you how sorry I am."

Kaplan looked at him as straight on as his skewed eye would allow. "You know?"

"Small town."

What he knew about the affair between George Kaplan and Louise Esterville he'd learned in the same way as everybody else—rumor. Aurora was isolated from the world by a hundred thousand acres of national forest land. Gossip was a pleasure and a plague. He'd heard about the affair soon after Louise began attending the AA meetings held in the basement of St. Agnes Catholic Church. The meetings were among the few things that also brought Kaplan to town. At first, Cork dismissed the rumors. He knew that affairs between members of the same AA meeting group were frowned upon. It was called thirteenth stepping, but it was not just that. George Kaplan was a hard man, tempered to a hard silence by the brutality of his experience. Cork had seldom heard more than a few words pass his scarred lips at any one time. He couldn't imagine Kaplan involved in a conversation long enough to lead to a woman's bed. When he allowed himself the unspoken honesty of his own prejudice, Cork couldn't imagine any woman desiring Kaplan's head on the pillow next to hers, even a woman as plainly unhappy as Louise Esterville.

"Something's not right about this," Kaplan said. The muddled skin along his jawline trembled.

"What do you mean?"

"She isn't drinking now. She's been sober for over seven months."

"People fall off the wagon, George. Happens all the time. It's understandable having to live with a man like Oren."

"She's leaving him. She's got an appointment to see a lawyer about a divorce."

Laughter broke out from the booth where the deputies sat. The young waitress stood with a coffeepot poised above the table.

Chip Ledbetter said, "We'll find her sooner or later. She's probably a Popsicle by now."

"What happens then?" the waitress asked.

"A case like this," Ledbetter said with authority, "not sure of the exact cause of death, they'll autopsy her. Ever seen an autopsy?"

"No," the waitress said. She sat the pot on the table and scooted into the booth next to Ledbetter.

"Ever gut a fish?" he asked. "Same thing, basically. They make these long incisions here, here, and here." He drew a big Y across the front of her uniform and she smiled as his finger moved. "They pull out the organs, weigh 'em, cut off little pieces to put on slides for their microscopes. Then they saw around the skull just like opening a tin can and they take out the brain."

McDougal saw Kaplan listening. He spoke low and harsh to Ledbetter.

Kaplan was quiet. He reached out and took the saltshaker in his hand. The top of the shaker was shaped like the head of a moose; he fiddled with the antlers awhile. "He's right, isn't he?" Kaplan said.

Cork wished there was something to say to make it easier, but more or less, Ledbetter was correct.

"There's not a single scar on her body," Kaplan said. "Her skin is perfect, absolutely perfect. All her scars are inside."

"George," Cork began because it was painful to see Kaplan go on.

"Look at me," Kaplan said. His eyes were glossing with tears. "She thinks I'm beautiful. Me. Can you believe it?"

"Go home, George," Cork said.

"Not till I find her."

"It's the coldest night in a quarter century. The honest to God truth is, if she's out there, you can't do her any good. No one can do her any good. Look, I'm sorry, George, I really am, but I'm going to pull the men off. In this cold and dark, it's too great a risk to go on looking."

"I hope to Christ she's not out there," Kaplan snapped. "But if she is, I'm not leaving her."

Jude lay at his feet. Dogs weren't allowed in the

café, but nothing had been said when Kaplan brought him in because no one would suggest leaving a dog out on a night like that. The big Saint Bernard lumbered loyally to his feet as Kaplan swung out of the booth. "I'm going to find her," Kaplan said. He grabbed his parka.

Cork stood up and put his hand out as if to hold the man back. "George, you're only going to hurt yourself or the dog."

"I'm not going to hurt Jude," Kaplan said. He brushed aside Cork's hand and headed for the door.

As Kaplan paused to pull on his mask, Cork called to McDougal, "Give him the keys to the Land Cruiser."

McDougal drew the keys out of his pocket and tossed them to Kaplan. Kaplan looked back at Cork.

"Warm up often," Cork told him. "And get on the radio every half hour to let us know you're okay. Understand?"

Kaplan nodded. "Thanks." He headed out with his dog into the night.

Cork drifted to the window. McDougal joined him.

"My grandma Dilsey never spoke a word of English until she was fifteen and met my grandfather," Cork said. "She lived her whole life after that in the drafty cabin he built next to a school. She wouldn't come into town to stay with us, even in the worst of winters. She believed all things had spirit and if you respected that, you could live with anything." Cork watched Kaplan struggle through the snow and wind toward the Land Cruiser. "I wish she were here to tell me what the hell is the spirit in this."

"You sure it's a good idea to let him go?" McDougal asked.

"Maybe not," Cork allowed. "But I can't help thinking what if it was someone I loved out there, Jo or one of the kids. I wouldn't want to give up either."

Kaplan pulled out slowly through the drifts in the parking lot. In only a moment, the taillights were gobbled up in the blizzard. Through his own reflection on the window, Cork stared onto the face of the storm confronted by a spirit he didn't understand in the least. He felt tired and helpless and very grateful it wasn't someone he loved out there.

"At least I could give him a little help staying warm," Cork said.

"Seems to me," McDougal replied, "you gave him everything you could."

Not long after midnight the wind finally died. In the early hours of darkness, the plows hit the roads. They cleared the highway through Sand River Crossing but left Cedar Lake Road untouched. At first light, Cork had nearly thirty men, deputies and volunteers, scouring the length of road from the bridge over the Sand River to the Esterville place. George Kaplan wasn't among them. After they combed the snow over the road, they spread out through the woods and across the ice of the lake. They didn't find Louise Esterville.

George Kaplan lived alone in a small cabin north of Aurora. A beautiful stretch of the Superior National Forest was his backyard. He had a small barn. Next to it was the kennel where Kaplan kept the dogs he trained as hunters and as trackers. When Cork and McDougal drove up, the dogs rushed out and set to barking. Kaplan appeared a moment later, coming from the barn. He turned and slapped the padlock into place, then limped toward Cork and McDougal.

"We just stopped by to get the Land Cruiser," Cork told him, "and I'd like to talk to you a minute if I could."

Kaplan reached into his pocket and handed the keys over to McDougal. "Thanks," he said.

McDougal got into the Land Cruiser and headed back toward Aurora. Cork followed Kaplan to the cabin. Kaplan looked even more like hell than usual. The skin across the tops of his cheeks and around his eyes was blistered from frostbite. His limping indicated that he'd probably frostbitten some toes as well. The last communication from him the night before had been at 1:45 a.m., when he radioed to let the department know he was finally giving up. Cork could understand why he declined to join in the search that morning. Jude lay on the couch, his paws carefully bandaged. The cabin was cold, very cold. Kaplan took off his parka. Underneath he wore a thick brown sweater, hand-knitted. Cork wondered if Louise Esterville knew how to knit.

"We haven't found her," Cork said. Kaplan waited. "I suppose there's still an outside chance someone picked her up, but no one's reported anything to my office."

"You tell Esterville?"

"Yes."

"How'd he take it?"

"All things considered, pretty well."

"I'll bet."

Cork hadn't been inside Kaplan's cabin in a long time. He remembered it as a bachelor's kind of place, not much thought to order or cleanliness. The cabin looked good now, tidy. There were even flowers in a yellow vase on the coffee table. A photograph in a small gold frame caught Cork's eye. It sat on a shelf near the front window next to Kaplan's Purple Heart, glinting in the sunlight that slanted through the panes. The photo was of Kaplan and Louise together smiling at the camera. They both wore jeans and flannel shirts with the sleeves rolled back. Their arms were around each other, and at their feet lay one of Kaplan's big dogs. They looked relaxed and happy, as if they'd been together forever.

"George, you said Louise had stopped drinking. Are you sure of that?"

Kaplan went to the couch and gently stroked Jude's massive head. "Absolutely."

"You also said she was planning to talk to a lawyer about divorcing Oren. Do you know who that was?"

"Michael Greenway."

Cork felt an icy draft coming from under a closed door at his back. Daisies in a white teapot adorned a small lamp table next to the door. The flowers hung over, dying in the cold.

"Baseboard heater went out in the bedroom," Kaplan explained when he saw Cork looking. "I've been using an electric heater, but that went out, too. Now I'm having trouble with the propane heater in the kennel. The cold gets to everything sooner or later. No matter how hard you try to fight it, the cold always wins." Kaplan gave Jude's head a couple more thoughtful strokes. Then he said, "He killed her, Cork. That son of a bitch killed her."

"We don't even know for sure she's dead, George. All the possibilities have to be considered. Maybe someone picked her up. Maybe she just got tired of Esterville and took off."

"She wouldn't leave without telling me."

"What I'm saying is that without a body, it's difficult to tell exactly what's happened. It would be hard to prove anything."

"You don't need her body to know I'm right," Kaplan said.

"No," Cork admitted, "but I'll need her body to prove it." He glanced again at the closed door with the cold draft coming in underneath. "Mind if I take a look in there, George?"

"Just a bedroom. I'm not even using it anymore, it's so cold now. Been sleeping on the couch here."

"Then there's no reason I shouldn't look?"

Kaplan eyed him, considering. Finally, he said, "No reason in the world."

Cork opened the door. All that greeted him was an empty bed and the cold of the room where the thing that had warmed it was long gone.

Cork dispersed several deputies to canvas the liquor stores within ten miles of Aurora. Then he went to talk to Michael Greenway. Greenway confirmed that Louise Esterville had made an appointment to see him, but he didn't have any idea what she wanted to discuss. The deputies had no luck that day. The next morning, Cork instructed them to widen the area of their inquiry.

A little before noon, Chip Ledbetter reported in from Yellow Lake, more than fifteen miles south of Aurora. Although the clerk at the liquor store there wouldn't swear to it, he thought he recognized the photograph of Oren Esterville. Esterville might have been the man who had come in a few days earlier with the storm well under way just as the clerk was starting to close up and head home before the roads became impassable. Although the clerk wasn't certain about the man, he remembered the purchase very well. A bottle of the best red wine they carried, Stonebridge Merlot 1992, and a bottle of Tanqueray.

Cork had McDougal check the trash company that serviced the Esterville place. Two days later he and McDougal sifted through the contents of the two big plastic garbage bags Ed's Rubbish had picked up there. They didn't find an empty Merlot bottle, but they did find something else. Something they were anxious to ask Esterville about that afternoon.

Esterville offered them coffee. Cork and McDougal declined.

Esterville said, "Pretty cold out there. Need to use the bathroom?" He smiled as if they were friends and it was a good joke.

"No, thanks, Oren," Cork said. "I just wanted to see how you were holding up and check in with you on a few things."

Esterville had been reading a book, *Play It As It Lies: A Guide to Better Golf.* He'd put it facedown on the coffee table when he went to answer the door. Now, he marked his place by folding over the corner of a page. He closed the book and turned patiently back to the man. "I'm doing fine, all things considered. When I get a call from Louise telling me she's been with a friend the last few days, I'll be even better."

"I hope that happens, Oren. I truly do."

"What did you want to check in with me about?"

"Just a couple of questions. You say Louise had fallen off the wagon?"

Esterville nodded. "Yeah, I'm afraid so."

"In her attempt to stay sober, were you supportive?"

"Of course I was. Christ, O'Connor, you think I like having a wife who's a drunk?"

"I'm sure it's not easy, Oren."

"You bet your ass it's not easy."

"Any idea how she got the gin she was drinking when she disappeared?"

Esterville raised his hands in bewilderment. "She was a magician at conjuring up a bottle when she needed one."

Cork slapped his gloves lightly against his leg a couple of times and nodded thoughtfully. "You say when Louise left she was going to buy cigarettes at Sand River Crossing?"

"That's right."

"Dying for a smoke, huh?" McDougal said.

Esterville glowered at him. "If that's meant to be funny, it isn't."

"What brand did she smoke?" Cork asked.

Esterville thought a moment. "Winston Ultra Lights, I believe."

"That's interesting. Did you know, Oren, that there was almost a full carton of Winston Ultra Lights in your trash this week?"

Esterville considered them both carefully. "Yes," he finally said. "I threw them there myself."

"Why?"

Esterville put his hands in his pockets and let his shoulders drop. "I found them after Louise disappeared. I've been concerned for some time that she was seeing someone. I believe the cigarettes were just an excuse so that she could leave for a rendezvous." He settled soulful eyes on Cork. "I didn't want anyone to know. You understand?"

"Why did she take the Mustang?" McDougal put

in. "A convertible? I know she's got a Volvo, a good snow car with an air bag."

"She was drunk. Go figure." Esterville shrugged hopelessly.

Esterville was a big man, six two, Cork figured, weighing maybe 230, and in good shape. He was rumored to be in line as the next chair of the Independent Republican State Committee, a rough job. So, a big man in a lot of ways. Tough, but not big enough or tough enough apparently to keep a small, quiet woman from heading out into the worst weather in a quarter century, drunk, without proper clothing, and driving a car that had no business on the road in the dead of winter.

"Is that all, Sheriff?"

"For now," Cork said.

In the Land Cruiser, McDougal smashed his fist against the dash. "Christ, Cork, he's lying, I can feel it. Like slime over everything he says. He juiced her up, faked that accident, and left her out there to die. That son of a bitch!"

"I guess it was too much to hope he'd be drinking the Merlot," Cork said.

"He's got it in there somewhere, I'd bet on it."

"All right, Mac," Cork said. "Let's see if we can take a look."

Judge Robert Parrant had been a good friend of Louise Esterville's father. Like him, Parrant came from Iron Range money. In Parrant's case, the wealth was built from timber, mostly at the expense of the magnificent white pines that at one time were the lords of the great North Woods. Parrant was an old man, a powerful figure in the state Independent Republican party and rigid in his views on politics and the law. Cork had been at odds with him many times. More often than not, dealing with Parrant was like sliding naked down a splintered board.

Cork laid out the evidence and his concerns about the disappearance of Louise Esterville and asked for a warrant to search the Esterville place.

The judge rocked back in his leather chair. "Corpus delicti," he said. He used the glowing end of a lit cigar and jabbed it at the air as if torturing the two words as they hung there before him. "You understand that doesn't necessarily refer to the need for a body, but the need for a sufficient body of evidence to indicate that a felony has been committed. As I see it, you have neither. In my estimation, Oren Esterville has provided you with a reasonable explanation for all your concerns. The circumstances surrounding his wife's disappearance suggest a tragic misjudgment on her part, nothing else." He took a deep, unhappy breath. "We live in harsh country, Cork. We have to accept the harsh realities of life here."

When Kaplan opened his door, Cork reacted with horror. "Christ, George, you need a doctor!"

Kaplan's face was falling apart. The frostbitten, blistered skin was peeling away. The hard mottled red had become a swollen inflammation. His eyes were puffed to slits. Cork stepped into the cabin. The place was a mess—unwashed pots on the stove, open cans on the floor with crusted spoons still inside. The cabin had been chilly when Cork was there last; now it was frigid. The flowers hung down the sides of the yellow vase, dead things in the cold.

"George, you've got to get the heating fixed."

"I don't care about the cold," Kaplan replied. He

limped to the sofa, sat down, and wrapped a blanket around himself. He had thick red wool socks on his feet.

"Your pipes are going to freeze," Cork warned.

Kaplan looked up at him a long time, the damaged face impossible to read. "Let 'em freeze," he finally said. "You're not here to advise me about my pipes. You're here with bad news."

"Not good anyway," Cork admitted. "I think Oren bought the gin that we found in the Mustang. I think I can prove it, but I need to get into Esterville's place, and Judge Parrant has refused to issue a search warrant."

"Cronies," Kaplan said.

"I want to use your dogs again to go over the whole area carefully. I think now that the wind's gone and the snow's not drifting anymore, we'll find Louise, if she's there."

"So you can autopsy her?" He said the word as if it were a profanity.

"I need something more than I have right now, George. I'm after the truth."

"The truth is that it wouldn't matter." Kaplan looked at Cork with calm resignation. "You can't have my dogs."

"I'll just call Alvin Tabor down in Moose Lake and ask him to bring his dogs up."

"Do what you have to do."

George Kaplan seemed broken. Cork understood how the weight of all the circumstances could do that to a man, but it was a hard thing seeing it happen. "I'm going to keep at Esterville," he swore. "I'm going to keep at him until he breaks, George."

A bitter little laugh escaped Kaplan's lips. "You don't have to throw me any bones. Oren killed her and he's gonna get away with it."

"If I could find her body—" Cork began.

"It wouldn't do any good," Kaplan broke in. "Suppose you cut up her perfect skin and found alcohol inside her, would you be able to prove he'd forced her to drink it? If you found a wound on her head, who's to say it didn't come from hitting the windshield? Oren's not smart, but he's rich and well connected. He'd hire the best lawyer money could buy, and you know all that lawyer would have to do is point to me and ask the jury, do you really believe any woman would leave her husband for a thing like that?"

Kaplan pushed himself up and walked painfully to a window. Late afternoon sunlight angled through in a long, solid shaft. He looked out where the snow stretched toward the woods, sparkling like a field of jewels.

"Winter's beautiful," he said, "but it's a lie. Just look at how pure the snow seems, even though everything it touches dies. And that sun, same as a summer sun, but it won't keep blood from freezing." He reached to the photograph of Louise on the shelf by the window. The room was cold enough that ice had formed along the edges of the frame. "I've known one beautiful thing in my whole life, really beautiful and true. That's more than some people ever get. I guess I should consider myself lucky." Kaplan turned to him, a small smile on his lips. "I fixed the propane heater in the kennel; the dogs are comfortable."

"Let me take you to see a doctor, George."

"Don't worry, Cork, I'll take care of things. I look pretty bad, I know, but, hey, I'm the king of accepting hard realities. Thanks for your concern."

Cork left Kaplan standing in the cold sunlight, holding in his hands Louise Esterville's frosted photograph.

That evening, Cork called Alvin Tabor and asked him to bring his tracking dogs up from Moose Lake the following day. Tabor promised to be there by noon. As things turned out, that was too late. At 9:47 the next morning, the Tamarack County Sheriff's Department received a call. Cork and McDougal were the first to arrive on the scene. Minnie Willard, who cleaned the Estervilles' home twice a week, met them on the road a distance from the house.

"I couldn't stay there," she said, "not with him like that."

They could see Esterville in a wooden chair on the front porch, sitting very still as if enjoying a warm summer morning. As they came closer, they saw icicles hanging from the rope that bound him to the chair. One very long icicle hung from the end of his nose. In his lap sat a frozen bottle of Merlot, Stonebridge 1992.

McDougal said, "It looks like he was doused with water and left to freeze to death. Wouldn't take long in this cold."

Cork bent close and studied a large bruise under the ice near Esterville's right eye. "Probably knocked out cold before he was tied to the chair and then brought back around."

McDougal pointed to the frozen blood that hardened the ropes around his wrists. "He must have fought like hell to get loose. Whoever did it to him wanted him to feel every minute."

Cork stepped back from the body. "I suppose we ought to talk to George Kaplan."

The dogs went crazy barking when Cork and McDougal drove up. The door of the small barn stood wide open. They checked it first. Sunlight slanted in, cold and hard as ice, showing a clean room. Bags of dog food stood neatly stacked against a wall. Bales of straw that Kaplan used as bedding in the kennel filled most of the barn. Two bales had been broken open, the loose straw piled carefully in one corner like a makeshift bed.

"You don't think someone's been sleeping out here?" McDougal said.

"In this cold?" Cork shook his head.

"Let's check the cabin."

Kaplan didn't answer Cork's knock. McDougal tried the knob, and the door swung open. Frost encased the kitchen sink. The contents of an unopened beer bottle on the coffee table had turned to ice and had shattered the glass as it expanded.

The door to the bedroom was ajar. Cork and McDougal stood at the threshold taking in the sight. The windows were wide open, letting in a steady flow of bitter arctic air. Louise Esterville's frozen body lay on the bed. It was blue-white, like snow at twilight. Kaplan lay with her, naked as the day he was born, holding her in a protective embrace. The warmth of his body had melted the ice that sheathed her skin. When he had no more heat to give, the ice had reformed, fusing their bodies together.

"What do you think?" McDougal asked. "He found her out there that first night?"

"That would be my guess."

"My God," McDougal whispered. "He must have loved her something awful."

"Get the coroner out here," Cork said.

McDougal turned away.

Cork stood in that frigid bedroom, a place in which George Kaplan and Louise Esterville had undoubtedly shared many things. It was death they shared now. But Cork didn't feel especially sad for them. There were worse things than death, and between them, George and Louise had known more than their share. Looking down at the sculpture the ice had made of the two lovers, Cork couldn't help thinking that Kaplan had at last become part of something beautiful and forever.

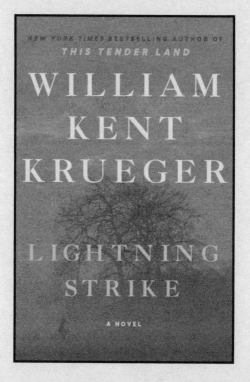